The Guava Tree

A Novel

Written by Andrew Diaz Winkelmann
Book cover illustrated by Courtney Strickland

www.1010Publishing.com

Dedication

To my abuela Ines, and the immigrant's journey. Your courage and strength inspired this story.

Acknowledgement

This novel wouldn't exist without the people I'm about to name. If it wasn't for the encouragement of my parents, Craig and Lourdes Winkelmann, and their nightly readings growing up, I may have never discovered my love for writing. Thank you both for always being honest with me and for reading and listening to countless early drafts, of both this novel and other stories, while I worked to get everything closer to right each time.

This story in particular was born from the oral stories shared with me by my abuela Ines, and the feelings those stories evoked. Her life, and the life of the other Lebanese immigrants living in Cuba who were then forced to escape the island to find a new home, colored my understanding of the world from an early age. I was aware of a mysterious, far away land that had once been home to my family. That could have been, maybe should have been, my home as well. I was aware that a Government could so easily shape the destiny of the individual, unless the unimaginable decision to leave one's home was taken. But it wasn't the loss of this far off homeland that inspired this story. No, this story was inspired by the courage and strength it took to leave everything behind, in order to create a better life for one's family, for my family, for me, and for that, my gratitude cannot be explained in words. This story is my thank you.

The actual writing of this story wouldn't have gone anywhere without the love and support of my wife Melissa Winkelmann. From late nights to early mornings, you encouraged me to keep writing, to stay focused, even when the world around us seemed to be screaming at me to quit. I never quit, and you're the reason. You've listened to and read more of my work than anyone else, and you always share your unfiltered truth. You've kept me grounded and told me that you'd always be my biggest fan. It's you I will always write for, Melissa. I love you.

This story being told in novel format is almost entirely thanks to my professor, Gray Stewart. It was your encouragement to take my short story, "The Cuban Dream," and expand it into a novel that led to *The Guava Tree*. You helped edit and shape its early form, from abstract to concrete. Without you, Gray, this novel would not have existed.

With keen eyes for both story and granular detail, my professor John Williams went above and beyond to ensure he read and edited the novel in its entirety (even though we started working together halfway through this project). I want to thank you, John, for believing in this work, for believing in my writing, and for helping to bring it all home.

I'd like to also thank my other professors at the Etowah Valley MFA Program, Michael Lucker, Director Bill Walsh, Dr. Donna Coffee Little, and Anne Corbitt for imparting upon me countless hours of sage-like writing advice as I learned and grew immeasurably under your tutelage.

While the writing and editing are important, I need to thank Nury Castillo-Crawford for believing in this story enough to champion it into existence. You, Nury, are an inspiration to the entire Latino community, and it's my honor to have this novel published by your publishing house, 1010 Publishing. It's you, and people like you, who act as beacons of hope to countless students, young adults, and Latinos who still haven't found their home and just need the right guide to show them the way. Thank you for believing in this story, for believing in what this story means, and for continuing your work in our community.

From the bottom of my heart, thank you all.

Introduction

If you go back far enough, we're all immigrants. It's a through line running down the spine of human history: we are nomadic creatures. Beings who strive for something more, something better, for opportunities waiting just on the other side. If they don't yet exist, we create them. There's a commonality here that gives all people, especially Americans, both old and new, the frontiersman spirit: the desire for "the American Dream." This story was born from that idea, both directly from the stories passed down to me by my older Cuban relatives and indirectly, as a personal desire to be better and never stop searching. What is it exactly that we're all searching for? I think it's home. Somewhere to belong while continuing our endless growth.

I'm the product of an American father, with German ancestors, and a Cuban mother, with Spanish and Lebanese ancestors. One side of my family spoke English, and the other side spoke Spanish. From a young age, I've seen the world as a space for dualities, for dichotomies and differences to exist that allow for newer, often better things to come into reality. Growing up, I'd hear stories about this distant land, an island speckled with dancing palm trees and surrounded by turquoise water, called Cuba, which was magical, whimsical, but then evil came and took everything away. It sounds like a fairytale and recalls countless stories, but there's good reason for that. Many of those fictional stories—at least the good ones—were inspired by true events, and it's in that truth, that something, or someone, powerful can change the course of both someone's personal history, and the world's history, for better or for worse, that we *feel* something when reading these stories. It's felt just beneath the surface of conscious understanding and inspires emotions the words wouldn't have been able to conjure alone.

While this novel in your hands is a work of fiction, loosely inspired by some of the stories shared with me as a child, stories with my own family members as the protagonists, it's the feeling and truth of the immigrant's journey that this story is meant to capture. There are two questions I had, which made this story impossible not to write. The first was, "were there 'American dreams' in countries other than America?" And the second, "what would it be like as a young child to move between continents, to have your entire life uprooted, then as an adult, having to make the same impossible decision for your own family?" When these two questions were met with my love for my Abuela Ines, the woman whose courage and strength inspires me to this day, whose name was my first word, whether I wrote the story no longer existed as a question. The question became when.

Initially, the first chapter of *The Guava Tree* existed as a short story I'd titled "The Cuban Dream," and was a direct interpretation of the story my Abuelo Rene and Abuela Ines shared with me as a child of the day they left Cuba. I'd heard the story dozens of times throughout my entire life, and even if some details changed or were added in over the years, the feeling I felt when hearing it was always the same. I wrote from that feeling, and when I finished reading the short story to my Abuela Ines, translating from the written English to spoken Spanish, she began to cry. Then, she looked up at me, and said, "es exactamente lo que senti." *It's exactly what I felt.* The Guava Tree is a love letter to my grandmother, an ode to the immigrant, a story of losing home and having both the courage and strength to find it again.

Chapter 1

Ines was cutting vegetables in the kitchen the day her home was taken from her. The thin wooden door slammed open and warm air swirled inside. Her son, Renecito, was in the doorway, his face painted with fear. He should have been outside playing.

"Mami, *soldados*!" He panted the words, his shirt soaked with sweat.

She looked up at him from the reds, greens and yellows on the cutting board, her mind slowly processing his words.

"There are soldiers outside," he repeated. "They're almost here."

We aren't ready.

She looked down at her feet to make sure she was still there and began to feel small in the kitchen, like she was shrinking, and the last thirty-two years of her life in Cuba now meant nothing.

She dropped the knife she'd been using, and it clattered on the counter. Her mind raced and her throat became tight, like it was covered in coffee grounds. Rusted bicycle brakes squeaked outside, and she knew they'd arrived. Ines rushed over and pulled Renecito behind her, closing the front door and locking it. His eyes, filled with panic, looked up at Ines as she peered through the linen curtains her mother had sewn for her. Two men in green uniforms sat on dark blue bicycles in front of their home. Gravel crunched as they planted their feet, and dust rose in clouds around their ankles. They spoke to each other and looked down at a dirty piece of paper. When they looked up, Ines was sure they saw her through the window. Her nails dug into her palms as they confirmed the address to their assigned house in gruff voices and stepped off their bicycles.

She took Renecito by the arm and ran for the back door.

Are they here because of the raffle? Or to arrest us? She needed to find Rene. *Had he seen the soldiers? Had they seen him?* He'd been out in the backyard roasting a pig leg, one that he'd purchased from the black market, and she knew they could take him for it.

"Ines! Ines! El Telegrama," her neighbors yelled from outside. Their warnings came too late and only confirmed what she already suspected: the telegram had arrived.

She pushed open the screen door at the back of the house and almost fell through it as she ran to where Rene was cooking near her vegetable garden.

"The soldiers are here. Get rid of it," she told him.

Knowing washed across his dark features, and he immediately lifted the half-cooked hunk of pork from the grill. He tried to throw the still-sizzling meat over the fence into the neighbor's yard, but it didn't clear the wooden points. Instead, it hit the side of the fence with a wet smack and tumbled over, landing with a dull, metallic thud onto the neighbor's low aluminum roof— the one that clanged when it rained—completely missing the softness of the grass.

Did the soldiers hear it?

Ines looked to Rene and held her breath. His tan skin took on a whiteness she'd never seen before, and she realized that she wasn't the only one who was terrified. With a look over Rene's shoulder, she saw the large guava tree that still, after all those years, stood proudly in the garden. Ines prayed the soldiers wouldn't find what was buried there. What *she'd* buried there. Her mind went to thoughts of what would happen to her family, her parents, her brother, if the soldiers discovered what she'd done, what they'd all done, but she pushed the thoughts from her mind and followed Rene back inside, still holding onto Renecito's wrist.

When they reached the living room, the front door was rattling from the fists slamming against it.

"Señor Diaz, we're here with news from The Prime Minister of Cuba, Fidel Castro. Please open the door."

Rene stepped in front of Ines and the children. Renecito reached for his father's hand, but Ines tightened her grip on his shoulder, and kept him by her side. Their daughter Lourdes sat in front of the couch, playing with a small wooden horse, unaware of the chaos around her, but Renecito was aware, and he was afraid. He knew that something was wrong, that something was about to change.

As Rene opened the door, a fist stopped an inch away from his face. The soldier was preparing for another set of knocks against the wood.

"Señor Diaz, buenos dias." The soldier in front, his skin tanned and sweaty, greeted Rene and ignored Ines, who stood behind him like a shadow. "May I come in?"

It wasn't a question, and Rene stood aside as the soldier entered their home.

"We're here to let you know that your names were selected in the raffle. You'll be going to the United States of America. *Immediately.*"

He had the voice of someone who smoked several cigars a day. The last word hung in the air and seemed to hum. *Immediately.*

Ines felt bitter relief when the soldier confirmed their business with them. They would be going to America. If they'd seen the pig or if they were there to punish them for another crime against the revolution, things would have been much different. The moment of calm quickly disappeared as her mind filled with thoughts of leaving. Most of her life had been spent in Cuba, and now they were expected to leave it all behind. There was still hope in her, buried away with other forgotten things, that the revolution would fulfill its promises, or a new government would step in, but it had been years, and things were as terrifying as they were in the beginning. She had two choices: leave and face the unknown or stay and be subjected to what she already knew to be true. The soldiers in her home made the decision more real, more final. It made her question everything.

Are we making the right choice? Is this the right thing for our family?

"Okay," Rene said to the sweaty soldier, "now what?"

"Are your things packed? If not, I'd get to it."

The soldier looked at his wristwatch.

"Okay," Rene said. The color still hadn't returned to his face.

Ines looked at her children, saw the fear in her son's eyes, the confusion in her daughter's, and realized that they'd become strangers in their own home. It was as if she was an outsider seeing this happen in someone else's home to someone else's family. She needed to reclaim her power. When she finally found her voice, it sounded foreign to her.

"Would you like something to drink?" she asked through dry lips.

"Yes—" the soldier by the door began but was interrupted by the other soldier who was standing in their home.

"We're fine."

The soldier outside had a rifle slung around his shoulder, but it looked awkward, like a plastic toy as it wrapped loosely around his body.

"Ines," Rene said, "we need to pack."

She nodded and made her way to their bedroom while Rene stayed with the soldiers, ensuring no harm would come to their children. The bedroom already felt empty and cold. Even though they were still there, to the government, they were already gone. On the mantle, the glass elephants her mother had brought from Lebanon glittered in the daylight. They seemed to look at her with their round, black eyes while their trunks and tusks reached out above them. She had a name for each elephant and had been convinced they'd brought her good luck back when she believed in such things, but they couldn't go with her. She could only take the necessities.

The suitcases they had in their closet didn't fit the regulations given to her, so she pulled down four drapes from the bedroom windows and tied the thick fabric into sacks. They would do. She began with her things, including the dresses her mother had sewn for her, her high heeled shoes, and the jewelry Rene had given her. *What are the necessities?* The question was numbed by the task at hand as she folded and piled clothing into her makeshift bag. She looked at all of the things she knew couldn't go with her and felt the tears coming but held them back. The things themselves didn't matter, they were lifeless objects that carried a value decided by barters and vendors. What mattered was the meaning attached to those things and they all seemed to mean something to her. They were memories from the past, many from before things changed in Cuba. They were laughter over family dinners, birthday celebrations with children running barefoot in the gardens, her wedding when she walked down the aisle with her father to the flicker of candlelight after the power had gone out. Those memories were what mattered, it was those things she would be leaving behind.

Ines fumbled with trembling hands and did her best to fit as much into the sack as possible but kept dropping things. She began filling a second bag with bundles of Rene's things. The buttoned-up shirts he used on the ranch, his stained cowboy hat, the one he wore when they'd first met, and everything else that would fit. There was no sense of accomplishment once she finished. Their entire lives, memories and all, thrown together into the two thick, fabric curtains that could hardly contain them. Now she had to do the same for the children.

She walked out of the bedroom and headed for the room her children shared. The same bedroom she had shared with her brother many years before. With each step, she felt the blood rushing inside her head, pounding desperately at her temples, as if looking for an escape. Part of her wished she could escape with the blood, become invisible in a current of crimson and take her family far away from there to a time when life made sense. She wondered what they were talking about in the living room as she heard the men's voices carrying down the hallway.

When she entered her children's bedroom, thoughts came like water entering a ship's broken hull, overtaking her. *Who will use my children's bedroom now? Some politician? A high-ranking military officer?* No, she'd seen the houses the commanders had taken as their own; they preferred beautiful, large mansions like her parents' home in town, not her small house in the countryside. Whoever took their home wouldn't be very important, probably a low-level lieutenant or judge. Regardless of whoever claimed their home, Ines knew that what meant so much to them would mean so little to someone else. She was sure her daughter Lourdes wouldn't remember what her bedroom looked like, but she would always feel as if she'd had something amazing once that was taken away.

What will she have in America? A fresh start or an empty beginning? Will she always feel like she is missing something that she doesn't remember? A life that she never lived but should have?

Ines felt dizzy with the thoughts and sick to her stomach. She sat down on the bed and waited for the moment to pass. Just a few years before, Ines couldn't have imagined any of this, this backwards world that had become their new reality.

Renecito's toys were scattered on the floor from his playing earlier that morning. Little airplanes, toy soldiers and figurines of Zorro were lined up, ready for a war that would never come. Ines wondered whether or not Fidel existed in her son's imaginary world. The light in the room dimmed slightly, but Ines didn't look up as it was nothing unusual. Since the revolution took power, electrical outages had become routine, the energy being drained away to help the regime achieve "a greater good." That's what the flyers said. Ines wondered what amount would be enough. She looked to the small dresser where she kept Lourdes' clothes. When the lights had gone out a few nights before, Renecito was using a candle to get dressed and dropped it at the foot of the dresser. It would have burned the dresser, maybe even the entire home, if Rene hadn't seen and put the fire out. Ines smiled at the thought. She'd been so angry, but as she sat on the bed, with the world spinning around her, it didn't matter at all. She would miss those moments most of all.

"Señora Diaz, are you almost done?" the soldier called from the living room, "We have four more houses to visit today."

Once she finished packing the children's things into the bulging curtains— which somehow seemed to be filled with more things than hers and Rene's— Ines walked back out into the living room dragging their luggage behind her. No one was speaking when she entered the room. The soldier was sitting in Rene's favorite recliner. Beads of sweat streamed down his arms and stained the yellow fabric brown. Rene sat on the couch next to Renecito and Lourdes and didn't seem to notice that the world had gone upside down. Birds chirped outside.

"I think we have everything," she said.

Ines looked to the balled-up curtains she'd dragged into the room. The soldier's eyes followed hers and his forehead creased into dozens of tiny wrinkles.

"No suitcases?" he asked with an amused expression.

"None that would fit," Ines replied.

"Wait—I think you're confused," the soldier smiled a small, greasy smile that looked out of place in the room, "the rule is only one bag per family. I see four bags here."

"What do you mean?" Ines asked.

She was convinced she'd heard him wrong. It was impossible to fit what little they were taking with them into just one bag.

"Yes, ma'am, only one suitcase per family." He coughed a wet sound and smiled again before continuing, "and judging by the clinking sounds those bags made, you have some jewelry in there.

That can't go with you either. No money or jewelry. That all belongs to the revolution."

"I thought it was one bag per person…" Ines muttered, unable to move.

"They'll search your things at the airport, I'm just trying to save you the embarrassment," the soldier said, a gold tooth visible as he continued to smile.

Ines looked to Rene. He didn't say anything, but his eyes spoke for him, begging her, *it's fine, leave them. Don't make a scene.* She realized then that Rene was more prepared to leave than she was. Her mind was still filled with doubts, compounded with thoughts of how much she would be leaving behind. They would be the first of their family to leave, and with so little to start with in America, what sort of life would they have? Cuba was her home, and this wasn't the way she imagined leaving, with one small bag of shared memories, and an armed soldier, who held all of the power, sweating in her living room.

"Okay," Ines said.

She looked at her daughter and son who she knew wanted nothing more than to run to her. A sob she'd been holding back escaped her, and she began to cry.

Rene moved to stand, but the soldier reached an arm out, stopping him.

"Why are you crying?" the soldier asked, "You're getting what you want. Soon you'll be an American, so you should be happy," he said and stood up from the armchair, placing his hands on his hips in a pose.

The soldier at the door laughed at this, which made Ines cry even harder.

"I'm very happy," Ines said, tears wetting her lips.

Both soldiers were laughing then. The sweaty one sat back down into the recliner.

"I'll give you ten more minutes before we all have to leave. We've already spent too much time here," he said, his smile disappearing entirely.

Walking down the hall the second time was even harder than the first. Ines felt powerless. A man had entered their home and from the moment he stepped over the threshold had taken complete control of their life. He pulled it from her as easily as one would pick a ripe guava fruit from a low hanging branch. Had her life not been worth more? Denser, more unmovable? Or maybe it was when things finally had value that other people came to take them away.

The bedroom was a mess, drawers left half opened, and the closet door wide open. Ines felt as if she would drown in the mountains of clothing that surrounded her and when she looked at herself in the mirror, she realized her blue eyes were red from crying, and that she looked as distraught as the room itself. She sat down in front of the closet and began to take everything out of the bags, deciding what of her family's would stay behind in the Cuba that no longer belonged to them. It was in that moment she saw it, surprised she hadn't noticed it before. In the back of the closet, partially buried beneath a pile of clothes, was a small, wooden box. The box was white, decorated with purple violets and had once belonged to her grandmother. Her own mother had brought it with them from Lebanon and had given it to Ines when her grandmother passed away.

Ines pulled the box out and opened it without thinking. Inside was a mix of seemingly unrelated things she'd collected since she was a young girl. There were photographs, newspaper clippings, even a journal that she'd kept up with as often as she could before Fidel arrived. She couldn't believe how easily those memories would have been left behind. She moved the contents of the box around, and took them out, one by one, placing them in her lap. Her hand brushed a white seashell and a wooden toy horse, before moving to a doll she'd all but forgotten, *Aleia.* That was the name she'd given the doll, her grandmother's name. When she grabbed hold of Aleia, the world around her seemed to melt away and her mind filled with memories.

Chapter 2

It was their first day at sea and a storm was raging. As wind and water crashed against the ship's metal body, barnacles clung to its hull, holding on tightly against the exploding waves. Ines Aude and her family were like those barnacles, holding on to everything they could, leaving behind the only home they'd ever known. The passenger ship was beautiful, but in the common dining room, on that specific day, it smelled like sweat. Ocean water sprayed across the deck, splashing the wood and metal that became more slippery as the day wore on. It was a large ship, especially to Ines, who had never seen anything so big in her seven years of life. While she'd seen many ships pass through the harbor in Beirut, nothing compared, and once on board, everything was different, somehow even more beautiful, than she'd imagined. The crew barked to each other in French, a language she couldn't understand while her parents and their fellow passengers spoke Arabic, the language she had spoken all her life in Lebanon. She'd been told by her parents that a wonderful new life waited for them on an island called Cuba, where palm trees cast shadows across endless white sands and the perfectly blue waters of the Caribbean.

None of those things mattered to Ines who wondered what had been so wrong with their old life that they needed to find a new one.

Ines and her brother Michel rocked back and forth between their parents in the cavernous dining area where many other passengers with families had taken refuge to wait out the storm. There must have been hundreds of people crammed together in that room. It was a cacophony of coughing and laughing, shushing and crying as needle-like rain buffeted the creaking ship. The wooden bench groaned beneath them as they swayed at the mercy of the storm. The pattering of rain against metal was soothing, but Ines feared the flashes of lightning and crackles of thunder that waited for her outside. She shut her eyes and held her doll Aleia tightly against her chest while she rested her head on her mother's pregnant belly. It gave her comfort to be near her parents and her baby sister. Michel told her there was no way she could know if the baby in Mama's belly was a girl, but Ines was sure of it. A little girl who looked just like Mama had visited her in a dream and since then, nothing could convince her otherwise.

"God wouldn't punish me with another sister," Michel had teased her.

On that day, as the storm raged around them, while Ines wanted to stay as close to Mama and Papa as possible, Michel was itching to get out of the stuffy hall and out onto the deck. The curtains on the long windows were drawn shut, so the only light came from the yellow, incandescent bulbs that flickered off and on each time a strong wave pounded the ship's exterior.

"Mama, can I please go see the rain?" Michel pleaded, looking up at their mother who said nothing. Ines cracked an eye open, curious to see if her mother would allow Michel out in the rain. Their mother placed one hand on her pregnant belly, the other on the bench, and looked over to their father.

"Salim," Mama said.

Their father placed the book he'd been reading down on the bench beside him and rubbed at his eyes.

"Here, son," he said, reaching into the brown satchel that was resting on his lap. He rummaged around in the bag, his forehead pinched, until finally, he brought out a book with a cover that was a faded red color and torn at the edges. Ines was convinced her father had an infinite number of books in his satchel, but he only ever gave them to Michel. If she ever protested, her father would remind her that Michel was older, and a man, so it was his duty to read. This only made her want the books even more.

Michel's eyes went wide, as if the book were made of solid gold instead of paper and ink. To Ines, he looked like a frog, or one of those insects with eyes that seemed to explode out of their oddly shaped heads. Michel outstretched his hand and tried to grab hold of the book, but Papa raised it just out of reach. If she hadn't been so sleepy, Ines would have laughed.

"This is my favorite book," Papa said.

"Yes, Papa." Michel nodded.

"Don't lose it," Papa added.

"I won't," Michel said, straining to grab the book.

"What do I tell you?"

"The mind is sharper than any sword and louder than any cannon," Michel recited.

"Correct," Papa said.

He handed Michel the book with a smile that sent his large mustache curving around his lip like a half-halo. Both of Ines's eyes were open now.

"I want a book too," she said.

"Oh, the little princess is awake," her father said and began to tickle her. They both laughed until there were tears in their eyes.

"I'm serious, Papa, I want a book too."

But her father said nothing. He'd stopped smiling as his gaze fell upon the spectacle of a large man who crawled on his hands and knees between the rows of benches and tables. Ines turned her head and looked at the man as well. He was crawling in their direction. The man moved one big hand in front of the other, his knees shuffling behind, like he was a human-sized worm. He paid no attention to the other passengers who began to murmur and point. He stopped a few feet away from where Ines and her family sat. The man bent his head, his back extending upward like a stretching cat, and he vomited onto the wooden floor. Ines placed her hand over her doll's eyes and closed her own, but quickly reopened them as curiosity got the best of her. She watched as the puddle began to spread across the floorboards, and the smell moved along with it. The family sitting nearest the sick man got up and hurried to another part of the room. Ines' mother turned away and covered her face with a handkerchief while her father looked more interested than surprised, and Michel did nothing at all, his attention focused on his new book. The room around them erupted with laughter.

The man became red in the face and attempted to wipe up the spreading liquid with the bottom of his long-sleeve shirt, which only made the mess worse. Ines's mother whispered something to her father who nodded and grabbed a towel from his satchel.

"Watch your father," her mother said, "this is how a man should act."

"Grab more towels," Papa said to a ship attendant who seemed as amused as the other passengers were. The attendant looked surprised by her father's command, but her father was firm. "Go on." The ship attendant listened and disappeared through a nearby door.

Ines watched as her father walked over to the crumpled mess of a man and glared at the other passengers who were still laughing loudly. For them, the monotony of the day, while waiting out the storm, had been broken at the man's expense.

"Are you alright?" her father asked, kneeling down and resting a hand on the man's large back. It was heaving with heavy breaths and drenched in sweat.

The sick man looked up, his green eyes streaming with tears. There were chunks of food in his brown, tangled beard.

"I've never traveled by boat before," he said, spitting onto the floor. "My wife and children are fine, but it looks like I was never cut out to be a sailor." He wheezed a laugh through his congested throat and smiled weakly.

"Sailor, no, but maybe a pirate?" Papa said, laughing as well. The man did look like a pirate. He had long, dark hair and a bushy beard that looked as if a family of birds could have been living in it.

Her father helped the man stand. He must have been over six feet tall, towering over Papa. Even though Papa wasn't very tall, Ines had never seen anyone look so much bigger than him. The man looked like a mountain, his muscles and rolls of fat flexed against the stretched and now stained linen shirt.

"Thank you," he said and reached out his hand, "My name is Abraham."

Papa looked at the outstretched hand, which was bigger than both of his combined. Whispers filled the room then as if asking, *will he take the man's hand?* Papa knew they watched, and he wouldn't embarrass him. Their hands shook.

"A pleasure, Abraham. My name is Salim Aude. Where are you coming from?" Papa asked.

"Beirut," Abraham said.

"We are from Beirut as well." Papa smiled and clapped his hand against Abraham's back.

"Thank you, Salim," Abraham added quietly.

"I can't have you taking all the spotlight," Papa said and looked back towards his family. Ines noticed her mother smile at him. "Would you like to sit?" Papa asked Abraham.

"I should get back to my family soon, but yes, I'll sit for a moment while my stomach settles."

They spoke for hours. Papa instantly took a liking to the large man. They discussed the women's movement and how quickly things were changing in Lebanon. Papa shared memories of being raised in the family business. The orchard farms where they grew the sweetest peaches and pears. He described how they looked in the early morning when the dew was fresh and unbroken. He could smell the fruit even before piercing their skins. Papa told Abraham that even as an adult he would get lost for hours between the trees and branches, looking for breaks in the browns and greens, searching for the bunches of colorful fruit that peppered the countryside like stars on Earth. Ines had heard those stories many times, but she couldn't get enough. The world was so colorful back then, before her parents felt they had to leave. By the time Papa and Abraham finished talking, the storm had ended, and everyone returned to their cabins.

A few days after the storm, the warmth of the Mediterranean was replaced by a chill as the ship docked in Russia, a country Ines had never heard of before. The day they arrived, Ines joined her family and hundreds of other passengers on the deck. They looked out at buildings Ines thought resembled giant pieces of candy, hints of a world she was sure only existed in fairy tales.

"Are we going to get to see those buildings up close?" Ines asked her brother.

He shrugged.

"Look," he said and blew out a cloud of air from his lips. The cloud didn't disappear and seemed to float weightlessly in front of them.

"Wow," Ines said, "how'd you do that?" she asked, only then realizing that clouds were escaping her lips as well.

Ines had never before experienced that sort of cold, which made the warm clothes she had on, the only warm clothes her mother had packed for her, hardly enough to keep the cold at bay. She had to move her feet from side to side to keep her teeth from chattering.

"My little penguin," her father said and laughed as he watched Ines' dance to keep warm.

That was the last time she would see her father smile or laugh for several days. What was meant to be a brief stop prolonged their voyage several weeks, due to issues with the Russian government. Until they were resolved, they were to remain docked, and no Lebanese citizens were allowed to disembark. Ines heard rumors floating around the ship that they'd never be allowed to leave as clouds of doubt hung over the ship and its passengers. This was the first time Ines realized something powerful could take control of people's lives and tell them what they could and couldn't do. Michel explained to her that each country had a government, and each government had control of what their people did. This concept made little sense to Ines, but it scared her, the idea of an imaginary force able to swoop down at any moment, making one a prisoner in their own country, or, in their case, on a ship.

But in their cabin, though Papa hadn't heard many updates from Abraham or the other men he'd met while onboard, Mama ensured they stayed positive, her worries alchemized into prayer, something she did daily, both morning and night. Ines joined her mother in prayer as often as she could. She understood, on some unconscious level, that in the same way she moved her feet to keep warm, her mother prayed for a similar reason. After several weeks surrounded by a cold Ines was sure would never end, the ship was allowed to leave Russia, and they continued on their voyage to Cuba, their delay quickly a distant memory. The air became warmer the farther south they went and without any sort of warning, the ocean soon surrounded them on all sides.

Ines made the most of her new life at sea. She felt like an explorer from one of Michel's books, any of the islands visible from the deck a potential new adventure. She knew they only had one stop, Cuba, but she still daydreamed. She imagined running along the white sandy beaches with her doll Aleia, knocking against coconut trees, cracking open their thick, hairy shells and drinking deeply of the sweet water Michel had told her they contained. In reality, she had no idea what waited for them in Cuba, the island her parents swore would give them a better life than they had before. Ines still wasn't convinced, but she hoped they were right, and still felt sure that one day they would return to Lebanon. She already missed the way her sandals clacked against stone as she and Michel chased the ships sailing along the waterfront.

Michel reminded Ines constantly how much he hated the ship, claiming boredom, when she suspected fear.

"But how will you ever be an explorer if you don't like ships?" Ines asked him.

"I like ships, just not this one. Anyway, I can fly to my adventures," Michel said.

"You can't fly. You're not a bird," Ines said.

"You're so ignorant," Michel said, and wouldn't tell Ines what ignorant meant when she asked.

Although Michel was only two years older than Ines, he was wise, and knew that once they arrived in Cuba, there was little chance they'd return to Lebanon. Even though their father had explained that much to Ines, she still didn't fully understand the finality of their voyage. *How would they not return home?* But they passed the time by exploring the many corridors of the ship, looking to find secret hiding places where Michel was sure the French crew members kept their jewels and other treasure. Michel spent hours reading the book Papa had given him as well as other books he'd brought with him, but the ship's passengers talked loudly and made too much noise when he wanted to read, so much of Michel's time exploring the ship was spent searching for pockets of quiet. Ines wasn't bothered by the noise and entertained herself by playing with her doll when she and Michel weren't running along the deck and hallways of the ship.

The cabin they slept in was small, made up of a double bed and a tiny cot that was springy and uncomfortable. While Ines was lucky enough to sleep in the bed, between her parents, two large mountains on either side of her, she worried that one morning she'd wake up crushed beneath Papa's back. There was a porthole in the room that looked out onto an ocean so vast Ines was sure it extended out in all directions until the ends of the Earth. When she told Michel this, he laughed and said it was impossible. It never looked like they were moving at all when she looked out through the porthole. The thought occurred to her that they weren't actually making any progress, that they were all being tricked by the ship's crew, and they would never reach Cuba after all.

It was late morning. They had been on the ship for several weeks and were finally nearing the end of their voyage. A cascade of soft light came in through the porthole, illuminating dust particles as they danced around the cabin. Papa was out somewhere on the deck with Abraham and other men he'd met during their time on the ship.

"I'm dressed," Michel said.

He stood by the door with his hands clasped together in front of him.

Mama was sitting on a chair by the porthole, knitting while she looked out at the ocean. She turned from the porthole to look at Michel.

"Did you brush your teeth after breakfast?" she asked.

He moved his finger along his teeth, making them squeak.

"Good…" She waited a moment, "Are you forgetting something?"

Michel had a smaller version of the satchel Papa used around his shoulder. He reached his hand into the satchel and jangled the coin purse. He then squeezed the book Papa had given him with his other hand.

He shook his head.

"Are you sure?" Mama asked and nodded towards Ines who was sitting on the bed, combing her doll's straw-like hair.

"Do I have to?" Michel pleaded.

"Michel," Mama said.

"Ines, you'd rather stay in here with your doll, right?" Michel asked.

"Take me around the ship, Michel. Aleia needs the fresh air," Ines said without looking up. She heard her brother's sigh and wanted to laugh but kept brushing Aleia's hair so her mother or Michel wouldn't notice.

"She only says that to annoy me. It's not fair. She'd rather stay in here and play with that stupid toy," Michel said.

"You're her big brother, Michel," Mama said and turned to Ines, placing a hand on her feet, little mounds in the bed covers, "Ines, put on your clothes and go with your brother. The voyage is almost over, so make the most of the ship," Mama said. "Your sister is kicking a lot today, and I need my rest," she added, more to herself than to her children. Mama turned back towards the porthole, rubbed her hands along her large belly and looked out towards the sea.

Chapter 3

If she'd known the sort of day that waited for her, Ines would have stayed in the cabin with her mother and wouldn't have left her side. She stepped out of the cabin and into the corridor, swishing her pink dress around how she imagined a moving picture star like Mary Pickford would, grateful to no longer be needing warm clothes when out on the deck. Ornate light fixtures illuminated the hallway floor, which was covered in red carpet. A painting hung to the left of their cabin door that showed the Eiffel Tower and the word "Paris" in bold, white letters. It was bordered by a huge, golden frame that Ines swore was made of solid gold, but Michel had told her it wasn't. She'd never experienced anything as luxurious as that ship. The simplest things brought wonder, both in their novelty and in their beauty.

Michel was sitting against the wall, directly underneath the painting, his cap pushed down over his eyes as if he were taking a nap.

"Come on, Michel. Aleia wants to go around the ship," she said, holding her doll loosely by her side, "Mama said we need to be back in an hour, so we can go eat lunch with Papa."

Michel grunted and lifted his cap to look up at her.

"I don't know why Mama thinks I need to take you with me every time I go around the ship," Michel said, pushing himself up, "and dolls don't have names. Why'd you name it after grandmother Aleia, anyway?"

"Well, this one does, and she's mine, so I can name her whatever I feel like," Ines said, "Where are we going? Do you want to see the pool again?"

"Nope," Michel replied, already walking down the hallway towards the exit to the deck.

"Then where?" she asked, trailing behind.

"Ice cream," Michel said without looking back.

Ice cream. The words echoed in her mind and filled her head with memories of barefoot summers in Lebanon. Her cousins would chase her through their family's orchards, careful not to knock down any of the dangling fruit and risk punishment from their parents. They would laugh for hours, getting lost in the labyrinth of small trees. Ines was the best at hide and seek, but when she'd been hiding too long without being found, she'd run out of her hiding spot, no longer wanting to be at the mercy of the hot sun. She would cry out that she'd won and run towards her home as fast as she could before they could catch her and accuse her of cheating. Every time she swung open the wooden door that creaked loudly—no matter how many times her father fixed it—her mother was there in the kitchen, ice cream ready in glass bowls. The ice cream ranged in color from yellow to red to green, all fruit from the orchard processed into melting orbs of cream and sugar.

Everything that came from the orchard was some sort of magic to Ines. Even when Papa explained to her that the fruit orchard was a family business and that one-day Michel would take it over, the magic wasn't lost, although she never understood why she wouldn't be the one to take care of the orchard. After all, she was the one who watched over the fruit trees, warning Papa of any patches that seemed to be growing slowly, and always on the lookout for infestations. In her mind, she was the perfect candidate while Michel didn't want anything to do with the orchard.

"I want to be an explorer," he would tell Ines.

Like the heroes in his favorite books, Michel wanted to see the world, traveling to Africa and other dangerous places, finding lost treasures and hidden things. He didn't want to be a farmer, stuck in Lebanon for the rest of his life, doing exactly what Papa had done, but Ines did.

With thoughts of ice cream as motivation, Ines followed Michel up the flight of stairs that led out onto the deck. Sunlight splashed across her face, instantly warming her skin. The sky was a light blue with only a few spread out clouds that looked like scoops of vanilla ice cream themselves. It was the perfect day for ice cream. At the same moment she felt the sunlight, a wave of sound crashed over her, voices yelling and laughing. It was as though a circus had come to life on the deck of the ship, but the roar of the lions, and the cheers from the audience were replaced by the sounds of hundreds of passengers moving around the deck. Whenever the circus came to

Beirut, Ines would beg her parents to take them, but now, in the middle of the ocean, the circus was there, just steps from her bed.

"Where do you think the ice cream man is?" Ines asked.

Michel shrugged and tugged on his cap.

"But I'll find him," he said with a grin.

It was Michel's signature grin, brimming with confidence. The same grin Michel would flash in Lebanon whenever he wanted to show off for Ines and their cousins, who were all girls. When they had rock skipping competitions at the pond near their home, Michel would get angry and storm off if he was ever beaten. Mama would scold Ines and her cousins, even when they swore that they'd done nothing wrong. She would make Ines go find her brother, who was always reading under the huge tree that cast long shadows along the west side of the orchard. Even when her cousins would snicker and make fun of Michel for running off, Ines defended him. While his idols were in books, swinging along vines and crashing through jungles, Michel was her hero, but she would never tell him that.

There were so many people on the deck that Ines was afraid finding the ice cream man was going to take much longer than the hour her mother had granted them. She inhaled the smell of fresh-baked bread as they walked by the outdoor café where tables were lined up and filled with people who were eating French pastries, smoking cigarettes, and drinking coffee. Ines noticed a group of men sitting outside of the café who were pointing and laughing between drags of their cigarettes. She looked to where they were pointing and saw women playing deck shuffleboard. The women were using long sticks to push discs along the floorboards, cheering when they knocked other discs away. She didn't understand the rules of the game, or the fascination with it, but the women's beautiful hats and sundresses drew her in. They looked like the Americans she'd seen in the magazines her older cousins had shown her the Christmas before they'd left Lebanon. She heard kids' voices to their right and saw a group of children playing tug-of-war with a thick rope, their faces red with effort. One side celebrated with laughter when the other group fell to the ground in a huge heap. Ines tugged on Michel's shirt.

"Let's play with them," she said.

"No," Michel said. "We're on a mission to find the ice cream vendor, remember?" Michel grabbed her hand.

They walked across the deck among people of all shapes and sizes. Some of them had smiles on their faces while others looked uneasy, as if they could feel the choppiness of the waves below them. Before they'd left Lebanon, Papa had shown Ines a map of the world, and pointed to where Cuba was. It was so tiny on the map that it looked like a smudge, painted on by mistake, God's afterthought, but Ines didn't say this to her father, who seemed so excited by what the island promised. It didn't look too far away from their home, only a few fingers in distance, so she couldn't believe it would take weeks to arrive. As they walked along the deck, Ines looked out at the sea and imagined where they were on the map, knowing that their delay in Russia had pushed back their arrival date significantly.

She held on tightly to Aleia, making sure no one bumped into her. It was her responsibility to take care of the doll. Her grandmother had sewn it herself and had given Ines the doll the night before they boarded the ship to leave Lebanon. She'd explained to Ines that she needed to keep the doll company, so she wouldn't feel lonely on their voyage to Cuba. Ines knew she was just cloth and scratchy fabric, filled with life-less stuffing, but it was the last thing her grandmother Aleia had given her, and she wouldn't let any harm come to her.

Michel led Ines to a part of the ship where a large group of people were standing around some sort of commotion. The crowd was made up of almost as many children as adults. The adults were talking to the children excitedly, pointing to something that Ines couldn't see over the treelike bodies around her. Standing on her tiptoes, Ines tried to get a glimpse of what had everyone else so intrigued, and it was then that a section of the crowd parted, and she saw it. Walking out towards the center of the deck, raised above the head of a little girl with pigtails, was an ice cream cone topped with a huge scoop of chocolate ice cream. Ines looked at Michel who smiled at her, a look of victory on his face. They'd found the ice cream vendor. Michel pulled Ines behind him as he attempted to squeeze through the crowd. Ines could feel her hand losing its grip with Michel's as he rushed through the throng, only slowing to find new routes around the people who were like rocks in their path.

"Oh, it's so great to see you!" a voice above Ines yelled.

Ines looked up, but before she could do anything, an adult foot came down hard on her own, and she was knocked to the ground. The outline of a large woman towered over her, almost blocking the sunlight completely. She was wearing a white bathing suit and matching swimming cap that made her head look like an egg.

"Watch where you're going, little girl," the woman hissed.

Ines stood up slowly and hugged Aleia closer to her body, grateful she was still there, but realized she didn't see Michel anywhere.

The woman's eyes squeezed together like dark beetles as she stared at Ines.

"Did you forget how to speak? Where are your manners?" the woman asked.

"But…" Ines began, looking down at her left foot, which throbbed in its once spotless white shoe, "But you ran into me," she said, looking back up at the woman.

"What did you say?" the woman asked, spitting as she spoke.

"I said—" A hand grabbed Ines by the arm, and she turned to see Michel had come back for her.

"I'm sorry, ma'am, my sister is very young," Michel said as he stepped in front of Ines.

Ines wondered how long he'd been standing nearby.

"Your wild animal of a sister here just ran into me. I should call security to have her put on a leash," the woman said, "but I won't if she apologizes. Are you sorry, little girl?"

Michel nudged Ines with his elbow.

"I'm sorry," Ines said in a quiet voice.

"What was that?" The woman took a step forward.

"I'm sorry," Ines repeated more loudly than before. The woman snorted.

"You *should* be sorry, little girl. I spent a lot of money for first class passage on this ship, and my trip is not to be ruined by rude little girls who don't watch where they're going. Do you understand?"

No words came out when Ines tried to speak as she was cold with fear. She'd never been punished by an adult who wasn't Mama or Papa. The woman's face twisted into an angry mask, making her look like one of the gargoyles Ines had seen in a painting on the ship. The painting was of a huge French cathedral that Michel explained was famous in France and had stone gargoyles that protected the French people by scaring away any evil spirits that wandered through the city. In that moment, with the woman standing in front of her, Ines was certain that the woman wasn't scaring away evil but was actually evil herself.

Ines tried to make sense of the woman's words, but she had no idea what "first class" meant and assumed it had to do with school. Her mind wandered to little desks and creaky seats as she imagined a black board covered with Arabic letters in white scratches of chalk. She thought of the clock on the wall, to the right of the teacher, and even though she still couldn't tell time, knew that when the hands were positioned in just the right angle, school was about to be over, and she could go back to the fields and play outside until the sun went down. Ines was sure that couldn't have been what the woman meant. Who would be excited for being the first to go to class? And why would she spend a lot of money for it? Ines did her best to keep tears from escaping and bit her lip so it wouldn't quiver, her confusion only making her fear more profound.

"I should really find your parents, shouldn't I?" the gargoyle woman asked.

Michel pleaded with her not to while Ines said nothing, her body still frozen. In her mind she prayed that the gargoyle woman wouldn't try to find their parents, but she couldn't do a thing, as if she were a prisoner in her own body. When the gargoyle woman exhaled a sound like a deflating balloon and her eyes once again focused on Ines, she was sure the woman would grab her by the ear and parade her around the ship, in search of her parents. Instead, the woman looked past Ines and Michel, exhaled once more, and walked away, in the direction of the swimming pool. Ines watched as she walked away then looked to Michel as they stood in silence. She wanted to thank him, but also wanted to explain that it wasn't her fault, that the woman had run into her, but Michel didn't give her a chance to say a word.

"Come on, the ice cream man's through here," he said.

Michel took hold of Ines' hand again and pulled her with him through the crowd, but this time, even as people yelled at them, some with raised fists, as they squeezed and nudged their way through, Michel held on even more tightly, careful to not let go. Ines heard the ice cream vendor before she saw him. There was the tinkling of bells and a warm, hearty laugh that boomed over all the other sounds around them. Between the people circling the ice cream vendor's cart like hungry piranhas, Ines caught glimpses of a jester hat that drooped in five points, each with a bell attached. Her heart swelled. She'd never seen anyone wear a hat like it outside of the circus.

"We're almost there," Michel said, looking back over his shoulder.

They continued pushing forward until they were next to the cart, and Ines was able to get a better look at the ice cream vendor. She realized then that the bells weren't just on his hat. He had dozens of silver bells threaded through the thick bristles of his beard and looked more like one of the clowns she loved to watch in the circus than someone who should be on a ship selling ice cream. Seeing the ice cream vendor up close, she forgot completely about the woman from before, and the question about first class that had still been floating around in her mind. Now all she could think about was ice cream.

On the side of his metal cart were the words "Crème Glacèe" in huge red letters. Michel pointed to the words and explained that they meant ice cream in French. He told Ines that he'd heard the ship's crew members say it once. Just once. While Ines, on the other hand, hadn't learned any French words, other than "Merci," and "S'il Vous Plait," throughout their entire journey, but that's just how Michel was. He remembered everything, even things Ines found boring. If Papa asked him what the capital of any country in Europe was, Michel would know. Papa was so proud of Michel's abilities that he'd quiz Michel in front of his professor friends who would gather around his study, listening eagerly to Michel's answers, which were always correct.

"Michel, come to the study!"

That was how they would know Papa had company.

Ines wanted so badly to impress her father, to remember things like Michel did, but as hard as she tried, she never could. She wanted to know how Michel did it. So, one night, Ines snuck into her brother's bedroom when everyone else was asleep. He was in bed reading a huge Encyclopedia. She only knew what it was because it belonged to Papa, and he'd shown it to her once, taking it from the old wooden bookshelf in his study. Ines told Papa the next morning that she'd seen Michel reading his encyclopedia. Instead of getting angry, Papa bought Michel his very own copy, a newer copy.

Michel also knew the capital of Cuba, which he would often remind Ines was Havana as if he thought she'd forgotten. He knew the language they spoke, which wasn't Cuban, or Arabic like she'd originally thought, but Spanish, a language Ines assumed they only spoke in Spain. She wondered how they would be able to speak with the locals when they arrived in Cuba if none of them could speak the language. This answer had come without the question ever being asked aloud when, while they were still docked in Russia, Mama had announced that she'd found a way for them to learn Spanish on the ship. She'd met an old woman who had lived in Spain as a child before moving to Lebanon. Mama asked her to teach them Spanish in exchange for scarves and other pieces of clothing that their mother spent all day knitting. Ines didn't remember a day go by when Mama wasn't knitting and remembered her mother arguing with the old woman before and after every lesson, begging her to take some form of payment outside of the clothing she'd made, but the old woman would never accept.

Ines and Michel called their Spanish teacher Mrs. Parrot. They named her this after the large parrot she kept caged in her cabin. It was light blue in color with splashes of yellow around its neck and talons. Whenever they went to the old woman's cabin for their lesson, the parrot would squawk and shake its wings furiously as if trying to shake loose from its feathers. Mrs. Parrot had yellow, see-through drapes over the porthole that made everything in the room glow orange. Ines hated the lessons, and the way Mrs. Parrot treated her pet. She shuddered whenever Mrs. Parrot used her cane to bang against the cage. It only made the bird angrier, squawking louder and louder, sometimes saying words that Ines didn't understand, but made Mrs. Parrot hit the cage even harder. Ines wanted to set the parrot free from its cage, so it could fly off to a distant island and enjoy its life in the trees, away from its owner. She had gotten close once before her brother had seen and stopped her, scolding her later when they were back in their own cabin. Once, when Mrs. Parrot had lost her temper at the bird and slapped her own leg in frustration, Ines and Michel laughed, and the old woman heard them. She raised her cane as if to hit them instead of the cage, but she didn't, calming herself before teaching Ines and her brother the names of colors in Spanish.

Ines was so glad to be outside in the warm sun and not in a lesson with Mrs. Parrot. The ice cream vendor's cart was swarmed by people, all yelling out the flavors they wanted scooped out for them, like ants crowding a dropped piece of mango. There must have been a dozen high-pitched voices rattling off flavors all at once while waving their hands in the air. The ice cream vendor seemed flustered, his eyes darting from one face to another, trying to figure out who was next. Ines felt bad for the man and didn't join in on the yelling.

The ice cream vendor finally lifted up a large copper bell and rang it with one hand until everyone was silent. He then asked that everyone form a line and wait their turn patiently, or he'd be forced to close early for the day. Ines had never seen so many children, or adults, move so quickly. The ice cream man's demeanor returned to normal, and he let out a hearty laugh as he pointed to the first in line. Ines and her brother were near the end. There must have been at least ten children in front of them—there were even two adults, and they looked almost as excited as Ines and Michel were. They waited for what felt like hours.

The sun was beaming down hard in the way it did around midday, making the water that surrounded the ship look refreshing. Ines felt beads of sweat pooling along her forehead until one broke free and ran wild down her face, as if trying to escape. She wiped at the trickle of sweat as fast as she could, swiping it away with the back of her hand. Ines looked around, but no one was looking. Her mother had taught her that ladies should never sweat in public, that it was impolite, and that only men who worked with their hands or little boys playing, were meant to sweat. After a few more minutes in the boiling sun, minutes that moved like snails through honey, Ines and Michel were one person in line away from their ice cream. Ines felt lucky when she looked back and saw at least six more kids lining up behind them.

The girl in front of them had on a light-yellow dress with white polka dots that burst from the fabric. Her hair was dark blonde like Ines', but Ines noticed that unlike hers, which was curly and sprouted from her head like tendrils of smoke, the girl's hair ran down her back like a river of velvet and almost reached her waist. Her hair was the most beautiful Ines had ever seen. The ice cream vendor handed the girl with the beautiful hair a cone filled with two scoops of mango ice cream that looked ready to fall over. When she turned around, Michel seemed to also be in awe of her hair because his cheeks turned red, and he seemed to be standing up even straighter than before. The girl looked to be a little older than Michel. She had a large smile on her face and stared intently at her ice cream.

"You look like an angel," Ines said to the girl as she walked past.

The girl didn't react, but Michel's cheeks became even redder, and he scooted Ines forward towards the cart.

The ice cream man was cleaning off his silver scooper with a stained towel and looked up as they approached.

"Good day, children. What flavor would you like?"

He spoke in Arabic with a thick French accent that made it hard for Ines and Michel to understand him. The ship's crew all had the same accent when they spoke Arabic, which is why most of them didn't even bother and instead communicated using their hands and the occasional grunt. It was a language everyone on the ship had learned to use, speaking to the crew members with broken phrases, their arms wielded like pens writing messages in the air.

"I can't see the ice cream," Ines said as she stood on her tiptoes, her hands resting along the rim of the cart.

"You know you're just going to get vanilla," Michel said.

"How do I know that for sure? I want to see. Maybe Aleia wants something different."

She whispered a question to the doll then lifted its face to her ear before looking back at Michel.

"She says she wants to see what the choices are. So come on, lift me up," Ines said.

The ice cream vendor let out a deep laugh. The bells on his hat and in his beard jangled, and his large belly bounced up and down beneath his white apron. Michel looked at Ines, his eyes narrowed for a moment, but without another word, lifted her up. Even though she'd asked him to, Ines immediately regretted having her brother lift her into the air. He wobbled and strained as he held her up just enough just to see the ice cream flavors on display in the cart. It wasn't like when Papa would raise her up onto his shoulders, strong and unmoving, like a tree that not even the most violent gusts of wind could knock over. She always felt safe when she rode Papa's shoulders through the air, as if she was still completely attached to the ground, but Michel just made her armpits hurt.

Her eyes went wide when she saw the different colors of ice cream. She recognized some of the flavors, but there were some she didn't. Pistachio was green and had little lumps in it. Mango, pear, and raspberry all looked refreshing, but weren't exactly what she wanted. She made her decision.

"Vanilla," Ines declared.

"See, I told you," Michel said and placed her back onto the deck.

The ice cream vendor chuckled and pressed his silver scooper into the mountain of white ice cream and scooped it out into a cone which he handed to Ines. As soon as she licked the ice cream, Ines wanted time to slow down.

"And for you, young man?"

"Two scoops of pistachio, please," Michel said, trying to make his voice sound deeper than it was. Ines giggled to Aleia. It entertained her when Michel tried to make himself sound more like Papa when speaking with strangers.

"How much do I owe you, sir?" Michel asked, echoing the words he'd heard Papa say when buying or bartering with merchants in Beirut. He reached into the bag slung over his shoulder and pulled out his coin purse. Ines hated the sight of that coin purse, reminding her how much their father trusted Michel. Papa hadn't given her any coins, saying that she was too young to be responsible with them, but Ines knew her father was wrong.

The ice cream vendor put up two fingers and Michel handed him that many French coins.

"Have a great day, children," he said in his rough Arabic.

Michel turned from the cart with his ice cream held proudly in hand. The light green scoops reminded Ines of the ocean. It looked like seaweed or one of those slimy ocean things that stuck to her legs when she played along the beach in Lebanon. It was piled up so high that she was sure Michel couldn't finish it all. Ines had never seen Michel eat two scoops of ice cream before and she thought maybe it had to do with the girl in the yellow dress who had two scoops of ice cream herself.

When they turned to walk back towards the cabin, the girl in the yellow dress was standing there, looking right at them.

"I love your doll," she said to Ines.

"Thank you," Ines said with a smile, "her name's Aleia. My grandmother made her for me."

"Wow," the girl reached out to touch Aleia, but Ines took a step back, shielding the doll with her arms.

"I'm sorry about my little sister," Michel said, stepping in front of Ines for the second time that day, "I'm Michel. What's your name?"

"My name's Ines," Ines interjected, peeking out from behind Michel.

The girl smiled and said, "My name's Johara."

Wow.

To Ines, even her name was beautiful, Johara meaning jewel in Arabic. She wanted that name, a name that brought to mind images of princesses, castles, and shiny things. Ines wasn't sure what her own name meant, or if it meant anything at all, but felt the pangs of curiosity inside of her as she wondered.

"Would you guys want to come and eat with me?" Johara asked.

"Sure," Michel said without hesitation.

Ines tugged at Michel's shirt. "Mama said we have to eat lunch with her and Papa today."

"We need to eat our ice cream either way," Michel whispered.

"But she said to be back in an hour. Has it been an hour?"

"Not yet. We have plenty of time." Michel turned to the girl. "Lead the way."

Johara waved for them to follow her as she turned and walked across the deck. This time, Ines had to grab on to Michel's hand before he took off after her.

"Come on. We need to keep up," Michel said.

Michel looked like he was in a trance. He didn't seem to blink, as if afraid that if he did, Johara would disappear. Ines secretly hoped that she would. She didn't want to get in trouble with Mama or Papa. They ate lunch together every day, always around the same time. It had become a temporary tradition, something that gave their life aboard the ship consistency. It was a sense of normalcy that had been left behind half a world away. Even though she hoped that they would lose Johara in the crowd, and Michel would have to take them back to the cabin, Ines knew it would be almost impossible. The girl's dress seemed to glow as it reflected the sunlight. The fabric flowed around her as she moved. She was graceful, like a dancer, dodging and swishing around the people walking along the deck who in comparison appeared to be moving in slow-motion.

Johara led them in the opposite direction of their cabin. Ines looked up as they went past one of the huge smokestacks that coughed out dark clouds into the sky. There were three huge smokestacks on the ship, which acted as her landmarks. She had the ship mapped out into three sections in her head. The first section contained their cabin, the dining hall, and the café. The second was the main deck, where they'd found the ice cream vendor and was also where the swimming pool and a theater were located. The theater showed French movies on a large white screen. Ines never understood what was going on during the movies, but she enjoyed them all the same, and once they ended would ask Michel what had happened. The third part of the ship, the one farthest from their cabin, was where Johara took them that day. That area was the most unknown to Ines and Michel.

They reached a dead end in the form of a rope that wrapped around a metal handrail and connected to a column on the deck. There was a sign in French that Michel told them said, "ship personnel only."

"I always wondered what that said." Johara lifted the rope and urged them through.

"Are you sure we should?" Ines asked Michel.

Michel didn't say anything. He walked past the rope, and she had no choice but to follow.

The walkway in this part of the ship became much narrower, and Ines noticed that there weren't any other people at all. Johara put a finger to her lips and told them to walk quietly. Ines kept thinking about her mother. Was she still looking out at the ocean from their cabin? Or was she walking around the ship, looking for them?

A door to their right swung open and a man walked out backwards with a bucket in one hand and a mop in the other. They ducked behind a column, hoping he hadn't seen them. He was singing something in French and had on the white uniform that the crew members wore. He turned for a moment and stood near the railing, only a few inches away from Ines. She didn't breathe, afraid to make a sound. Ines wasn't sure what would happen if they were caught in this part of the ship. He turned, water sloshing in his bucket, and walked away.

Johara and Michel began to laugh once the man was far enough away.

"Did you see how close he was?" Michel asked.

"How did he not even see us?" Johara said.

Ines didn't laugh, and looked at Aleia, who stared back with her button eyes, clearly unamused.

"Can we leave now?" Ines asked.

"We're almost there," Johara replied.

"See, Ines, we're almost there," Michel said.

As they continued down the walkway, Ines looked out over the railing to see water frothing white along the side of the ship. Every time they passed a door, she held her breath, imagining a crew member coming through the door and becoming angry with them for sneaking around the ship.

"Let's eat our ice cream here," Johara said in a part of the ship that to Ines, looked the same as the others.

Johara sat by the railing that looked out over the ocean. She dangled her legs over the side of the ship and Ines felt a current of fear run through her. Ines looked at the crashing waves below and imagined what would happen if the girl they'd just met were to somehow slip under the rail. Johara smiled and patted the deck next to her.

"Here, give me your doll while we eat our ice cream," Michel said to Ines and opened his satchel.

"No." Ines shook her head.

"Why not?"

"You might lose her," she said and took a step backwards.

"I'm not going to lose her. I have my ice cream money and my book in here," Michel said.

"Well, what if you drop your bag into the water? How will you get her out then?"

"I won't drop her. You want to eat your ice cream without worrying about Aleia, don't you?" Michel asked. It was the first time he had ever referred to the doll by their grandmother's name.

After some hesitation, Ines agreed and handed Michel the doll, which he stuffed into his satchel, her cloth head sticking out from the leather awkwardly, and then went to sit down next to Johara. Ines sat down next to her brother who told her to let her feet hang down over the edge. With all of the courage she could muster, Ines listened to him, and all three of them looked out at the water below as they licked their ice cream. Johara's hair blew around her, and to Ines, she really did look like an angel. Ines wished that her own hair could look like that, even if only for one day.

They finished their ice cream and talked about what they were most excited about in Cuba. Michel spoke the most, going into detail about all of the amazing things he would discover. Ines could tell Johara was becoming bored with Michel's habit of speaking more than listening, and without warning, Johara reached over and grabbed hold of Michel's bag. Before Michel could react, she pushed herself up, and ran along the deck the way they had come, waving the bag in the air.

"Well, if you're such a good explorer, come catch me!" she shouted behind her shoulder.

Ines saw Aleia's button eyes looking back at her from the opening in the satchel.

Michel said a string of words Ines had only heard Papa say and got up to run after Johara. Ines watched as they ran off, but couldn't go after them, her body paralyzed with fear as she sat at the edge of the ship, her legs dangling over the side.

Chapter 4

Ines was completely alone then, in a part of the ship she didn't recognize, and without Aleia. She began to cry. Her hands wrapped tightly around the metal railing as sea spray, carried by the wind, splashed up at her from the crashing waves below. She sat there for several minutes, waiting for Michel, or even Johara, to return, but neither of them did. They'd both forgotten her.

Ines looked down at the ocean through blurry eyes, which were red and burned from crying. She imagined the sharks circling below her dangling feet. The sharks were hungry, waiting patiently for something to fall from the ship and into the ocean that would make them less hungry. With this image, she pulled her feet up and crossed them, but still couldn't make herself stand up on her trembling legs. She shut her eyes, which only made things worse. The ocean, the waves and the wind were louder with her eyes closed and somehow seemed more violent. In the darkness she saw the sharks even more clearly and squeezed the slick railing as hard as she could. Her stomach felt weightless at the thought of falling into the water filled with the sharks, their enormous bodies, bunches of sinew and muscle, cutting through the water like blades. Ines knew they were moving right below the surface of the water, in a circular pattern that felt infinite in its motion. They were so close that they could smell her fear.

When they'd first arrived on the ship, Ines began having nightmares of being eaten by sharks, which alternated with nightmares of being lost at sea. She dreamt she'd never reach the island of Cuba or any other island, just float, lost in the ocean, on a small wooden raft that was only big enough for her and Aleia, while large, dark gray shark fins circled them. Mama would stroke her hair when she woke up from those nightmares and whisper softly to her until she fell back asleep. When it was morning, and she shared these fears of the ocean with Papa, he explained that the ship was moving too fast for the sharks to keep up with them and that the ship's captain and crew knew exactly where they were going, so they would never become lost. He explained that the ship was a miracle created together by God and man, one of the greatest achievements of all time, and that they were completely safe while onboard. He added that all of the sharks were still in Lebanon without any idea that they'd left, hundreds of miles in distance between them, so the sharks weren't able to find their way to Cuba.

"Sharks aren't sea turtles, after all," Papa would remind Ines, whom he'd taught that sea turtles would travel great distances in their long lifetimes, searching and finding new homes entire continents away from where they started. Her father's words didn't make her fear the sharks any less. They only made her wonder if she was in fact a sea turtle herself, and would spend the rest of her life swimming, never finding a place to call home.

Ines began to pray, hoping God could hear her so far from home and over the sounds of the waves and wind. She asked that her brother come back for her soon, so she could be back in time to eat lunch with her parents. Prayer gave Ines more strength than anything else. She and her mother had prayed every night before bed since arriving on the ship, the same way they'd done in Lebanon. She was like a perfectly wound clock, and never once forgot to pray, but she still wondered if God could really hear her. They were so far away from their home now that Ines wondered how He could still hear her, but Ines wouldn't dare ask Mama or Papa, so the question drifted around like a thundercloud in the back of her mind.

Don't just sit there. You have legs that work. Go find Aleia.

The words came from nowhere. Ines opened her eyes and looked around, sure someone had spoken. She was surrounded only by the wind as it whipped through her hair and burned her tear-streaked cheeks. A sudden thought occurred to her. Did the voice belong to God Himself? Had he heard her? Was He returning the prayer, assuring her that all was going to be alright? She wiped her eyes and looked around again. There were still no people, only rows of doors that led to parts of the ship she wasn't familiar with.

Be strong, Ines.

There it was again. But in that moment, she recognized the voice, and it reminded her of rain tapping gently against fruit trees and days spent running against the cool, Lebanese breeze. The voice belonged to her grandmother Aleia, who she pictured sewing the doll she'd made for her as she rocked on her old, wooden rocking chair. It had only been a few weeks since leaving, but she'd already forgotten exactly how her grandmother's face looked. She remembered her how she looked in dreams, slightly different, a sketch of the original, but she was still with her, and that was enough. The images of sharks disappeared from her mind, and she saw her grandmother's white hair and frail hands, filling her chest with a warmth she hadn't sensed since leaving home. Her grandmother was her best friend and while the other grandchildren called her grandmother, Ines called her by her name, Aleia. On several occasions her parents had asked that she call her grandmother, but Ines refused, and so did grandmother Aleia, who reminded them all it was her name that first crossed Ines' lips when she was a baby. She would often tell this to her friends, proud it was her name that Ines had said even before Mama or Papa.

Mama told Ines that her father's mother was once an incredibly beautiful woman, known to turn heads and break hearts, a strong-willed, free-spirited woman who had lines of men courting her from all around Lebanon, even from some neighboring countries. Ines loved hearing about her grandmother when she was young, but Papa refused to speak of her, angry with his mother for not wanting to go with them to Cuba.

"I'm too old," her grandmother told Papa when he pressed her, "I have lived a full life here, and I will not die away from my home, on an island you claim is a paradise. You all still have much life left in you. It's your turn. Go find *your* home."

On the night before they left Lebanon, when Aleia handed Ines the doll she'd made her, Ines decided that she'd name the doll after her. Her grandmother laughed so much then, a bright laugh that Ines could still hear in her mind, half a world away. Ines was hopeful she would see her grandmother again, either the day they returned to Lebanon or the day her grandmother changed her mind and agreed to join them in Cuba. Michel reminded her how foolish this was, but Ines didn't listen. Hearing her grandmother's voice while she sat alone on the ship renewed her hope and sent a surge of courage through her. It was her responsibility to take care of her doll, Aleia, the last thing her grandmother had given her. With this, she held onto the railing above her, and pulled herself up, careful not to slip out and into the churning waters below.

A man stepped out of a nearby door, which slammed shut behind him. Ines held her breath as she'd done before and watched the man. She waited for him to storm over in anger and take her to the captain, or worse, her parents, but instead he slapped on a hat and walked in the direction of the main deck, not seeming to notice her at all. Ines followed the man as she was sure he would lead her out towards the main deck. Her white dress shoes clicked loudly against the deck, and she needed to be as quiet as possible to keep from being heard. She removed her shoes and followed, ducking behind columns and peeking around them to make sure he hadn't noticed her. As she snuck quietly down the narrow corridor, Ines realized that she'd stopped crying. It was as if there was a fountain of fire inside her and nothing would get in the way of her finding Aleia. With this thought, an image of Johara flashed into her mind. She no longer seemed like an angel to Ines, who imagined Johara running through the ship, her perfect hair swirling around her, while Aleia bobbed up and down in Michel's stolen satchel. She remembered the words her grandmother had repeated often, when Papa wasn't nearby.

"Be most careful with the strangers that seem the friendliest. They are like lions pretending to be kittens. They are the worst of all."

She hadn't understood them before, but now she did, and wished she'd been more cautious.

Ines almost cried out when she saw the same rope and sign that they'd passed when following Johara. The man unhooked then re-hooked the rope as he stepped through, and Ines followed, ducking under the rope as she had before. This time it felt as if she'd gone underwater and had come up on the other side, breaking through the surface to fresh air. She looked around the deck for any sign of Johara or Michel but found none. There were more people in this section of the ship now, enjoying the weather as they rested in long chairs under the shade of umbrellas. Ines was greeted by the whooshing of handheld fans, which sounded like the swishing of bird's wings as she walked by. Finding an empty chair, Ines sat for a moment to put on her shoes. She shielded her eyes from the sun and looked up to see one of the three smokestacks she used to guide her around the ship. The smokestack seemed to be moving with the ocean, which made her feel a twinge of nausea, but gave her a better idea of where she was.

I'll find you.

Ines stood and ran along the deck, no longer caring that her shoes clicked loudly, towards the main deck where she was sure Aleia had been taken.

When Ines approached the main deck, the circus had once again come to life. The wave of sights and sounds hit her even harder than before, as there were even more people outside enjoying the midday sun. She looked around at the mass of people moving around like fog, hiding Aleia from her. She knew her doll was somewhere on that deck. Ines imagined the paths Michel had taken to chase Johara, watching them move in between people like a game of tag. Outside of her imagination, there were no signs of them.

"Help, someone's overboard!" came a woman's voice to the left of the crowd.

Ines glanced in the direction of the voice and saw a woman standing by the railing, pointing, yelling, and waving her arms as if she were signaling another ship. Ines felt her body go cold when she realized it was the same woman who'd accused Ines of running into her, the gargoyle woman. The woman's eyes seemed desperate, ready to come out of her head as she pointed at the ocean below. Ines wanted to know what she was pointing at, but it was what was in the woman's other hand that grabbed her attention. The woman clutched Aleia between her gargoyle claws. A group of men went over to her and looked to where she was pointing, but it didn't seem like they could see what she was seeing.

"I know what I saw," Ines heard the woman say, "someone is in the water, I'm sure of it."

Ines wondered who had fallen into the ocean, and if they were alright, but she needed to find a way to get Aleia back. With more people joining the woman at the railing, it would be difficult to grab the doll without anyone noticing. Ines stepped over to the crowd, squeezing between the adult bodies until she was standing next to the gargoyle woman. The fear that had paralyzed her before tried to creep back in, but Ines pushed any thoughts away as she was so close to Aleia.

"Excuse me," she said.

The woman didn't hear Ines or ignored her outright. She continued to yell and point, doing her best to convince the onlookers that someone had in fact fallen overboard.

"Excuse me," Ines said again, this time a little louder.

Still being ignored, Ines reached out and grabbed the woman's thick wrist.

The woman let out a cry and brought her hand to her chest, the one with Aleia. She looked down at Ines as if she'd been attacked.

"You just scared me half to death," the woman said.

"I'm sorry, but that's my doll," Ines said.

The gargoyle woman looked as if she'd recognized her after all.

"No, it isn't," the woman said, "You've already bothered me enough for the day. Go away." She turned back towards the ocean.

A few members of the ship's crew had joined in the commotion and were asking what had happened.

"They think someone's fallen in," a man in a straw hat told them.

One of the crew members used a pair of binoculars to look out at the ocean while another ran off to inform the captain.

Ines looked up at the woman. A strong gust of wind blew through her hair and ruffled the bottom of her dress. She reached back up.

"Can I please have my doll?"

The woman spun to look at Ines, spit flying from her mouth as she spoke.

"This can't be your doll, little girl," the gargoyle woman said, "I found this doll right here by the railing. There's someone overboard in the water down there. Whoever's doll this is must have fallen into the ocean. You aren't in the ocean, are you?"

Ines shook her head and tried to look down to where the woman was pointing.

"That's right. You're here, on the deck, *bothering* me. I'll ask you again, go away," she said.

Ines felt incredibly light, as if the wind could pick her up and take her away. Was it true, had someone fallen into the ocean? The ship was tall, and even though it was water below, her father had taught her the dangers of falling. She knew that if someone had fallen, they would have been very hurt or even worse, but there had to be some mistake because whoever fell overboard had Aleia, according to the gargoyle woman. Ines looked down and saw her legs planted on the light brown wood then touched her arms and felt warm skin. She was alive.

Could Michel have fallen in?

Before she lost herself to panic, Ines wrapped both hands around Aleia's cloth body and pulled as hard as she could. Aleia came free immediately. Ines was already running across the deck by the time the gargoyle woman turned to yell. She was numb with shock and could only think to run. She ran in the direction of the cabin, to find her mother, who would know what to do.

Could Michel have survived if he had fallen? Where was Johara? Why was Aleia left alone?

Ines fought to push the questions away, but they seemed to chase after her as she ran. So did images of Michel falling into the ocean, surrounded by the open jaws of hungry sharks. She squeezed Aleia, whose fabric body felt rough in her hands. Ines noticed a drop of water on one of Aleia's button eyes and couldn't help but think she was crying.

When Ines reached the entrance to their living quarters, she descended the stairs as if the ship was on fire and almost knocked into a man who yelled at her to slow down. It was as if she didn't notice a world existed around her and only her brother mattered to her then. Her mother was still sitting in the chair by the window when she entered the cabin. Everything looked the same as it had when they'd left that morning. She was knitting a pair of white, frilly socks that seemed to glow against the afternoon sunlight that entered through the porthole. Ines knew Mama was making the socks for her and wanted so badly to put them on and forget everything that had happened since leaving the cabin that morning, but she knew it was impossible.

"Mama," she said, panting.

Mama jumped in her seat and looked up at Ines.

"Where have you both been? First your father is late and now… you left the door wide open," Mama said, looking behind Ines. "Where's Michel?"

Ines said nothing as she tried to gather her breath.

"Is everything alright?" Mama asked, shifting in her chair.

"I—" Ines began.

"What's happened?" Mama asked, panic entering her voice, a hand reaching for her belly.

Ines finally began to speak. She relayed everything, from the ice cream vendor to Johara to finding Aleia by the railing. When she told Mama the last part, of the person who may have fallen overboard, Ines hoped her mother would explain how silly she was for worrying, that Michel couldn't have fallen overboard, but she didn't say those things. Mama only sat there. She parted her thin lips and let out a sound unlike any Ines had ever heard before. It was a croak, as if she were trying to speak, but couldn't. The sound filled the small cabin like a nightmare.

"Mama?" Ines asked.

Like water being poured slowly from a glass, Ines saw the color leave her mother's face.

"Mama?" she asked again.

If she'd heard her, Ines couldn't tell. Ines looked out through the porthole, hoping to see something that could fix everything that had happened. The ocean's waves looked so still.

"I'm sorry," Ines said.

She began to beg her mother for forgiveness, sure everything had been her fault, if only she hadn't told her. Then, as if someone had set the world back into motion, Mama burst into tears. She gripped her belly with a pained expression, and Ines began to cry as well. Ines wasn't sure how long they cried.

"We have guests."

Ines turned towards the door, wiping at her eyes. Her father was standing in the doorway with Abraham towering behind him.

Papa continued, "I brought Abraham and his daughter to visit."

Mama buried her face into her hands and wouldn't look at Papa.

Papa paused, looked at Ines who still had tears rolling down her face and then to Mama. "Is everything alright?" he asked.

Ines couldn't pull her eyes away from the doorframe. There, in the corridor, were two more people. They stepped into the cabin after Papa and Abraham. One of them was Johara and the other, Michel.

Chapter 5

The rest of their time on the ship bled together. All of Ines' thoughts revolved around her mother, and the cabin that had become her jail cell. Her mother couldn't leave the cabin, and Ines refused to leave her side, not allowing Mama or Aleia out of her sight. Ines sat in the wooden chair next to the bed where she had an equal view of the ocean through the porthole and of her mother. The chair was comfortable enough, but it looked old, and smelled like moth balls.

"Mama, how are you feeling?" Ines asked often.

"Better, thank God," her mother would say followed by a weak smile.

Even though Ines didn't believe her mother, and the smiles looked forced, she waited desperately for those replies. They were precious to her.

At Papa's request, the ship's doctor examined Mama several times.

"The baby may be at risk from the shock," the ship's doctor said to Papa in rough Arabic, "No matter what, Mrs. Aude must stay in bed."

"Okay," Papa said in reply, grabbing hold of Mama's hand.

Papa wanted another doctor to look at her, preferably one who spoke better Arabic, so he asked around the ship. Abraham told him there was a fellow passenger, a doctor from Lebanon, who had helped him with his seasickness. Although he was on vacation with his wife, the Lebanese doctor visited their cabin at Papa's request. Ines was surprised when he stepped into their cabin. She didn't think he looked like a doctor at all, more like one of the young men she'd seen hanging around in groups around the ship. After inspecting Mama with the small kit he'd rolled out onto her bed, the young doctor came to the same conclusion as the ship's doctor. He recommended bed rest for the remainder of the voyage and that she be taken to the hospital as soon as they docked in Cuba. Whenever the doctor said anything, Papa nodded his head and said, "okay."

Ines was convinced that if the doctor asked Papa to stand on his head and cluck like a chicken, he'd nod his head and say, "okay." Papa wasn't a loud man, but his voice was almost non-existent whenever the doctor was in the room. Mama was even worse, not saying anything at all, just listening absently while she rested her hands above the bed sheets that covered her belly. Her eyes searched the room as if she wasn't entirely sure where she was, and Ines knew how much her mother hated hospitals, but when the topic was mentioned, she didn't utter a word of protest. Ines wanted to cry out and wave her arms in front of her, just to make sure she was still there. Instead, she sat quietly and did her best to listen to everything the doctor said.

Listening and understanding were two different things entirely. She had no one to explain the technical things the doctor said as she was ignoring Michel, who Ines felt had abandoned her on the ship, and her father refused to discuss her mother's condition with her and constantly urged her to leave the cabin to enjoy the fresh air. Ines refused and felt if her mother was condemned to the cabin, she was too.

"This isn't your fault, Ines," her father reminded her, "your mother wants you to see the ocean. We only have a few days left," Papa pleaded.

Although her mother agreed from the bed, Ines was firm in her decision.

A day later, her father brought her a leather journal and a fountain pen and ink.

"I bought it from a man on the ship. He makes these journals. Do you like it? You can write in there, maybe go out onto the deck and note down what you see? There are many beautiful things left to see."

Ines thanked her father, knowing he only wanted to distract her from staying in the cabin, but there was nothing anyone could say or do that would take her away from her mother's side.

This wasn't the case for Michel who couldn't stand being in the cabin, especially after what had happened. He barely looked at Mama when he entered, as if he were afraid of what he might see. Instead, he played with Johara and her little brother on the deck, only spending time with Mama when it was time for bed. They no longer ate as a family, Papa and Michel eating in the dining hall like they all had before, while Papa brought back food for Ines and her mother to eat in the cabin. Ines noticed that her father went to the smoking parlor with Abraham more often than he had before. Ines would sometimes wake up in the middle of the night, her father just returning, with the smell of sour smoke clinging to his clothes and hair. The smell would balloon around the cabin and make it difficult to breathe. During the day, Ines would keep the porthole open to let out all of the smells of smoke from the night before.

"I'm opening the porthole, Mama," Ines would say, which garnered only a grumble from her mother.

If her mother had been herself, she wouldn't have allowed her father to come back home so late and would have been upset with Ines for keeping the porthole open, inviting the cold ocean air the opportunity to make them sick, but she said nothing about either. Ines couldn't understand how her father and brother acted so normally while her mother was sick and found it even stranger that her mother didn't seem to mind either. Ines missed her family as they were before and hated the shadows that had seemed to replace them. Every night, after she prayed, Ines wrote in the journal her father had brought her. Sometimes she wrote about the ship, and what she'd done before her mother's sickness, but mostly her words were expressions of her anger, doubts, and fears about her mother's condition and what it all meant for their new life in Cuba.

Ines directed her anger towards Johara, whom she blamed even more than she blamed herself. She was sure that if Johara hadn't run off, Mama wouldn't have become sick. Her father tried to find out if someone had actually fallen overboard, but they never found out for sure. Between witnesses and the passenger log, the people Papa spoke to claimed that everyone was accounted for. Ines thought that perhaps it had been a mermaid the gargoyle woman had seen, and as she felt excitement at the thought, quickly remembered where she was and that her mother was still feeling ill.

On one of his visits to the cabin, the young doctor brought two members of the crew with him, who announced it would be only a few more days before they reached Cuba. The men stood in the cramped cabin and looked at Mama as if she were a piece of furniture that they were tasked to move from one place to another. Ines glared at them with distrust. They asked Papa questions and nodded as he answered while Michel read a book on his cot.

"We'll move her before the official offboarding begins. That way you and your family can get to the hospital as quickly as possible," the older of the two men said.

The younger crew member nodded in agreement. Papa thanked the doctor and both crew members, but for just a moment, Ines saw fear on his face.

The day they arrived in Cuba was very different than Ines had imagined. Her father jostled her shoulder softly until she opened her eyes. It was early morning, so early that the sky looked purple through the porthole and there were only hints of the sunrise to come. She hugged Aleia to her body and stretched out her legs. Ines had dreamt of her baby sister and wondered if she was doing okay inside of her mother's belly.

"We're here," Papa said softly, his hand brushing hair from her face.

It was then that Ines realized what day it was. She shot up from the bed and ran into the bathroom with a bundle of clothes, including the socks Mama had been knitting her before she'd gotten sick. As the crew members had promised, the Aude family was the first to get off of the ship that day. Soon after they were all awake and dressed, the two men were at their door, tapping lightly against the wood. When they entered, they pushed a long gurney into the cabin and apologized as it smacked against the doorframe. The young doctor entered behind them.

Ines and Michel watched as their father and the other men helped lift Mama onto the gurney.

"They use that for dead people too," Michel whispered to Ines.

Ines didn't say a word. She looked at her mother where she lay on the creaky table with wheels.

"We're ready," one of the men said.

Papa and the younger crew member grabbed their luggage and led them down the corridor. Ines stayed by Mama's side as she was wheeled out of the cabin. Her large belly rose up from under the gurney's sheet like a snow-covered mountain. It took all four men to help lift and guide Mama up the stairs as they went to the main deck. Ines had never seen the deck so quiet. The few people who were out stared and whispered as they went past. There were more crew members waiting for them near the side of the ship, including the captain. Ines realized how strange it was to be let off of the ship like this when they'd been near the last to board in Lebanon.

The young doctor greeted the captain who smiled as Ines and her family approached. Papa explained to Ines that the doctor was friends with the captain, and it was because of him they were allowed to leave the ship so early. The captain wished them well before leading them to a ramp that was still being set up by several crew members. While they waited, Papa grabbed hold of Mama's gurney and pushed it closer to the railing. Ines and Michel followed closely behind. The rising sun washed over them as they looked out from the ship. There were buildings everywhere, surrounded by palm trees that erupted through the paved streets. The sky was the color of tangerines and made the city look as if it were made of gold. Even the palm trees glowed like flickering birthday candles. Ines stared off towards a stretch of the island where a huge castle loomed above the glittering water below. She wondered if princes and princesses lived there.

"That's Havana," the Lebanese doctor said as he joined them by the railing, pointing to the harbor they'd entered.

Although it was early in the morning, the city felt as if it were already awake. The bustle of Havana sounded like the gentle shushing of the sea.

"We're home," Papa said, hunching over to speak into Mama's ear.

"Yes," Mama said and smiled.

The doctor told them it would be his third vacation to the island as both he and his wife loved it. If it wasn't for his family's medical practice in Lebanon, he would have moved to Cuba long ago. Seagulls flapped their wings only a few feet above their heads. Ines wanted to reach up and touch one, wondering if Cuban birds sang different songs.

"Havana awaits," the captain said, motioning towards the gangplank.

Papa thanked everyone once again before hurrying them along, but it was difficult for Ines to look away from the view of the city, as though she were under a spell.

"Come on, Ines," Michel said, grabbing her arm.

They moved down the ramp cautiously, as if any sudden movements would cause Mama to shatter into a hundred pieces. The doctor and the two crew members who had been helping them also came down the ramp. Ines wondered if everything her parents had told them about Cuba was true. They'd said it was the most beautiful place anyone could ever live, that they would find a new home there. Ines couldn't deny it was beautiful, but the island itself was still a stranger to her, and just as Johara had harmed her, maybe the island would too.

Once she stepped down from the gangplank and onto the dock, a warmth wrapped around Ines like a blanket. She shielded her eyes from the newly risen sun and looked around. There really were palm trees everywhere, and the dock was much busier than the ship had been that morning. Dock workers and officials hurried past each other while the crew members who had helped them returned to the ship. The doctor led them to a tent where several officials waited.

"Hola," one of the officials said.

He coughed into a clenched fist and sat down behind the table. He was an old man with tan, wrinkled skin. The whites of his eyes were tinged with yellow, and he didn't look like he'd expected to see anyone this early in the day. He looked them up and down, his gaze pausing over Mama lying on the gurney. He motioned toward the ship they'd just arrived on and said some words in Spanish that Ines didn't understand. When he moved his hand, it smelled like Papa did after coming back from the ship's smoking parlor, making Ines feel nauseous.

"He's asking if you're here on vacation. I'll tell him you're immigrating. Go ahead and give him your Visas," the young doctor told Papa.

Ines understood little of what the official and the doctor said as they spoke, realizing then that Mrs. Parrot hadn't prepared them as well as her mother had hoped. The words flew by her ears like buzzing mosquitoes as she snatched at as many she could, most of them sounding more like noise than the language she'd studied on the ship.

Papa reached into his satchel and placed a stack of documents onto the table while the doctor translated between Papa and the official. The old man squinted his eyes as he went over the documents.

"If they don't like you, they may not let you in and you'll have to go back to Lebanon all by yourself," Michel told Ines.

Her stomach clenched as she wondered if Michel was telling the truth. Ines wanted to ask her mother, but she was resting her eyes. Ines watched the man behind the table closely as he continued to read over the papers Papa had given him. It looked as if he were checking for the smallest of errors. Swatting at something near his head, the man looked up from the documents. He looked directly at Ines and fear surged through her as she pictured herself all alone on the voyage back to Lebanon. She knew in her heart that no matter what, her parents would never leave any of their children behind, but the fear remained. Part of her wished the man would tell them that none of them were allowed to stay in Cuba at which point they would all be forced to go back to Lebanon together.

Without a word, the official lifted up a stamp, pressed it firmly into a pad of ink and brought it down hard on each document. He then stood up and handed them to Papa.

"Bienvenido a Cuba," the old man said.

He whistled over to a group of men who were squatting and throwing dice under the shade of one of the palm trees. The men slapped on their caps and ran over to them.

"They'll help you get sorted out from here on out," the doctor said and gestured towards the Cuban dock workers, "A car is waiting to take you to the hospital. It's parked on that street over there. I'll tell these men where to take you."

"Thank you," Papa said, shaking the doctor's hand, "How can we repay you?"

"I'll be repaid when your wife gives birth to a healthy baby," the doctor insisted, "and if I don't help a countryman in need, what sort of doctor would I be?"

He told her father about an acquaintance he had from Lebanon who worked in the hospital. He then handed Papa a piece of paper containing the phone number of the hotel where he and his wife would be staying, along with the name of his acquaintance.

"Doctor Karam," Papa read aloud from the paper.

The doctor nodded and encouraged Papa to ask for Doctor Karam as soon as they arrived at the hospital and to call him at the hotel if there was anything else that they needed. The young doctor looked at his wristwatch before telling Mama and Papa that he had to get back to his wife. Ines waved at the doctor as he left, realizing she didn't know his name.

One of the Cuban men the official had whistled over grabbed hold of her mother's gurney and pushed it along while the other two grabbed the luggage Papa had been carrying, except for his own suitcase, which he refused to hand over. They led the Aude family along the dock and kept looking back over their shoulders as they spoke a Spanish none of them could understand. Papa nodded, acting as if he understood whatever it was they said.

"Hospital," Papa said in Spanish.

It was one of the few Spanish words Papa could say in Spanish, which made the men laugh then point in the direction they were headed.

"Hospital," they repeated as they walked.

The dock was much bigger than it had appeared from the ship. Everyone stopped as Papa placed his suitcase down and wiped at his forehead with a handkerchief he pulled from his pocket. He then walked over to Mama and patted her face dry as well. Even though it was early, it felt hotter than it had on the ship, and to Ines, the sun itself seemed brighter and more orange somehow.

They were all drenched with sweat by the time they made it to the sidewalk, but a car was waiting for them like the young doctor had promised. When the driver saw them approach, he got out and helped them with their luggage. He said something in Spanish to the dock workers that made them laugh as he took the heavy bags from them. When the car was loaded, one of the dock workers walked up to the driver.

"Hospital," he said, then patted Papa on the shoulder and headed back towards the dock with the other workers.

Chapter 6

They'd been in Cuba for several hours by the time they arrived at the hospital. The comforting warmth Ines had felt when they'd first arrived had become an uncomfortable heat. Her mother had her eyes closed during the car ride, her jaw clenched tight, and small beads of sweat trickled down her face. It looked as if her pain was becoming worse the more they drove. Ines sat next to her in the back seat and wouldn't let go of her hand, which was cold and sweaty. Ines stared out of her window as they passed by statues of huge eagles, their wings spread as long as cars and stone soldiers who raised their swords up into the sky. The buildings were even more beautiful than they'd looked from the ship. They looked a lot like the figurines Papa collected in Lebanon. He kept a huge display case in his study full of miniature figurines of castles, bridges, and detailed archways. Ines never cared much for those small replicas, but she couldn't deny how beautiful the city of Havana was.

When they entered the hospital, Ines was surprised at how big it was, its walls and floors as white as the uniforms the nurses wore. One of the nurses saw them coming and ran over with a wheelchair for her mother, who was being helped inside by Papa and the driver. The gurney hadn't fit in the car, so they had to help her in and out of the car as delicately as possible. Ines wanted to help too, but her father wouldn't let her.

"Gracias," Papa said to the nurse.

He asked her for Doctor Karam as he held out the piece of paper the young doctor from the ship had given him. She looked at the name before disappearing down the long hallway and returning a few minutes later with a tall man who wore a doctor's smock and had a long, bushy mustache like Papa's.

"Doctor Karam," Papa said and greeted the man in Arabic.

Doctor Karam smiled, clearly happy to hear his mother tongue, and echoed the greeting. Ines watched as her father explained their situation to the doctor, a complete stranger, as if he could truly understand. The doctor asked questions and nodded while a look of curiosity remained on his face. Ines looked over at her mother whose breath was coming out in short gasps that sounded like a broom's bristles brushing against the floor.

"Papa, I think something's wrong with Mama," Ines said and tugged at her father's trousers.

Doctor Karam noticed and walked over to her mother and placed a hand on her neck. Within a minute the same nurse who had brought the doctor was wheeling Mama away from them. Ines tried to run down the hall after Mama, but her father stopped her. The hallway looked endless to Ines as she watched her mother disappear down it.

"She is in the hands of the doctors now," Papa said, bringing Ines close to his body.

Doctor Karam led them to a waiting room before he himself went down the hall. Ines was convinced that the hallway was somehow magical and sent anyone who walked down it to another world.

Most of the seats were empty, so her father chose the closest to the hallway and sat down. Ines refused to sit at first, but after a few minutes of standing, she sat next to him. The room was stuffy and felt no better than it had outside, but she was lucky in that the chair she'd sat in was in the direct path of a metal fan that whirred as it moved side to side. Michel begged her to switch seats with him, but Ines shook her head. She turned in her chair and looked out at the street through the windows behind them. It was a busy road, but after watching dozens of cars pass by, she became bored, and looked around the waiting room.

An old woman sat a few seats away and coughed repeatedly into an embroidered handkerchief. A man who looked about the same age as her father sat across from the coughing woman, his head arched back against the seat of his chair. A woman, who Ines assumed was the man's wife, sat next to him. They reminded her of her parents. The woman noticed Ines and smiled at her. Ines quickly looked away, her eyes landing on a stack of magazines that rested on a wooden coffee table in the center of the room. The magazine on top showed the cartoon drawing of a man with a big white beard as he stood next to a cow. The words underneath his photo were in Spanish, but Ines understood them: *All is well, in Cuba.*

Ines remembered her grandmother, who would always repeat those words to her when she couldn't sleep.

"All is well, little one," she would say, rocking Ines on her lap.

"Will everything be okay?" Ines asked her doll, hoping somehow her grandmother could hear her.

A breeze would flow in through the entrance of the hospital whenever a new patient walked through the doors. The warm air moved softly against Ines, and her eyes became too heavy to keep open. She fell asleep without wanting to, her dreams dark and frightening. Ines saw her mother splayed out on the gurney she'd used on the ship as doctors surrounded her, their faces stretched and contorted like demons with eyes that burned bright red, and teeth that were too long for their mouths. They clutched rust covered axes in their claws, dozens of bent teeth reflecting the yellow light from the exposed lightbulb dangling above them.

A hand brushed the hair from her face, causing Ines to wake up with a start.

"Shhh, it's only me," her father said, brushing aside another strand of hair.

Ines rubbed her eyes and looked outside, realizing night had come. It was only her, Papa, and Michel in the waiting room.

"Where's Mama?" Ines asked.

"She's still with the doctors," her father said, "do you want some dinner? The nurses brought us food."

Ines shook her head, but her father reminded her she'd need her strength for Mama.

They ate their food in an empty cafeteria. Whenever a nurse walked by, Papa relied on Michel to ask them for updates on Mama's condition, but every update was the same, their mother still hadn't gone into labor.

"She will soon," the nurses would add.

Eventually, after they'd received the fourth update that nothing had changed, Papa told them that they would be staying the night in the hospital.

"Will we even have beds?" Michel asked, but their father didn't reply.

Ines said nothing, but she thought to herself how strange it was that on their first night in Cuba, on the island meant to be their new home, they would spend it sleeping on lumpy hospital chairs. Their father promised that they'd all be going home soon, but Ines had no idea where that was. Lebanon was still her home, so part of her thought that perhaps after all that had happened, they would have no choice but to go back.

Multiple hospital workers stopped by to check on them throughout the night. One nurse with dark, curly hair, and kind eyes, brought them blankets and pillows to use. She helped Ines and Michel push some of the seats together, so they could make makeshift beds. Papa slept sitting up in his chair and fell asleep quickly. Ines couldn't fall asleep at first and decided to stop ignoring Michel. They whispered for hours, talking about Mama, their baby sister, and Cuba.

When sleep finally came, Ines dreamt of her baby sister again. She repeated the words of her grandmother to her unborn sister, "All is well, little one."

When Ines woke up the next morning, Papa was standing nearby and speaking with Doctor Karam. The doctor was surprised they'd spent the night in the waiting room.

"Where are you living?" he asked.

"Las Piedras," her father said.

"Las Piedras?" the doctor asked, using the proper pronunciation.

Papa nodded and the doctor smiled. He explained he'd grown up in Las Piedras, having arrived from Lebanon as a young child around the same age as Michel, and that his mother still lived there. In fact, he told Papa, he could give them a ride there once his shift ended.

No! Don't listen to him. Ines imagined her mother waking up all alone in the hospital.

Papa refused at first and thanked the doctor. At that moment, a nurse returned with an update on Mama, explaining that it would still be several hours at least until labor began, maybe even until the next day.

"You see, you will all have to stay here at least for another night. Come, let me take you home," Doctor Karam said.

Her father reluctantly agreed.

Ines begged her father to let her stay, but he refused.

"The hospital is no place for children," he said.

"But what about my little sister? She's going to be born here and she's even younger than I am," Ines said.

Papa chuckled at this, which was the first time Ines had seen her father laugh since her mother became sick.

"Your little brother or sister will be home with us soon. You want to have everything ready in our new house for Mama and the baby, don't you?" Papa asked.

A little while later, when Doctor Karam's shift was over, Papa sat in the front seat of the doctor's car while Michel and Ines sat in the back. Ines noticed that his car was much nicer than the one that had picked them up from the dock. Papa whispered to them that it was a very expensive American car, which made them both look around in wonder. The windows were down, and wind rushed past as they headed out of the city. Ines' hair flew all around her face as she leaned out of the window to look at everything they drove by. People walked under the shade of palm trees and tall stone buildings, filling the sidewalks completely. The ocean looked beautiful in the distance, and so much cleaner than the Beirut harbor she was used to. Ines wondered if Las Piedras looked like Havana.

She realized then that the first time she'd heard the name of the town where they'd be living was when her father told Doctor Karam. She knew less about their new home than the doctor, who was still a complete stranger.

"Did Papa tell you the name of the town?" Ines asked Michel.

The car was noisy with the wind coming in through the windows, bringing in the sounds of the engine and passersby from outside.

"What?" he asked.

"The town, did Papa or Mama tell you that it was called Las Piedras?"

Michel thought for a moment.

"I think Papa did before we got on the ship," Michel said and turned back to look out of the window.

Ines looked back out through her own window. She wondered how Las Piedras would compare to Beirut. Could she see the ocean or the cliffs from her window? Could she smell the saltwater on the wind as she ran barefoot through the fields? Would she ever be able to pick large, ripe fruit fresh from their branches? Ines knew she would miss the orchard most of all.

As the doctor drove, he talked constantly. He explained that Las Piedras had been named after all of the rocks that were found in and along the huge river that ran through the town and its surrounding countryside. Like a huge blue vein that connected every part of Las Piedras, the river was crucial to the people who lived there and was the town's most prominent feature. Las Piedras was bordered by large mountain ranges and filled with long stretches of countryside ideal for farmers and ranchers. While Las Piedras wasn't as much of a tourist location as Havana, or other towns that had nearby beaches or famous shops and restaurants, he shared that the river brought locals from other parts of Cuba, who swam and rafted down it almost year-round.

When Papa showed the doctor the address where they would be staying, he grew even more excited, explaining that he knew the house. When he was a child, his mother would occasionally cook for the woman who lived there, and he'd deliver the food to her. He told them that there was a huge guava fruit tree on the property and that the woman, who he said was named Nayibe, would let him pick a guava fruit every time he visited. The ripe guava from that tree were the best he'd ever had.

"What's a guava?" Ines asked Michel.

Michel shrugged and asked the doctor.

The way the doctor explained guava fruit to them made Ines feel as if she was still in Lebanon, eating fresh pears from the orchard. She hoped that the guava tree was still there and thought of it as they continued down the road. She imagined what Las Piedras might look like as the city streets of Havana began to change into country roads that led them further away from her mother and closer to their new home.

Chapter 7

Ines was filled with wonder as they drove over the large bridge that passed over the river, just outside the Las Piedras town square. Once they were over the bridge, the countryside became even more overgrown and wild. While the houses in town were similar to the buildings they'd seen leaving the hospital in Havana, most of the houses outside of town were unlike any Ines had ever seen before. Their roofs were made of palm fronds and had walls that looked as if they'd been sculpted from tree bark, as if they still belonged to the nature from which they were borrowed. The doctor stopped his car in front of a dirt road that was surrounded by bushes. He apologized as he explained that the car couldn't make it all the way to the house. A wooden bridge nearby crossed over a stream that was filled with stones. Water rushed over the stones, creating small waterfalls that reflected the late-afternoon sun. The stream was only a small offshoot of the even bigger river they'd seen as they arrived in Las Piedras, a town that seemed quieter than Havana had. Ines wanted to explore the town, but her father insisted they go home and unpack. "You'll have much more time to explore," he told her.

"Can I at least help you with your luggage? It's really only a short walk to the house," the doctor said to Papa.

"Not at all. You've already helped us more than you know," Papa said.

As soon as Ines got out of the car, she tried to see the house from the road, but her view was blocked by large, green plants whose leaves looked like sharp knives that sprouted out in all directions as well as tall, skinny trees that had large fans of green on top of them. The trees looked to be as tall as buildings from where Ines stood next to the car. The doctor helped Papa and Michel unload the luggage, while Ines lifted Aleia above her head, hoping maybe *she* could see a sign of the house or the guava tree. Ines stared at the dirt path that wound between the bushes and wondered if Mama would be able to walk all the way to their new home once she left the hospital. She could only imagine her the way she was on the ship: tired, feeble, and bedridden.

Papa thanked the doctor and asked Ines and Michel to do the same.

"Thank you for taking us away from Mama and splitting our family apart," Ines thought, but said, "thank you," instead.

The doctor smiled and wished them all farewell before he reminded Papa that he'd be back in the morning to take him to visit their mother in the hospital. Ines knew her father wasn't used to such kindness from strangers and could only imagine how he felt accepting it.

They watched as the doctor drove back down the bumpy road, leaving behind a cloud of dust that stung Ines' eyes. Her father made them wait until the car was completely out of view before turning toward the dirt path and making their way to their new home. He carried three suitcases, two in his hands and one balanced between his chin and arms. Ines carried a small bag that was heavier than it looked while Michel struggled to drag one of the heaviest suitcases behind him. They had to stop several times while her father readjusted, fumbling with the luggage. He finally decided that they'd leave some of their things on the trail and come back to get them once they reached the house.

The stream was beautiful. Rocks rested all along its bank and little green shrubs burst from between them. The rocks looked like little heads and the shrubs looked like the frilly collars that kings and queens wore around their necks. To cross the stream, which was a lot wider up close, they had to walk over a wooden bridge that, to Ines, seemed unsafe to step on. The wood looked old and was covered in a layer of light green moss. It looked like the planks would break the moment they walked over them. Ines dropped her bag, crossed her arms, and refused to cross the bridge.

"I'm not going to walk over that," she said.

"Come now, we need to cross here. It's the only way over," her father pleaded, "I still need to go back for the rest of our luggage."

"What if there are sharks in the water?" Ines asked her father.

Papa put his luggage down and knelt in front of Ines, placing a hand on each of her shoulders.

"I promise you, there are absolutely no sharks in this water. This stream is so far from the river, and even farther from the ocean. It wouldn't be easy for a shark to get here."

Papa looked at her hopefully, but his explanation didn't make her feel any better. She remembered the ocean, and the woman screaming at the railing, *someone's overboard!*

"Do you know how many people have crossed this bridge before us? Does it look like it's ever broken before?"

Ines shook her head.

"Exactly. It's a strong bridge, one of the strongest bridges I've ever seen. Look, if I can cross it, then you will know it's safe, right?" her father said.

Ines thought for a moment then nodded.

"Good. Come," Papa motioned to Michel, "let's cross."

They crossed the bridge, which creaked loudly with every step, but didn't break.

"See, Ines? We're fine."

Ines squeezed Aleia and stepped onto the bridge, the layer of moss slick under her shoes. She looked at the water flowing next to her. The stream wasn't very deep, and she could see little fish swimming with the current. Several droplets of water splattered against her forehead. At first, she thought a fish had splashed her, but then she looked up to see dark clouds forming in the sky above them.

"It looks like there's a storm coming. We need to get inside before it really starts to rain," her father said.

There was a flash of lightning that seemed to cover the world in light followed by booming thunder.

"Whoa, did you see that?" Michel cried.

Ines ran across the bridge, no longer afraid of the water below her feet.

"Let's get inside quickly," their father said once she made it across.

The dirt path wove between bushes and short grass until it ended at a fork. Michel was sure they should follow it to the right, but their father had them go left. As they walked down the path Papa had chosen, the rain, which had begun as a light drizzle, became a total downpour. Ines felt her hair become heavy as beads of water rolled down her face.

"Papa, don't you think we should have gone back the other direction? The doctor said it was a short walk to the house," Michel said.

"No, we are still on the path. It should be just a little bit more. We are walking very slowly after all."

Their father was wrong. They walked for several more minutes in that direction without seeing the house until Papa told them to turn around. Michel smiled and told him that he'd been right all along, but Papa continued to walk and said nothing.

When they finally reached the house, it had stopped raining, but their clothes were drenched, and the sun had set. Insects made noises all around them as they approached the porch. There were two lanterns hanging on either side of the front door. From what Ines could see with what little light the lanterns provided, the house looked smaller than their home in Lebanon. Papa walked up to the door and knocked. Ines thought it was strange that her father would be knocking on the door to their own house, but it was even stranger when the door opened, and an old woman greeted them in Arabic and ushered them inside. Ines was convinced they'd somehow walked all the way back to Lebanon.

Papa thanked her and asked her to forgive their wet and muddy appearance.

"That's the weather in Cuba. It comes and goes without a hello or goodbye."

When the old woman laughed, something about it reminded Ines of her grandmother. Once they were inside, Papa introduced Ines and Michel to the woman, explaining that she was the owner of the house and had been childhood friends with their grandmother Aleia. Ines' heart leapt when her father mentioned her grandmother's name. He went on to explain that they'd be staying with her until they were able to buy their own house in Cuba. Ines looked at Michel who seemed as surprised as she did, but neither of them said anything other than, "hello." Ines wondered how many more things she still didn't know and stared at the old woman whose white hair was pulled back in a tight bun that made her face look stern.

"Please, call me Nayibe. Consider my home yours," she said as she began to show them around.

It was as small on the inside as it looked from the outside. There were three bedrooms in total and Papa explained to Ines and

Michel that they'd be sharing the bedroom on the left while he and Mama would have the room across the hall.

"Oh, that's right, is your wife still outside?" she asked.

Papa explained that Mama was still at the hospital. When he mentioned the doctor, who had driven them, the old woman's eyes came alive.

"I remember that young man. He was a little troublemaker who I had to shoo away from my guava tree. His mother would cook me food to pay me back for the stolen fruit. I'm glad that he's become something more than a fruit thief."

"Do you still have the guava tree?" Ines blurted out.

"I do. Tomorrow we can go check on it and see how it looks. That tree is older than I am."

Ines imagined the tree outside in the darkness, waiting for her.

After the brief tour, Papa made them change into dry clothes while he went back out to get the rest of their luggage, which he'd forgotten in the rain.

Ines looked around the bedroom she'd be sharing with her brother. There were two small beds in the room, a large, wooden dresser, and a window, but Ines could only see her own reflection against the glass. The room was bigger than their cabin on the ship, but smaller than their bedrooms in Lebanon. Ines knew her brother hated the idea of sleeping in the same room as her but was surprised when he didn't complain.

"I want this bed," Michel said, getting into the bed furthest from the window.

Ines sat down on the other bed, which she secretly preferred and tried her best to see out through the dark window. She'd forgotten what a bed felt like without the ocean moving beneath it and was grateful that the earth below them was solid. Michel fell asleep before their father returned, but Ines was restless. She whispered to Aleia, asking her the questions she would have asked her grandmother if she were there beside her. Ines wanted to know if she could trust the old woman they would be staying with and was curious how she had known her grandmother.

When her father returned, the two leather suitcases he carried were as soaked as his clothes. If her mother had seen him, she would have rushed him into a warm bath, so he wouldn't catch pneumonia.

"You're still awake?" her father asked when he checked on them.

"I was waiting for you to come back," Ines said. "Can we pray?"

Her father agreed and knelt beside her bed, and Ines joined him. She prayed for her mother in the hospital and that God could still hear and protect them in Cuba. Ines opened one eye and looked over to her father. He wasn't making a sound, but tears wet his face. Ines quickly shut her eyes and pretended she hadn't seen. When they finished, and Ines opened her eyes, she noticed her father had wiped his tears away.

"Can I go with you to see Mama tomorrow?" Ines asked.

Her father shook his head and explained that she'd be home soon, but as he'd said before, a hospital was no place for children. Ines expected that answer and knew arguing wouldn't do any good.

"Can you at least tell her we prayed? Tell her I'm praying every night like always, until she comes back."

Her father nodded and wished her goodnight before walking across the hall and closing his bedroom door. He left the door to their room open. An oil lamp rested on a table in the hallway and sent a soft, orange light into their bedroom. Shadows danced along the walls as the flame from the oil lamp flickered. As Ines pulled the sheets tighter around her, she realized she still didn't know her little sister's name.

"Michel," Ines whispered, looking over to the other bed.

There was no reply.

"Michel," she said again, a little more loudly, but quietly enough that her father wouldn't hear.

Michel turned in his sheets.

"Huh?"

"What's our little sister's name?" Ines asked.

"It doesn't matter, let me sleep," Michel groaned.

"Why not?"

Michel said nothing.

"Why doesn't it matter? Don't you want to know her name?" Ines asked.

"How many times do I have to tell you, there's no way to know if it's a girl. And we don't even know if the baby will come back home from the hospital," Michel said.

Silence fell over the room.

"What do you mean?" Ines asked, her mouth suddenly dry.

"I heard the doctors on the ship say the baby is going to be born too early," Michel said.

Ines didn't ask her brother any more questions. She looked up at the ceiling and listened to the rain tap against the window as she fell asleep thinking about what it meant to be born too early and whether or not her sister would have a name.

Chapter 8

When Ines woke up, Michel was still asleep in his bed. She heard the clanging of pots and pans and heard the buzz of the radio coming from the kitchen. Ines noticed that her father's bedroom door was wide-open, and his bed was made. She crouched down as she entered the hallway and crept by the low wall that separated the kitchen from the dining room. Lifting her head over the wall, she saw Old Lady Nayibe cooking and singing along to a Cuban song as she jostled a smoking pan. Ines noticed that the only reason the house hadn't filled with smoke was because all of the windows and doors that led outside were open, allowing the early morning air to filter throughout the house like a river current. The air felt warm and soothing against her skin, and it was freeing to have the outside world inside, making her wonder what her mother would think.

Ines kept as quiet as she could and watched Old Lady Nayibe cook on the other side of the low wall. She sprinkled pinches of spice into an iron pan and stepped back as eggs popped droplets of grease across her apron. There was cooked ham piled on a plate on the counter, the smells making Ines' mouth water. The woman, although familiar in ways Ines couldn't describe, was still a stranger, and Ines wanted to know why they were staying with her. Over the sounds of breakfast and Spanish singing, Ines heard what sounded like hundreds of birds chirping from the bushes and trees just outside the front door. The old woman clicked off her radio and began to hum along with the birds. Ines was filled with the desire to see what the house looked like in the daylight but didn't want to speak to Old Lady Nayibe without her parents home. She looked back over the dividing wall and waited until the old woman turned her back to her. At that moment, she ran to the open door. A small block of wood was propping open the front door, and as Ines ran, she accidentally kicked it away. The front door slammed shut behind her, which caused the birds in the trees to fly away in an explosion of color. Ines looked all around her. The sky was the bluest sky she'd ever seen, the sun even brighter than it was the day they'd arrived in Cuba, and the bushes and trees vibrated with life. Miles and miles of green and yellow earth stretched out in every direction. She stepped off the porch and turned to look at the house, which, although small, was beautiful and painted a light yellow, the color of lemons. Behind the house, stretching out like sleeping giants in the distance, were huge mountains partially covered by morning fog. The mountains were dark brown and peppered with small splashes of green that must have been entire forests of trees.

"Beautiful, no?"

Ines jumped when she saw Old Lady Nayibe standing by the front door.

"I will always have fond memories of Lebanon, but the second I arrived in Cuba all those years ago, I knew this was where I wanted to spend my life," Nayibe said as she joined Ines at the front of the house.

They stared at the mountains together.

"How did you know that Cuba was your home?" Ines asked, the warmth of the sun on her neck.

"I just did."

"Oh," Ines said.

Nayibe looked at Ines and smiled.

"You'll know your home when you see it."

"Papa said you knew my grandmother?" Ines asked and turned to look at Nayibe.

She nodded. "I did, she was my best friend."

"So why did you leave her in Lebanon?" Ines asked.

Nayibe cleared her throat but didn't say anything and began walking towards the side of the house.

"Want to see the guava tree? It should be very happy after last night's rain," she asked without looking to see if Ines was following behind her.

Old Lady Nayibe led Ines behind the house. A long clothesline dipped under the weight of drying clothes and separated the front of the house from the backyard where the large guava tree stood alongside several other fruit trees. The grouping of trees cast shadows along a vegetable garden and other little shrubs and flowers. The colorful vegetable garden was surrounded by dozens of small, wooden stakes that pierced through the soil and had metal wire webbed between them. Ines felt as if they'd walked into a miniature version of their family orchard where their rows of fruit trees had been squeezed down into a single backyard that was enclosed by thick shrubs. Even though the land went on for miles and miles, the shrubs acted like a wall that surrounded the backyard from the rest of the property, the only entrance around the side of the house and under the clothesline.

"Without the shade from these trees, all of my vegetables would die," Nayibe said as they walked around her garden.

"Why?" Ines asked. "Don't vegetables need the sun?"

"Very good. I forgot that you grew up on an orchard." Nayibe chuckled. "They do, but the sun is very strong on this island."

Old Lady Nayibe explained that she had avocado and nispero trees as well but that the guava was her favorite. Ines walked closer to the guava tree and looked up at the heavy fruit dangling from its limbs. Fresh morning dew beaded and rolled down the light green skin of the guava.

"What does it taste like?" Ines asked.

She stood up on her tiptoes and reached up to pluck one, but Nayibe stopped her.

"This one's not ready yet. The longer they stay on the tree, the better they'll taste," she said, "but don't worry, I have guava inside that's ready to eat, we can share one with our breakfast."

Ines didn't want to leave the garden, but her stomach grumbled loud enough for both of them to hear, and they walked back to the house. Michel was awake and sitting at the dining room table when they got back inside, a plate of food in front of him.

"Sorry," he said, "I was hungry."

They ate with the doors and windows open. Ines had never tasted anything so simple yet filled with so much flavor. She shoveled the food into her mouth, mixing the eggs with the ham and fried plantains, and was grateful her parents weren't there to see her lack of manners. Old Lady Nayibe served them slices of guava once they finished their breakfast.

"Let's eat these on the porch," she said.

Ines and Michel sat down on the porch steps as Old Lady Nayibe made herself coffee. The birds had returned to the trees and once again sang their songs. Ines didn't like the guava at first, but the more bites she took, the more it grew on her. The inside was pink and felt sandy against her tongue, but the sweetness was unlike any fruit she'd had before, and the warmer the sun became, the better it tasted. Michel didn't seem to like it, and took slow, pained bites. When Nayibe came back outside with her coffee, Ines had already finished the slices of guava from her plate.

"Hungry, are we?" Nayibe asked in Spanish, switching over from the Arabic she'd spoken that morning.

For the rest of the day, Old Lady Nayibe refused to speak to them in Arabic and would ignore them if they didn't speak Spanish.

"I hate this," Ines told her brother, "Why can't we speak Arabic?"

"They speak Spanish here. We have to learn it somehow," he replied.

The language frustrated Ines, and she became even more frustrated with how easy it was for Michel.

It wasn't until their father returned from his visit to the hospital later that night that Old Lady Nayibe reverted to her mother tongue. Ines was excited to see her mother, but she wasn't with her father when he walked through the door. Instead, Papa announced that he'd brought someone who wanted to see Old Lady Nayibe before standing aside for Doctor Karam who smiled and removed his hat as he stepped into the house.

"Great to see you, Señora Nayibe. Remember me?" he asked.

"The guava thief," Nayibe said with a serious face before letting out a chuckle.

She invited Doctor Karam to eat dinner with them that night and asked Ines to help her cook in the kitchen while Papa, Michel, and Doctor Karam sat in the dining room. Ines wanted to stay with the men, so she could hear any news about Mama, but her father wouldn't allow it.

"Now pay attention, little lady," Nayibe said, once again speaking Spanish, as she minced beef, chopped onions, and readied a pan on the stove, "this is my secret recipe for Picadillo. Not even the Cuban natives can make it this good."

Ines only understood some of the words she spoke but did her best to watch everything Nayibe did as she moved around the kitchen as if she were dancing. Even though practicing their new language frustrated Ines, and she wanted to be in the dining room with the men, she enjoyed spending time with Nayibe. She realized that the old woman's voice was similar to her grandmother's, soft but stern, and even her eyes were the same shade of brown.

Every so often, Ines went near the entrance of the kitchen so she could try to hear what her father and Doctor Karam were saying. She glanced out to see Michel sitting at the table as if he were already an adult and felt anger well inside her.

"Come along, we're not done yet," Old Lady Nayibe called over to her when she noticed Ines looking out into the dining room.

Ines helped Nayibe stir tomato paste into the minced beef and onions she had cooking on the pan. Little by little the old woman added other things like raisins, olives, and fragrant spices, which Ines was sure wouldn't taste good with the ingredients they'd already used.

"Okay, almost ready now. Go on and set the table."

Nayibe motioned to a folded tablecloth with silverware stacked on top. Ines gladly accepted the excuse to go into the dining room. When she entered, Ines thought she'd heard mention of the hospital, but their conversation changed quickly.

"This island is rich in opportunity. Look at you, a Lebanese man, an immigrant, now a doctor. A man can make much for himself here," Papa said.

"True, but even Cuba isn't without its flaws," Doctor Karam replied.

Ines felt like a ghost in the room. She wanted to slam the utensils she carried against the table.

"I'm here. Look at me, I'm a person too," she shouted in her mind but didn't make a sound as she finished setting the table.

Old Lady Nayibe called her back into the kitchen and served steaming picadillo, rice, and fried plantains onto decorative plates. Like one of the French waiters she'd seen on the ship, Ines walked each plate into the room and placed them in front of Doctor Karam, her father, and reluctantly, Michel. Nayibe brought out her and Ines's plates as she entered the room.

"This looks lovely, Nayibe," the doctor said, and Papa agreed.

"You need to thank Ines here. She's a natural," Nayibe said.

As they ate, Ines listened for any mention of her mother or baby sister, but instead the adults spoke of meaningless things. If Ines asked a question about Mama, her father would ask her not to interrupt the doctor, who always seemed to be telling a joke. Her father laughed loudly when Doctor Karam mentioned he'd visited his own mother, who lived nearby in Las Piedras, more in the last few days than he had in the last few months.

"She owes you all many thanks," Doctor Karam said.

Ines didn't understand his joke. If she had a car and could go visit her mother in the hospital whenever she wanted, she would have been with her even then. It was as if everyone had forgotten that Mama wasn't with them.

When they finished eating, Ines helped Nayibe clear the plates. Doctor Karam joined them in the kitchen and thanked them both for dinner. He then fumbled around in his jacket pocket and brought out a small, light brown button that he presented to Ines.

"The doctors that are helping your mother are very good, the best in our entire hospital, and from what I've heard from your father, she is a very strong woman. She will be back home with you soon."

The doctor handed Ines the button.

"This has brought me luck and now it will bring you luck as well," he said.

"It's just a button," Ines said, looking at it closely where it rested in her palm.

"That's like saying a guava tree is just a tree. This isn't just any button, it's a magic button. Make a wish and put it under your pillow tonight, see for yourself."

Ines rubbed the button with her fingers and felt its smoothness. It wasn't until the next day that Ines found out her baby sister had been born. Her mother had gone into labor during the night and when Papa returned from the hospital that day, he shared the news.

"Is it a girl?" Ines asked.

"Yes, a little girl, and she's doing much better than the doctors expected," her father said.

"I knew it," Ines said and clapped her hands.

Michel groaned when he heard that her divination was correct and he would be having another sister, but Ines was so happy she didn't even think to ask what exactly the doctors had expected. She ran into her bedroom and grabbed the button Doctor Karam had given her from underneath her pillow.

You were magic after all. She placed it back under the pillow to make sure none of the magic would wear off and ran back into the living room.

"Are you sure it's a girl?" Michel asked their father.

"I'm sure," he said.

"What's her name?" Ines asked.

Her father explained that their mother wanted to tell them their sister's name when they were both back home from the hospital. This struck Ines as odd, and she remembered what Michel had said about their sister being born too early and a wave of panic crashed over her. She needed to know her sister's name.

"Let's go to the hospital then," Ines said and ran to the front door.

"Ines is right, can we at least go see her?" Michel asked.

Their father didn't move and refused to take her or Michel to the hospital.

"Your mother and sister are weak, so the doctors need a little more time with them," was all their father said.

Old Lady Nayibe watched motionlessly from the kitchen. Ines wanted her to say something to Papa, anything at all, but she didn't say a word. It was then that their father announced that Old Lady Nayibe had agreed to have Abraham and his family over for dinner the next day. "It will be good for you both to have your friends visit," her father continued.

Ines thought of Johara seeing their new home before her mother and baby sister.

"They're not my friends," Ines shouted.

"Ines, that's no—" her father began, but before he could finish, Ines burst into tears and ran through the front door. She heard the door crash behind her as she rounded the house towards the vegetable garden.

Ines sat in the shade of the guava tree and didn't move to wipe away her tears. There wasn't a cloud in the sky, but thunder boomed in the distance. The sound sent a shiver through her as she imagined lightning striking both her and the guava tree. Her father appeared from around the house and paused when he saw her. With going back and forth to the hospital, it was the first time he'd seen the garden.

"Like Lebanon," he said as he walked over and sat down next to Ines under the guava tree.

Ines put her head down between her knees and continued to cry.

"Your mother is okay, Ines," he said.

The wind rustled the leaves and bushes, blowing against them.

"Why can't I see her?" Ines asked, her voice muffled by the fabric of her dress.

"You will soon."

Thunder once again echoed in the distance.

"Will she have a name?"

Ines looked up at her father.

"What do you mean?" he asked.

Ines told him what Michel had said about the baby being born too early.

"Ines, your sister already has a name. We just wanted to tell you together when your mother arrives home from the hospital," Papa said.

"So, she's going to live?" Ines asked and wiped her eyes with the side of her dress.

"Ines," her father said, moving closer to her, "of course she is."

Her father was silent for a moment then smiled.

"Look, I told your mother I wouldn't say a word until we were all together, so this will be our secret, okay?" her father said.

Ines nodded.

He paused, then said. "Your sister's name is Aida."

As they walked back to the house, the thunder roared, and sounded closer than before, but Ines was no longer afraid.

"Aida," she said before going inside.

Chapter 9

Ines spent the long days waiting for her mother and baby sister to come home from the hospital by helping Old Lady Nayibe with chores around the house and in the garden. She wanted the house to be beautiful for them once they arrived. Her father agreed not to have Abraham and his family join them for dinner until her mother's return as long as she agreed to stay with Nayibe during the day. Ines agreed without hesitation. She woke up earlier than Michel, but somehow never early enough to see her father leave with Doctor Karam to the hospital. Old Lady Nayibe would already be in the kitchen by the time she woke up, convincing her that neither adult truly slept, and went on with their days long after she and Michel had fallen asleep. Her father returned home at the same time each afternoon, so she'd wait by the front door, hoping her mother would be with him. Her spirits would fall when he entered the house alone, but she'd begin the next day with the same hope she had the day before.

On the day her mother came home, the morning hadn't given any indication that it would be a special day. Old Lady Nayibe and Ines prepared breakfast as usual before getting started in the garden pulling out weeds and planting new vegetable seeds that Papa had purchased from the market near the hospital. Ines was sweaty and covered in dirt by lunch time, so Old Lady Nayibe asked her to go inside and change into clean clothes before they sat down to eat. Once they ate lunch, Ines waited by the front door for her father to arrive. Like every other day, she watched the door handle closely, anticipating the slightest turn.

"You know, watching it won't make him come home any faster," Michel reminded her, but she ignored him.

When he came through the door that day, the world became fuzzy, and Ines felt as if she were in a dream. Her mother was with him. She sat in a wheelchair and held a bundle of blankets in her arms, but her skin had color again, and her smile was real, not broken as it was on the ship.

Her mother burst into tears the moment Papa wheeled her through the door, but she was still smiling, and had even begun to laugh with joy.

"Don't cry, Mama," Ines said as she ran over to her mother and hugged her.

"I've missed you all so much," she said.

Ines looked at the blankets and lost her breath when she saw her baby sister Aida peeking out through the folds. She looked so small, like some sort of vegetable instead of a real person. Ines wondered if she had been that small when she'd been born. She stared into her baby sister's eyes, which were large and brown like the nispero fruit Old Lady Nayibe grew in her backyard.

"Mama!" Michel yelled.

He came running out of their bedroom where he'd been reading and joined them by the front door. Their mother told them that their baby sister's name was Aida, and Ines noticed her father watching closely as she acted as if she were hearing the name for the first time. Old Lady Nayibe watched from the kitchen, pretending to clean dishes with a rag until Papa called her over and introduced her to Mama. Ines touched her sister's hands, which felt so soft and swollen. She looked up at her mother who was laughing as she spoke to Old Lady Nayibe. For the first time since arriving in Cuba, Ines felt as if she were home and had an overwhelming desire to keep that feeling close to her, to protect it, so she wouldn't ever lose it again. She didn't leave her mother's side for the rest of the day and at night she slept in the bed with her parents while Aida slept in a bassinet at the foot of their bed. Before Ines fell asleep that night, she watched her mother's belly rise and fall under the bed sheets, just to make sure she was really there.

After a few weeks resting in bed at Old Lady Nayibe's house, Mama regained all of her strength. She no longer needed help getting around the house and would wake up early with Old Lady Nayibe to prepare food, clean, and tend the garden. Ines would join them on some days but spent most of her time playing outside with Michel and Aleia. With her mother home, she didn't feel the need to keep up with as many chores. Other things had changed as well. Since her mother had come home, the days of open doors and windows, being barefoot in and outside of the house, and staying up late had ended. Although

Ines protested her mother's strict rules, she was grateful to have them. Her mother spent hours knitting every day, making clothes for baby Aida. One night when Old Lady Nayibe had seen some of the clothes Mama had made, she clapped her hands together and disappeared into her bedroom. She returned a few minutes later with a dusty sewing machine.

"This is yours now," she said before placing it on a table in Mama and Papa's bedroom.

Mama protested at first, but Nayibe insisted.

"I hardly ever use the thing. Just make me a beautiful dress, and we're even," Old Lady Nayibe told Mama.

Mama promised that she would.

After a month or so had passed, they all had dozens of outfits that Mama had made with the sewing machine. She'd made several shirts, bottoms, and piles of socks. True to her word, Mama also made Old Lady Nayibe a beautiful yellow dress, which Nayibe wore often. Ines loved to help her mother change Aida into the small clothes she'd made. Her baby sister was like a living, breathing doll. Ines sat with her for hours by the crib that her father and Michel had built her and begged her mother to let her take Aida outside, finding it hard to imagine being held captive in a bassinet for hours at a time.

"She's still too young to play," her mother would say.

Instead, Ines entertained her sister with stories she'd bring back from her time playing outside with Michel and Aleia.

With her mother back from the hospital, it was as if her father had come back to life. He spoke loudly and excitedly about his plans to begin his business in Cuba, reminding Nayibe that once he made his fortune, he would pay her back many times over. One night over dinner, he announced his idea to buy land from Old Lady Nayibe and make a large farm that would be the biggest in Cuba. Using his experience from the orchard, Papa was sure he was capable of making the farm successful. After trying the nespiro, avocados, and guava from the trees in the backyard, Papa decided that those fruits would be his staple crops. He talked about exporting the product back to Lebanon and to other countries all around the world, wanting to share them with as many people as possible.

"It would be a sin not to share such treasures," he would say.

Ines watched her mother smile as he spoke. While she didn't understand most of what her father said, the idea of having a farm excited her. She imagined running with Aleia and Aida through their thousands of fruit trees, just like she used to do with her cousins in Lebanon.

Papa spent much of his time with Old Lady Nayibe out in her garden, learning everything he could about the different crops. Ines would listen to them speak as she played outside and wondered if her father would let her help with this farm or if he would give it to Michel like he'd planned to do with the orchard. Just like in Lebanon, her brother didn't seem interested at all in their father's plans. When he wasn't reading, Michel would ask Ines to explore the land with him. They sometimes followed the river deep into the countryside and would return after dinner time. This would result in a scolding from their mother, but the punishments weren't enough to keep them from running alongside the rushing water, rolling large rocks into it, or trying to catch lizards as they darted out from under their hiding places. They played outside for hours, finding the biggest bushes and best bases of trees to build their forts and hiding places.

Of all of the forts they made, there was one that they were both especially proud of. It was a huge outcrop of bushes that backed up against a calm part of the river. Unless someone knew where it was, the small entrance was almost impossible to find, making it the perfect place for their home base. The inside of the bush fort felt cavernous to Ines, who would help her brother by bringing rocks and sticks into the bushes until they ran out of space. Michel found two small boulders by the river that he wanted to use in the fort as seats, but they were too heavy for him to move alone, and Ines wasn't much help. After much debating, they agreed to let their father help them roll the boulders into the bushes. He was the first and only adult to know where their fort was hidden. They called it "La Casita," it is how Old Lady Nayibe referred to her own "little house." Once they'd finished the fort, they both spent much of their time outside playing in it. Ines would play with Aleia, brushing the doll's hair and making up stories while Michel read his books using the light that filtered in between the leaves.

Every Sunday Doctor Karam would pick up the entire Aude family, including Nayibe, in his car and take them all to the large, stone cathedral in Las Piedras. Ines hated the trips, which were both uncomfortable and cramped. She sat in her father's lap while baby Aida lay in their mother's, and Michel sat comfortably in his own seat, looking carelessly out of the window. Nayibe, no matter how much she protested, would sit in the front next to Doctor Karam. Whenever church was about to begin, the bell tower echoed throughout the town and people wearing their finest clothes filed in through the tall, oaken doors. Ines and her family would sit with Doctor Karam and his mother, who lived only a block or so away from the cathedral. The sermons were in Spanish, but Ines understood more and more each week. Old Lady Nayibe answered any questions she had after the sermons ended and would help her to fill in any blanks. Each time they went, Ines felt encouraged that God could, in fact, still watch over them so far from Lebanon.

From where she sat in the pews, Ines often stared at the huge beams and pillars that held up the ceiling from collapsing as the Father spoke. She breathed in deeply when the smells of frankincense wafted nearby. The Cuban natives, who filled the wooden pews to the point of some having to remain standing by the entrance, reminded Ines of their old neighbors in Lebanon, but livelier. They were silent when the priest spoke, but when told to participate, the church erupted with sound. When a verse was to be repeated, one deep, unified voice filled the cathedral and reverberated against the stone walls.

When church ended and everyone returned to the town square, the streets came to life. Vendors took to the streets or positioned themselves at the bottom of the steps to trap potential customers in conversation. Everywhere Ines looked, the Cuban people spoke with passion and moved their hands, arms, even legs around to make their points. Often after church Ines and her family would walk around Las

Piedras, between the beautiful Spanish buildings that looked old and proud, as if they'd been around longer than the island itself. When they ate in town or visited the shops after church, Ines would watch in wonder as people called out her father's name, or he would approach a store owner, in his broken Spanish, and they would embrace as if they'd known each other for years. Her father had the ability to become friends with anyone and having been helping Nayibe sell her fruits and vegetables in town as part of their rent, he was becoming as confident as he'd been in Lebanon. Even their mother had been making friends at church, which made Ines both happy and sad. As she became used to their new life in Cuba, she began to remember less and less of her old one.

A few weeks after their mother returned from the hospital, her father announced it was time to have Abraham and his family over to celebrate baby Aida. Ines hated the thought of seeing Johara again, but she was grateful to be with her sister and mother.

"Are you sure it's alright to have guests at your home?" Ines heard her mother ask Nayibe after her father's announcement, when he had walked outside to pick fruit and vegetables from the garden to take into town, "I know how excited Salim gets, sometimes he forgets his own manners."

"Of course, it's alright. My home is happier with you here, and I'm looking forward to meeting your friends," Nayibe said and wouldn't listen to any more apologies from Mama.

The day of the dinner, Papa had gone into town early in the morning to purchase goods at the market. It wasn't a very long walk to town, but between the walking and time spent at the market, a trip back and forth took half the day. When he returned later that afternoon, his face was serious, and he asked everyone to join him in the parlor.

"If you could join us as well, Nayibe."

Mama balanced Aida in her lap and rocked her slowly as they waited for Papa to begin speaking. He spoke quietly, his voice missing the infectious excitement he'd exuded since Mama had left the hospital.

"Your grandmother Aleia has died."

Her father said the words so quickly that Ines thought perhaps she'd misunderstood.

"When?" Mama asked.

"While we were still on the ship, only a few days after we left Lebanon. My cousin sent me the telegram, but it was delayed."

Mama began to cry while Ines absorbed the words. Michel looked as solemn as Papa, but Ines could see his face tighten to hold back tears.

"No, she can't be dead," Ines said, hugging Aleia, the last thing her grandmother had given her, tightly to her body.

"How did she die?" Mama asked.

"In her sleep," Papa said, "peacefully."

"Thank God for that," Old Lady Nayibe said as her eyes seemed to drift to things far away.

"She can't be dead, Papa. I heard her voice when we were on the ship. She can't be dead. She can't be…" Ines' words trailed off, "can we at least go see her?"

Ines stared at her father who looked back at her as if his heart were breaking.

Without a way to let Abraham know what had happened, they were forced to go on with their dinner celebration. All Ines wanted to do was go to her bed and sleep, so she could wake up the next morning to find that the words her father had spoken were just part of a horrible nightmare. Instead, Mama asked Ines to help her and Old Lady Nayibe cook their dinner, which was a medley of traditional Lebanese cuisine and the Cuban food Nayibe had been teaching them how to prepare.

"This will be a dinner to remember your grandmother as well," Mama told Ines as she scrubbed dirt from the vegetables, her eyes still filled with tears.

They cooked in silence, and by the time Abraham and his family arrived for dinner, the reality of what had happened slowly set in. Memories of her grandmother came back to Ines more vividly than they had since they'd arrived in Cuba, and she realized her grandmother would never meet her new baby sister. The thought confused her as she couldn't imagine her own life without her grandmother. She'd never met any of her other grandparents, but she had Aleia. Who would Aida have? Ines felt as if she'd stolen something, like the time she enjoyed so much with her grandmother was limited, and she'd spent it all before Aida could even get the chance to meet her. She wanted so badly to hear her grandmother's voice again, as she had on the ship, but the house was only filled with the sounds of cooking. These thoughts were interrupted when their guests arrived.

Ines watched from the kitchen as her parents welcomed Abraham and his family into Nayibe's home. Abraham had to duck as he entered through the door. Her father laughed and welcomed his friend with a handshake and clap on the back. Abraham's wife was the second to enter. Ines hadn't seen her on the ship, but she was beautiful. When Johara trailed in behind her, Ines felt as if she were transported back to the ship, and a pit formed in her stomach. Johara was even more beautiful than her mother, and looked like an actual princess, but to Ines, she now carried a cloud of guilt around her that tarnished her beauty. For a moment, Ines looked at her own clothes, a light pink dress her mother had made her, and a pair of white dress shoes she had worn often on the ship and was grateful her mother had made her wear them. Bashir, Johara's younger brother, was the last to enter, and didn't seem as excited as the rest of his family to be there. When Ines saw her mother say hello to Johara, she gripped at the sides of her dress and couldn't understand how her parents acted as if nothing had happened, wishing it was only Abraham, his wife, and son who had come to visit.

"Come Ines, let's introduce everyone to baby Aida," Mama said, grabbing her from the kitchen.

Ines went to the parlor where Aida rested in her bassinet. She looked to be asleep, but when her mother approached, tiny wails and hiccups came from the wicker basket. Everyone took their turns looking into the bassinet as if her sister was some sort of creature on display in its enclosure.

"She's so beautiful," Johara's mother said.

Old Lady Nayibe joined them in the living room.

"This is Nayibe," Papa paused and cleared his throat before continuing, "a close friend of my mother's. Nayibe is letting us stay with her."

The living room came to life with sound as everyone seemed to begin their conversations at once. Mama took Aida into her bedroom, so she could sleep without being disturbed. Ines tried to sneak off to her own room, but her mother stopped her in the hall as she softly closed the door to her and Papa's bedroom.

"It's rude to go to your room when you have guests," she whispered.

Ines argued that her sister was allowed to rest in her room, but her mother wouldn't have it, and led her back into the parlor.

The adults shared their memories of Lebanon. Ines sat on the couch next to Mama, who went back and forth to the kitchen with Nayibe, bringing out appetizers whenever a platter was finished. Ines felt as if the drone of stories would lull her to sleep at any moment.

"These are delicious, they taste just like home," Abraham said, approaching the couch where Ines and her mother sat.

He looked to Ines and asked, "And how do you like them, little princess?"

She sat with a plate of rice rolled in grape leaves on her lap. Ines thought Abraham was funny, and enjoyed being around his seemingly endless happiness, but that was before she knew he was Johara's father. Now she just wanted to be left alone and wished so badly for the day to end.

Michel approached the couch with Johara and Bashir behind him.

"Mama, can I show them my fort?" Michel asked.

Before their mother could answer, Ines stood up.

"No! That's our secret place!"

The room went quiet.

"It's not fair," Ines said and began to cry in front of their guests.

Without a word, Mama walked Ines out of the room and down the hall to her bedroom, shutting the door behind them.

"I know how much your grandmother meant to you, but some playing outside with your brother and your friends will do you good."

"I won't play with her," Ines said. "She's the reason you became sick."

"Who is?"

"Johara. If it hadn't been for her, I would never have told you Michel had fallen overboard and nothing bad would have ever happened," Ines said.

Mama pulled Ines to her chest.

"No one made me sick, my sweet girl. Not you, not Michel, not even that little girl. I was the same way when Michel was born, and that was God's will, nothing more."

"Really?" Ines asked.

Mama nodded.

"Everything happened as it was meant to," her mother continued, "and nothing could change that. This is our home now, and we're all together and healthy. Your grandmother Aleia lived and died the way she wanted. She's in Heaven now, and she will always be with you." Mama paused before clapping her hands suddenly. "Here." She walked over to her closet and reached into it, bringing out something Ines hadn't seen since they'd arrived in Cuba: the beautiful, white box covered in purple violets where Mama stored her jewelry. "Your grandmother gave this to me when I married your father and now, I want you to have it," she said.

"But it's yours," Ines said.

"And now I give it to you, so it's yours," her mother said as she placed her jewelry out onto her vanity before handing the box to Ines.

Ines took it with both hands, tracing the intricate violet carvings with a finger.

"Thank you," she whispered.

"She will never leave your heart. Now, let us not keep our guests waiting. Go have fun with your friends," Mama said.

Ines felt as if a weight had been lifted from her. She went to her bedroom and put the white box on her dresser before grabbing Aleia and walking back into the parlor. Michel, Johara, and Bashir were already outside playing. The adults were all looking at Ines when she and Mama came down the hall.

"Your father told us what happened to your grandmother. We're very sorry," Abraham said.

Ines nodded and tried to smile.

"Don't get dirty before dinner," her father said before kissing her forehead.

"Okay," Ines said and went outside.

The sun was low in the sky, but not completely set. Ines ran towards their fort as quickly as she could. Even though she felt better, she didn't like the thought of strangers playing in their secret place without her and Aleia. Michel was drawing symbols in the dirt when she crashed through the small opening. Ines recognized the symbols immediately as he'd shown her the same several times since they'd arrived. He was explaining to Johara and Bashir that somewhere on the property there was treasure buried.

"How do you know there's treasure?" Johara asked him.

Only Bashir looked up as Ines took a seat on one of the smaller rocks. Johara was sitting on the boulder Ines had claimed as hers.

"Because I have the treasure map," Michel said.

He opened a book and showed them the picture of a map. The trails in the dirt hardly looked like the drawing from the book, but Michel insisted he had the location burned into his memory, and that even without the book, he was going to find the treasure on the island.

"That's *Treasure Island*," Bashir said, "My mother has read me that book before. It's not about Cuba."

Johara giggled and Michel's face turned scarlet.

"How do you know it's not this island? Did she tell you that?" Michel asked.

"Well… no," Bashir admitted.

Ines wasn't sure whose side to be on.

"You'll see. I found hundreds of treasures in Lebanon, I even found some when we were on the ship, but now I'll find the biggest treasure of all, right here in Cuba."

"What treasure on the ship? We never found the treasure you said the crew had hidden away," Bashir said.

Johara looked at Ines and smiled while their brothers argued over the treasure. Ines noticed Johara's smile seemed to dim when she saw Aleia in her lap.

"How does it feel to have a sister?" Johara asked Ines.

She was surprised by the question, but before she could answer, a voice from the porch called out, "Dinner!"

Michel took the stick he'd been using and wiped away the markings he'd made.

"Now only I can find it," he said to Bashir, making his final point as they funneled out of the fort and back towards the house.

As they ran, Ines watched Johara. Although she was smiling then, Ines could only think about how sad she'd looked when asking about her sister.

The dinner table looked beautiful. A long white tablecloth with frayed edges was draped over the wooden table and covered in a mix of Lebanese and Cuban dishes that when placed side by side looked more similar than different. Even though she'd helped her mother and

Old Lady Nayibe prepare the food, Ines was surprised by how delicious it all looked when set in the glass bowls and serving trays. Her mother asked Ines to put her doll back in her bedroom before claiming her seat next to Michel. Bashir sat on the other side of Michel and had to duck forward or lean backwards whenever Michel told a joke or said something to Johara, who sat to the right of Bashir.

Once they were all seated, Papa led them in prayer. When he mentioned her grandmother, and how she was with God now, Ines squeezed her mother's hand tightly. Papa's face was serious when he finished the prayer, but he quickly flashed a smile and encouraged everyone to eat. Serving spoons clattered against glass and ceramic as they filled their plates with food. Ines observed Old Lady Nayibe. She looked more like her grandmother than she'd noticed before. The way she served food for Abraham and his wife, the way she passed the pitcher of water with lemon to Papa, and even how she chewed her food in small, rotating motions. Ines thought of her sister Aida who was resting in their mother's room. While she would never know their grandmother, maybe she could have Old Lady Nayibe instead.

The dinner was loud, full of talking and laughing, but Ines hardly said a word to anyone. She was captivated by Abraham, who waved his fork, glass, or whatever else was in his hand around in the air while he spoke. Occasionally Papa and Abraham would say a Spanish phrase they'd overheard the locals say and did their best to pronounce the words exactly as they'd heard, but their thick accents made them sound as if they were speaking gibberish instead. Old Lady Nayibe would correct them, which made both Mama and Abraham's wife laugh. Abraham's wife seemed kind and asked Mama countless questions about Aida and how she was doing since leaving the hospital. Michel and Bashir had forgotten all about the treasure they had argued over and began discussing the huge river that they'd seen on their way through Las Piedras. The dining room was warm and filled with Arabic and laughter, making Ines feel for a moment as if she were still in Lebanon until she looked outside and saw the orange Cuban sun as it began to set.

"Can we play with your sister after dinner?" Johara asked Ines when Michel's attention was turned to Bashir.

Ines hadn't expected the question, but she said, "Okay."

Once dinner ended, Ines helped her mother and Old Lady Nayibe clear the table. Abraham's wife insisted that they help as well and so did Johara. They then took the desserts out from the refrigerator and brought them out into the dining room. The plate Ines carried was stacked high with her mother's baklava, the thin, golden crust glistening with honey. Ines set the plate down next to a Cuban dessert Old Lady Nayibe had made.

"This is guava flan, made from the guava that grows outside. You've tasted nothing like it," she promised.

Ines looked at the jiggling custard as her mother brought out a tea kettle filled with warm water and chamomile tea flowers.

"Can we go see the baby now?" Johara whispered.

Ines nodded when she saw that her mother was still preoccupied with setting the table. Johara smiled and followed Ines as they walked down the hall towards her mother's bedroom.

"Sometimes I come in here and rock her in Mama's chair and tell her stories," Ines told Johara.

"Bashir would never sit still when he was a baby. Girls are just better," she said.

Ines wondered how much Johara could remember from her brother being a baby as she was only a year or two older than him herself. As they opened the bedroom door, light from the hallway cut through the darkness and illuminated Aida's bassinet. They walked into the room expectantly, but Aida was fast asleep. Ines stood on her tiptoes and stared down at her sister and Johara did the same.

"I want to hold her," she said.

Ines reached into the bassinet and could feel Baby Aida stirring as she grabbed her under the armpits.

"What are you two doing in here?"

Ines spun around to see her mother standing in the doorway like a shadow.

"Out, out, out," her mother said with her arm pointed towards the hallway.

When they returned to the table, everyone had begun eating their dessert and drinking tea.

"What were these two troublemakers up to?" asked Abraham's wife.

"Paying the baby a visit," Mama said with a smile.

A slice of Old Lady Nayibe's flan jiggled violently on a plate in front of Ines. She pressed her spoon into the soft custard. Michel and Bashir had both already finished theirs, so Ines knew it couldn't be as strange tasting as it looked. When she took a bite, the sweetness of the caramel and creaminess of the custard made her forget the way the flan moved.

"It's so tasty," Ines said to Johara as she stared at her own flan.

The dessert and tea lasted even longer than the dinner had, their parents talking for what felt like hours. Johara forced Bashir to switch seats with Ines, so Ines could sit next to her. When Ines stood up from the table to change seats, Abraham's wife complimented her dress, and everyone turned to look. Ines felt as if she were on display for the entire table. Her face became hot, and she stared at her dress shoes. It was a beautiful dress, but she still didn't look like Johara.

"Thank you," Ines said as her hands bunched the sides of the dress, "Mama made it for me."

"Oh really? I had no idea you were so talented," Abraham's wife said, turning to look at Mama.

Ines felt relief as the attention went away from her.

Before her mother could say a word, Old Lady Nayibe interjected, "She made me the most beautiful dress as well."

"Really?"

"Along with all of Baby Aida's clothes," Old Lady Nayibe continued.

Old Lady Nayibe left the table and returned with the yellow dress Mama had sewn her. Everyone stared at the dress as she held it out in front of her. Ines noticed her father staring at her mother as he smiled.

"This is gorgeous. I was meaning to ask where you'd gotten the baby's outfit when I arrived. I was sure it was the work of some sort of seamstress," Abraham's wife said as she ran her fingers along the fabric.

"She's better than any seamstress I've known," Old Lady Nayibe said.

"Truly, it's been so hard to find clothing that I like since we've arrived in Cuba, but this dress is gorgeous," Abraham's wife said.

Mama raised her hands and shook her head.

"I'm really not that good. My mother was an amazing seamstress, so I learned some things from her. Just a nice way to pass the time."

"I wish I could create things half as beautiful when I passed the time," Abraham's wife laughed, "I'm serious, I love it so much I'd like to buy one myself."

At the insistence of Abraham's wife and Old Lady Nayibe, Mama brought out more of her designs from the chest in the corner of her room. Old Lady Nayibe draped the clothing over the couch and chairs in the parlor until the room looked like the inside of a closet. Abraham's wife, joined by Johara, became more impressed with every new outfit presented to her. Michel and Bashir both sat at the table, looking as If they were ready for bed while Ines watched the women look at her mother's work from her father's lap as he spoke with Abraham.

"I see the farm providing food to the entire island of Cuba and even exporting out what we can," her father said.

"That's a big goal, alright. You'll need to raise a lot of money, Salim" Abraham said.

"I know." Papa rubbed his eyes with the backs of his hands. "We don't have much money left over from what we'd brought with us from Lebanon, so I'll need to find a local investor of some kind. Someone who sees my vision."

"Why don't you sell some of these?" Abraham asked.

"Some of what?" Papa asked and stopped rubbing his eyes.

Ines followed Abraham's gaze towards the clothing her mother had sewn.

"You said you need funds to get started, but you already have them. Those clothes will sell."

"I'm a farmer, not a salesman," Papa said.

"Nonsense. Even a farmer can sell water in the desert," Abraham said and nodded towards the parlor where Abraham's wife was still admiring Mama's clothes. "Just look at them in there. I've tried to buy my wife dresses for the last ten years and almost always she makes me take them back the moment I step through the door," Abraham said with a laugh.

Her father asked Ines to run into his bedroom and bring back his satchel. She went as quickly as she could, not even stopping to see if Aida had woken up. When she handed Papa the satchel, he pulled out a leather journal, quill, and bottle of ink. She watched as he observed the women in the parlor, asking questions and scribbling notes in his journal as they replied. Abraham offered his help to Papa, which led them to discuss where they would buy the sewing materials in bulk and the best ways to sell clothing to the locals seeing as neither of them were able to speak very good Spanish. They spoke in circles until Ines fell asleep at the table.

Ines woke up with her head bobbing softly against Papa's shoulder as he carried her down the hall. Ines could see Michel helping Mama and Old Lady Nayibe fold the clothes that had been laid out all across the furniture.

"Is everyone gone?" Ines asked, only half awake.

"Yes," her father said.

He placed her down gently into her bed.

"What about grandmother Aleia?" Ines asked.

Her father paused.

"What do you mean?"

"How do we know if she really made it all the way to heaven?"

Papa knelt down beside the bed and rested a hand on her shoulder.

"Why do you ask that? Of course, she's in heaven," Papa said after a few moments passed.

Ines was too tired to ask any more questions and before she knew it, had fallen back asleep.

Her grandmother came to her in her dreams that night. She and her baby sister were playing outside in Old Lady Nayibe's garden, picking fruit from the guava tree. The sunlight was beaming down, but it didn't feel good, instead it felt like a boiling kettle was being pressed against Ines' skin. Her sister stood next to their grandmother and looked much bigger than she should have. Ines heard a voice calling to her from far away, but she couldn't make out what it was saying. The voice sounded like her father's, but she couldn't be sure. Ines looked around them. The ground seemed to be burning and she realized that it wasn't the ground on fire, but her mother's clothes piled up all around them as they burned, sending thick, black clouds into the sky. Her grandmother and baby sister both turned to face her, the guava fruit gone from their hands and juices running down their faces.

"Ines," her grandmother said.

"Ines," her sister repeated in her grandmother's voice.

Ines was sitting up in her bed when she woke up, her skin cold with sweat. Michel was still sleeping calmly in his bed while her mother and father stood by her bed.

"What's wrong, Ines, you just screamed?" her mother whispered and pushed damp hair from Ines' forehead.

"Bad dreams?" her father asked.

Ines nodded. They stayed with her until she fell back asleep.

Ines had that same dream, or one similar, every night for several weeks following the news of her grandmother's death. She was afraid to go to sleep most nights, so her parents would read or talk to her for as long as it took until she fell asleep. Michel quickly grew annoyed by this and would tease her in the morning. Ines would have been angry with Michel, but sometimes when she woke up in the middle of the night, she heard Michel crying in his bed and she knew he missed their grandmother too. Eventually, the nightmares went away.

Chapter 10

In the months that followed, their life centered around Papa's plans to sell the dresses and accessories Mama made. Abraham and his wife took several of the dresses back home with them and began to show them to people in their town. Abraham visited once a week to pick up more dresses and show Papa all that he'd sold. Over dinner, Ines listened intently as her father shared how well the clothes were selling. He would walk to Las Piedras early every morning with a large bag filled with the clothes Mama had sewn slung over his shoulder. He visited each and every shop, even the ones that didn't sell clothing, and offered them his wares. Several times a week he asked Michel to go with him to help him translate if there was an especially difficult customer. He continued to take Old Lady Nayibe's fruit and vegetables to the market, but each week took less, filling the space with more clothes that Mama made daily. Instead, he would give Nayibe a share of whatever he sold from the clothing. A salesman rode his wagon from the country into town each day, and Nayibe begged Papa to sell his wares to him along with her fruit and vegetables, but he refused.

"Why pay someone when I can do it myself?" Ines heard her father ask.

Although he was adamant in his decision, the man riding his wagon into town inspired Papa to do the same and so it became his goal to make enough to buy his own wagon and horses, so he could distribute deeper into the country and to neighboring towns.

Whenever Ines joined her father on his trips, Old Lady Nayibe handed her a basket filled with fruit that she and Michel took turns carrying. Nayibe allowed them to keep any of the money they made. Ines used the money she earned to buy ice cream or candies in the Las Piedras dulcería after church while Michel saved for books from the bookstore. After making his daily rounds to the stores, Papa would roll out a mat in the town square next to the other vendors who sold everything from wooden toys to miracle medicines. When Papa let Ines join him on his trips, she enjoyed watching the vendors as they called out to people as they passed by.

One of the vendors was a dark-skinned man who sold creams and would shake the bottles violently above his head as he called out to people as they walked by, "You, with the big hat, I know you could use this cream. It will protect you from the sun!"

Ines and Michel would laugh at the reactions of passersby as they stared at the man who looked crazy and hurried on their way as he yelled after them.

"You haven't tried bananas as good as these, take a bite, and you'll be swinging through the trees!" another vendor shouted as he proudly displayed his banana stand.

Dozens of voices called out as people walked through the square. During the week the square and surrounding stores were relatively busy, but the weekend was something else entirely when hundreds of people milled around, and tourists packed the streets. Some of the tourists were from other countries, but the majority were visiting from other parts of Cuba. Everyone wanted to see the beautiful town where a river flowed through its center. The bridge that overlooked the river was only a five-minute walk from the town square, so Ines and Michel would sometimes take their breaks on the bridge to watch the water as it rushed beneath their feet. Cars passed them slowly as they dropped rocks or took turns spitting and watching as their projectiles disappeared into the white, frothing water. If they took too long to return to their father, he would join them and watch the water with them, sometimes even looking around before spitting into the river as well. Afterwards they would laugh and walk back to the town square together. Ines felt more free than ever before.

They wouldn't begin school until the following year, but their selling trips into Las Piedras taught them many things. Ines and her brother watched as the vendors either attracted customers or failed miserably, learning from both. Pedro, a short, bald man who sold wooden toys, taught them how to bring in customers. While some of the vendors were envious of her father's wares, and unwelcoming at first, Pedro was helpful from the very first day, and Ines enjoyed hearing the man speak with honey in his voice, instead of merely yelling at people as they walked by. Papa continued to set up next to Pedro as he too began to enjoy the older man's company. Pedro spoke quickly, as if someone was about to cut him off, and he'd talk as if everything he said was of the highest importance.

When Pedro was about to give them a lesson in selling, he would raise a finger and say, "Watch how I work."

His demeanor changed completely. He wouldn't shout or talk in his usual animated tone and instead walk calmly up to passersby, always those with children, and present the child, not the parents, with one of his wooden toys. Every time, without fail, the children would beg their parents for the toy, and eventually the parents would reach into their purses or wallets for money, sometimes even coming back later in the day, begging Pedro for another of his handmade toys.

"Always sell to the one who will be using the thing," Pedro said. "Who will use your dresses?" Pedro asked with a smile as he handed Ines a wooden, toy horse. Ines accepted the gift gratefully and inspected the horse's details.

"Can I have it, Papa?" Ines asked.

"This one is a gift," Pedro told her father when he reached for his wallet to buy it.

Ines smiled and looked up at her father who was also smiling.

From that point on, Ines watched as her father began to target women who were walking with their husbands or suitors. While her father wasn't as loud as the other vendors and wasn't able to say very many words in Spanish, he was persistent, and used every tool at his disposal. Ines and Michel ran after potential customers, dresses streaming behind them as they held the fabric above their heads. They then led the couples back to Papa who would show them even more dresses and shawls. Sometimes when their father was busy with another customer, or taking a break, Michel would pick the most serious looking person out from a crowd and dare Ines to bring them back. After a while, it became like a game to them, but it wasn't always without risk. If the police saw anything they disliked, they would force the vendor to leave the square. This rarely happened, but Ines knew to save her more aggressive sales tactics for when the officials were nowhere to be seen.

Ines looked forward to their trips and as they sold more, her father brought her with him more often. When they weren't helping Papa sell, or learning from the other vendors, Ines and Michel spent their time scaring the birds that flocked in the square, sneaking into shops and spying on shop owners, or going back to their favorite spot on the bridge and dropping things off it. After church, they spent less time exploring the town and more time selling. At first their mother didn't approve, but Papa convinced her that the weekends were the busiest times to sell, and she would sometimes join them after church. She was nervous to see the reactions of the customers as they perused the clothes she'd made, but eventually grew to enjoy it, and the selling became a family affair every Sunday.

Ines watched her mother work during the evenings, barely keeping up with the high demand. Sometimes from her bed Ines could hear the sewing machine whirr as her mother worked through the night. Abraham still visited once a week to take new dresses with him but began to take larger stacks and returned with even more money that he'd share with Papa, who trusted him completely and would never count the money his friend brought back with him. While there were other clothing vendors in Las Piedras, none had clothes as beautiful as Mama's. With the money coming in, Papa was finally able to buy a horse and wagon. This increased the amount of product he was able to take with him, which in turn meant even more sales. Like the fruit orchard in Lebanon, Ines watched as this new business completely consumed her father. He would disappear for entire days at a time only to return sweaty, dirty, and with hardly any clothes leftover in the wagon. Some days he would skip dinner or eat quickly in the kitchen, to her mother's protests, before going into his bedroom and closing the door behind him.

While her father had allowed Ines to go with him to Las Piedras, he wouldn't allow her to go with him on his longer trips into the Cuban countryside, even though he had no issue taking Michel along.

"Where did you go selling?" Ines would ask her brother when he returned with their father.

He would then describe the countryside and all of the obstacles they faced with details that rivaled his adventure books.

"It's nothing like when we sell in Las Piedras," Michel told her.

Eventually, her father stopped taking Michel with him, which relieved Ines of her jealousy, but made her even more curious as to where her father went. He no longer sold in Las Piedras during the week, having found more success in neighboring towns. There were times she would only see him once or twice during the week as he left early in the morning, before she woke up, and most nights went straight to bed as soon as he returned. Seeing how exhausted her father was made her imagination run wild. Images of large dragons, old witches with crooked noses, and bandits running through the fields filled her head. Ines missed spending time with her father and wanted more than anything to see where he went during the week.

Ines began to pay attention to when Papa left in the morning. The moment Old Lady Nayibe switched on her radio, Ines shot out of bed, ran down the hall, and out the front door to see that her father was already on his wagon, halfway down the path that led to the road. She woke up earlier each day until she was finally up before her father left.

"Is everything alright?" her father asked, puzzled when he saw Ines waiting for him in the hallway as he prepared to leave.

"I want to go with you," she said and rubbed her eyes.

"Not today, my love," he said and led Ines back to her bed before leaving on his wagon.

One morning, Ines woke up before her father. On that day, all of the lights in the house were still off and the sun hadn't risen outside of the windows. She snuck outside, making sure not to wake Michel as she left their room. Night insects were still chirping and croaking in the bushes and trees around her as she inspected her father's wagon. There was a thick linen blanket covering several sacks filled with clothes, protecting them from the smell of the horses. Ines climbed in and squeezed between the sacks before covering herself with the blanket. Roosters crowed as she waited for what felt like hours, trying to breathe as quietly as possible. Her eyes began to close, and she almost fell back asleep when she felt the wagon jostle.

"Good morning," Ines heard her father say as he attached his horses, "are we going to have a fruitful day?"

The horses exhaled and snorted in reply. Ines could feel her heart pounding as she prayed that her father wouldn't pull back the blanket and find her.

"In you go," her father said and grunted.

Ines gasped as something heavy landed on her legs, causing the wood to rock on its wheels.

Did he hear me?

When the horses neighed and the cart began to move, Ines exhaled softly and didn't mind the weight of whatever it was her father had thrown into the wagon.

The ride was bumpy and uncomfortable, the sacks of clothes shifting on top of her as they went down the path that led to the road. Ines couldn't see out from under the blanket but could hear the stream as they passed over it and felt the wagon's wheels crack loose rocks along the road. Her father let out the occasional cough or cleared his throat, but those were the only sounds other than the birds and roosters welcoming the morning. The farther they went, the more difficult it was to inhale the thin air that filtered through the blanket. Ines waited as long as she could before finally raising the edge of the blanket, poking her head out from under it and breathing in deeply.

The morning air ruffled her hair as clouds of dust billowed from where the wheels met loose dirt. Ines pushed off the sack her father had thrown onto the wagon and looked around. The sun was rising above the mountains in the distance and sent beams of light onto the surrounding fields, making the morning dew glitter as it clung to the crops and plants in the field like small, liquid diamonds. With a jolt, half of the wagon dipped down and then back up. The horses protested, raising their front legs as the wagon came to a complete stop. Ines threw the blanket back over her head, feeling the weight of the wagon shift as her father climbed down.

"It's okay, my friends, only a small hole." Her father's voice came from the right of the wagon, not far from where she was hidden. Ines kept her eyes closed under the blanket as if she were invisible until she opened them. Once she felt the wagon begin to move again, Ines began to doubt her decision to go with her father. From where she hid, she could hardly see the countryside and as the sun rose further in the sky, the heat under the blanket became unbearable. The back of her dress clung to her sweaty skin, making her itchy. There was no way of knowing just how long she would have to hide under the blanket. All she knew was that her father returned home late most days, sometimes once the sun was already gone from the sky. Ines imagined her body melting from the heat and that when her father lifted the blanket when they finally returned home, there would only be a puddle where her body once was.

As she imagined her death, the wagon once again came to a stop.

"Buenos dias, señor." Ines heard her father's voice from the front of the wagon.

His greeting was met with a grunt. Ines froze as she felt something lifted out of the wagon. She waited for her father to pull the blanket away, but nothing happened. She waited a little while longer before raising the blanket slightly and peering out from under it.

Her father stood at the back of the wagon across from a man who wore a large, straw hat. The man's face was deeply tanned, and his lips were cracked like scorched earth.

"I have clothes here that will make your wife very happy," Papa said in his broken Spanish.

The man spit onto the road.

"I don't have a wife," the man said before asking, "Where are you from?"

Papa continued, "These clothes are becoming very popular in the Las Piedras market and—"

"I don't care about that town or your clothes. I asked you a question," the man's voice was deep and filled with gravel.

A younger man appeared next to him. He held a large machete that he slapped against his leg. Her father paused and looked at the younger man.

Tap, tap, tap went the machete.

"I can see you're not interested in my wares; I'll be on my way." Ines watched as her father began to walk around the side of the wagon, but the first man grabbed him by the arm.

"I asked you a question. Where are you from?"

"Las Piedras," her father replied.

"No. Where are you really from?"

There was a pause before Papa said, "Lebanon."

The man clucked his tongue like a chicken and let go of her father's arm.

"A moro. I knew it," he said. "You need to work on your Spanish."

Ines had never heard the word *moro* before and wondered how her father could be one, wondering if that meant she was a moro too.

"Why do you people keep coming to our island?" the other man asked as he continued to tap his machete.

The sun reflected from the blade, making it look both beautiful and terrifying. Old Lady Nayibe was the only person Ines had ever seen use a machete. She'd used it to clear the overgrown bushes that surrounded her garden, and, on one occasion, Ines had seen her cut the head off a snake that had slithered out from the shrubbery. Ines had been paralyzed with fear when she'd seen the snake slithering along the grass through the garden, and she felt the same helplessness as the men spoke to Papa.

"It's bad enough the Americans are infecting us like a plague, but at least they leave after they visit. Your kind stay behind like fleas," the older man said, pointing a finger at her father's chest.

Ines watched breathlessly as her father said nothing and put the sack of clothes back onto the wagon.

"I'm sorry if I offended you in some way," he said.

The younger man clanged the machete against the wood of the wagon, which caused Ines to imagine the headless body of the snake, and the red streak of blood on Nayibe's machete.

"Don't ever come back out here to sell your moro clothes," the man in the straw hat said.

Although Ines had never seen her father do business before, she had a feeling that what was happening wasn't normal. He walked back towards the front of the wagon as the two men watched him. The younger man continued to tap the machete against his leg.

Tap, tap, tap.

Ines let the linen blanket fall back over her and shut her eyes. The men were worse than the gargoyle woman on the ship, worse than any of the monsters she'd ever imagined, and even worse than the snakes that slithered around Old Lady Nayibe's house. Ines tried to understand what her father had done wrong but couldn't. *Had they not liked the clothing her mother had made?*

The sacks shifted against Ines as her father turned the wagon around in the road. With her eyes closed, Ines still saw the machete as the sun reflected off its blade. The harder she squeezed them shut, the easier it was to see the blade as it flashed through the air of her imagination. After a while, she poked her head back out from under the blanket and looked up at the bright blue sky. It was marked by the smallest, paint brush strokes of clouds. Ines didn't think she could stand the trip back to Old Lady Nayibe's house, but the bumpiness of the wagon ride didn't bother her as they made their way back.

"You can come on out now," Papa said, slowing the wagon, "I'm not angry with you, Ines, come on out."

A moment later, the wagon stopped completely, her blanket was pulled away, and she saw her father staring down at her.

"How did you know I was here?" Ines asked.

Her father didn't answer and helped her down from the bed of the wagon and lifted her up to sit at the front with the horses.

"Your mother doesn't know you're here, does she?"

Ines shook her head.

"Do you know how worried she must be?" her father asked as he climbed up next to her.

Ines looked at her father, her hand shaking slightly as the wagon bumped along the road.

"What's a moro?" she asked.

She waited for her father to reply, hoping he could help her understand what had happened.

After hesitating, her father said, "It's a word they call people like us." He didn't look at Ines as he spoke.

"Like us how?" she asked.

"From the Middle East."

"Oh."

Ines looked out at the countryside. The mountains in the distance seemed to shimmer under the afternoon sun.

"Why were they angry with you?" Ines asked. "Do things like that always happen?"

Her father shook his head.

"They weren't angry with *me* exactly, and no, nothing like that has happened before," he said.

"With me then?" Ines asked.

"No, no of course they weren't angry with you. I'm sure they didn't even notice you were there, thank God," he said, not taking his eyes away from the dusty road in front of them. "They're just afraid."

"Of what, Papa?"

Ines found it hard to imagine how someone could be afraid when they held a weapon in their hand.

"They're afraid that people like us will take their home from them," he said as he let out a sigh.

"But I thought this was our home too." Ines looked to her father then back to the fields.

Neither spoke again until they arrived back at Old Lady Nayibe's house. That was the last time Ines went with her father on one of his trips into the country. Neither of them discussed what had happened that day. But from that day forward, when Ines heard the horses neighing in the morning, she imagined the machete as it glinted in the sun, and prayed her father would return safely, before the sun came down.

As their success grew, Ines noticed her mother began to visit church every morning instead of two or three times a week. She walked to Las Piedras and spent hours praying in the stone cathedral, bruises covering her knees by the time she returned home.

"We need to give more thanks than ever before," her mother would tell Ines when she asked why she would go each day.

Sometimes Ines and Michel would join their mother, and on one such trip, a Saturday, they walked by a man whom they hadn't seen before. He was announcing a lottery that would be drawn soon, asking anyone who was walking by if he could bend their ear.

"What's a lottery?" Ines asked Michel.

Michel wasn't sure, so they both asked Mama. She explained that the lottery was a game of greed, where people spent their money only to chase after the promise of more money. When she mentioned that the winner of the lottery would receive a large amount of free money, Ines noticed her brother's eyes light up.

"Please, can we play, Mama?" he asked.

"Didn't you listen to what I just said? Do you not know of greed, Michel? It's a sin, and the lottery is filled with it."

Ines looked up to see the man who was announcing the lottery walk towards them. Her mother's eyes narrowed as he approached.

"I'm sorry, Señora, I overheard you speaking with your children." The man removed his hat and wiped the sweat from his brow. "I just want to clarify, the lottery isn't a sin at all. The drawings are announced over the radio later today by the orphans taken in by the church. Most of the money goes to them and to help fund the church itself."

He introduced himself as a government representative who worked for La Renta de la Lotería, the organization in charge of the official lottery in Cuba.

"This isn't an ungodly, unofficial lottery, señora," he continued and went into detail about the "unofficial" Cuban lottery,

La Bolita, *Little Ball,* which he claimed was run by criminals and thieves. He nodded towards the church, as they stood in its shadow. "Go ahead and ask the priest after today's mass, he'll tell you."

After the homily ended, Ines watched as her mother did as she was asked, and went up to speak with the priest, sure the man outside was some sort of thief.

"No, he's right, the proceeds go to help both the government and church," he reassured Mama.

The lottery official was still standing outside under the hot sun when church had ended. Ines and Michel followed their mother as she walked straight towards the man.

"For the children of the church," she said and asked to buy several lottery numbers.

She'd already donated when they were inside, adding money to the collection basket as it was passed around, but to her, helping the church and those in need was a blessing in itself. Ines knew her father didn't agree with her mother, having overheard several arguments when she and Michel took turns pressing their ears to their parents' bedroom door. They could hear their father asking if she knew where the donations actually went while their mother defended the church and the faith involved. When they returned home that day, Ines expected a similar argument to erupt between her parents. Her father was outside on the porch with Old Lady Nayibe, having just gotten home from one of his selling trips. When her mother greeted them, she said nothing of the lottery tickets.

Remembering that the numbers would be announced soon, Michel ran into the house and into the kitchen where he clicked on the radio. Ines ran after him and stood there as he fiddled with the knobs, looking for the frequency the man had told them to find. Their mother joined them in the kitchen and looked over her shoulder towards the front door. Ines listened for the metallic croak that came through the speakers before and after every program, but when the announcement finally came, it wasn't what she'd expected. Ines imagined that the voices of the orphans would be angelic as they announced the winning numbers, but instead they sounded distorted and almost frightening through the metal radio. Ines looked up at the piece of paper Michel held out in front of him. Her stomach fluttered each time a new number was announced and when the final number came in through the radio, both Ines and her brother looked at their mother who said nothing as she stared at the radio, which buzzed with static as the announcement ended. Michel handed Mama the piece of paper.

"We got them all," Ines exclaimed.

She joined her brother who began to celebrate by stomping around the kitchen and yelling, "We won!" while their mother stood in utter disbelief.

"What's going on?"

Ines turned to see her father come in through the front door.

"We won, Papa," Ines said, not fully understanding what it was they'd actually won.

He joined them in the kitchen and went speechless when their mother showed him the paper and explained that she'd played the lottery. Ines thought maybe he would be angry with them for using their money in such a way, but instead he hugged Mama and then joined them in their jumping and dancing around the kitchen. None of them realized how much they'd actually won or even how to collect their prize, but they celebrated all the same. That was the day their lives in Cuba would change completely, but none of them could have realized just how much.

Chapter 11

While Mama wanted Papa to use the fortune that they'd won to buy the farmland he dreamed of, he had other plans. One day after returning from a trip to Havana, he presented the designs for a factory an architect had drawn up for him.

"We will use your designs and make the biggest clothing factory in all of Cuba," he told Mama.

He wanted to build the largest factory Las Piedras had ever seen and it was all he spoke about in the days following his announcement. Ines was sad that her father was leaving behind his dream of making Cuba's largest farm, but he told them that once the business was able to run smoothly, he would build his farm. While this made Ines feel better in the moment, the factory never did run smoothly enough and would be all consuming from the moment it was built.

Soon after her father announced his new plans, construction began on the factory, and they moved into the town of Las Piedras, only a short walk away from the town square. Ines cried every night leading up to the day they left Old Lady Nayibe's house. When the day came for them to move, Ines refused to leave. Michel and Papa were already waiting in Doctor Karam's car with Aida and only Ines, her mother, and Nayibe stood outside of the house.

"This isn't goodbye," Nayibe told her, "You're only a few minutes away. You can visit every afternoon if you want to, but I doubt it. You'll be so busy with all of the wonderful things in town. You may even forget about me."

"I'll never forget about you," Ines said and stamped her foot down, "I won't leave."

"How about this, we'll come visit on Saturday, once we're all moved in?" Mama said.

Ines still refused to leave, but finally, after some more convincing, she joined her family in the car, and they made their way into town.

The house they moved into looked like a castle to Ines and was so beautiful it made even the French ship they'd sailed on pale in comparison. Although she still missed Old Lady Nayibe, the house captivated her. There was a private courtyard in front enclosed by a tall, stone wall and an iron gate. Ines spent many hours sitting in that courtyard, watching the water from the fountain splash against the cobblestone or in the gardens behind the house that were filled with the most beautiful flowers. The inside of the house was even more impressive, at least double the size of their farmhouse in Lebanon and triple the size of Old Lady Nayibe's house. Ines and Michel had their own bedrooms and almost every room downstairs had a chandelier.

The house was like something out of a fairy tale, which made Ines skeptical that it was really theirs. She would often ask her mother and father when they'd have to leave again.

"We never have to leave. This is our home now," her mother reassured her.

While Ines hoped her mother was right, she worried that they'd leave just as easily as they'd left all of the other homes they'd had before, and she loved this one the most.

There were seven bedrooms in all, and only five of them were being used. Ines and Michel had the entire upstairs of the house to themselves, while her parents had their own, spacious bedroom on the main floor where Aida slept with them in her crib. Soon after moving in, her mother hired a housekeeper who also lived on the main floor, in a room behind the kitchen. Her name was Bernita and while she helped take care of Aida, cooked their meals when their mother was too tired, and kept the house in general order, Ines quickly grew to dislike her. She missed living with Old Lady Nayibe, whom she had grown to trust, and compared Bernita to her constantly. There were no secrets between Ines and Bernita, and if the older woman saw anything that she deemed dangerous or inappropriate, she would tell Ines' parents without hesitation. Ines felt as if she were a spy who was always looking to get her into trouble, and if Bernita entered a room she was in, Ines would scurry to another one where she could escape her watchful gaze. Using this method, Ines was usually able to steer clear of Bernita entirely.

Ines' bedroom window looked out to the courtyard, which was across the street from the factory that was still under construction, making it the first thing she saw when she woke up in the morning and the last thing she saw before bed. It took several months for the clothing factory to be completed, so she became used to the clanging hammers, the yelling of the workers, and the sounds of saws cutting wood. She spent less time with Michel as they no longer had the countryside to themselves. They were now surrounded by sidewalks and busy streets. Michel often closed himself in his room for hours, coming out only when Johara and Bashir came over to play with them. At first this wasn't often, but when Abraham and his family moved nearby, Michel would see them almost every other day. The more time Ines spent with them, the more she enjoyed their company, especially Bashir's. She would show him around their gardens, pointing out all of the flowers whose names Old Lady Nayibe had taught her during one of her visits to their new home. Bashir seemed to enjoy the flowers as much as Ines did and stared at them as they sat on benches in the backyard, smelling the dampness of the soil after a summer rain.

"Our father says he's going to be working at the factory with your father now," Bashir told Ines one day as they played.

"That's only because our father hired him," Michel interjected.

Ines hadn't noticed that Michel and Johara had joined them in the garden. While she had once overheard her father telling her mother something similar, Bashir's face looked so sad that she couldn't bring herself to agree with her brother.

"What do you know anyways?" she asked Michel. "Come on, let's go play over here."

Ines led Bashir to the front of the house where they played in the street and watched the workers as they finished their work for the day.

Later that night, as she was getting ready for bed, Ines asked her father if Abraham worked for him now. He looked at her for a moment before explaining that while the initial investment came from the money her mother had won, as well as the income from the clothing they sold, Abraham would be her father's partner in the business.

"We will work together as equals," he said.

Ines couldn't wait to tell this to both her brother and Bashir.

"So, what do you think we should name our factory once it's finished?" her father asked.

"The ice cream factory," Ines said.

Her father laughed and tickled her.

"If we were making ice cream, that would be the perfect name, but we need something that brings to mind fashion and beauty. Ines, what's the most beautiful thing in the world to you?"

Ines remembered their voyage from Lebanon, and her favorite sea creature of all.

"A mermaid," Ines said.

A few weeks later, Ines watched from the courtyard as workers fit a large, wooden sign onto the side of the building. The sign read, *La Sirena*, the mermaid. Papa had a beautiful, wooden sculpture of a mermaid installed below the sign, which he convinced Ines was sculpted after her likeness. She later grabbed her doll Aleia and asked Michel, Bashir, and Johara to join her in front of the factory. They looked up at the sign and at the wooden mermaid while she explained what her father had told her.

"It looks nothing like you," her brother said.

"I think it does," Bashir said.

"I do too," Johara said and smiled at Ines.

Ines looked triumphantly at her brother who didn't say a thing as he asked who else wanted to play games in the house. Ines stood there long after everyone else had gone to play and stared at the sculpture.

"I think you look like me," she said as she looked up at the mermaid.

She felt as if the smooth, wooden eyes were aware of her, somehow watching over Ines and her new home, keeping her family from moving again and ensuring that their new life wasn't just a dream.

When the factory was finally completed, it took up an entire street corner and was made up of three buildings that had previously been separate businesses. Her father had explained to Mama that none of the businesses were doing very well when he had offered to buy them, so their previous owners parted with them easily. He had the buildings gutted, repurposed, and outfitted with ten long, rectangular tables equipped with benches on either side. Each had at least a dozen of the most up-to-date sewing machines and enough seating for as many seamstresses to work. Next door to the factory was a converted storefront, where her father drew passersby by displaying her mother's designs on lifeless mannequins, how he explained they did in Paris, the pinnacle of fashion. At night, Ines could make out the shapes of the mannequins from her window and imagined them coming to life and moving through the factory when the workers were away.

On the days Ines wasn't playing, she visited her father in the factory or helped her mother at the clothing store, which she decided was better than working in an orchard, under the hot sun. Her father spent every day in the factory, except for Sundays, the days all workers would have off. At first, her father managed the factory alongside Abraham while also managing the storefront, but after realizing the impossibilities of being in two places at once, he allowed Mama to manage the store where she also custom fit customers with their purchases.

"Salim, this is my store as much as it is yours," her mother would say when her father had second thoughts of her working.

She would then wink to Ines and whisper, "Never let a man do a woman's work."

When Ines joined her mother in the store, the hum and clicks of the sewing machines from the factory next door sounded like the buzzing of bees during springtime. She loved hearing them and when her mother took a break for lunch, Ines would enter around the back of the factory the same way her father and Abraham did. The back entrance took her through her father's office where she could look through a large glass window that faced out towards the rows of seamstresses at their sewing stations. Her father was always in his office, usually on the phone while Abraham walked along the factory floor. There were over one hundred sewing machines going at all times and there always seemed to be a problem her father and Abraham needed to solve.

"Buenas tardes, Señorita Ines," the seamstresses would say as she stepped out of her father's office into the factory.

When Abraham saw her, he would walk over and twirl her around in the air and say, "Look how heavy you've gotten, little princess," or something else that always made Ines laugh.

She walked between the lines of tables and watched as the strings changed from thin, colored lines into beautifully intricate pieces of fabric and eventually, clothing. Her parents disliked her spending too much time on the factory floor, so she would hurry through, saying hello to each and every seamstress before returning next door. If her mother was with a customer, Ines would quietly wait in the chair by the door or check through inventory in the storeroom until her mother was finished tailoring or showing a new design. Ines waited patiently, hoping her mother would call her over as she sometimes did and ask for her input.

"So, what do you think, Ines, doesn't Señora Martinez look stunning?"

Ines always nodded when she asked her, and it was never a lie. Her mother's dresses were beautiful and with the help of the seamstresses, she was able to finish so many more than she could before, which meant she could now sell to even more customers. The word of La Sirena spread throughout the island and people from all over Cuba came to visit the store. On Saturday mornings, there was a line of women outside waiting for their turn to see her mother's newest work.

Taking advantage of the crowd, a pastry vendor rode his cart up and down the street, in front of the line of women every Saturday morning. As he pulled his cart behind him on his bicycle, the smells of freshly baked pastries followed.

"Sharks always come to blood," Ines heard her father say as he shooed the man away from in front of his businesses, but every Saturday, as sure as the sun, the man came back as if nothing had happened. Eventually, her father let him be, but complained of the man who he felt was taking advantage of his own success.

When her father wasn't looking, Ines would use some of the money she made helping sell Nayibe's crops or from working with her mother to buy pastelitos from the vendor. Ines waited until the man crossed the street to a part of the road difficult to see from the warehouse windows before she approached him.

"Buenos días, señorita Ines," the pastelito vendor said.

When he handed her the pastelito wrapped in a sheet of paper, Ines could feel the heat radiating from it and her mouth began to water. The layers of crust fell apart so easily as she bit into it. The cream cheese and guava filling reminded her of Nayibe's guava tree.

Ines expected the rest of her life to be the same as it was then, playing with her brother, visiting with Nayibe, or working at the store with her mother, but one morning, as she was preparing to go outside to play with Michel, her mother called them both downstairs.

"You both will be starting school next week," she told them before walking into the kitchen and leaving them speechless at the bottom of the stairs.

Since their mother's announcement had come without warning, Ines and Michel agreed not to acknowledge what she'd said, thinking that their mother may forget if they said nothing, but when the following week came, much to their disappointment, she hadn't forgotten. The morning meant to be their first day of school filled Ines with dread. She imagined the new students as they looked at her, something so strange, different from anything they'd seen before. Her light skin and grayish-blue eyes didn't match her thick accent, making it almost impossible for anyone to guess where she'd come from. If anyone did guess she was middle eastern, they wouldn't know what Lebanon was, where it was on the map, or what the Beirut harbor sounded like as the early morning sun rose above the water. Ines imagined that the other children would mock her, keep her at arm's length, and remind her that her true home was thousands of miles away, halfway across the world.

The school her mother chose for them wasn't very far from where they lived, but to make things worse, Papa insisted on driving them on their first day. Ines was afraid to ride in the car with her father who had never owned a car in Lebanon and had only recently purchased one after they'd moved into town. He now practiced his driving around Las Piedras, the car jerking wildly as it stopped and stalled at his growing frustration. The car was a sore reminder of the horses that had pulled her father's wagon, which he'd sold when they moved, just as Ines began to grow fond of them. Like everything else, Ines wasn't given any say in the matter or even a chance to say goodbye. Now her father's deliveries were made in the hunk of steel that smelled of oil and gasoline and roared to life with the sound of thunder.

"Can we please walk, Papa? I've passed the school on the way to the park countless times," Michel said.

Ines knew he was as afraid of their father's driving as she was.

"Don't you want to show up to school in such a marvelous machine? How many of your friends will be jealous of you then?" their father asked.

Ines wanted to mention that they had no friends, other than Johara and Bashir, who would be going to a different school, but she said nothing.

The moment they entered the car she held onto the bottom of her seat as her father set the car into drive and began unsteadily down the road. When they arrived at their new school, a faded pink building that was surrounded by palm trees, Ines wished she could stay in the car with her father, willing to risk another trip with him if it meant not having to walk inside. Other children, many in groups, ran across the stone sidewalk towards the huge wooden doors that were parted open. Michel exited the car and waited for her on the sidewalk farther up the street, not wanting the other students to see their father's car.

"Go on, Ines. I know it's scary on your first day, but through those doors is endless opportunity. Part of me wishes I was in your shoes," her father said.

Ines said goodbye to Aleia, whom she'd brought with her in the car, and placed her onto the seat before stepping out and walking towards the school with Michel. Ines stared up at the large wooden doors that in her mind looked like the gates of hell she'd learned of from Michel. She didn't see the endless opportunity her father mentioned and felt nothing but fear as she approached the building, not understanding how anyone could have wanted to be in her shoes.

Chapter 12

A little over five years had passed since they'd first arrived in Cuba, and although they had a beautiful new home, and a thriving factory, Ines still felt like an outsider. The other children teased her for her accent which they said made her sound congested as if she had a cold. She ignored them, hardly speaking while she was in the classroom, and instead focused on the daily lessons. As soon as the school day ended, she hurried home, running past the vendors who stood behind the iron gates surrounding the school, waving to the ones she recognized from her time selling with her father in the town square. Ines spent the day after school playing with her doll or with Aida, who at five ran around the house like a wild animal, much to Bernita's frustration. Ines spent less and less time with Michel who had no issues making friends and would have them over often, joining him, Johara, and Bashir as they played in the streets and alleyways outside. Ines didn't join them, afraid of the Cuban children who treated Michel as their leader.

"Playtime?" Aida asked when Ines came home.

They explored the house, imagining tea parties and royal balls taking place behind every door while they steered clear of Bernita and their brother's friends. Sometimes Bashir would play with Ines and Aida as well, but whenever Michel called him back to his group, he went without protest.

"We can play later," Ines would tell him as she led Aida around the house, or their garden, searching for the next adventure.

Aida spoke Spanish without any accent at all and sounded like one of the natives. She only knew a few words in Arabic, which Ines had taught her in secret. They were only allowed to speak Spanish in their new home, a rule her father had borrowed from Nayibe. While Michel's accent wasn't perfect, his grammar was, and he would even correct Bernita if she spoke incorrectly, which made Ines' parents proud. Ines was the only one who hadn't conformed completely to the rule.

"Do you want people to mock us?" her father asked her when she spoke in Arabic.

"Do you want to forget Lebanon entirely?" Ines would retort, usually landing her a trip to her bedroom, where she would remain for the rest of the night.

She felt it was wrong to forget one's past but wouldn't push the issue further when she remembered the man with the machete who threatened her father for being a "moro." Ines was sure her parents only meant well, but at times felt like she didn't belong in her own home, and only felt truly comfortable around Aida, who kept their lessons in Arabic a secret, and Bashir, who would sometimes speak Arabic with her, when no adults were watching.

These efforts to hold on to her mother tongue didn't go unnoticed by Mama, who made it her personal goal to break Ines of the habit. To do so, she hired a tutor, but after a week of working with her, the tutor resigned, claiming Ines to be unteachable. This happened two more times. Ines found ways to make her tutors so frustrated they had no choice but to give up. Eventually, her mother hired Señorita Mariela, a young woman who was studying to be a teacher in Havana and came recommended by Mama's friends from town. Although Ines tried her usual antics to get Señorita Mariela to quit like the other tutors, she stayed.

"No matter what you do, I won't give up on you," Mariela told Ines.

Eventually, Ines began to enjoy her time with Mariela, seeing her more as a friend than a teacher. The young woman wore colorful dresses and didn't act like the stern teachers from Ines' school. A week before Mariela's birthday, Ines begged her mother to make her a custom dress, which she did, and they both presented it to Mariela after one of their lessons. When her mother asked how the classes were going, Ines would reply, "very well, thank you," in a Spanish she felt confident in. After several months of tutoring, Ines began school again. She still kept mostly to herself during classes, but her Spanish had improved immensely, giving her a confidence that she hadn't had before, even though her accent took longer to tame.

"I want to be a teacher one day," Ines told Mariela after returning from school one evening, "not one like the teachers in school, but like you." It was both a promise to herself and a thank you to Mariela.

Ines' heart broke when Señorita Mariela had to return full-time to Havana to finish her studies, but she would never forget the young teacher who had given her more than even she could have known.

While Ines had grown accustomed to their life in town, miles from the countryside, she visited Old Lady Nayibe once a week, sometimes bringing Michel or Aida with her, but often going alone. On the days her father couldn't drive her, she'd walk more than an hour each way. The days she visited weren't the same every week, but Old Lady Nayibe always seemed to be waiting for her when she arrived.

"You're late," Nayibe would say with a laugh, if several days had gone by since her last visit.

They would pick ripe fruit from the garden and eat them outside before sipping café con leche, dark coffee clouded by fresh milk, on her porch. Her mother didn't like Ines drinking coffee at home, saying that it made her wild and would stunt her growth, so she took full advantage during those visits. Sometimes Ines would drink a second cup before the afternoon was over.

Her trips to La Casa de Nayibe, as her parents called their previous home after they'd moved, had become something sacred.

Spending time with Nayibe was like spending time with her grandmother, and she would invent any excuse she could to visit.

"I'm taking food to Nayibe," Ines would say as she loaded food from the pantry into a wicker basket.

Sometimes she would go by the bakery in town and surprise Nayibe with a warm loaf of bread she would carry under her arm. Old Lady Nayibe reminded Ines and her parents constantly that she didn't need food, and while Ines used it merely as an excuse to visit, her mother felt sorry for the old woman, who lived alone without a husband while her father felt indebted to the woman who had taken them in when they'd first arrived. After she delivered the food, or whatever she used as her excuse that day, Ines visited Nayibe for hours, sitting on her porch while they sipped their coffee and ate their fruit and bread.

She told Ines stories of the past, sometimes mentioning her husband and son, who had both died while she still lived in Lebanon, although she never told Ines how they died, and she would become quiet and far away whenever she mentioned them, quickly changing the subject to the mountains that surrounded her childhood home, which were similar to those in Las Piedras, or to something else entirely. Ines' favorite stories were those about her grandmother Aleia, who Nayibe claimed was almost exactly like Ines. Ines loved hearing about the schemes Nayibe and her grandmother dreamed up, reminding her of the games she and Michel had played when they were younger. As they got older, Nayibe and Ines's grandmother became known in their town for being strong, independent women, which both scared away and attracted many suitors.

"Why didn't she come with you to Cuba?" Ines asked.

A pause followed that seemed to take up space. The wind blew against them as if joining in on their conversations.

"Well, by then your father had been born and your grandfather was still alive. If it was any other man besides your grandfather, I think she would have left with me for another one of our adventures."

"You never saw her again?"

The old woman shook her head thoughtfully.

"Not with these eyes," she said, "but I've felt her often."

Ines thought of the voice she'd heard on the ship, but didn't say anything, remembering that the last time she'd mentioned it to her mother, she'd asked her not to speak of things such as ghosts and spirits.

Nayibe continued, "Once in a while, I would see her in my dreams. We exchanged telegrams for many years but as time went on, the telegrams became less frequent until they stopped completely. Before I received the telegram telling me that your family was moving here, it had been several years since we'd spoken last."

Neither of them said a word as Nayibe slathered cream cheese and a guava paste she'd made onto the bread Ines had brought with her. It was a sort of meditation for both of them, Nayibe in her spreading of the condiments and Ines in her watching of the seemingly meticulous process.

"Did you miss her?" Ines asked once Nayibe was finished dressing her bread.

"Of course, I did. I still do. She was my best friend."

Ines realized then that she too would probably never see her cousins or childhood friends again, which made her cry quiet tears as she walked home that day.

Soon after that visit, Old Lady Nayibe sold parts of her land and construction of several homes began immediately. Ines watched as her father's retired dream, of converting Nayibe's land into acres of farmland, turned into houses filled with neighbors. No one else seemed to notice what had happened, not even her father, who instead congratulated Nayibe on the "wise business decision." Only Ines grieved for his dying dream, which was completely replaced by La Sirena, and the racks and car loads full of the clothing that they sold weekly. The neighbors were kind and kept mostly to themselves, but whenever Ines visited, she felt as if she'd once again lost part of herself. This time, instead of leaving the land behind in another country, she remained, while the land itself changed and was no longer hers to explore. When Ines asked Old Lady Nayibe why she'd sold part of her land, Nayibe explained that everything belonged to God, and she was only borrowing it.

"It's a sin not to share such a beautiful place with others, don't you think?"

Ines didn't agree and couldn't understand how anyone could give away their home so easily. She was grateful that Nayibe still had her garden, especially the large guava tree that would forever remind Ines of when they'd first arrived in Cuba.

When Ines was still twelve, only a few weeks before her thirteenth birthday, and with her mother's help, she was accepted into the most prestigious Catholic school in Las Piedras, El Sagrado Corazón, *The Sacred Heart*. Ines detested the idea of changing schools, and although she didn't care for her previous school, she knew this change was the final piece in her mother's plan to make her the same as everyone else in Cuba. Everywhere they went that summer her mother would tell whoever they encountered where she would be going to school that year. Whether they were shop owners, customers, or her friends from town, she would tell them all about the school they all seemed to be familiar with.

"That's one of the best schools in all of Cuba." The response was almost always the same, no matter whom she'd told.

"I'm so proud," her mother would say then look at Ines as if she'd been hand-picked by the nuns who ran the Catholic, all-girls school.

This was Ines' turn in the conversation, at which point she nodded and feigned a smile as she looked at her mother who glowed with approval. Ines never once told them of the countless cakes her mother had baked or the many dinners she'd made for the priests and nuns who would eventually have her accepted into the school. Michel knew the truth and teased Ines for it the entire summer before her classes began, but she didn't pay him much attention; instead, she focused on her work at La Sirena, helping her mother with a sense of purpose that distracted her from thoughts of the new school. On the days she wasn't helping her mother at the store, she would go to the large park in the center of town where she and her siblings spent sun-drenched afternoons playing with Bashir and Johara as well as Michel's friends, whom Ines had warmed to over the years. She still hadn't made friends of her own, without the help of her brother. Even the thought of speaking to someone without an introduction brought on a crippling fear that made it difficult to eat and even sleep when the thoughts crossed her mind. Only a few blocks away from the park was El Sagrado Corazón, a looming reminder that within a few short weeks, that always seemed to go by faster than the rest of the year, she would start in her new school.

On her first day at El Sagrado Corazón, Ines felt as if a clock had been reset, and the same fear she'd felt on her first day of school in Cuba had returned, making her bones feel like icicles as she walked through the park towards the school, a beautiful stone building, similar in appearance to the large cathedral in Las Piedras. If she hadn't been so nervous, Ines would have noticed and even admired the beautiful building as she stepped closer to it. Instead, the first thing she noticed was the absence of vendors waiting around the fence as she walked up the cobble stone path towards the entrance where at her previous school they would have been waiting outside, underneath the shade of the palm trees. There was no one outside of El Sagrado Corazón other than students filing in through the front door. Ines wondered if it was the nuns or God Himself who scared the vendors away, having heard stories from her brother of how the temper of a nun was similar to a violent, island storm.

When her first class at her new school began, she stood at the front of the classroom while a nun, her teacher, Sister Francesca, stood behind her.

"My name is Ines Aude."

In that moment, her tongue felt too big for her mouth and the words she'd mastered in the years prior once again felt foreign to her.

"Qué dijiste?" *What did you say?* One of the girls called out.

Ines felt the familiar heat wash over her skin as she blushed and looked down at her feet. She knew the girl had understood her but was making a point to her friends and classmates: *Look, something strange is trying to enter our world.*

There were snickers around the room that were quickly ended by Sister Francesca.

"Enough!"

Ines jumped and turned to look at the nun just as she brought a ruler down onto her desk with so much force that the wooden ruler snapped into two pieces. One of the pieces remained in her hand while the other flew up into the air, hung there for a moment, as if in slow motion, while Ines watched it soar towards her, becoming larger before striking her an inch above her left eye. Ines heard seats scrape against the ground and imagined everyone sitting up straighter than before but couldn't see past the pain. She felt a warmth sliding down her face that she reached up and touched, but quickly pulled her hand away as if she'd touched a hot kettle. Ines looked at her fingers, which were wet and red.

"Sangre!" *Blood,* a girl in the front row cried out, pointing to Ines.

Ines looked at Sister Francesca. When the nun saw her, her mouth opened wide as if she wanted to speak, but then her eyes rolled to the back of her head, and she crumpled to the floor. It was then that Ines could no longer see through her left eye as a curtain of red replaced her view of the fallen nun. No one moved or made a sound, except for two girls near the back of the class who ran up to Ines as if they'd seen that sort of thing many times before.

"Give me your dress," one of them told Ines.

Ines' school uniform went down to her ankles and was so long that when she handed the girl the hem of her dress, she was able to press it against the spot above her eye where the warmth was radiating. The girl pressed against Ines' forehead so hard that she saw stars as another jolt of pain went through her body. She felt dizzy and tried to pull away from her.

"Stop, you're hurting me," Ines cried out.

"Never mind that, let's get you to the nurse. Quick, come on!"

The girl who'd pressed the dress against Ines' face grabbed her arm and pulled her behind her as the other girl followed closely behind them. Ines heard the classroom erupt with sound as they left, but they were already running down the hall before Ines was able to make out what the voices were saying. As she looked back towards the open door, a group of girls had come out and into the hallway to watch them as they made their way to the nurse's office. Small droplets of blood trailed behind them on the otherwise spotless floors, and Ines worried that the stains would never be washed away.

When they entered the nurse's office, she was tidying up the room and jumped when they crashed through the door. One of the girls told the nurse that Sister Francesca had fainted. After taking a look at Ines' forehead and handing her a towel, the nurse ran out towards the classroom.

"I'll be right back. Press down hard on the towel," she yelled over her shoulder.

Ines watched through the small glass window as the nurse and a group of sisters ran towards the classroom they'd come from.

"Are you okay?" one of the girls asked her.

"I think so," Ines said, only then realizing how lucky she'd been that the ruler hadn't struck her eye.

"I've never seen anything like that before," the other girl said.

"Thank you for helping me," Ines said.

"Don't mention it, I'm Concha by the way," the girl who had pressed the dress to Ines' head said.

Concha reached over to a plate of sliced papaya the nurse had left on her desk and looked out into the hall before grabbing one and putting it into her mouth.

"This is Isabella," Concha said as she ate the fruit.

"Hello," Isabella said, "your name is Ines?"

Ines marveled at the two girls who seemed to be exact opposites of each other. Concha had light hair, like Ines,' and seemed to be full of life, unafraid of anything, while Isabella had dark hair, and was timid in both how she spoke and in how she carried herself. They stayed with Ines until the nurse returned and asked them both to go back to class.

"Feel better," Isabella said as they left.

"We'll see you back in class," Concha said.

And Ines thanked them once again.

The nurse told Ines that she was lucky not to need stitches, but she didn't feel lucky at all. As the nurse rummaged around in one of her drawers, Ines began to explain that it was Sister Francesca's fault for slamming the ruler against the desk, but before she could get any more words out, the nurse quieted her, "Be quiet. You'll only get into more trouble."

Ines was able to leave early that day and Sister Francesca let Concha and Isbaella walk her back home. Her dress was stained with blood, and she worried what her mother would say.

"It's really not that bad," Concha told her, "No matter how strict the nuns are, there are always ways to have more fun."

The sun felt good as Ines enjoyed her freedom outside, away from the school, walking with the two girls.

"Wow, your house is beautiful," Isabella said when they arrived at Ines' home.

"I live close by," Concha said.

Ines was grateful that the girls had walked her home, but she thanked them and went inside quickly, embarrassed by everything that had happened. She hoped the girls and everyone else would forget about her the next day.

When Ines woke up the next morning, she refused to get dressed for school.

"I'm not going back to that place ever again," Ines told her mother who came upstairs only to find her still in bed.

"Your face is already healing, it was only just a scratch," Mama said as she checked under the bandage.

But as her mother spoke, Ines only heard the voices of the laughing girls, and the slam of the ruler echoing in her head.

"No, I won't go."

Ines watched as her mother walked out of her bedroom and back down the stairs without another word. She was surprised at how easily she'd convinced her, so Ines got up from bed and walked out after her. When she looked out over the banister, Mama was looking out into the courtyard.

"You'll have your friends walk to school alone?" she asked, looking up at Ines from the bottom of the stairs.

Ines rushed to her window and looked out to see both Concha and Isabella standing in the center of the courtyard, running their hands through the fountain's splashing water.

Walking to school with them that morning, Ines felt that at any moment, the two girls would begin to laugh, and so would all of the other girls hiding in alleyways or inside bushes and behind palm trees that they walked past, as they announced it had all been a joke, that it was impossible for anyone to actually want to walk to school with her.

After all, Sister Francesca had asked them to walk her home the day before, but this time, it seemed as if they'd decided to on their own. But the further they walked with nothing happening, the more Ines' doubts dissolved, and she realized it wasn't some cruel joke they were trying to play on her, they actually wanted to be there. She began to enjoy their walk, laughing along with them when they pointed out a dog with three-legs who every morning would pee against the fence that surrounded El Sagrado Corazón.

"It's like a yellow alarm clock," Concha said.

The three girls burst into laughter as they walked. They only spoke briefly of what had happened the day before, as if they'd seen it in the cinema and it wasn't very important. Ines felt at ease around them, as if she'd known them all her life, and they didn't mention her accent once. Even when they entered the classroom, they sat on either side of Ines, as if protecting her from the rest of the girls, who stared and whispered when she arrived. It wasn't until after school that day, when Ines was lying down in her bed, looking up at the ceiling fan as it spun slowly, warm air coming in through her open window, that she realized she'd made her very own friends in Cuba. Ines prayed that they would remain her friends forever, and that she wouldn't lose them or be forced to leave them behind, as she had her friends in Lebanon.

Chapter 13

From that point on, the girls were inseparable. They walked to and from school together, passed notes to each other during class, and spent all their time together when the weekends came. The nuns quickly realized how much trouble they were and did everything possible to keep them apart during the school day, but whether they were assigned new seats or spoke with their mothers, their bond only grew stronger. The nuns became exasperated, and with nothing working, the three girls were assigned to a new classroom that belonged to Sister Clara, who was the strictest nun of all.

Sister Clara scared everyone, including Ines. Her face was covered in pits that some girls whispered came from a battle she'd had against the devil himself while others swore that she burned herself before she'd become a nun, and that's why she'd joined the sisterhood. Concha and Isabella didn't believe either of those stories and were convinced that Sister Clara was actually the devil himself and that under her nun's veil, where her hair should be, were two pointed horns.

"Look, Ines, don't you see them?" Concha asked one day in class.

She pointed to the front of the room, where Sister Clara stood at the black board.

"Which of you can recite all of the ten commandments without reading from your Bible?" Sister Clara asked over her shoulder.

As some of the girls began to recite the commandments, Ines squinted her eyes and stared at the back of Sister Clara's head. She did seem to have some sort of bump under her veil.

"You see?" Isabella whispered to Ines.

"That's just her hair," Ines said.

"Are you sure?" Concha asked.

Ines didn't believe the other girls, not even Concha and Isabella, but she needed to see Sister Clara without her veil to be sure.

Later that week, on the warmest afternoon since school began, they went on a field trip to the large park near the center of town. It was a beautiful day, so the sisters wanted to give an afternoon lecture outside, and Sister Clara decided on the park because it was across the street from the cathedral and filled with benches situated along the walking paths. Sister María was also with them that day, as they wrangled the students along the sidewalk, down the street, and into the park. Sister María was far less strict than Sister Clara, but she taught the younger girls, and Ines only ever saw her when the younger girls were gone for the day, and Sister Clara needed her to help chaperone. Unlike Sister Clara, she smiled often, and her skin was perfectly smooth.

Although she was kind, Sister María watched Concha, Isabella, and Ines as if at any moment they would try to make an escape or do something foolish. Her smiling face seemed to darken when she noticed them whispering or pointing, having grown wearier of the three girls after their last field trip. On that trip, they were walking in a line down the sidewalk in front of the school and were supposed to be reciting prayers in their heads to keep their minds clear of distractions, when they all saw a beautiful bicycle complete with colorful streamers on the handlebars and a large, blue horn. Her classmates began to whisper and point to the bicycle, and Ines couldn't take her eyes away from the blue horn. It was the bluest thing she'd ever seen, bluer than any sky or ocean, as if it were begging for someone to reach out and honk it. As her classmates walked by the horn one by one, Ines watched as many of them brushed their hands against the rubber ball or through the colorful streamers. When it was Ines' turn to walk by, instead of brushing against the bicycle, she grabbed hold of the rubber ball and squeezed down as hard as she could. The ball let out a satisfying honk that sounded like a clown's nose at the circus, only louder. As Sister Clara and Sister María stopped walking, pausing the procession to look in the direction of the noise, Ines could hear both Concha and Isabella giggling from behind her, which made her giggle as well. Both of the nuns' eyes locked on Ines, who was still standing by the bike.

"Ines Aude," Sister Clara said before grabbing her by the ear and leading her back to school.

Ines was punished by Sister Clara, who also spoke sternly to Sister María for not watching her properly, and since that day, Sister María treated them differently than the other girls.

"Come, children," Sister Clara said and took a seat on a bench in the park.

She gestured to the grass in front of the bench. They all hurried to sit and huddle around. Sister María remained standing and used her finger to quietly count that each and every one of the students were still there. When she reached Ines, her eyes quickly went to Concha and Isabella.

"All here," she said.

"Good," Sister Clara said, her face stern.

As the lesson began, Concha whispered into Ines' ear when she felt the sisters weren't looking.

"You should do it now," Concha said.

"Do what?" Ines asked, but she already knew the answer.

She'd told her friends of her plan to one day lift Sister Clara's veil, so they could be sure of what was underneath. Her constant curiosity made the other girls see Ines as bold, even though she was as afraid of Sister Clara as they were. Ines felt her hands grow sweaty as she looked at the veil, and the Sister's face wrapped within it, looking stricter than ever before. Ines looked around at her classmates, whom Concha must have told of her plan because they gestured forward towards the bench, encouragingly.

As the lecture ended, Sister Clara stood up and brushed off her habit. Ines knew it was her chance. She crept up to the bench, while

Isabela distracted Sister María with a question, and stood on top of it, behind Sister Clara. With a quick motion, Ines pulled up the veil and exposed Sister Clara's head. There were no devil horns. A stream of long, brown hair that was matted down with sweat spilled down the sister's face. She spun around.

"You—"

If Sister Clara had said anything else, Ines didn't hear it. She saw a flash of white and then stars as she fell off the bench and onto the grass below. When Ines stood back up, all of the other girls had scattered around the park, and she felt her burning cheek where Sister Clara had slapped her.

"Wait, children!" Sister María called out and held her dress as she ran after Ines' fleeing classmates.

Only Concha and Isabella remained, sitting frozen in the grass, looking on in horror.

"You…" Sister Clara wheezed, "niña malcriada!" *Brat*! She yelled so loudly that the birds in a nearby tree flew away.

From that day forward, Sister Clara wanted nothing more but for Ines to be expelled from the school. She did her best to convince the other nuns and one day, took several of them to join her for a visit with Mama, whom they all knew well from the fruit baskets and other peace offerings she gave in penance for Ines' misbehaving. It became routine for the sisters to visit Ines' home, sometimes several times a month, to collect the gifts from her mother. That day, with Sister Clara leading them, was no different, and no matter how much Sister Clara tried to rile up the other nuns, they still sided with Mama, agreeing to forgive Ines.

They still watched her more closely than the other girls, but instead of becoming angry and punishing her, the nuns would say, "Let's go visit your mother, shall we?"

Sometimes they'd march her home where her mother would open one of the large, wooden front doors as if already expecting them. Other times the nuns would wait until after school had ended, sometimes even until the weekend, but never on Sunday, and wait outside in the courtyard for Mama.

"I'm so sorry, sisters," Mama would always say as they left, waving to the nuns as they crossed the street and went back to their home with baskets of food in their arms.

When her mother would close the heavy front door, she would look at Ines sternly and tell her how ashamed she should be for causing trouble for such Godly women. Ines couldn't remember exactly how many times she'd received those scolding's, from the nuns or her mother, but they didn't seem to keep her out of trouble. It was a group of girls in their school who were finally able to get Ines, Concha, and Isabella to behave in class.

One day while visiting church during a field trip, Veronica, the biggest girl in their class, came up to them while they knelt, praying, and waiting for the nuns to take them back to school. Ines felt a flush of nervousness as the girl approached, having only just received a yell from Sister Clara moments before for talking with her friends during prayer.

"Do you guys know what happened to the last little girls the nuns didn't like?" Veronica whispered, a smug smile on her face.

Isabella didn't say a word and kept looking at the figure of Jesus that stared at them from the cross hanging over the sanctuary. She was afraid of Veronica because she was the only girl taller than Isabella, and everyone knew that Veronica would fight anyone who crossed her. Concha, on the other hand, wasn't afraid at all.

"Go away, Veronica," Concha hissed.

Two of Veronica's friends joined them in the pews. For once Ines hoped the nuns would notice and tell them to leave them alone, but no one looked over or said a word.

"See those walls?" Veronica whispered.

She pointed to a section of the thick, stone wall near the back of the church. They all turned and looked, even Concha.

"You know what's in there?"

Veronica's friends looked at each other and smiled.

"I said go away," Concha repeated, but Veronica continued.

"No guesses? I'll tell you, then, it's the last girl who made the nuns angry. She was buried in there… alive," she said, smiling wide and showing a gap in her mouth where one of her adult teeth still hadn't grown in.

Ines imagined Sister Clara's face being the last thing she saw before a large stone slid into place over her coffin in the wall and shivered, picturing the craters that covered her face.

"And over there is where they buried her friends." Veronica pointed to the front of the church, where a large pillar connected the floor to the ceiling.

One of Veronica's friends joined in, "they say that you can hear the girls crying out for help because their spirits were damned by the nuns. They will never find their home with God and will spend eternity trapped in the walls of the cathedral."

"Do you hear that?" one of them asked.

They all listened. Concha grabbed hold of Ines' hand, her stubborn face marked with fear.

"Heeeeeeelp meeeee."

Ines, Concha, and Isabella screamed, realizing too late that it was Veronica who had wailed.

"Quiet!" Sister Clara's yell echoed throughout the cathedral, "Ines, Concha, and Isabella, this is my last warning. Do not forget where we are," she said before kneeling back down and squeezing her rosary beads between her interwoven fists, letting them dangle over the pew in front of her.

Veronica and her friends laughed but pretended to be praying when Sister María walked by to check on them. Ines began to pray that Veronica would get into trouble, that the nuns would realize she hadn't done anything wrong, but they didn't.

The following Sunday when Ines went to church with her family, as the sermon ended, she was convinced that she'd heard the wails of the damned girls. She asked Michel if he'd heard anything, but he shook his head. Ines refused to misbehave in class from then on. While she knew Veronica and her friends were only trying to scare them, it didn't mean the story wasn't real, and knowing how much the nuns disliked her, she wasn't willing to take the chance that they may bury her alive in the walls of the church, her soul forever trapped in damnation, unable to go home to Heaven. Isabella felt the same, but Concha still tried to pass notes to them in class and make jokes when she thought the nuns wouldn't hear them, but eventually, even Concha stopped, which meant their usual antics were reserved for the weekends or afternoons spent outside playing after school.

While this kept them from trouble with the nuns, they were able to find their fun in other places. Sometimes they played jokes on unsuspecting passersby or ran wildly between the palm trees in the park, or even hid from each other between the people and Spanish-style buildings and monuments in the Las Piedras town square. There was one woman in particular, whom Ines and her friends had nicknamed, "Modesta la Loca," who especially disliked the three girls. If she saw them playing in the street or along the sidewalk in town, she would yell at them, as if she were possessed by spirits. Ines wasn't sure what had caused the woman to see them as her enemies, but sure enough, if she saw them, she would yell, "troublemakers in the streets. Get them out of here before they burn everything down," or something similar, always drawing attention to both herself and the girls.

The girls retaliated by singing the name they'd given the woman and running away from her if she ever chased after them.

"Modesta la Loca, Modesta la Loca, Modesta la Loca," they chanted, giggling to each other as the woman grew even angrier.

When Ines wasn't with her friends, she wasn't as bold, and felt shy around strangers. On a Saturday, as she went to the market alone to pick up a surprise to take to Nayibe during one of their visits, Ines saw Modesta la Loca walking between the stalls, and immediately hid behind a crate of bananas.

"Little Ines?"

She looked up to see the banana vendor standing behind the stall where she was hiding.

"How's your father doing—," he paused, "what are you doing hiding back here?"

Ines raised a finger to her lips to quiet the banana vendor, but it was too late, and Ines heard a shrill shriek, "Peluca de Maiz!" *Corn Hair*.

It was the name Modesta la Loca called Ines.

Ines stood up from behind the crate and saw Modesta la Loca coming towards her.

"Peluca de Maiz, where are your troublemaker friends?"

"I've got to go now, I'll tell Papa you said hello," Ines told the banana vendor before running off into the crowd.

Modesta la Loca chased Ines through the town square, along sidewalks, and between the crowd, until Ines turned into an alleyway and ran in the direction of La Sirena. When she arrived at the clothing store, she hid in the storeroom behind the clothes racks as her mother asked what had happened. Later that afternoon Ines told her friends that the older woman had chased her farther than ever before and they all laughed, mimicking the woman's shrill yells as they played until dark.

When classes ended for the summer, Ines saw her friends almost every day. Both girls lived nearby, so they agreed to meet at the large park in the center of Las Piedras every afternoon that their parents allowed. From there they explored the town, played jokes on Michel, their favorite target, or spent time in each other's homes. Ines loved visiting Concha's house because it was even bigger than hers, and looked even more like a castle, with four stone pillars that seemed to Ines as big as the ones that held up the cathedral and long windows that let in more light than she'd ever seen inside a home. In the backyard there were palm trees surrounding a swimming pool that was big enough for a family of elephants to bathe.

"That's the biggest swimming pool I've ever seen," Ines said when she first saw it.

She hadn't seen many swimming pools up until that point, but it was even bigger than the swimming pool on the passenger ship, which had previously been the largest one she'd ever seen.

Concha explained to her that her father owned one of the largest sugar fields in Cuba, which had made him "exceptionally rich." She also told Ines and Isabella that her father always had Americans and government officials visiting him in his private study, where he would never let Concha enter. It reminded Ines of her own father and his friends in Lebanon, who would call Michel in to entertain them with his intelligence.

"We should spy on them," Ines said.

Her friends loved the idea. They snuck around Concha's house on many occasions, tiptoeing or crawling near her father's study, especially when he had guests over. Some of the men visiting her father wore military uniforms complete with badges and medals that dangled from the fabric of their jackets while others wore guayaberas and bowler hats as they puffed on their cigars and laughed loudly. On the hottest days, the girls played in the pool for hours until the sun came down and Concha's mother reminded them that their parents would be getting worried if they weren't home soon.

Ines spent many afternoons that summer playing by the pool, sometimes just her, Isabella, and Concha, while being waited on by Concha's housekeeper, Roseline. Unlike Bernita, Roseline was kind. Her skin was dark, and she spoke with a strange accent that reminded Ines of her own. When she thought no one was watching, she sometimes sang lullabies to her young son or spoke in hushed whispers, using a language Ines found enchanting. It was filled with many words and sounds she'd never heard before but reminded her of the French she'd heard spoken by the crew members on the ship.

"What language is that?" Ines asked her, but when she realized she'd been overheard, Roseline acted as if she hadn't heard the question and quickly left the room.

"She speaks Haitian Creole," Concha told Ines later, "but my father won't let her speak it in our house."

Ines felt an instant kinship with Roseline, but from that point on, no matter how often she tried to approach Roseline to learn more about her language, the older woman avoided her. Concha and Isabella seemed as interested in the mysterious language as Ines was, so they often spied on Roseline, doing their best to catch her speaking in her mother-tongue. The three girls even tried to make their own version of the language, which eventually became a secret form of communication among them that no one else understood, not even Michel or Aida. Ines never told her friends that the language they'd created was filled with Arabic words she'd added in, making the language a mixture of Arabic and short phrases they overheard Concha's housekeeper say. They used their language often and giggled at the confused looks they'd get from strangers or classmates.

"What is that language?" Concha's father asked them as they played in the pool one Saturday afternoon.

He was sitting on a stone bench in the shade of one of the many palm trees in their backyard. He'd heard them speaking their shared language as they splashed water at each other.

"What language?" Concha's mother asked as she arrived with a tray of mamey milkshakes. Concha's father ignored the question and looked at them with eyes that resembled pinholes.

"Where on Earth did you hear that racket?" he asked. He first looked at Concha then Isabella before resting his gaze on Ines. Concha's mother stood like a statue, the mamey milkshakes dripping beads of condensation onto the silver platter.

A swell of fear rose inside Ines, and the pool water became uncomfortable, like she was no longer being warmed by the afternoon sun, but had instead become a lobster, being boiled alive in a large pot.

"It's my language," Ines thought, but couldn't say the words.

He asked them once more.

"We heard Roseline speak it," Concha croaked.

As if burned by fire, Concha's father shot up from his seat and marched over to the small house in the far corner of their backyard, where Roseline lived with her son. Minutes later, Ines watched from the pool as Roseline left through the back gate in tears, a small bag in her arms, and her son dragged behind her. Ines looked over at Concha who watched in horror. They never saw Roseline again. Not in Concha's house or in Las Piedras. It was as if when she'd stepped through the gate and out of the yard, she and her son had disappeared from the world completely. A few days later, Concha had a new housekeeper, an old Spanish woman who Ines thought was much stricter than even Bernita.

The guilt burned at Ines for the rest of the summer. She'd created the language that had resulted in Roseline being fired and sent from the house but couldn't understand what she'd done wrong. Ines wondered if this was why her parents forbade her to speak Arabic in their home. Although it was her first language, it was as if speaking it had become a sin, and she feared she too would be banished from her home and disappear like Roseline if she were found out.

When Ines returned home from her days spent with Concha and Isabella, Michel was usually still playing with Bashir and Johara or his friends from school. There were times when Ines and her friends joined Michel and his friends to play, but for whatever reason, Johara seemed to dislike Concha, who would always talk to Michel as if he was the only one in the room. When they played hide and seek or tag together, Johara reminded Concha constantly that she had no way of knowing all of the best hiding places in the house, because she was new to the group. Johara hardly said a word to Isabella who was already soft-spoken and seemingly unbothered by what anyone said, but Concha wasn't as soft-spoken, and would often argue with Johara. On most days, Ines and Michel played separately, Aida joining whichever group would have her that day. It was as if two worlds were now available to Ines, one from her life before, and a new one, where she was sometimes as courageous and outspoken as Concha.

Ines and her friends filled that summer with all of the adventures and dangerous stunts they could think up. One of their favorite ideas was jumping from the second story down to the foyer with nothing but one of Ines' mother's umbrellas. Ines imagined using an umbrella to float ever since seeing wind seemingly lift Bernita off the ground and up into the air during a particularly dangerous storm when she went to the garden to bring delicate flowers inside. She had never had the courage to try it, but when she shared the idea with her friends, both girls agreed that it was possible, believing the air would slow them as they went and plop them down gently onto the ground below. They placed pillows from Ines's bedroom onto the stone tile that lined the foyer. They tested the padding by jumping up and down on the pillows; however, there still wasn't enough cushion, so Ines ran up to Michel's bedroom and then Aida's, taking the pillows and sheets from their beds and placing them on top of the pillows from her bedroom.

"Who should go first?" Concha asked.

They stared down from the top of the stairs at the mound of pillows and sheets below. Ines regretted her idea as she noticed for the first time just how high their stairs went, fumbling with the umbrella in her hands.

"It wasn't my idea," Isabella said and looked at Ines.

Ines felt a hollow feeling start from her belly then spread to her limbs.

"Go or I'll go," Concha said.

Ines looked to Concha then to Isabella, her two friends, her only friends, then she closed her eyes, opened the umbrella, and jumped.

The thought of jumping made her stomach drop but the falling itself made her feel weightless. Instead of drifting slowly to the ground as they'd imagined, like a leaf on a gentle breeze, Ines crashed down like a coconut dropped into the sand, hitting the pillows and sheets with a whump. Her friends rushed down the stairs.

"Are you okay?" they asked, moving the pillows.

"I want to go again," Ines said as she laughed.

They took turns jumping into the pile of pillows for the rest of the afternoon until Bernita put an end to their fun. The moment she saw them jumping over the banister into only a small pile of pillows to break their fall, she turned and yelled, "Señora Aude! Señora Aude!" and ran out of the room. She came back a few minutes later with Mama who was so furious when she saw what the three girls had been doing that she sent Concha and Isabella home. Ines went a week without seeing her friends, banished to her room, but eventually, the punishment ended, and the summer continued.

Near the end of that summer, Ines experienced her first encounter with death. The day was overcast, and the entire week had been filled with storms, but the weather seemed to be holding, at least long enough for the day to be enjoyed. It was a rare occasion when Ines and Michel both wanted to play together, agreeing to visit Nayibe's house, so they could show their friends the house where they used to live. Ines wanted to catch lizards that hid under the rocks along the banks of the river while Michel wanted to check in on their old fort and show Johara and Bashir more of the countryside. It was the first time Concha and Isabella went with Ines to visit Old Lady Nayibe, but her mother still wouldn't let Aida join them. She looked at her little sister who watched Ines and her friends from the porch, where she held her mother's leg, crying that she wanted to go with them.

"Hold on," Ines told her friends.

She ran back inside and up the stairs to her bedroom where she pulled out a key she kept hidden under her socks in the dresser and used it to unlock the box she kept under her bed. Ines pulled Aleia out of the box where she kept her for safe keeping. She ran back outside with the doll.

"Here," Ines handed Aida the doll.

Aida's eyes went wide.

"You need to take good care of her while I'm gone today," Ines told her, "I'll bring you back the biggest lizard of all."

Ines ran back to her friends.

"Be back early today, children. There's another storm coming," her mother yelled out after them.

Michel and Bashir rode their bicycles and circled Johara, Concha, Isabella, and Ines while they walked away from town. Concha and Johara wouldn't walk next to each other, but they weren't fighting as they normally did. The air felt sickly against Ines' skin, filled with humidity, a promise of the rains to come. Ines and her friends picked up rocks as they walked and skipped them along the road, seeing who could send them the farthest.

"Hey!" Bashir yelled out when one of the rocks Ines threw bounced off the ground and hit his bicycle. "You'll make me fall."

"Sorry," Ines said and giggled.

Bashir smiled at her.

There weren't many cars or wagons on the road, and the sky was filled with dark purple storm clouds, the sun peeking through in glimmers, making the humidity even more uncomfortable.

"We should've gone to the ocean instead," Johara said.

"Or my pool," Concha replied.

"Where are we even going again?" Johara asked.

"I already told you guys. We're going to La Casa de Nayibe. We can't catch that many lizards by the pool and they don't like the ocean," Ines said.

"You're the only one who wants to catch lizards," Michel said as he rode his bike towards Ines and turned at the last second.

"Watch it," Ines yelled at Michel who laughed as he rode past her.

She turned to Concha and Isabella and said, "Trust me. You're going to love Old Lady Nayibe's house."

Ines was excited to share the magic of Nayibe's home with her friends, but part of her worried they wouldn't enjoy themselves.

The heat and far away rumbles of thunder aside, they talked and laughed the entire way. When they arrived, the sun was at its peak and everyone was glistening with sweat. Michel and Bashir abandoned their bicycles by the small wooden bridge that ran over the stream leading up to Old Lady Nayibe's house. She was outside in her garden, swinging her machete at the stray blades of a bush and wearing one of the dresses Mama had made for her.

"Good afternoon, children," she said, smiling as she wiped a gloved hand along her forehead.

Although she wasn't expecting Ines that day, much less all of her friends, she welcomed them as if she had been. Ines introduced Concha and Isabella to the old woman who had previously been her only friend. She watched as Nayibe looked them both up and down.

"Would you children like anything to eat?"

"Have you all tasted guava before?" Ines asked her friends.

They both nodded.

"Well, you certainly haven't had any like mine. I just picked some this morning," Nayibe said as she went inside.

"I'll help," Ines said and went inside behind Nayibe.

Ines brought out a pitcher of water filled with ice and enough glasses for all of them. Her friends sat down beside Michel, Johara, and Bashir along the steps of the porch and Nayibe placed a ceramic platter laid out with slices of guava between everyone. Ines passed the glasses out as she poured water into them, feeling as though her friends were also her guests.

"This is delicious," both Concha and Johara said.

Isabella echoed their praise.

"We used to pick them all of the time when we lived here," Ines said as she joined them on the steps.

Nayibe smiled and watched as Ines continued to share her memories of picking fruit and playing around the house. While Ines had been in Cuba for several years, the year they had lived with Old Lady Nayibe had felt like an entire lifetime that overshadowed the rest. When she spoke to her friends that day, as they ate their fruit on the porch, she felt for the first time that they were the visitors in *her* country, and that she had lived in Cuba all her life. As they sat on the porch and ate, she saw one of Nayibe's neighbors in the yard, hanging clothes on a long string, with three small children hanging from her legs and running around her like swarming bees. She realized then how much everything had changed, even Nayibe's home was so different than what she'd known as a child, making her wonder what else would change before the world finally settled and let her keep something as her own.

Once they finished eating, Ines led Concha and Isabella down a dirt trail that took them to the deepest part of the river, where the most rocks were piled along the bank. The further away they went the fainter the whacks of Nayibe's machete became as she swung it at the bushes in her yard. Michel, Bashir, and Johara didn't join Ines and instead stayed closer to the house, setting off to explore the old forts Ines and Michel had built several years before.

"It's higher than usual," Ines said when they arrived at the river.

The normally calm stream was now swollen with water that rushed off between the trees. The water level completely covered some of the rocks that were usually visible above the surface.

"Wow, look at all of these rocks," Isabella said.

"What type of lizards can you find out here?" Concha asked as she flipped over a sand-colored stone.

Ines didn't know there were different types of lizards, but she answered that there were several kinds around the river, you just had to find them. She walked over to a smooth rock and flipped it over to search the exposed soil where it once rested. She found a few centipedes and worms that wriggled in the moist soil, but no lizards darted out. The three girls continued flipping over rocks, some of which tumbled down into the water with a splash or a quiet plop. They searched for several minutes but didn't find a single lizard.

"That's weird," Ines said.

"Let's try down there," Concha pointed downstream to where the flowing water cut between the trees and into the forest.

Ines imagined all of the wild animals that hid in the darkness and shuddered.

"I've never been down there," she said.

"So? That's even better. Let's go before your brother and his friends find us."

"But we haven't found any lizards yet," Ines said, drying her hands on her dress, which to her horror had become stained with mud. She knew her mother would be angry with her when they returned home.

"Forget the lizards, maybe we'll find iguanas in the forest," Concha said.

Isabella said nothing but seemed to agree silently.

Ines felt as if her day had been taken from her, but she knew there wasn't any use arguing, so she followed Concha and Isabella down between the trees alongside the overflowing stream. She looked at the darkness of the forest, underneath the canopy of overgrown trees and her mouth became dry. She prayed silently, hoping neither of her friends noticed her fear.

"Why have you never explored in here before?" Isabella asked Ines as they followed Concha into the forest.

Ines shrugged, her eyes scanning the bushes around them. She wouldn't tell them that it scared her, that the unknown darkness made her remember nightmares and monstrous things. Not even Michel had gone very deep into the forest.

"Come on, guys, keep up," Concha said.

A quiet hung above the thick forest. There were no sounds outside of the moving water, the occasional rustling from the canopy above, or the whistling of invisible birds. Ines shuddered as she imagined what else might be watching them from the trees. Ines looked back at the entrance to the forest to make sure it was still there, feeling as if the world behind them had disappeared, and they'd gone somewhere else entirely. They followed the river closely because the forest was dense and difficult to pass through unless they stayed close to the rushing water. Long finger-like vines fell from the trees, which Ines thought looked like hands reaching down to touch the earth.

They reached a clearing where the sunlight came down in beams along the water. The river had become much deeper, and she could hardly see any fish darting around.

"Maybe over there?" Isabella pointed.

A rock wall, part of the mountain that rose above the forest, was completely covered in greenery outside of a small cave mouth that was shaped like a heart.

"There's probably iguanas in that cave," Concha said.

"But that's on the other side of the river," Ines said.

"We can probably get across there," Isabella pointed again.

There was a small path of rocks that led across the river, which looked slippery as they glistened with sunlight.

"Great idea," Concha said.

"Do we really need to? Let's go find lizards somewhere else," Ines said.

She imagined the sharks that had haunted her as a child, swimming up the stream towards them. If they fell in, the water's current would take them back to the sharks' home in the ocean, where they would never be seen again.

"You wanted to find the lizards, didn't you? We already saw there were none in the spot you showed us," Concha replied.

Isabella and Concha removed their shoes as thunder roared above them, a dull, delayed echo as if the rain hadn't made up its mind whether or not it would fall.

"It's about to storm," Ines said, "let's go back before it starts to rain."

"Well, I'm going," Concha said and began to cross the river.

Isbaella walked towards Ines, who still hadn't removed her shoes.

"We're already here. We might as well see what's in that cave," Isabella said, her voice quiet and thoughtful. "Besides, it's pretty, isn't it?"

Ines looked at the cave — the vines hanging down in front of it looked like green hair as they cascaded across the opening in the rock face.

"Okay," Ines said, before taking off her shoes and following behind Concha along the patch of stones in the river.

Ines matched each of Concha's steps. She almost fell in the first time her foot brushed along the slick moss but began to gain confidence the closer they came to the other side.

"I wonder if this goes all the way to the ocean," Isabella said.

Ines thought of the sharks again, but focused on Concha, who was almost across.

Between each rock she stepped across, Ines made sure her footing was steady, before bringing her other leg across. It was a dance, simple, yet requiring a balance Ines had only just learned to achieve on a bicycle a few years before. It began to rain when Ines was halfway across, but she continued, at the urging of Isabella behind her. Drops of rain plopped into the river with a gentle tapping that sounded like fingers on glass. In less than five minutes, after multiple near falls into the water, all three girls made it across and stood in front of the opening in the rock wall. Ines stared into the cave as the rain began to come down rhythmically around them. The inside of the cave was a void, a black deeper than any she had seen before. It looked as if she were staring into a bottle of ink, like the one she used to scribble her notes in her journal or how she imagined the night sky would look without any stars.

"What are you guys doing all the way out here?"

Ines turned and saw Michel, Bashir, and Johara walking along the other side of the river.

"We followed you guys over here," Michel yelled over at them, "our old fort was gone."

Her brother's voice was raised to carry over the sound of the rushing water, and the falling rain. The water had turned brown from the mud that had been stirred up from the bottom by the rising waters and faster than normal current.

"Come over here… if you're not afraid," Concha challenged him.

Ines noticed Johara look at Concha with what appeared to be anger as she stepped closer to Michel who was looking at the stones where Ines and her friends had crossed moments before.

"I don't want to go over there," Johara said.

"I do," Bashir said.

"What's in that cave?" Michel said, "I've never seen it before."

"We're looking for iguanas," Concha said and turned to step into the cave.

"I'm coming too," Michel said.

Michel threw off his shoes and began to step out along the rocks towards them.

As the rain continued to fall, the water's already swollen height seemed to rise even more, which filled Ines with a sense of dread.

"Michel, wait until it stops raining, it's too slippery now," she cried out.

Bashir removed his shoes and followed behind Michel, neither one listening to Ines' pleas for them to stop.

"It's okay, Ines, it's not that slippery," Bashir said as water sloshed above the stones and over his feet.

Concha stood at the entrance of the cave and called out to Bashir and Michel, "Guys, I think Ines is right, go back until the rain stops."

"If you girls could do it, we can too," Michel said and looked back at Bashir, "right?"

"We're not afraid of any rain," Bashir said with a smile and nodded.

Ines looked across the river at Johara where she stood frozen. Her long hair was drenched with rain, and her face was full of fear.

There was a flash of lightning followed by a boom of thunder that sounded out all around them and seemed to shake the forest itself. The sound made everyone jump, including Bashir, which caused him to lose his footing and slip into the swollen stream.

"Bashir!" Ines and Johara both cried out.

His head went under the surface, but appeared a moment later, farther down the river.

Ines looked around her and saw a large fan of leaves, which had turned gray from being detached so long from its tree. She ran over and grabbed it from the ground, pushing it into the water towards Bashir, who fumbled for it, but the current was too strong and pushed him even further away.

"I'm coming!" Michel said.

"Wait, Michel!" Ines cried out, but with a splash, her brother was in the water after Bashir.

The two boys went under and resurfaced multiple times, gasping for air, and yelling out as the current carried them farther away. Ines and her friends ran along the river on one side, Johara on the other, as they tried to reach them, but the water was too fast, and the rain was making it harder for them to see.

"Here, use this to float!" Ines shouted and threw a long stick, that Concha had given her, into the water.

She hoped they'd heard her, but as the rain came down in hard sheets, they were lost from view.

"What should we do?" Isabella asked.

Ines felt panic take hold, but somewhere inside of her, she heard the same voice she'd heard as a child when on the ship, her grandmother's voice. *Downstream.* In that instant, her fear turned to action.

"The river will carry them downstream. It should loop around behind Nayibe's property on the other side. Let's go," Ines said.

The rest of the day was a blur to her. She remembered leaving the forest and telling Nayibe what had happened, so she could get help from one of her neighbors who had a telephone, while they checked the sections of the river where Michel and Bashir could be. Johara was in tears and crippled by her fear, and Ines knew she would have been too if it wasn't for her grandmother's voice that sounded from somewhere within her.

"I d-d-don't know w-w-what—" Johara stuttered between sobs.

"Stay with Nayibe," Ines said and left with her friends to search for Michel and Bashir.

They started at the river crossing half a mile or so behind Nayibe's home then worked their way around to check along the bank and anywhere else the current may have taken them. After several hours of searching, they found nothing.

"Let's go back, Ines, maybe they got out in the forest and are at Nayibe's now," Concha said.

"Maybe they're looking for us?" Isabella said.

"You guys go back if you want, but I'm going to find them," Ines said.

"We're not leaving you," Concha said, and Isabella agreed.

It was almost dark and still raining by the time they returned to Nayibe's house, unable to find any sign of her brother or Bashir. When they returned, Ines' parents were there, rain tapping against the metal hood of her father's car. Her mother ran to her when Ines approached the porch.

"Thank God you're alright. We just arrived and were about to go looking for you," she said, hugging Ines close to her, not minding her soaked and muddied clothes.

"We need to go to the hospital in Las Piedras," her father said, "Michel and Bashir are there."

Ines had so many questions but was too exhausted to ask them. The adrenaline had left her depleted, but unable to sleep as she sat cramped in the back of her father's car alongside Johara, Concha, and Isabella. For once she did not mind her father's erratic driving.

"Who found them?" Isabella asked Johara whose eyes were swollen from crying.

"A farmer found them washed up on the riverbank." Johara didn't say anything else.

Please, God, keep them safe.

Ines repeated the prayer silently as she looked out of the window. It was still raining. When they reached town, they crossed the large bridge over the river, making Ines wonder if her brother and Michel had crossed below them just hours before. Ines wondered how far they'd been taken by the current. *Had they made it to the ocean? Were they even still alive?* She looked through the window and watched the river rush past.

<h1 style="text-align:center">Chapter 14</h1>

School began several days after the accident, and no matter how much Ines protested, her parents forced her to go. Michel and Bashir were still in the hospital, both in and out of consciousness. Ines didn't understand what that meant when she'd heard the doctors say it, never having been unconscious herself, but when allowed to see them, she thought of a candle as its flame went in and out with the breeze. She'd also overheard the doctors telling her parents that when the farmer had found them on the riverbank, both boys were barely conscious and had cuts and bruises all over their bodies most likely caused by the large rocks in the river that gave the town its name. Her mother, along with Bashir's, went back and forth between their homes and the hospital, while Papa and Abraham continued their work at La Sirena, going to the hospital only in the evenings. The hospital in Las Piedras wasn't as equipped as the hospital in Havana, so she heard her father and Abraham on the phone with Doctor Karam constantly, doing everything they could to get Michel and Bashir transferred to the capital. But for the time being, they were told a transfer was too dangerous.

While her brother was fighting for his life in the hospital, Ines had to sit in class and listen to Sister Clara lecture, her voice clawing at her ears. Ines hardly spoke and although Concha and Isabella did their best to cheer her up, there was nothing anyone could do. To make things worse, everyone seemed to know what had happened to Michel even though Ines hadn't told anyone in school, which made her angry with her friends as she knew they must have told them. There was no relief when she returned home in the afternoon. The house felt empty without Michel, and her parents hardly spoke to each other.

"How long will Michel be away?" Aida asked her the day after the accident. She looked up at Ines as she clutched Aleia, whom Ines had decided to let her keep until Michel returned from the hospital.

Ines said nothing because she didn't know and normally when she didn't know something, she'd turn and ask Michel. She felt completely alone those first few days. When she saw her friends at school, images of Bashir falling into the water filled her head. It was as if she were transported back to that exact moment, with the rain coming down, her clothes cold and wet, pressing against her skin, and the smell of guava juice lingering on her lips. Could she have done something differently? Even her dreams were filled with these memories, waking up in the night, thinking she was standing next to the river, this time close enough to reach out and grab her brother.

Her mind kept racing when she went with her mother to visit Michel and Bashir at the hospital. They went every afternoon once school ended. Bashir's mother and Johara were always there by the time they arrived.

"Any news?" Mama would ask.

"The same," was the reply.

While they waited in the hospital, Ines' mother showed her and Johara how to knit using the yarn and needles she brought with her. The doctors let them visit with Bashir more than Michel as Bashir had regained consciousness, but he seemed exhausted, looking up at them with a weakness Ines had only seen once when her mother was sick before giving birth to Aida. When they visited her brother, the room was draped in an unnatural silence. Michel looked as if he were sleeping, but no matter how much Ines spoke to him, he wouldn't turn over and tell her to leave him alone. Ines heard the doctors tell her mother and Abraham how lucky the boys were that they'd survived, but that they were still fighting for their lives.

"What can we do?" Mama asked the doctor.

"Pray," the doctor said with tender eyes.

When they returned home, Ines prayed alone at the foot of her bed. Her mother and father stayed with Aida through the night; her inability to sleep the first night kept them all awake as she cried and called out Michel's name. In the morning when they ate breakfast, Aida was more quiet than usual and moved the food around on her plate as if it disgusted her. Ines tried to distract her by telling her stories, taking her to the park, or listening in on their parents' conversations, but nothing took either of their minds from Michel.

When Mama and Papa thought Ines and Aida were upstairs, they spoke in hushed voices in the kitchen. Aida stood behind Ines as they watched through the crack in the kitchen door, trying to hear what they were saying.

"No. I won't allow it," Ines heard her father say.

"It's just one day, Salim."

It was rare to hear her mother use her father's name.

"Won't allow what?" Aida whispered to Ines.

"What are you two doing?" Bernita asked from the hall.

"Getting water from the kitchen," Ines said at the same time that Aida said, "Listening to Mama and Papa."

"Upstairs the both of you. The adults must talk without your curious little ears listening to them." She shooed both girls upstairs.

Later that night, Mama and Papa called Ines and Aida into her bedroom and explained that she would be traveling to a church, so she could pray for Michel. It was in a different part of Cuba, so she would be gone for most of the day.

"What's wrong with our church?" Ines asked.

Her mother explained that it was a special church, a shrine to La Virgen de la Caridad, *Our Lady of Charity.*

"She's the protector of the Cuban people," her mother said.

"But we aren't really Cuban, are we?" Ines said with an anger she didn't expect to hear in her own voice.

"Go to your room," her mother said.

"Take me with you," Ines begged, but her mother shook her head.

Ines looked up at her father, but he wouldn't return her gaze.

When her mother left the house early the next morning, Ines watched her from the window. She didn't walk towards the church in Las Piedras, and instead turned right out of their courtyard in the direction of the bus stop. Ines changed into her school clothes and crept out of the house after her mother. There weren't many people on the street, and her mother didn't look behind her, but Ines stopped at every intersection to make sure she hadn't seen her before crossing. Ines wasn't sure what her mother would do if she saw her. Ines smelled gardenias as the wind blew her mother's perfume towards her, conjuring up memories of time spent in their garden.

The quiet emptiness of the street was replaced by the sound of people as Ines reached the bus stop. Men and women, but mostly men, piled onto the bus once it had pulled up along the street corner. She waited for her mother to get on the bus and for several other passengers to get on behind her before Ines went in herself. She tried to make herself as invisible as possible, her head down, a thin Pashmina shawl bundled up around her neck and pooling at the bottom of her face. It was all Ines could think of to conceal her identity from Mama, but she knew she would still most likely be recognized, the shawl one of her mother's designs after all.

Ines took the first empty seat that she saw, next to an overweight man who was focused on something outside of the window and looked behind her. Her mother was seated a few rows back, sitting next to a young woman who had already closed her eyes and was resting her head against the bus window. Ines' seating arrangement wasn't as comfortable. The man next to her smelled like day-old cigars and took up more than just his seat. White stubble covered his face, and he scratched at it from time to time. When he glanced at Ines as if hoping to make conversation, she looked away quickly and pretended not to have noticed. She hoped that he'd get off the bus much sooner than she did and would leave her alone for the majority of the bus ride. The brakes gasped, and the bus began to grumble down the road. Although Ines was only thirteen, and still a few months from fourteen, she looked much older for her age, a fact that scared her parents, but made her life easier when needing to do adult things. She was beyond grateful in this situation, knowing that if her age were discovered, and she was traveling on the bus alone, there would be questions. It was the first time she'd ridden the bus alone, even though her mother was only a few feet away, and the feeling of adventure and maturity made her stomach flutter.

Ines had no pocket watch with her and wouldn't dare ask the man what time it was, fearing a conversation that would reveal her age or be loud enough to alert Mama, so she based her sense of time on the sun and its proximity to the mountains that were in view once they drove over the bridge and out of town. When they'd boarded the bus, the sky was purple, the sun still a baby not yet ready for the world. But as the minutes passed by, and the sun rose, Ines knew they were getting closer to their destination. She had no idea what to expect, or if the driver would advise them once they'd arrived, so she paid close attention to her mother, sneaking glances to where she sat every few minutes. Her eyes grew heavy on several occasions, but she pinched herself throughout the trip, afraid that if she closed her eyes even for a moment, she would fall asleep and wake up somewhere she didn't recognize with her mother gone.

Several hours went by as many passengers disembarked and few boarded, while her mother remained.

How much longer until we arrive?

Ines had never heard of the town or the shrine they would be visiting, but she spent much of the trip imagining La Virgen de la Caridad. She remembered her lessons from school and saw the image of her hovering over the ocean, a boat containing three lost men at her feet. The legend was that two Native American brothers and an African slave child encountered a dangerous storm, which almost sank their boat, but as they prayed to the Virgin Mary, she appeared in the form of a statue with the words La Virgen de la Caridad attached to a plank of wood, and the storm was kept at bay. Although Ines believed prayer was powerful, she still maintained her doubts, knowing how badly her brother and Bashir were hurt.

"You're traveling far," the man next to Ines said.

He was one of the few remaining passengers who had originally boarded in Las Piedras, but she'd never seen him before in town. It wasn't the first thing he'd said, but Ines had ignored him, acting as if she'd fallen asleep, or had become entranced by something out of the window. Now with the bus as empty as it was, she feared her mother would notice if he kept trying to get her attention without a reply.

"Yes," she said, pulling up her neck wrap.

"Where are you headed?" he asked.

The man pushed their window up, and the smells of saltwater mingled with his cigar musk.

We must be near the ocean.

Only then did Ines realize just how far from Las Piedras they had to be.

"So?"

Her hands grew sweaty, and she glanced back to check on her mother. The woman next to her had gotten off the bus, so she'd taken the seat closer to the window. Ines jumped as the man slammed the window shut.

"I'm not sure," she said, turning to look at him.

The man made a huffing sound and looked around.

"Is that so?" he asked and leaned closer to Ines.

A wave of discomfort came over her, and she felt as if she wanted to hit him or cry out, but she did nothing.

"You can tell me. I'm really a nice guy."

Ines could feel the hot dampness of his breath, his face then only a few inches from her own. She decided that if he came any closer, she would have to do something, but her body seemed paralyzed. They'd gotten far enough from Las Piedras, and she knew that even if her mother found her out, they'd already traveled too far for her to make Ines ride the bus back, but still, no words escaped her lips. She wasn't supposed to be there, she was supposed to be in school and for a moment, she wished that she'd never followed Mama that morning. She prayed, swearing that she'd never skip her classes again if only the man left her alone, but he didn't move his face from where it was. His breath was heavy and as he blew out, strands of her hair shuddered. His hand moved towards her, and Ines felt as if her heart would burst with fear as her stomach turned in disgust. Her fear had become primal, irrational, everything felt fuzzy and unreal. Before his hand reached her, the bus stopped, and the man stood up.

"My stop." He smiled as if nothing had happened and pushed past Ines before she could make room for him, his large thighs pressing roughly against her knees.

The smell of day-old cigars lingered in his seat even after he got off the bus. It made Ines nauseous, but she didn't want to bring any more attention to herself by changing seats, so she opened the window and let the fresh, ocean breeze wash over her.

No one else boarded the bus, but before the bus began to move, a woman walked up to the driver, only a few rows in front of Ines and worked to get his attention.

"Excuse me, sir. How much longer until we arrive at El Cobre?"

Ines quickly realized the woman was her mother, so she pulled the shawl tighter around her face.

The bus driver grumbled and looked at a pocket watch he pulled from his breast pocket, "at least another four hours," he said.

Ines didn't see her mother's reaction, but she must have been shocked because she then said, "There must be some mistake."

The driver assured her there was no mistake.

"I can leave you here, or you can ride the bus with me to El Cobre. Either way I need to get going." The bus driver reopened the doors.

Ines imagined they had been riding for over five hours at that point, so another four would have meant a nine-hour drive, making it the longest trip either Mama or herself had taken since their voyage from Lebanon. Ines knew her mother had intended to be back the same day because of what she'd overheard her tell her father, and she would never stay anywhere overnight without her family.

"Close the doors," her mother said to the bus driver.

She sighed and sat down only two rows in front of Ines, who could feel her heart pounding in her chest. The bus driver shook his head, shut the door, and the bus began moving again.

Ines didn't raise the window back up. Instead, she enjoyed the breeze as it flowed in while she stared out of the open window. The thought of another four hours on the bus made her eyelids grow heavier and, eventually, she fell asleep.

When Ines woke up, her mother was sitting in the seat next to her. She reached for the shawl, meaning to pull it higher up her face, but it wasn't there.

"How was your nap?" Mama asked Ines.

The shawl was in her mother's lap, and she was running her hands through it.

"Did you think I wouldn't notice you?"

Ines looked around the bus. There were only a few other passengers left, most of them sleeping.

"I'm sorry, Mama."

"Don't be sorry to me. Do you know how worried your father will be when you don't return home tonight after school?"

"I didn't know it was so far away," Ines said, immediately regretting her words.

Her mother lectured her for the rest of their trip, which totaled over two hours. Ines begged her to understand why she'd decided to come, and even though Ines knew it wasn't right, she felt it was her only way to help her brother and Bashir. She said nothing of the man who had been sitting next to her before, afraid that would only prove her mother's point further.

The sky was growing dark by the time they arrived at El Cobre. Ines walked in front of her mother, like a prisoner being escorted by her jailor, as they exited the bus. Ines hopped from the bus onto a dusty street that was filled with shirtless children playing and laughing. Throughout the bus ride Ines had pictured what El Cobre would look like, but the town was very different than she'd imagined. There was dust everywhere, as if God Himself had poured a bucket of sand over the buildings once he'd finished creating it, but beyond the dust, in between all of the buildings and houses, there were green bushes and beautiful pink flowers that Ines hadn't seen before. It was as if the forest hadn't realized a town was in its way and had grown around and through it. In the distance, an impressive temple loomed above the town and cast long shadows along the streets below.

"That's it," Mama said, nodding towards the shrine.

Ines noticed her mother's anger seemed to subside when she saw it.

The building was the color of white sand but had three rust-colored domes capping off large towers that rose above the trees. At its center, under the middle tower, was an ornate design that resembled the sun.

"Come, let's get there before the sun goes down completely," her mother said, grabbing Ines by the hand.

Ines felt like a small child again. It had been years since she'd held her mother's hand while in public, but she didn't mind it, grateful the lecture seemed to be over, and to her surprise, she welcomed feeling like a little girl again. She noticed her mother's hands seemed thinner than they had when she was younger, and her skin had become rough, like coarsely grained paper.

The shrine wasn't as close as it looked from where the bus had left them, and although the sun was low in the sky, it was still hot, and the walk was strenuous. They walked through the entire town before finding the way up the mountain. They had only found the path by asking a boy about Ines' age which was the fastest route to the shrine. He pointed towards the forest, where they saw the entrance to the long, winding path that led uphill through the trees. Animals called out to them as they walked below the thick canopy. The sounds of the forest reminded Ines of the accident, which instilled in her an even stronger sense of purpose as they walked up the dusty path. They paused several times, taking turns to drink from the flask of water Mama had purchased from a vendor in town.

Ines could see the shrine the entire time they walked along the path, the stone towers cresting above the trees. Her mother said nothing, and Ines was afraid to mention anything of Michel that may upset her, but it was difficult not to speak of her brother when it was all she could think of. The silence suited them both. There was no one else walking up the path with them, which made the noises of animals, and the whispering of the trees, the only sounds around them. As they reached the clearing containing the shrine, Ines was overwhelmed by its beauty. Of all the churches Ines had seen in the past, the temple in El Cobre was the most beautiful of all. While most churches Ines had seen were surrounded by other buildings, stone and wood, man-made structures that confined them to the material world, in El Cobre they were surrounded by nothing but green mountains and trees. Ines felt that the shrine looked happier somehow, if such a thing were possible, as if it was allowed to be free and belong completely to the divine.

By the time they opened one of the heavy wooden doors that led inside, their clothes were soaked through with sweat. They'd finished all of the water Mama had brought with them but found a bowl of fresh water by the entrance that they used to refill the canteen after Mama ensured it wasn't holy water they would be drinking so liberally. Ines and her mother were the only two people in the cavernous cathedral, which Ines absorbed slowly, its beauty even greater than what she could see from the outside.

The sun's remaining light for the day splashed in through the circular, stained glass windows that framed the statue of La Virgen de La Caridad at the back of the church. It was a strange, beautiful place, with some of the walls gray, others bright blue, and some a burnt orange that was the color of rust. Ines stood in awe of where they had entered. The statue, Mother Mary in her robes, which glowed golden in the final rays of daylight, seemed to illuminate the room around her. The empty, wooden pews had beautiful silhouettes carved into them that resembled the towers that rose from the outside of the shrine. Stone statues of saints were on display in every crevice and ornate black and white stars were stained onto the marble that covered the floor, but it was the statue of La Virgen de La Caridad that her eyes kept going back to. Ines wanted to absorb the beauty that surrounded her, so she could take some of it back home with them to Las Piedras, but her mother hurried them over to the front row of pews, and she remembered once again why they were there.

As they knelt on the cold, marble floor, Ines began to complain that her knees hurt, but her mother interrupted her.

"This is for your brother." Ines had never heard her mother's words so sharp.

She didn't say anything else and watched as her mother bowed her head and clutched her rosary in her hands. Ines took one last look at the statue, before bowing her own head, closing her eyes, and praying. Even with her eyes closed, all she saw in the darkness behind her eyelids was the statue. It was as bright as the sun, burning away at the darkness that surrounded it. Ines repeated Michel's name in her mind, turning it over, sounding different each time. The word became a hum, like music. She prayed that both her brother and Bashir would be safe and protected by the blessing of the Virgen de la Caridad. The face of the statue smiled at her through the darkness. Ines felt as if she were dreaming, but she could still feel the cold marble against the skin of her knees. Behind the statue, a world exploded into view, a dark sky filled with flashes of lightning illuminating her surroundings. She was in the ocean. Large waves crashed all around her, but her head remained above the surface. The statue of La Virgen de La Caridad was larger than a palm tree and at her feet, being rocked in the rough waters, was a wooden boat. Ines saw Michel and Bashir on the boat, staring up at the angel in front of them. Ines tried to call out to them, to get their attention, but the roar of the ocean and the thunder drowned out her voice. Ines could feel the wind on her face as well as the ocean spray as it splashed into her eyes, knowing with certainty that the coldness of the water against her skin was real. Then, as if nothing had happened, Ines opened her eyes. Her mother's hand was on her shoulder, and she told her it was time to go.

Ines never shared her experience in the shrine with anyone, and she lacked the words to describe it fully. When she asked her mother how long they'd prayed, her mother wasn't sure. Sunlight was no longer coming in through the stained-glass windows, and the room was illuminated only by the orange glow of candles.

"Who lit those candles?" Ines asked.

She looked to her mother. Ines was sure the candles weren't flickering when they'd first arrived, and there wasn't a sign that anyone had been there while they'd been praying.

Her mother glanced around them, a confused look on her face, but she only shrugged and said nothing.

When they stepped outside, the sky was dark, a deep purple, and filled with stars. It had felt to Ines as if they had prayed for only a few minutes, but it must have been hours. What she knew for certain was that God and His angels had heard her. Ines looked out down the hill towards the town. It seemed to shimmer as lights came in and out like fireflies. They stood in silence, looking at the town in its quiet beauty, before walking towards the path with only the stars and moon to light their way. The sounds of the forest seemed louder and more dangerous than they had on their way to the shrine. Her mother looked around as if at any moment they would come under attack by creatures reserved for their nightmares. Ines felt her own fear as well, a constant thing she'd lived with for many years, but realized then, under the stars and trees, so close to the shrine, she wasn't as afraid. Whatever had happened in the church had changed her. When an exceptionally loud screech was followed by a rustle in the bushes nearby, her mother grabbed hold of her arm as if their roles had been reversed.

"We're almost there," Ines told her mother.

While she wasn't sure whether or not that was true, after they walked a little longer, they were back in the town of El Cobre. They both knew it was too late to take the bus back, but there was no one out in the street, and all of the houses were quiet, outside of the occasional barking of dogs. Still with her mother's arm looped through hers, without speaking, they walked around El Cobre, searching for an inn to stay the night.

"Should we sleep outside?" Ines asked after some time.

The thought didn't bother her, although she'd never slept outside before. Michel had once, in the backyard, under a teepee he'd made, the design from one of his books. She hadn't joined him then, afraid of sleeping outside of their home, but there in El Cobre, under the blanket of stars, she would have preferred it.

Her mother bit her lip and shook her head.

"God will guide us," she said.

Ines could see the sadness on her face, the thoughts of Michel that she knew were keeping her from thinking of anything else.

Insects chirped as they walked, but otherwise, the night continued in silence. A firefly appeared near Ines' shoulder and seemed to fly along with them for a little while, pulsing with light every so often as Ines watched it with fascination. It flew slowly towards a house where Ines heard voices from inside. A dim light from one of the windows illuminated the wooden porch, which was overrun with crawling vines, and looked as if it were used less often than the porches of the other houses that lined the street.

"Let's try this house, Mama," Ines said.

She noticed her mother hesitate as they approached, so she squeezed her mother's hand as they stepped up to the door. Mama tapped on the wood. The voices stopped, but the door remained closed. For a moment Ines thought her instincts to follow the firefly had been wrong. Reaching up without thinking, she knocked against the door, harder than her mother had. Mama pulled Ines down the steps and back out onto the street and looked at her as if she were once again merely a young child.

"People may be sleeping," she said in a hushed whisper as if someone would be awakened inside by their whispering voices in the street.

But as soon as she spoke, a crescent of light splashed across the vine-covered porch.

"Good evening," a voice said.

Ines' eyes had grown accustomed to the darkness, and she could just make out the silhouette of a woman who stood in the doorway.

"Hello," her mother said, "I'm sorry to bother you so late, but my daughter and I are in need of somewhere to stay. We can't find an inn, and the buses aren't running to take us back home. Do you know of anywhere that could take us in for the night? We're willing to pay, of course."

Ines envied her mother's confidence with strangers and wasn't sure if it was her mother or father who was the braver of the two. Even when she should be the most afraid, facing a night sleeping outside, in a town where she and her daughter were strangers, she pushed back her fears, and acted. Ines wondered if her mother had felt the same way she had as they stepped out of the shrine, and maybe it was that same feeling that gave her courage. To Ines, it was the feeling that God was with them.

"The inn is down the road, close to the path that leads up to the church," the woman told Mama, "But they had a fire last month and aren't taking on any guests."

She stepped out through the door frame, and the light washed across her features. Her skin was brown, like the bark of the guava tree. Ines noticed her mother's face darken, if only for a moment.

"But you both are more than welcome to stay with my daughter and me. It's just the two of us. If you're in need, we'd be more than happy to help for the night."

She radiated warmth and kindness. Ines saw a flash of light near the woman's head, and she realized that the firefly had stayed with them on the porch.

Ines waited for her mother to reply.

"Mama," Ines said.

Her mother looked at Ines then once again at the woman, her forehead filled with lines.

"Yes," she said finally, "thank you."

Ines realized then that this was the first time she would be staying the night away from home and also the first time she would be inside the home of someone of African descent. Both ideas filled her with a rush of excitement that gave her tired body a renewed energy.

"Thank you, God," Ines heard her mother whisper as they entered the house.

The soft light of a lantern filled the room with an amber glow that reminded Ines of the candles that were burning in the shrine when they'd left. The woman closed the door behind them and spoke into the house, "We have guests, Mirlande."

Her daughter came out from an unlit hallway and greeted them. She must have been several years older than Ines. Her skin was lighter than her mother's, the color of a coconut, and Ines thought she was as beautiful as Concha or Johara. When she spoke, her voice was quiet, and hardly carried across the room. Standing at her side, clutching her leg and rubbing his eyes, was a young boy who Ines thought must have been her younger brother.

"My name is Carmen, and this is my daughter Mirlande. Can we get you anything?" Carmen asked as she lit several more lamps and candles around the house.

Mama asked for water, and Ines asked for milk, but as soon as she did, her mother shot her a look, but Carmen didn't seem to mind.

She turned to her daughter and said something to her in a language that Ines didn't understand but had heard before. As Mirlande disappeared into the kitchen, Ines remembered the language she'd heard spoken by Concha's old-housemaid Roseline.

"You speak Haitian Creole," Ines said.

"That's right," Señora Carmen said, clearly surprised.

Ines noticed her mother shoot her a questioning look.

"We're immigrants too," Ines said and surprised herself with her own boldness.

The room went silent as they waited for Mirlande to return.

Ines noticed a rift in the room, a line drawn down the middle, separating her and her mother, light-skinned, Lebanese immigrants, and the Haitian family that took them in for the night. Ines and her mother were able to pass for Spaniards, or visitors from another European country, which meant they were easily accepted. It was only when they spoke Arabic, or their accents became prominent, that they drew any form of attention to themselves. While her parents did all they could to hide the stains of their homeland, Mirlande and her mother never could. While Ines was proud of the marks of Lebanon, part of her knew they would disappear completely over time. Her accent was already a light echo, and she could hardly remember how their old house on the orchard looked, or how the ships in the harbor sounded as the sun rose.

"Your milk," Mirlande said and handed Ines a glass of warm milk before sitting down on the couch, the young boy still by her side.

They sat in the parlor and ate soda crackers, guava paste and cream cheese as Mama drank water, and Ines drank her milk. The young boy had fallen asleep in Mirlande's lap, and she stroked his head softly.

"Your son?" Mama asked her.

Carmen straightened up slightly on the couch and looked at her daughter, who replied, "yes," and smiled as she looked at the boy.

Ines was surprised. It hadn't even crossed her mind that the boy could be Mirlande's son.

"Where's your husband?" Ines asked.

Carmen stood up without a word and disappeared into the kitchen. While she was gone, Mirlande explained in a quiet voice that the man she loved had died before they could marry. Carmen returned with a plate full of crackers and guava paste.

When they finished their food, Mirlande showed them to a small bedroom in the back of their home, which seemed to be used for storing things.

"I'm sorry there's not much space," Mirlande said.

"Not at all," Mama said as they stepped inside, careful not to step on anything, "thank you again for allowing us to stay in your home."

The springs creaked loudly as they climbed into bed, and Mama pulled the covers over them both. The window was open in the room, propped up by a small stone pressed against the hinge. Chilly air from the mountains blew in through the window, which made Ines grateful that she and her mother were sharing such a small bed. Ines felt as if they were once again staying in La Casa de Nayibe. She listened to the sounds of the insects through the open window, which she knew her mother wanted to shut, but wouldn't dare as a guest in someone else's home. As soon as Ines closed her eyes, she fell asleep.

Her dreams were dark and violent. She was back in the same ocean she'd seen while praying in the shrine, but this time not far from shore. The ocean crashed against large stones and black sands, but Michel and Bashir were nowhere to be seen. Lightning flashed, filling the sky with white light as the thunder that followed made the water around her tremble. She tried to grab onto something to keep above the water, but the current was too strong, and the waves were taller than any she'd seen before. When they crashed over her, she was thrust deeper and further out into the ocean, away from the shore. As she tried to cry out Michel and Bashir's names, water filled her open mouth. She saw them both in the distance, but they were no longer sharing a boat. They were both far from her, but Ines had the understanding that she could save one if she swam, but only one.

Ines woke up the next morning to the ringing of church bells and looked around the room as if seeing everything for the first time. Her mother was standing by the bed.

"About time you woke up," she said.

Ines rubbed her eyes and stretched out, becoming aware of the smells of something delicious cooking. She told her mother about her nightmares, which she remembered in vivid detail. A look of concern crossed Mama's features, but she made no comment.

"Let's eat quickly and then go pray once more before the bus arrives. You can sleep on the way back home."

Señora Carmen was already dressed and cooking in the kitchen when Ines and her mother stepped out into the hall.

"I take it you're going back up to the shrine before leaving?" she asked when they walked into the kitchen.

Mama nodded.

"Good, we'll be joining you, if that's alright," she said, looking at Mirlande who was setting the dining room table.

"We go every morning," Mirlande said, looking over her shoulder at them.

Ines remembered her experience in the shrine the day before.

"Does someone light the candles at night?" Ines asked.

"Maybe Father Enrique. Why do you ask?" Señora Carmen replied.

"When we were there last night, someone lit the candles, but I never heard anyone else come inside," Ines said.

"One can lose themselves while praying in the shrine," Señora Carmen said.

Ines noticed her mother glance over at their host as she served food onto their plates.

They ate their breakfast quickly before setting out. Mirlande left her son sleeping, explaining to Ines and Mama that like clockwork, he would wake up the moment they returned from prayer. The sky lightened as they walked the path up through the trees. Señora Carmen was funny and made jokes, reminding Ines of Old Lady Nayibe. She wished she were there with them and thought of La Casa de Nayibe and her brother as they walked.

As they reached the top of the hill, the sun was visible from behind the mountains in the distance and gave the horizon an orange haze that Ines knew could only be seen in Cuba.

"One good omen," Mama said as she looked over Ines' shoulder towards the sunrise.

The church bells rang once more, and they entered the shrine. Ines was surprised to see the pews almost completely filled. The night before, the church had seemed abandoned and cared for only by the love of God. Now dozens of people prayed silently, some raising their heads to gaze at the statue of La Virgen de la Caridad, which glowed in the morning light that streamed in through the stained-glass windows. Ines shuddered when she saw the statue and remembered more details of the visions she'd had. She wondered if any of the people there praying that morning would see something similar.

They followed Señora Carmen to a row near the back of the church where only a few seats remained. Ines knelt onto the cold floor once again, this time not saying a word. The odd cough or voice echoed off of the thick stone walls, but they were otherwise wrapped in silence. That morning when Ines prayed, she didn't see any of the visions she'd seen before. Curious, she glanced at Mirlande who looked completely peaceful, more beautiful in the daylight, like one of the angels or saints depicted in the stained-glass windows. Ines then glanced at her mother, whose face was stiff, her eyes shut tight as if even the smallest crack might snap her out of prayer. Ines couldn't imagine what her mother felt. She was afraid, unsure of what to do, but she had her mother to look to. Ines realized then that her mother only had God to guide her, someone she'd never seen before with her own two eyes. She was reminded of her fears of God no longer hearing them when they'd left Lebanon and wondered if He heard them now, whispering words that could bring with them salvation to her brother and Bashir. The fear consumed her then and filled her mind with thoughts of life without her older brother. She cried quietly as they prayed, hoping that no one around them noticed the tears that streaked down her cheeks.

When they left the church, Mirlande asked Ines who she'd been praying for.

"My brother and our friend. They're both hurt," she said.

Ines pictured them being fished out of the river by the farmer who had found them and their quiet bodies lying still on their hospital beds.

"I'm so sorry," Mirlande said, "I will include them in my own prayers."

"Who did you pray for?" Ines asked.

She looked up at Señora Carmen who was speaking with Mama as they walked.

"I pray for my mother," she said.

"Why?"

Mirlande paused before answering, "When my father died, my mother's world fell apart. She no longer had someone to cook for, clean for, and had somehow lost part of herself when he left."

Ines looked at Señora Carmen, who laughed and smiled with Mama as if nothing bad had ever happened to her.

Mirlande looked over to Ines.

"She's not usually like that," Mirlande said, "I think you and your mother visiting us has helped her. We've been alone in our house for so long," Mirlande said.

When she spoke, it was as if she were speaking more to herself than to Ines, who was realizing how difficult life must have been for the two women.

Ines didn't know how to respond, so she let the wind fill the silence. As they walked and passed people on the path, she noticed how they looked at Mirlande and Señora Carmen, somehow differently than they looked at Ines and her own mother. Eyes were always upon them. No one whom they passed could know that it was because of them that they hadn't slept on the street the night before.

The bus that would take them back to Las Piedras arrived at El Cobre soon after they did. Her mother said goodbye and thanked Señora Carmen, and Ines did the same. Señora Carmen asked them to visit one day with Michel when he was healed.

"He would love it here," Mama said.

"I'll pray for your mother too," Ines told Mirlande when she said goodbye.

The long bus ride back to Las Piedras allowed Ines too much time to think. Thoughts of the shrine as well as the way people stared at Mirlande and her mother clashed with images of Michel in his hospital bed.

When I get home, he'll be back in his bed at home, resting.

It was this thought that gave her the hope necessary to withstand the trip back. Mama stared out of the window, her face painted with thoughts that Ines was sure were similar to her own. Although Cuba had become her home, Ines couldn't imagine what her world would be like without Michel. Their house would be an empty thing, devoid of the sights and sounds that brought the stone and wood alive with laughter.

When they arrived in Las Piedras later that day, only Bernita was home. She explained that Papa had taken Aida to the hospital in Las Piedras that morning after receiving a telephone call. Ines and her mother rushed over to the hospital. They found Papa in the waiting room with Aida, who looked as if she'd been crying. Ines expected her father to be angry with her, but when he saw Ines, he said nothing and hugged her close to his body, which shook as he sobbed. Ines didn't need words to understand what had happened, but she asked her question all the same, "Can we see Michel?"

The next several hours were as unbelievable as what had happened in the shrine the night before. The doctor, a short man, who seemed to stoop as he walked, joined them in the waiting room where he explained to Ines and her mother what Papa had already been told, Michel had passed away. Ines remembered the day she'd thought Michel had fallen overboard into the ocean and wished that this day would end in the same way. Aida held Ines's hand with the conviction of someone who would never let go.

"I want to see him," her mother told the doctor between sobs.

Ines watched silently as her father tried to convince Mama against seeing Michel, but she was steadfast, and both he and the doctor eventually gave in.

The doctor told Mama that there had been some confusion that afternoon as to where Michel's body was, explaining that a nurse had taken him to where they kept the bodies of those who had passed away, but another nurse who was to be transferring him to the funeral home had been unable to find him when she'd searched just a few minutes before.

"I will find him," Mama said in a barely audible whisper.

"I want to go too," Ines said.

She wanted nothing more than for everything that was happening to be wrong, a dream of some kind, a nightmare, but it was her duty to be there for her mother, no matter how afraid or sad she was.

"No," her father said, but Mama put a hand on his shoulder.

"Let her come," she said and looked at Ines with tired eyes that were thick with tears.

A nurse led them down the hallway to a part of the hospital that seemed darker than where they'd come from. Ines noticed how much quieter everything was. There was no one running between the rooms or calling out the names of doctors, just a peaceful silence that gave Ines gooseflesh along her arms. The air smelled of wet stone and as the nurse opened the door that they would be stepping through, a cold gust of air blew against Ines, bringing with it a putrid smell she had only smelled once before, after running across the body of a dead mongoose when playing in the fields around Old Lady Nayibe's home.

What is this place?

Ines pressed the handkerchief her mother had given her against her face, breathing in the fresh smell of gardenia that did little to cover what she knew had to be the smell of death.

The room was poorly lit and looked like one of the dungeons she'd imagined after Michel shared a story from one of his books where pirates were being sent to their death.

Michel.

The nurse led them through the room. Ines followed her mother closely, afraid to touch or be touched by any of the corpses that were covered in sheets throughout the room. It still made little sense to her that Michel himself was hidden underneath one of the sheets, but as the nurse lifted one sheet after another, and Ines saw the paleness of the faces, some understanding crept in, and she knew that their life as she knew it would be ending that day as well. Ines held on tightly to her mother's hand and squinted her eyes so as to not see the bodies as clearly. Until the nurse removed the final sheet.

"Michel," her mother said finally in a pained voice.

Ines looked at her brother where he lay still with a white sheet pooled at his neck, only his face visible. He seemed so peaceful. For a moment, no one spoke, and Ines only heard the soft, stifled crying of her mother, who it seemed was doing everything she could to keep from bursting into tears. Then, without warning, a choking cough exploded past Michel's lips, and he moved his head towards them.

"Water," Michel croaked.

The nurse screamed then ran from the room, returning minutes later with another nurse and a doctor. Ines stood in wonder as she watched the world come back to life.

"El niño vivo," Ines heard the second nurse say. *The living boy.*

Ines and her mother were taken from the room and went back to wait with Papa and Aida. Ines explained what had happened, but Mama wouldn't say a word until the doctor came back out to get them.

"There was some sort of mistake. One I must apologize for on behalf of the hospital," the doctor said, looking down as he spoke, "Michel is alive."

And with those words, Ines smiled. Her life returned to what it was just days before, to the life she had prayed for, and she knew God, and La Virgen de La Caridad, had answered.

It was only three days after that Ines and her family discovered that Bashir had died, and he wasn't coming back like Michel had. Abraham and his wife came to the house, Johara running to Michel when she saw him seated quietly in the parlor. Ines was sitting next to her brother, who seemed constantly tired or hungry since he'd returned from the dead.

"Bashir is dead," Johara said, sobbing as she clung to Michel.

Ines felt as if she now existed in two different worlds. One where she was happy, her brother returned to her, weak, but alive, and the other, a world where Bashir was gone, and an empty space she didn't realize existed spread from inside her. She looked to Abraham who was sobbing at the entrance to their home while her father and Abraham's wife tried to console him. When she looked at his face, it wasn't just sadness Ines saw, but also anger. He seemed to be staring at Ines, and an icy chill ran through her, until she realized his eyes were looking past her and set on Michel. She was reminded of the eyes of the gargoyle woman from the ship, and those of the Cuban man with the machete who had forced her father away. She hadn't thought of them in years, but there, in Abraham's eyes, the man she considered family, she saw what she'd seen in both their eyes. It was the emotion she later learned to be hatred. Abraham left the house soon after arriving while Johara stayed with her mother and visited Michel the rest of the day.

Chapter 15

The year that followed was like a dream. Ines had seen the veil pulled back from the face of death, and it had made her more cautious, more distrusting of the world around her. With Bashir gone, there was a piece missing from her life that she hadn't been prepared to lose. For months she couldn't sleep through the night, her dreams betraying her with recollections of the day of the accident, the foul-smelling room in the hospital, or made-up horrors that woke her in a cold sweat. *Why did she miss Bashir so much? Had it been her prayers that had saved Michel, but not Bashir? Could she have only saved one?* While the nightmares only haunted her during the night, the constant barrage of thoughts followed her everywhere she went.

She was now fourteen, but went outside less often than before, only spending time with Concha and Isabella on rare occasions. At first, it hurt her to see them, sometimes it hurt her to even see Michel, who all reminded her that everything had changed. Abraham and his wife visited their home much less than they had in the past, and when Ines saw Abraham at La Sirena, he no longer called her "little princess." Abraham never spoke of Bashir, and if Ines even mentioned him, a happy memory or a wish that he was still with them, he would act as if she hadn't spoken.

The greatest change came from Michel, who had reverted to his childhood habits. He spent more time in the garden reading than he did with Johara, whom he seemed to avoid as much as he could.

"How are you feeling?" Ines asked her brother.

"I'm not going to suddenly die, Ines," he told her, but she wasn't convinced.

In her heart, she'd almost lost her brother twice. Once on the ship and once in Cuba, and both times something had broken within her and that broken thing seemed to come loose every day, needing Michel's reassurance that he wouldn't leave her again.

When they went into town, people who knew what had happened would call out to him, "el muerto vivo!" *the living dead!*

"Don't listen to them, Michel," Ines would remind her brother as they walked together to or from the park.

Aida went on with her life as usual, not seeming to understand fully what had happened to her brother. She had become more Cuban than Ines could have imagined; having been born on the island, she seemed to Ines as native as anyone else she saw in town. Ines spent most of her time with her sister, who was now eight years old, and had acquired a fascination with art. Ines would pose for her by the fountain in the courtyard or in the backyard by the gardenias while her sister sketched her and later gave the piece of parchment covered with smears of charcoal or paint to their mother who seemed to enjoy her youngest daughter's work more each time. Other times her sister would run through the house singing political songs that she'd learned in school or chasing after large lizards in the park as they fell from palm trees. Those moments with her sister were some of the only times Ines found escape from her thoughts. She even refused to visit Old Lady Nayibe, whose house only reminded her of rushing water, and the quiet forest that was the setting of many of her nightmares. While Nayibe would sometimes visit them in Las Piedras, Ines missed her weekly trips to the country, but couldn't bring herself to go.

They still had dinners as a family every evening, and while they were quieter than before, her father and mother did everything possible to fill the silence with small talk.

"How did you like driving the car today?" Papa asked Michel.

Michel, who had been helping their father at La Sirena since recovering from the accident, had recently learned to drive the car Papa used to make deliveries into other towns. He was a much better driver than her father, who declared Michel in charge of major deliveries once he mastered the vehicle.

"Very much," Michel said and filled his mouth with ropa vieja, so he wouldn't have to continue speaking.

"Does anyone have any news?" Papa asked the table in his usual manner.

No one replied. Not even Aida, who normally announced if she had new classmates or had painted something that she found interesting.

"Well, in that case, I have an announcement," he said.

Ines turned to look at her father as she took a bite of the mashed potatoes on her plate.

"La Sirena has been having unparalleled success," he paused and looked around the table before continuing, "and I have been in talks with someone who can help us take our clothing to every part of the island." He let his words float in the air, the excitement on his face disappearing slowly as no one else seemed to share his enthusiasm.

"Aren't we already going to every end of the island?" Michel asked.

His voice was deeper then, almost as deep as Papa's, who looked at Michel with both pride and something else that Ines couldn't quite place but thought it resembled fear.

"This will bring us possibilities outside of the island as well," Papa said, pausing again as he stared at Michel.

"That's wonderful news, Salim," Mama said, patting his arm with her hand.

A silence once again followed, but it was broken by Ines, "I want to be a teacher," she announced.

Ines waited for Michel to make a comment, to make fun of her, but he said nothing.

"What are you going to teach?" her father asked as a smile crept onto his face.

Her mother also smiled.

"Kindergarten," Ines said.

She was sure her parents thought she was making some sort of joke.

"You can teach *me*," Aida said.

Ines smiled then as well.

The next day Ines shared her newfound conviction to be a teacher with her friends as they ate their lunch outside.

"Me too," Concha said.

"I also want to be a teacher," Isabella said.

Ines watched as a bird passed overhead and a plop of white fell onto the shoulder of her dress.

"Good luck!" Concha exclaimed as Ines stood up and rubbed the bird poop onto the leaves of a nearby palm frond.

"I didn't know you both wanted to be teachers," Ines said as she did her best to clean the "good luck" from her dress.

Isabella nodded.

"How come you never told me?" Ines asked.

"This is the first time in a long time we've talked about anything other than Bashir," Concha said.

Ines saw the color drain from her friend's face and noticed Isabella shoot Concha a look that she tried to conceal.

"It's okay," Ines said, "I'm okay."

She looked down at her feet for a moment then back to her friends.

Other girls looked over at them as they ate nearby. Some giggled, some pointed, and Ines knew most of them were talking about the accident. She had become infamous in her school. No longer a troublemaker, she was instead seen as a totem of bad luck. A girl whose friends die and whose brothers' become zombies.

"I was telling Isabella that I have an idea," Concha said.

Ines saw Isabella shoot another look at Concha, but Concha continued as if she hadn't seen.

"Well, seeing as it's our last year with *these* nuns," Concha said, pointing her thumb back towards their school, "we should do something to celebrate. Who knows if we'll be together after this?"

"We will be if we're all going to be teachers," Isabella said.

"That's beside the point," Concha continued, "We haven't gone on any adventures in such a long time. I was thinking, why don't we take a trip to Havana?"

At first, Ines was against the idea, but the more she thought about it, the more she realized how much she missed spending time with her friends.

"Okay, but how will we get there?" Ines asked.

The buses to Havana would take too long with all of the stops, and none of their parents would let them stay elsewhere overnight, especially Mama, who'd kept a close watch on Ines since she'd followed her to El Cobre.

"I was thinking we have Michel take us," Concha said.

"And you just ask it like that?" Isabella asked.

"Well, I know he's been driving for your father, Ines, so I thought—"

"No, that's a good idea," Ines said.

Both girls seemed surprised by her reply. They all shared a giddiness as they finished their lunch that afternoon.

A few days later, on a Friday, the day before they planned to go to Havana, Ines approached Michel while he read in their garden. She'd dreaded asking him all week, afraid of his inevitable reply. The idea of the trip had become exciting to Ines, who wanted nothing more but to escape the house she felt was suffocating her since Bashir's death. Michel put his book down in his lap and looked up at Ines.

"Yes?"

He no longer joked as he did previously and spoke matter-of-factly, the excitement for life he'd had before missing from his voice. Ines hated this change and prayed her brother would come back to them completely, like their mother had years before. She sat down next to him on the bench and looked at the book Michel had resting on his lap. It was the book her father had given him on the ship. One he must have read dozens of times.

"Let's go on a trip," Ines said.

She detailed her and her friends' idea to Michel who looked at her as if he were looking through her to the bright flowers that filled the garden. When she finished, Ines was certain his answer would be no, and they would have to find another way to get to Havana.

"Okay," Michel said and lifted his book and once again began to read.

Ines hugged her brother and kissed his cheek, but he didn't say a word as she walked back into the house.

Concha and Isabella arrived early the next morning and waited on the street just outside the gate to Ines' courtyard. She saw her friends through her bedroom window and rushed to get ready. Michel was loading up the car with clothing her father asked him to deliver that day. It was one of the first deliveries her father had trusted Michel to make alone, without him or Abraham to help him, and if her father learned Ines and her friends would be joining Michel, it would most likely be his last.

Ines joined her friends outside, and they walked in the direction of the park, but stealthily turned left the street before and waited for Michel to pick them up.

"Maybe he changed his mind," Isabella said after minutes went by and Michel still hadn't arrived.

"He's coming," Ines said and hoped she was right.

Moments later, Michel arrived, and helped them into the car, which was filled with clothing wrapped in sheets of plastic and parchment paper.

"I'll sit in the front," Concha said and looked over at Michel who sported a face masked with indifference.

Ines sat in the back of the car with Isabella, clothes piled between them and at their feet. The drive was quiet at first, but as they left Las Piedras behind them, a light seemed to return to Michel's face. Ines looked at her brother and hoped the light would stay. Wind blew into the car and Concha led them in songs as they coasted down the highway towards Havana.

"Ines, it's your first time to Havana, right?" Concha asked over the roar of the wind that ripped through the car, swishing the plastic covering Michel's deliveries.

Ines shook her head.

"We came here when we were young. When we'd first arrived," Ines said.

Michel was silent.

Ines looked out of the window and remembered the hospital where they'd slept their first night in Cuba. She hadn't returned and hadn't wanted to before then. While she remembered how the city looked in general, she hadn't really seen it as a child. It was there as a backdrop to a time that was clouded with confusion and fear.

Today I'll see Havana with open eyes.

"I've been several times with my father, and I can tell you, it's nothing like home," Concha said. "It's beautiful."

As they drove, Ines remembered everything she could of the city, but her thoughts went back to the hospital then back to Michel and Bashir. The coldness she'd wanted to leave behind in Las Piedras, if only for the day, had followed them.

When they arrived in Havana, the early afternoon sun was high in the sky, and Ines felt her surroundings come to life. They drove along the Malecon, searching for parking. Cars rushed past on their left while the ocean roared and flung itself along the rocks to their right. Ines had never seen so many people walking through one place and imagined they all had stories that had led them to be there with them in that moment.

Ines felt the world shift around her. Her childhood in Cuba had glowed orange with sunlight, against a backdrop of greens and browns, but when she arrived in Havana on that day, at the age of fourteen, something changed. She came to exist in a bright new world, a world colored by scarlet. Once they parked, they walked into the large throng of people that moved through the city. Concha was their guide and led them around beautiful buildings and along busy streets. Havana seemed to breathe out the sounds of music and laughter. Singers sang while men played their horns and women danced in the streets outside of cafes. Ines was overcome with the desire to dance with them, to spin and jump as if on fire.

Michel carried the clothes he'd brought with him over his shoulder as they walked. With the help of Concha leading them through the city, he completed all of the deliveries Papa had asked of him within thirty minutes of arriving, giving them plenty of time to explore the city.

"It would have taken me all afternoon to get that done," Michel told Concha.

They stopped briefly at a café, ordering sandwiches and coffee. Ines ordered two black coffees and felt the rush of caffeine fill her head with a light buzzing that gave the scarlet afternoon a brighter glow.

"Let's go to El Barrio Chino," Concha said as they ate.

"I've always wanted to go," Isabella said.

"What's El Barrio Chino?" Ines asked.

Isabella explained that the Chinese immigrants who had come to Cuba years before had claimed a part of Havana as their own, bringing with them magical things from their homeland.

"What sorts of magical things?" Ines asked.

"You'll see," Concha said with a smile.

The first thing Ines noticed about El Barrio Chino was the smell. The smells of spices mixed with something sour that Michel pointed out was gunpowder.

"Hold on," he said, and went off for a moment to speak to one of the vendors that manned one of dozens of red and gold painted stalls that lined the street.

"I think I love your brother," Concha said.

Isabella giggled while Ines ignored them.

She watched as Michel moved his hands around and spoke with excitement to the man behind the stall. Ines wondered for a moment if the man was a recent immigrant, someone like them who had come from somewhere so far away to make a new life for themselves or had he and his family already been in Cuba for years, more native than she was? The vendor smiled as her brother spoke and reached down into his stall before handing Michel something Ines couldn't see. Her brother seemed at ease, happy to be in his element, away from the eyes of the people who saw him as "el muerto vivo," or pitied him in some way. There were no prying eyes in Havana or familiar faces that reminded them so easily of other things.

When Michel returned, Ines noticed the object he'd purchased from the vendor. It resembled a scroll that the priests would sometimes use during their sermons and looked to be covered with a piece of thin, red paper. He pulled out a string from the paper wrapping and explained that once you lit the string, which he called a fuse, it would travel until igniting the gunpowder, causing a small explosion that would send the object into the sky where it would explode a second and final time, sending beautiful sparks in all directions.

"They're called firecrackers," he said, "I'll show you tonight."

Like the firecrackers Michel had purchased, everything around them seemed entirely new.

"Let's try the food here," Ines said, pointing towards more stalls where steam and smoke rose and danced with the breeze.

She wanted to become lost among the sights and sounds in that part of Cuba that looked like another place entirely. They spent the rest of the afternoon there, trying different foods, some Ines swore were still alive when she bit into them, and watching the people who all seemed to know exactly where they were going as they walked up and down the streets. Before they went back to Las Piedras, they made a stop at a beach near Havana. It was a private beach where Concha's father had a membership, and everyone seemed to recognize her.

"These are my friends," Concha told one of the attendants who stood in front of a roped-off section of the beach club.

He reluctantly let them pass, reminding them all several times it was only members allowed onto the beach, but that he would make an exception.

"Please let your father know you saw me today," he said as Concha passed.

She squinted as she moved her face closer to the golden tag on his jacket.

"Gabriel," she said, "got it. I'll tell my father you said hello."

They made their way to the beach. Although it wasn't Ines' first time visiting a beach in Cuba, for someone who lived in a country surrounded by water, she had only been to the ocean a handful of times. When she had gone to the beach, it was normally full of both tourists and locals, but on that beach in Havana, it was as if they had an entire section of the Cuban coastline all to themselves. None of them had brought their swimming suits, but Ines waded into the water all the same, hiking up her dress to her knees, she felt the water lap and swirl around her legs. It was the first time she'd been in any ocean or river in the months following the accident. She feared the ocean, afraid that the current would take her off as it had Michel and Bashir, but the water felt warm and good as the last glimmers of sunlight washed across her.

At first, only Concha joined Ines in the water while Isabella and Michel sat in the sand and watched, but eventually they were all playing in the ocean, even Michel. He looked the way Ines remembered him before the accident – as if they'd been transported back to their childhood when her brother saw the world as a never-ending adventure. As the sun lowered in the sky, Michel pulled out the firecracker he'd purchased from the vendor and produced a box of matches. With a flash of orange and a whistling noise that sounded like hundreds of birds singing at once, Ines watched as the small rocket flew into the air before bursting into countless red sparks. The sour smell of gunpowder filled her nostrils. She looked at Michel. His face filled with wonder as it glowed with the last red glimmers of the explosion. She smiled. When Ines wrote in her journal that night, and said her prayers before bed, all she could think of was the new world she'd discovered that day in Havana. She wanted to go again the next day, and the day after that, and once again experience the scarlet afternoon when her brother had finally, truly, come back to life.

Chapter 16

From the age of fifteen, many suitors tried to win Ines' hand, but she was picky and uninterested, leaving almost every one of them broken-hearted. Although she was only fifteen, Ines looked like a woman of twenty — her blonde hair, which was once curly and unkempt, had grown into long, beautiful locks that reached down to the small of her back. Her blue eyes which had once been a gray the color of seafoam, seemed to have become bluer, more closely resembling the ocean itself. Young men from all around Las Piedras, and some from other parts of Cuba, now saw her differently than they had before. After enough suitors tried to win her hand, without any interest from her, she came to view the courtship as a game, one where, in the end, there was no true winner.

Ines spent hours walking among the manicured trees in the park or along the streets of Las Piedras, pondering the idea of marriage. She wrote questions into her journal, hoping that answers would appear below the black ink of her pen. *Did she even want to be married?* She missed Bashir in those moments deep in thought, realizing that if she could have married him, instead of a stranger, she would have. At least then she knew exactly how she would be treated and imagined herself running through the fields with him. She couldn't imagine belonging to someone else or someone else belonging to her, although the idea of being free from the watchful eyes of her parents and Bernita excited her. Bernita watched her closer than ever before, reporting back to Mama with whispers Ines would sometimes overhear from outside of the kitchen. When her mother spoke words that she was sure were put in her head by Bernita, Ines became angry and wanted nothing more than for Bernita to leave their lives entirely. If Ines even mentioned such a thing to her mother, she would be reminded how much their housekeeper had looked after the family since they'd arrived in Las Piedras and would be asked to pray for forgiveness.

Ines felt as if she were trapped and was unable to see the world in Las Piedras the way she had in Havana. She missed the dancers, the music, and above all else, the freedom. The house that she had once explored with wonder had become her source of confinement, a prison where she had all of the essentials, but wasn't truly living. Her trip to Havana had changed her in ways she herself didn't understand completely, but Ines knew if she were able to leave their home and be married, she would explore the entire island with her husband, or without him, seeing everything she still had yet to see. Ines also knew that marriage to the wrong man meant the opposite of the freedom she sought. She wanted things to be done on her terms, but in her position, as a woman of fifteen, she was granted little to no freedom regardless.

There was always a pressure, a current that tugged and pulled her in a direction in which she didn't want to go.

"Your daughter has become too beautiful to keep all to yourselves."

Ines overheard this and similar things told to her mother by the Cuban women who took pride in matching up would be suitors with their prizes. Ines felt that was how she was viewed, as a prize similar to the lottery her mother had won years before. Her mother's friends would visit her home often: nosey aunts, mothers, and grandmothers, all curious if the young Aude girl was finally ready to meet their "beautiful boy." Her mother wasn't one to be rude and would allow the suitors to visit with Ines on the porch, or walk with her around the park, but only if at least one of her siblings was present. Her mother walked the line between matchmaker and protector, but her father trusted no one with eyes for Ines. She saw fear etched into the lines of both her parents' faces as she stepped out of the iron gates of the courtyard and into the world beyond. They both tried to hide it, her mother better than her father, but she saw through them.

While Ines felt anxiety about her suitors, sometimes even excitement, she mostly felt boredom when they began to speak. Most of them were like fountains sputtering out endless streams of water as their words lulled Ines into a dull trance while she looked at the trees and flowers that surrounded them. She did nothing to hide her boredom, wearing a weak smile on her face as she sometimes nodded. If Aida was with her, she'd shoot her sister a look, which would be met with a giggle, and the occasional glance back by the suitor at Aida as she trailed behind.

Although her mother tried her hardest to transform Ines into a lady, one who nodded and smiled when spoken to, Ines was something else entirely. Her childhood spent running through the fruit orchard in Lebanon and then through the countryside in Cuba had made her careless around men, sometimes even wild. She felt her mother's efforts to chisel a marble statue from soil and sand were useless, but her mother tried all the same.

"Mama, do I have to keep seeing these boys?" Ines asked one Saturday afternoon as they waited on their porch for a suitor to arrive. She'd met dozens of suitors and not one interested her. She would much rather have been playing with Aida, running along the streets of Las Piedras or through the park, but she was seen as too old for such things.

Her mother ignored the question. She sat on a wicker bench while Ines sat on the stone steps that led up to the porch. The steps felt cool in the shadows of their home and it was from there that Ines had the best view of the front gate where at any moment a young man would be walking through to do his best to win her heart. Ines imagined that being the first to see whoever it was who walked through the gate gave her some sort of control over the situation. Perhaps she could run away before they saw her, right past Mama and back into the house. They would be forced to leave, and she would be spared a day of small talk and boredom. Although she knew this would never happen, the thought sustained her and gave her a false sense of freedom.

"Ines, come up here with me. You'll dirty your dress," her mother said.

It was an especially hot day, which gave mosquitos and other insects liberty to dart around the courtyard. Her mother had given Ines perfume that morning and sprayed it on her neck and wrists. The sweet scent of gardenias attracted the mosquitos to her like sharks to blood. She waved them away whenever one buzzed too closely, but the onslaught was relentless.

"I like it down here," Ines told her, blowing air through her lips at one especially courageous mosquito as it perched itself on the tip of her nose.

"Come up here before…" but her mother's words came too late.

The iron gate squealed open and her escort that day, German Perez, stepped into the courtyard. Her mother had explained that he was the son of a judge from Havana but was currently living in Las Piedras with his aunt whom she had met in church one morning.

"Good afternoon, German," Mama said and paused as she waited for Ines to greet their guest.

"Hello, German," Ines said after too long of a silence.

She was distracted by the largest mosquito she'd ever seen. It landed on her left arm and was large enough to be mistaken for a dot of spilled ink.

"Good morning, Señora Aude," German said. "Señorita," German nodded towards her.

Ines was taken aback by how handsome German was. His cheekbones and jaw were strong and proud, his nose pointed and straight. Mama had told her that Spanish blood ran through his veins, and in that moment, Ines understood what she meant, but unfortunately for German, most of her attention was on the mosquito that didn't move from her arm.

Go away.

She tried to subtly shake her arm, but the mosquito clung to her stubbornly.

"How are you both doing on this beautiful day?" German asked.

Without thinking, Ines slammed her right hand down against her arm, leaving behind a smear of blood and crumpled wings.

German acted as if he hadn't seen her un-ladylike action, but Ines knew her mother had and that was enough. She could feel Mama's eyes burning into the back of her head as she placed a hand on Ines' shoulder and squeezed.

"Very well, German, thank you," Mama said before waving goodbye to German and going inside.

Ines and German sat and spoke for several minutes before getting up to walk around the house to the gardens. Michel was busy helping Papa at La Sirena, and Aida was sick with a cold, so they weren't able to venture out to the park. Ines knew her mother would be watching them from one of the windows and looked up at the house but was unable to tell which one she was spying from. To her surprise, Ines didn't have to act as much as she normally did. German was as interesting as he was handsome and told Ines of his childhood, having been born in Spain and coming with his family to Havana when he was young. Ines was reminded of her own childhood and enjoyed looking into German's eyes as he shared his stories.

When they returned to the courtyard, German looked at Ines as if deep in thought.

"Yes?" Ines asked.

"It's just—" he said.

Ines waited for him to speak. She could feel heat rising in her face and chest, sure that a kiss was coming. She had never been kissed before, or even wanted to be kissed, but her mouth went dry at the thought.

"It's just… I'm very tall," he said.

She hadn't expected those words.

"Yes," Ines said, puzzled.

He *was* very tall. Maybe only slightly shorter than Abraham, who was the tallest person Ines had ever known.

"Well, I just don't think we're a match. I'm too tall." He flashed perfectly white teeth as he smiled at Ines.

She hardly found words to say as he said goodbye. Scratching at the angry welts on her neck where the mosquitoes had feasted, Ines watched as the iron gate clanged shut. She turned towards the house and saw Bernita looking out from the dining room window. Ines was sure she saw the hint of a smile play across her lips, if only for a moment, before she turned and disappeared to some other room in the house. When Ines walked back inside, she asked her mother to take her shopping for new shoes. Her mother became elated with the idea as Ines had never before asked to go to the stores with her. From that point on, Ines refused to leave the house without high heels, and she never told anyone why.

After their trip to Havana, Ines had once again found the courage to visit Nayibe at her home. Ines shared with her stories about the suitors as they ate their fruit and drank coffee on the porch. Nayibe chuckled after Ines recounted the story of German.

"I should get married tomorrow. I'd like to see how she'd like it then," Ines said.

She was sure that her mother was in no rush to see her married and living in a faraway home, in the house of a man she would only ever see in glimpses.

"Your mother is only doing what she thinks is best for you," Old Lady Nayibe said.

She went on to reiterate that the courting process, when done properly, took several years, something her mother had told her countless times. Those were years filled with letter writing, chaperoned dates, and measured meetings with family, all meant to ensure the right choice was being made.

"Is that how you met your husband?" Ines asked.

Nayibe looked away for a moment and stopped chewing her fruit.

"I'm sorry," Ines told her.

"Don't be," she said. "Yes, he wrote me many letters, but we married quickly."

"Really?"

"My family was not the most accepting at first, but once they realized the type of man he was, they loved him just as I did."

"See, that is what I want. Not these fake and boring boys. When will I find someone like that?"

Old Lady Nayibe paused, then laughed softly, but it seemed forced.

"You'll find him when the time is right."

After a while, their conversation shifted to Ines' studies to be a teacher.

Ines explained that she felt as if she'd fallen into teaching much the same way a fish is born into water and instantly begins to swim. She felt as if she had no choice in the matter.

"I always knew you'd be a teacher," Nayibe agreed, "The way you cared for that doll of yours – you did a better job than many women do with their own children," she said.

Without warning, Old Lady Nayibe burst into tears.

"I'm sorry," she told Ines.

Ines didn't press or ask why she was crying and instead put an arm around Nayibe. They sat in silence as the afternoon came.

Chapter 17

Only a few days after Ines had turned sixteen, a massive hurricane made landfall in Cuba. The Havana harbor, once filled with excited tourists and hopeful immigrants, was filled with broken ships and things dredged up from the bottom of the ocean. Broken wood and twisted metal floated above the water until they slowly sank or were washed up on the shore miles away. Mama was sure it was God's judgment upon the world, angry at Cuba for having become involved in a war that she deemed "a European War."

"We should just mind our own business. There are still many things to fix here in Cuba," Mama said often.

Cuba had officially announced its opposition of the Axis Powers several years before the hurricane, but during those years, every natural disaster, in the eyes of Mama, was divine retribution for Cuba's involvement. In reality, the war didn't affect the island as it did other countries around the world. Ines was sure it was the walls of water on all sides that kept the island safe, enclosed in its dream, undisturbed from the outside. But as time went on, many people did take sides, becoming increasingly aware of global affairs and the shortcomings of their own government. Papa and Michel became more vocal about politics, arguing their points as if their lives depended on the outcome. Unlike the rest of her family, Ines didn't make her political opinions known. She cared most for freedom and fairness for everyone but knew her ideas would sound radical to her parents, so she let Michel speak for her.

Papa sided with Mama and believed that Cuba should stay out of the war, one which he was sure would end the world as they knew it.

"How could you say that Papa?" Michel asked.

Michel believed it essential that Cuba stand as an example for Latin America and for the Caribbean, opposing fascism and promoting Western democracy throughout the world.

"And the disappearing men? What of them?" Ines heard her father say to Michel while they sat in his study.

It was normally at this point that Mama would bring them a platter of food or a pot of tea in an effort to silence them, afraid that if somehow the government heard of Papa's opposition, or Michel's passionate beliefs, they themselves would become disappeared men. While there were rumors that those who opposed Batista or the Cuban government would be taken in the night, never to be heard from again, no one Ines knew had disappeared. Those that went missing were always friends of friends, or some long distant cousin that no one seemed to know very well. Their names were whispered under the hot, Cuban sun like sinful secrets. The rumors frightened Ines, who wanted nothing more than for her family to be left alone by the outside world.

While she knew her father was a cautious man, he was also stubborn. The more time he'd spent in Cuba, running the factory and growing the business, the less he was willing to accept change. As a child, Ines remembered her father as a man who trusted strangers and believed that everything would turn out in the ways they were meant to, but he had changed, becoming someone who only trusted a man when it was earned. He now had an unwavering belief that working hard and taking control of one's life were the only ways to shape one's destiny. Ines never reminded him that it was her mother's faith and luck that had changed the tides of their fortune so quickly, but she was sure that somewhere in his mind the thought persisted, following him around like a shadow.

Against Mama's wishes, he'd have open political discussions when their friends visited the home. Papa entertained the men in his study, while Mama sat in the front parlor with the women, who always asked to see her latest clothing designs. Ines was an observer of both worlds. Not allowed in the study, she would pass by and listen, sometimes pressing her eye against the cold, metal keyhole to see the men who were visiting that day. She would then make her way back to the parlor slowly before taking her seat next to her mother while Aida played outside. Ines longed for her childhood and preferred spending her time in the park with Aida to hearing her family speak of politics or fashion trends.

During one of the more aggressive political arguments between Michel and Papa, Ines grabbed Aida's hand and left the house. Mama had gone across the street to La Sirena to check on the store, so she was spared from their arguing that day. The yelling drowned out the birdsong in the courtyard, and Ines heard fists slamming against tables as she closed the heavy front door behind them. They walked hand in hand towards the park, by the same trees and buildings she had walked by as a child. When they reached the park, they went straight for the tree they had claimed as their own. While all of the other trees were beautiful, well-groomed and maintained, their tree was wild, its branches twisting into the sky.

"The hand tree looks beautiful today," Aida said, looking at the tree framed in late afternoon light.

With its many limbs, the tree looked like a bundle of hands and limbs, and had been given the name by Aida, who would sit and paint it for hours on end. Ines no longer imagined as she once had. Now when she heard her grandmother's voice, or had visions in her dreams, she'd tell herself it was just the wind, or nightmares, and not signs of things to come.

"Look." Aida pointed up towards a large iguana that was splayed out on one of the thicker branches of the tree, above where they normally sat in the shade.

Ines laughed.

"You're not afraid of a little iguana, are you?" she asked her sister.

"There's nothing little about that thing," Aida said, taking out a piece of parchment and charcoal from the bag she carried with her. "I'll draw it."

"Draw me under it," Ines said and sat down in the grass below the tree.

The iguana didn't move and looked at Ines curiously with its small eyes.

"Why do they fight like that?" Aida asked Ines as she drew.

Ines blocked the beams of sunshine with her hand, so she could see Aida more clearly.

"We have a passionate family. They've been like this since before you were born," Ines said.

"They're worse than usual, like a tea kettle coming to a boil," Aida said.

Ines looked at Aida. Her face was young and innocent, but her words were always wise beyond her years. Before she could say anything in reply, the large iguana fell from the tree like a heavy fruit. It landed on Ines' lap with a smack, its claws scratching against the thin dress that covered her thighs. Ines screamed and jumped into the air while Aida's eyes went wide with surprise, and she also let out a scream that sounded out like a bell throughout the park. The iguana took off in a blur of green, skittering away into the bushes.

"Did you see that?" Ines asked.

"I told you it was a big iguana," Aida said.

They laughed until their eyes filled with tears, and Ines went back to pose under the tree, this time watching to make sure there weren't any iguanas on the limbs above her.

The rest of their time in the park went by quickly. Ines asked her sister if there were any boys that bothered her in class.

"Ricardo," she replied, "he never leaves me alone."

"That means he likes you," Ines told her.

"No way. That's disgusting. He still picks his nose," Aida looked at her sister and paused her drawing, "Do you miss Lebanon?" Aida asked as if it was a simple question.

Ines looked at her sister unsure of how to reply. Over the years, Cuba had become her home, but she still remembered parts of Lebanon, glimpses of a past she sometimes forgot had ever happened at all.

"I miss what I can remember, but Cuba is our home, and I wouldn't ever want to leave it," Ines said, then looked up at the large orange sun in the sky. "They're probably done fighting by now. We should head back."

"Can't we stay just a little longer?" Aida pleaded.

Ines recognized her voice so well. It was her own voice. The voice she had before she began her changes into womanhood, before Bashir had died, and before the world took on the color of scarlet. Ines wanted to say yes, that they could stay until the sun disappeared, sleeping under the stars and between the trees in the park until the birds sang their morning songs, but instead she said, "No, Mama and Papa will be worried if we don't get home soon."

As they stepped off of the sidewalk to cross the road, Ines saw a blur from the corner of her eye and heard an engine roaring. She turned to look and saw the car, a blue jeep, taking the corner faster than it should have as it barreled towards them without any signs of stopping. Ines pushed Aida back towards the sidewalk and didn't have time to do anything else. She heard the squeal of brakes and the metal creaking of the jeep's heavy body as it came to a stop only a few feet away from her. A cold sweat covered her as she hurried over to Aida where she'd landed, wide-eyed on the sidewalk.

"I'm okay," Aida said.

Ines dusted the grass from her sister's knees and was grateful to see no scrapes or bruises.

"Stay here," she told her sister.

She walked up to the jeep.

"You could've killed us!" Ines shouted.

The jeep had no doors or windows and was covered in splatters of mud. The front of the car had "Willy" written across it, which Ines thought may have been the driver's name. When she was close enough to see the driver, she was surprised that it was someone she'd never seen before. He was a boy, maybe a year or so younger than Ines, who smiled as she approached.

"I heard screaming," he said, his eyes looking to Aida then Ines.

His eyes were a light brown that swam like caramel around his pupils, his skin shadowed with the shapes of trees, and Ines noticed that he was completely calm. He wore a cream-colored cowboy hat that was slightly off-center. Ines had only ever seen men in the country wear hats like those as most people in town chose smaller hats, hats that were of the newest European or American fashions. From the stains that covered the brim, Ines could tell his hat wasn't a fashion statement, but something he used day in and day out.

"Who are you? And aren't you a little young to be driving?" she asked.

Ines found it strange for someone from the country to be driving such a nice American car. It was even stranger for the car to be completely covered in mud and to be missing its windows and doors. In Las Piedras, the only people with cars had money, and most people who lived in the country did not. Even Concha's family, who made their fortune in the sugar cane business, paid others to run their vast farmland, while they themselves lived in the comforts of town. Most people in the country resorted to horses or wagons to get around, like her father had before La Sirena's success.

"My dad bought that bank down there," he pointed behind him with his thumb.

Ines looked towards the street corner where he pointed and shook her head.

"Nice try, but the Martinez family owns the bank."

Ines and her family knew the Martinez family well, having had them over for dinner on several occasions.

"We bought it last week. My father asked me to come check on things before we hire someone to run it."

Ines wasn't sure she believed him, but her voice softened when she noticed a beautiful little girl in the passenger seat.

"And who's that?" Ines asked.

"My little sister, María. She wanted to come on an adventure into town with me today. And who's that?" he repeated the question, nodding towards Aida.

Ines looked behind her at Aida who was standing on the sidewalk, watching the driver of the jeep closely.

"My sister… you could've killed us," Ines said, remembering they'd almost been run over.

"I'm sorry," he said. "I can promise you I didn't mean to. I'm not used to these city streets yet."

When he smiled at Ines, something else, other than anger, rose within her.

"Let's go home, Aida," Ines called over her shoulder.

"What's your name?" the boy asked her as she took Aida's hand, and they began to walk away.

"Ines." She looked at him from over her shoulder.

He dangled the entire top half of his body out of the open window of his jeep and took off his hat.

"My name's Rene," he said.

"Good day," Ines said and kept walking.

They hurried back home to find Michel and Papa sitting on the porch while Bernita served them tea.

"Where did you two run off to?" Papa asked, peering at his pocket watch.

"The park," Ines said before walking past them into the house.

The weeks that followed, Ines saw the same blue jeep as it drove along the street in front of her parents' house. She thought it was a coincidence at first, until one morning she heard her name called as she sat in the courtyard.

"Ines!" a man's voice called out.

She looked around.

"Over here!"

She stood up from the stone bench where she sat and walked over to the iron fence, gripping the warm metal as she looked through the bars. On the other side of the street, parked in front of La Sirena, was Rene. He continued to call her name until she finally waved back. People who walked by on the sidewalks turned to look at him as he stood in the front seat of his open, blue jeep.

"Who is that?" Michel asked from behind her.

He was getting ready to leave for the day to take a shipment of dresses to several clothing stores in Havana. Ines badly wanted to go with him, but she had teaching classes that morning.

Ines shrugged. "I'm not sure," she said, looking at Rene.

"Are you sure you don't know? He just said your name several times." Michel looked at her, a wry smile on his face.

"Just go," Ines said as she began to smile herself.

"Okay, but don't let Mama or Papa catch you talking to that boy. I doubt he's what they mean when they want you to marry a "Cuban gentleman." Michel waved goodbye as he walked out through the front gate.

Even after Michel left, Rene continued to wave Ines over. He must have sat there in his car well over ten minutes as he waited for her to cross the street. Ines was finally about to give in, and see what it was that he wanted, when a group of girls who had seen him making a commotion walked up to his car. An anger she didn't expect stirred within her, and she wanted nothing more but to walk across the street and slap Rene. Instead, without looking back towards Rene or the group of girls who surrounded him like the sharks she feared as a child, Ines went back inside and closed the heavy door behind her.

The next morning, while they were eating breakfast, Ines noticed her father look at her several times, but when she returned his gaze, he would look away, back to his morning paper. They ate in silence. Mama, Aida, and Michel looked back and forth between Ines and Papa.

"Ines," he said finally.

"Yes, Papa?"

"Who did that car belong to yesterday? The one covered in filth," he asked.

"Which car, Papa?"

Ines felt her chest become warm. Michel chuckled as he cut into a fried plantain with his fork.

"Is that the same boy who almost hit you both while walking in the park?" he asked.

Ines looked at Aida and shot her a look that she usually reserved for Michel. Aida filled her mouth with chunks of egg and white rice.

"Well, he—"

"Enough," Papa said and let his fork clatter onto his plate.

A silence fell over the table.

"You will not see that boy again, understood?"

"But Papa, I haven't seen him, he—"

Ines felt her mother's hand on her knee and stopped speaking.

"End of discussion. If you want to continue your studies to be a *kindergarten* teacher," he said the word as if it were poisonous, "you won't see him again." He lifted his fork from his plate, and the sounds of breakfast filled the room once more.

For many months that followed, Ines listened to her father, and had nothing to do with Rene. On one of the occasions when he drove by their home, she told him to please leave her alone, and for a few days, he did. She continued to entertain the suitors her mother's friends sent her way, spent time with Concha and Isabella, and went to her teaching classes. She told herself that outside of her father's warning, Rene was too young for her and with the way the women flocked to him, she would never be at peace, but she still felt an urge to see him. Her thoughts continued to go back to the blur of blue from the corner of her eye, the caramel eyes, and the dirty cowboy hat. She even told Concha and Isabella about Rene in great detail, which she'd never done with any of her other suitors.

She told her friends as they ate their lunch outside of the house where they took their teaching classes. The house was pink and run by a woman who couldn't remember any of her students' names, except for Isabella's, referring to her other students, including Ines, as "you." Otherwise, Ines enjoyed the classes.

"Oh, I think I know who that is," Isabella said after thinking for a moment, "he and his father recently bought the bank near the park, right?"

"I've seen him too! He's handsome," Concha said, nudging Ines.

Ines didn't protest and laughed with her friends as they ate.

Back home, her father had grown even stricter, sure that Ines was still seeing Rene. This created a rift between them that Ines at times viewed as irreparable. In her eyes, she was a grown woman, a year away from teaching young students of her own, but he still viewed her as a helpless young girl and would remind her of that often. To make things even more difficult, Rene wouldn't give up. Only a week or so after she'd told him to stop driving by their home, a red jeep appeared. She came to find out later that he owned several cars, but at the time was surprised when he called her name. Normally when she told someone that she wasn't interested, she wouldn't see him again, but Rene was stubborn. This drew Ines to him even more. She saw freedom in the boy from the country, but she did her best to avoid him all the same.

Chapter 18

When the war ended, life in Cuba went on as usual. Ines had begun teaching, which was more fulfilling than she had ever imagined. She taught at a kindergarten in Las Piedras that wasn't far from home, and while Concha and Isabella had completed their schooling and begun teaching as well, all three women had been offered positions at different schools. They saw each other less than before, sometimes only briefly over the weekend, and even Rene had finally given up trying to win her hand. At times Ines wondered if someone else had caught Rene's eye and that was the reason he no longer drove by shouting her name. The thought sickened her. She threw herself into her teaching and helped her parents at La Sirena when time permitted, doing her best to forget about Rene entirely. Her father noticed this shift in Ines and began to allow her some of the freedoms that had been taken away.

While Ines focused on her teaching, Michel had begun spending more time with Johara, a fact they kept hidden from both Abraham and Papa. Only Ines knew of their relationship, which she suspected was even deeper than she herself was aware, but she knew

Michel could never tell her father. After Bashir died, Abraham and Papa's relationship became strained, which led to many arguments. They differed in their politics and in the way La Sirena should be run, and to her father's frustration, Michel often sided with Abraham. Despite their disagreements, La Sirena prospered in the years after the war. It had become the largest women's clothing factory not only in all of Las Piedras, but in all of Cuba, producing more dresses, shawls, and custom pieces than anywhere else on the island. Mama no longer worked at the clothing store but would sometimes make an appearance to help fit or customize clothing for certain exclusive customers. At the request of Michel, Papa hired Johara to work in the clothing store, with Aida helping her on occasion.

Papa announced one Saturday morning that they would be having guests over for dinner that evening and needed to make preparations. He went around the house speaking excitedly for the rest of the day. This wasn't anything new to Ines or her siblings as both Mama and Papa had their friends or business contacts over to their home. As a child, Ines enjoyed guessing who would be coming through the front doors that evening. However, after teaching her students during the week, she wanted nothing more than to rest or see her friends on her days off. Instead, more often than not, Mama would ask Ines and Aida to help her and Bernita prepare the house for their guests. On some of these occasions, her mother would orchestrate elaborate schemes and introduce Ines to would-be suitors and their families over dinner, denying afterwards that she'd done such a thing.

"Can Conchita and Isabella join us tonight?" Ines asked her mother, trying to find out more about their guests as they folded napkins and placed them onto ornate china plates.

She looked up at Ines and then back to her hands which were busy spacing out a fork and spoon.

"Whoever your father is having over tonight is very important. He hasn't told me exactly who they are, but if you want to invite your friends, ask him first."

Ines knew this was as good as her mother saying no without actually having to be the one to say it, but she was grateful that the dinner did seem to be an actual business meeting and not an attempt to find a new suitor.

After they finished setting the table, Ines went to her father in his study to ask if her friends could join them for dinner. Ines knocked twice on the open wooden door before looking inside.

"Come in," her father called.

He was in high spirits when Ines entered. He sat at his desk, surrounded by piles of papers that he stacked and sorted as if he were some sort of mad librarian. When Ines asked if her friends could join them for dinner, he said yes right away, surprising Ines.

"It may be good they come, in fact. Just make sure all three of you are on your best behavior, this could be a big deal for us," he said before pausing and looking at Ines. "He's bringing his son as well, and I'd like you to meet him. From what I understand he helps him run his business and has a mind for it."

Ines was surprised her father mentioned his associate's son, usually the job of her mother, but she didn't think much of it as her friends would be joining her. She ran to the telephone in the kitchen to invite Concha and Isabella.

At her mother's request, Michel had gone out to get flowers for the table, but when he returned home, not only did he have flowers, but Johara was with him as well.

"Johara will be joining us tonight for dinner," he told Mama, who agreed without mentioning him asking their father.

Ines couldn't understand how Michel got his way so easily with her, but she knew that if he had gone to his father, a fight may have erupted, and Mama wouldn't have that. Their mother acted as a middleman between Michel and Papa, saying sorry for them both when their pride wouldn't allow them to.

Concha and Isabella arrived an hour before dinner was set to begin. Ines excused herself with her mother who was looking on as Bernita dropped carrots into a large pot of soup as she stirred.

"Don't get dirty before dinner," her mother said.

"I'm not a child," Ines reminded her.

Ines knew her mother watched her as she left the kitchen, feeling her eyes burning into her back. She welcomed her friends who were waiting outside in the courtyard and sat with them on the porch at the front of the house. As they sat on the porch, Ines listened to the sounds of insects filling the silence as evening crept in.

"Who do you think it will be?" Isabella asked after Ines told them what her father had mentioned.

"I bet it's the President," Concha said laughing.

"Does he have any sons?" Isabella asked.

Concha flicked open a fan and moved it back and forth in front of her face. It was still warm outside even as the sun fell below the buildings and palm trees. Lights from the house splashed out onto the porch and the courtyard.

"Who do you think it is?" Concha asked Ines.

Ines looked at her friend as she waved the fan rhythmically.

"They're all the same, aren't they? Even if it were the president, it's just another old man who controls our island," Ines said.

She almost jumped when her father appeared on the porch behind them. He looked at his golden pocket watch, which was connected to a chain in his trouser pocket.

"Come inside, girls. They'll be here any moment," he said and held the door open for them as they went inside where they continued to wait for the guests to arrive.

Ines would have been less surprised if their guest that evening *had* been the President of Cuba. As Rene stepped into the house, Ines felt as if her body had gone numb. Ines was sure it was a dream or some sort of terrible joke her mind was playing on her. She felt her hands become sweaty and quickly wiped them on her dress as she stared at him. There was something different about him. His features were sharper, somehow more hardened than before, and Ines realized he wasn't wearing his cowboy hat. It was the first time she'd seen him without it, and she noticed his thick, black hair, which was cut short and styled as if he were some sort of movie star. Ines knew that despite the resemblance, Rene was no longer the boy who had almost run her and Aida over only a few years before or who had driven by her home countless times, honking and yelling like a madman.

"Hello," Aida said and waved to Rene.

Ines's heart sank when she realized her sister recognized him and prayed that her father wouldn't. Rene smiled at Aida then at Ines, but he didn't look as surprised as Ines felt.

"Welcome, Señor Diaz," Ines heard her father say as he entered the room with Mama by his side.

It was only then that Ines noticed an older man standing next to Rene, who she was sure was his father based on how alike they looked.

Bernita took their coats.

"Isn't that—" Michel began to ask, but Ines stopped him.

He began to laugh with the realization and whispered something to Johara. Ines had tried to kick at her brother's ankle but missed and hit Rene, who had walked over to them.

"I'm so sorry," Ines said as a warmth spread across her face.

Ines could hear her brother laughing even harder now, but Rene continued to smile as if he'd felt nothing.

"It's only a leg," he said and greeted everyone.

Before they sat down for dinner, Isabella and Concha took Ines aside and whispered excitedly.

"Is that *the* Rene?" Concha asked, grabbing her by the shoulders.

Ines looked over to the dinner table where everyone was taking their seats.

"Yes," she whispered back.

"Didn't your father forbid you from seeing him?" Isabella asked.

Ines nodded.

"Then what's he doing here?" Concha asked.

"I don't think Papa recognized him," Ines said, staring at Rene's features and looking away when he returned her gaze.

Concha and Isabella giggled as they all took their seats at the table.

Over the course of the dinner, it became clear to Ines why her father had been in such high spirits throughout the day. Rene's father, Domingo, was interested in buying cargo ships in order to transport goods from Cuba to America. While sugarcane was the biggest export, especially to America, he wanted to focus on other items that the American tourists purchased when they visited.

"Well, we can't ship over the casinos, but we can send over the next best thing," Domingo said as he bit into the meat Mama had prepared, "your clothing has become quite famous, especially with the tourists."

Ines knew this to be true after seeing all of the tourists waiting in line on Saturday mornings to visit her mother's store. She'd heard countless stories of people traveling from all around the world in order to visit the small clothing store in Cuba that was said to rival some of the best clothing stores in Paris. Ines tried to convince her father to open up more storefronts throughout Cuba, especially in Havana where the tourists flocked like migrating birds, but he wouldn't have it.

"There will be only one La Sirena," he told her.

Domingo also spoke of the other islands in the Caribbean, which were normally neglected, but could also prove profitable. Everything he said was met with excited agreement from Papa, whom Ines hadn't seen so animated since he and Abraham initially decided to create La Sirena. As the two men talked, Ines wondered why Abraham hadn't joined them for dinner.

"Permits will be the only issue," Domingo said between mouthfuls of food.

"What if we entered into a contract with the government?" Ines asked aloud without realizing it.

The sound of forks and knives stopped as the entire table turned to look at Ines. Papa's face was calm, but Ines knew how angry he must have been. He cleared his throat.

"Ines, this isn't—" her father began.

"Wait, let her speak," Domingo said to Papa and gave her his full attention.

If Papa wasn't angry before, Ines knew he must have been then. She looked to Michel who shrugged.

"If we give them clothing for their officials and soldiers, they may help to expedite our request to ship product outside of Cuba," Ines said.

"That's a great idea," Rene said.

Ines felt both her friends and mother looking at her from either side.

Once the dinner had ended, they walked their guests to the porch and said their goodbyes. When her father shook Domingo's hand, Ines knew the business agreement was sealed between them. She noticed her father watching her closely when Rene said his goodbyes. *Did he recognize him after all?* It wasn't until he approached her in her bedroom later that evening that she knew for certain. He pulled out the chair from under her desk and moved it to the foot of her bed.

"Is everything alright?" Ines asked.

Her father hadn't entered her bedroom for several years, and she felt as though she were a young girl once again.

"You may think me old and slow, but I still know you better than you realize," Papa began. "That's the same boy who used to drive by here often, the one with the cowboy hat and dirty car?"

"Yes, Papa."

She watched as her father closed his eyes and nodded as she answered.

"His father will be a great business partner for me. We have the opportunity to expand La Sirena into other countries around the world. Maybe even America. Do you know what that would mean for us?" he asked.

Ines nodded and waited for him to continue.

"Ines, tell me, what will happen if either of you become angry with the other, and my business relationship with his father sours because of it?"

Ines looked at her hands.

"We would lose everything that we've been working towards," he said.

"Don't we have enough?" Ines asked. "All you think about is La Sirena."

The chair that her father sat on creaked as he leaned forward.

"Rene is a cowboy like his father, and even worse, he was raised without a mother. You've heard the stories, I'm sure," her father said, ignoring her question.

Ines had heard the rumors. Over the years she'd heard much about Rene and his father, the wealthy cowboys, who had purchased the largest bank in Las Piedras. Rene's father, Domingo, had been an orphan, but had worked on his uncle's farm as a child and learned everything he knew from him. When he was still young, his uncle died, leaving Domingo to manage the farm as his uncle left behind only a wife and two daughters, and no sons. Domingo worked day in and day out, acquiring more and more land nearby and more cattle for his farm as the years went on. By the age of twenty, Domingo had become one of the most successful cattle ranchers in Las Piedras, and his fortune and business continued to grow. He eventually married and Rene was born soon after, but as his son came into the world, his wife left it. Devastated by the death of his wife, Domingo turned himself to the business completely and hired housekeepers to watch Rene, whom he had no idea how to care for himself. Eventually, Domingo remarried and had a daughter, María, the girl Ines had seen in the car the day she met Rene, but by the time Rene had a stepmother, he was no longer a young child, and the delicate guidance of a mother did not suit him.

"He will love his freedom more than he can ever love you," Papa continued, "I want you to marry someone who will give you everything that your mother and I gave you and more."

As Ines began to cry, for the loss of something she couldn't understand, her father didn't hug her as he did when she was a child. Instead, he stood up from the chair, put it back under the desk, and said, "One day, you'll understand. I only want the best for you."

Ines had a sick feeling in her chest and had trouble falling asleep once her father had left the room. Her mind turned his words over again and again, as if they were lost at sea, being battered by countless waves. She pictured the suitor her father did approve of, Carlos Estevez, the son of a doctor in Havana, and realized her prison would only change locations if she married him instead of following her heart. While there was nothing wrong with Carlos, she felt nothing when she was with him, and knew if they were to marry, it would only be to please her parents. where Rene was reckless, wild, and full of fire, Carlos was timid, controlled, and cold. Ines said none of these things to her father, or to anyone else other than Concha and Isabella, but the thoughts made it difficult for her to fall asleep. Ines didn't remember her dreams that night, but she woke up sure they were filled with heartache.

The next morning Abraham's booming voice filled the house. She heard her father's voice as well. It sounded as if they were arguing. She dressed quickly and went downstairs to find Michel and her mother standing outside of Papa's study.

"Don't go in there," Michel warned Ines.

"What's going on?"

"Business matters," he said.

Ines ignored her brother and opened the door to the study. The voices grew louder as she entered.

"And you told me nothing? I thought we were partners. My daughter was here, but you told me nothing!" Abraham bellowed.

"If I'd known Johara—"

"No, Salim, no excuses," Abraham said.

"Enough," Ines heard her father say. "We may be partners, but it's my capital we're using," her father said using a tone she'd heard reserved for fabric merchants.

"Not your wife's?" Abraham asked. "If I hadn't given you the idea to " Abraham stood up straight when he saw Ines standing in the doorway.

"Is everything alright?" Ines asked.

"I'm sorry if I woke you," Abraham said.

"You woke the whole house," Ines said with an uneasy laugh.

"Not now, Ines, we're having a discussion." Her father's eyebrows were pinched, and his jaw set tight.

Ines listened to her father and closed the door behind her as the arguing continued, muted through the wood. She felt powerless as she walked away.

Later in the day, Aida joined Ines in her bedroom where she was writing in her journal.

"I think this is for you," Aida said as she handed Ines an envelope. "I found it on the front porch this morning."

"Did you read it?" Ines asked, noticing that there was no seal.

"Of course not," Aida said.

From the time Aida was young, she was unable to lie, so Ines knew she was telling the truth. She thanked her and went out to the garden where she sat on a stone bench to read the letter in the sunlight. Ines had no idea who the letter could have been from. She turned the envelope around in her hands and looked at her name on the front, which was written in thick, heavy-handed letters. When she pulled the thin sheet of paper out, she knew at once that it must have been from a man. The handwriting looked like stains of charcoal scratched into stone rather than writing, like some sort of primitive cave painting, the kind that she taught her students about. She held the letter out in front of her as she sat on a bench in the garden. It took her several attempts to read it, but she finally realized who it was from and was grateful it had been Aida to find it and not Bernita or her parents. Rene's name was the only instantly legible part of the letter, big bold letters near the bottom of the page. Ines couldn't believe he'd been so bold to leave that letter out on their porch where anyone could have read it before her. It was an invitation to join him on his farm the following

Saturday. Ines counted the days in her head. Six. He'd pick her up from the park at 10 a.m., the same park where he'd almost hit her with his car nearly four years before.

Ines felt as if she were being pulled in two separate directions. Her heart swelled, and she imagined the farm full of vegetables and fruit, Rene holding her hand as they walked between the rows of color that looked like Lebanon, but then she remembered her father and her own doubts. Although Rene was charming at dinner, there was no way for her to know that he wasn't acting polite but would act entirely different the moment they were alone. She still remembered how the other girls looked at him.

Ines put the letter back into its envelope and looked towards the house to make sure no one had seen her. All of the windows were empty, and the curtains were still. Ines waited a few moments to be sure before walking over to a part of the garden that was well-shaded, where many stones covered the ground. She picked up a stone, one that was big, smooth, and gray. Insects squirmed underneath as they were exposed to the sun that crept in through the trees and a lizard darted out, a flash of green that disappeared into the bushes. If she were younger, she would have tried to catch it, but in that moment her thoughts were commanded by the piece of paper in her hand that seemed to throb with a life of its own. She covered the letter under a layer of dirt and put the rock back over it. She looked back towards the house once more, checking all of the windows to make sure no one would come out later to find what she'd hidden. She still didn't see any movement from the house. As she washed her hands of dirt in the kitchen, Ines almost jumped when Aida came up behind her.

"What did the letter say?"

Dirty water fell from her hands and into the sink as she scrubbed them.

"Nothing. Don't mention it to anyone else, okay?" Ines whispered to her sister.

"A letter?" asked Bernita as she entered the kitchen with a large basket full of food.

Aida looked at Ines, her eyes pleading to be saved from her uncontrollable honesty.

"I think you misheard," Ines said.

Bernita gave Ines a sour look but said nothing else as Ines walked over and helped her put away the food from the market.

The secret of the letter burned inside Ines all week. She told Concha and Isabella about it as they ate lunch one afternoon. They both urged her to meet Rene on Saturday.

"I saw the way he looked at you at dinner," Concha said. "If he's not in love, then he's about to be."

She bit into her sandwich.

"What's the worst that can happen?" Isabella asked Ines as she nodded her head in agreement.

Ines looked up at a palm tree as its fan of leaves danced with the breeze. She imagined her father and mother finding out. Though she was already nineteen, in the eyes of society, she still belonged to them. She knew her father could keep her from leaving home or force

Ines to quit her work as a teacher, or even worse still, pressure her into a marriage with someone like Carlos Estevez.

"Snap out of it," Concha said as she clapped her hands together.

Both Isabella and Concha laughed when Ines jumped.

"I know you like him, Ines. You've never given a man a second thought, but even years later, you haven't forgotten this one. Nothing will go wrong. Go see him Saturday," Concha told Ines.

"I agree with Concha," Isabella said.

When Ines returned home that afternoon, there were dirty paw prints throughout the house.

"Aida!"

For her birthday that year, her parents had given in to Aida's begging and had purchased her a puppy. The puppy was black with a small strip of white down its belly and had come from the market where a vendor who visited once a month from Havana sold foreign dog breeds, along with other exotic animals such as chimpanzees and colorful birds, from around the world. Ines knew her father had no idea what kind of dog he was buying, but Aida didn't care. While all of her wealthy friends in school had Havanese, small white dogs that resembled bundles of cotton, Aida loved her dog, who had grown to be large and unruly in its first year of life. She named him Sombra, *shadow*.

"Animals have a place and that place is outside, away from us humans," Bernita would say before their parents had brought Sombra home, but a few months of Sombra living with them changed her opinion entirely.

Bernita seemed to love the dog more than anyone else. If there was ever a mess or something broken because of Sombra, she would do her best to clean everything up before Mr. and Mrs. Aude noticed. The dog had become her own shadow, listening more to her commands than anyone else's, including Aida's. They had to shut the door to Aida's room in order to keep Sombra from sneaking out in the middle of the night and scratching and whining in front of Bernita's door. As Sombra grew, he became like a dark cloud that tore through the house, leaving broken things as he went. He would often bring in dead birds or track dirty paw prints throughout the house.

"Sombra made a mess," Ines yelled out again.

She walked towards the kitchen to see if Bernita or Aida were home, but she found her mother in the kitchen instead. Sombra was at her feet and a dirty sheet of paper was on the table in front of her.

"Sombra brought this in," she said, her eyes on the letter.

Ines went cold.

"Mama, I—"

But her mother held up her hand.

"This is the same Rene we had over for dinner the other night, the son of your father's potential business partner?"

Ines nodded and swallowed.

"Good. Well, he seems like a fine young man. I'll take care of your father, but you need to do something for me," Mama said.

She went on to explain that Ines was allowed to visit Rene's farm, but only if Aida went with her. Ines agreed without a second thought.

"But you'll be the one to convince your sister. I feel guilty enough keeping this from your father as it is," she told Ines.

Later that night, Ines told Aida that she would be going with her to Rene's farm on Saturday.

"My friend Cristina is having a birthday party on Saturday," she said.

Although Aida was only twelve, she was her own person. If she didn't want to go to the farm, she wouldn't go no matter how much Ines tried to persuade her.

"He has horses," Ines told her.

"Cristina's father will have ponies at her party and all of my friends from school are going," she said.

Ines spent the next several minutes trying to convince Aida, but she shook her head with every suggestion. Her only other option was to take Michel, but he had important deliveries to Havana that weekend, and had already left, most likely not returning until late Saturday afternoon. Ines felt crushed. She wanted to see Rene more than anything, as if every part of her was aligned to that purpose. It was then that she decided that she would take Aida to her party, meet Rene at the park, and then pick her back up once it ended.

"Okay," Aida replied after thinking for a moment, "but only if you'll take me to the beach the next time you go with your friends."

Ines agreed.

Her dreams that night were of flowers, sunshine, and blue skies filled with clouds. If she hadn't been planning to see Rene the next day, she would have stayed in those dreams for as long as she could.

Ines woke up before the sun. She wasn't sure what clothes to wear to the farm, but she finally decided on a long, bright blue dress that her mother had sewn for her the year before. It looked like a peony with its ruffles and folds of billowing fabric. When she'd finished getting ready, Ines went downstairs to find that her father was already awake.

"That's a nice dress to wear spending the day out with your sister," he said.

Ines said nothing, realizing that her mother had most likely told him that she would be taking Aida out to walk the town or to visit Old Lady Nayibe. Only Aida knew that Ines would be going to Rene's farm alone. Regardless, she left in a rush through the front door once Aida was ready to leave.

The birthday party was held at one of the largest houses in Concha's neighborhood. Ines didn't know the family who lived there, but she'd passed the house many times on her way to visit Concha. The house could fit at least five regular-sized houses inside of it and had a front lawn so large that it took them several minutes to get from the street to the front door. Although they were only a few minutes late to the party, Ines could already hear children's voices shouting and laughing from the backyard.

"They're going to have clowns, face painting, and even an elephant," Aida told Ines as they waited by the front door.

Aida fit in so perfectly that Ines sometimes forgot that they shared the same Lebanese blood, and she wasn't just some Cuban girl her mother had found one day in town. From the time she began school, her friends always invited her to play or go to the beach with them and their families. It seemed like there was a birthday party every other weekend, making Ines suspect that she had hundreds of classmates.

A tall man in a suit opened the door after Ines knocked twice using the iron knocker. He offered to take Aida to the backyard where the rest of the kids were playing.

"Pardon me, do you have the time?" Ines asked the man.

When he told her that it was only ten minutes until 10 a.m., Ines turned and ran without thanking him.

"I'll be back soon, Aida! I love you," she yelled over her shoulder as she ran towards the park.

The feeling of the wind on her face as she ran made Ines feel free once again. She hadn't run in public since she was a little girl. She seemed to rush past the world around her, which blended into waves of color. She moved with purpose, holding her dress up as she ran. Ines hoped that Rene would still be there when she arrived. When she arrived at the park, she saw Rene's Jeep and looked around to find him waving from a bench. She knew that she must have been late, but he'd waited for her all the same, without even a reply from her confirming his invitation. He had his cowboy hat resting on his lap and smiled as he saw Ines moving towards him at a slow walk as she tried to hide that she'd been running.

"Were you that excited to see me?" Rene asked with a smile while Ines fought to catch her breath.

Although he looked older, his large cheeks were still as round as they were when she'd first met him. It gave him a child-like appearance when he smiled. He looked at his wristwatch and tapped it.

"I thought you were going to leave me waiting here all day."

"What would you have done if I hadn't come at all?" Ines asked.

"I would have been sad, but there's worse things than sitting on a park bench for a few minutes," he said.

Ines appreciated that he never hid what he felt. His emotions and thoughts were obvious to her, as if she were reading a book. She didn't apologize for being late and instead, walked over to his Jeep and hopped into the passenger seat, hiding her smile as she noticed the surprised look on his face.

As he drove them farther from town, Rene asked her questions and hardly interrupted when she answered. Ines did her best not to give away how badly she'd wanted to see him. It was a feeling completely foreign to her and it scared her that another person, a man, was able to create those sensations within her. It was as if she were his hostage, and he had no idea that he was her captor.

The day was beautiful, and the wind ran through the Jeep in heavy gusts. The sun felt warm on her skin and her hair whipped wildly all around her head. Not once did she consider how her hair would look once they arrived. She felt as if she were running at the same speed as the car, the fields, trees, and mountains whooshing by as they sped along the dirt road. Ines could smell farmland and breathed in deeply, the bitter smells reminding her of La Casa de Nayibe. She was surprised that they weren't surrounded by fruit and vegetable crops. Instead, they passed by hundreds upon hundreds of cows and horses, most of them not even looking up as they sped along.

"How much longer?" Ines asked.

"We've been here," Rene said.

Rene accelerated and Ines looked back to see even more dust and dirt get kicked up behind them.

"We own all of this land," he said over the roar of the engine, "this is what we do. All of this."

Ines looked at him as if not completely understanding how all of the land could belong to them.

"We probably raised the dinner you ate last night," he said.

Without warning, Rene pulled off the road, taking the jeep through dry dirt and patches of wild grass towards a large fenced in area where at least a dozen horses were trotting or drinking water from long pails. Rene slowed the car and tipped his hat to a skinny, shirtless man who was working on a fence that had a wooden plank splitting away from it. The man paused his work.

"Señor Diaz," he said.

The man took off his own hat and wiped at his brow as Rene got out of the car and came around to help Ines down from the Jeep.

"I'm okay," Ines said, holding her dress with one hand and the car with the other as she jumped down onto the dirt.

"Raul, meet my guest," Rene said.

Rene didn't give her name, which was the custom, but she hadn't expected him to, knowing that he lived by his own rules.

"A pleasure, señorita," the man said and bowed his head.

Ines echoed his greeting and looked at the horses in the stable behind him.

"Are those your horses too?" Ines asked Rene.

He nodded.

She'd never seen so many horses all together in one place. The horses made grunting noises as they approached, scattering flies with flicks of their tails. They lifted their heads or turned to look at them but did so without excessive movement. Ines felt her heart pounding in her chest and wondered if they sensed her fear.

"This one's Charlie," Rene told her and ran his hand along the brown horse's side where its muscles rippled under the smoothness of its coat. Ines saw love in Rene's eyes as he looked at the horse.

Rene explained that Charlie was a funny horse, but hardly ever made a sound.

"So, you named him after Charlie Chaplin?" Ines asked with a laugh.

"And why's that so funny?" Rene asked, laughing as well.

Whenever Ines went to the movie theater in Las Piedras, she'd watch whatever was playing, but always enjoyed the silent films of her childhood, especially Charlie Chaplin, the most. She swore to

Concha and Isabella that if he ever visited Cuba, she would do whatever it took to see him.

"No reason," Ines said.

"Look." Rene pointed towards another horse, a smaller one that was the light gray color of a palm tree's trunk. "That's your horse today," he told Ines, "Her name is Palma."

"What do you mean *my* horse?" Ines asked.

Rene led Ines over to where Palma was drinking water. Where Charlie was strong and powerful, Palma looked majestic and serene.

"Have you ever ridden a horse before?" Rene asked.

"Never alone," Ines said.

"Well, then I'll just have to teach you," he said.

"Who said I'd agree to that?" Ines asked.

She turned to see that Raul was back to fixing the broken fence, not paying attention to them.

"It's just us out here, okay? Come on, let's learn the basics," Rene said and went to begin outfitting Palma with a saddle.

In the same way Ines felt her mother was a master seamstress, Rene was a master horseman. He showed her everything, from the parts of the saddle to the proper riding position to what to do if the horse was tiring and they were too far from the stable. Ines felt as though she was one of the students in her classroom, completely engaged by what Rene was saying. When he helped her up onto the horse, careful not to ruin her dress, Ines felt confident that she could ride it.

They began slowly at first, trotting out of the stables as Raul closed the gate behind them. The sun was beating down, but the air was cool. As Rene picked up Charlie's pace, Palma followed suit. Ines couldn't tell if she had any influence on the horse at all, but Rene turned to her and yelled over his shoulder, "You're doing great."

It was as if time had slowed as they rode. Every detail of the world around them came alive, and Ines noticed things that normally would have been hidden from her before as if only now they were ready to show themselves. There were birds, so many birds, and butterflies that danced around wildflowers growing out of the fields. The horses slammed their feet against the grass and dirt, kicking clouds of dust back behind them. In the distance, mountains and the shapes of trees rose into the sky, making Ines feel small, but part of something so much larger.

"That's our house," Rene said as he stood in his saddle and pointed to a large farmhouse that was surrounded by empty land.

After several minutes, the house had become a dot in the distance behind them and the grass became longer and scragglier. Ines began to feel as if Palma was beginning to understand everything she wanted without her having to say or do anything, as if their minds were slowly becoming one. Rene continued to call back to check on her, but she could only reply with smiles and laughter. All of her fears and worries had disappeared.

They stopped at a stream to let the horses drink water. Rene took a canteen from a bag on Charlie's saddle and filled it with stream water before pouring it along the backs of both horses. He then took off his belt and used it to remove excess water from their shining coats before refilling the canteen and repeating the process several times.

"If you don't wipe off the old water before adding more, they won't get any cooler," he told Ines.

Once Rene finished cooling them off, the horses ate grass from the field nearby while he filled the canteen once again with water and sat down on a large boulder next to the stream and invited Ines to join him. He offered her the canteen filled with stream water. Ines said no at first, but she was thirsty, and he reassured her that the water was safe to drink. Ines watched as he took a swig of water himself before handing the canteen over to her.

"The pebbles in the stream clean the water for us. The Earth is a wonderful thing," he said and stared off in the direction that the stream came from.

Ines drank from the canteen graciously. Small trickles of water appeared at the corners of her mouth, eventually dripping from her chin and onto the blue dress, darkening it where water met fabric.

If Mama could see me.

The fresh water seemed to fill every cell in her body with energy. She could taste how alive it was, still flowing with the river somehow even after Rene had bottled it. The world around them was silent other than the birds who always seemed to be calling out to one another.

Rene was still looking towards the mountains and trees where the stream disappeared. He seemed more like a statue than a man. When Ines had first met him, she saw him as an immature boy, but she realized that out here, where the land was still wild, he was wise beyond his years.

"How long have you been doing this?" Ines asked.

Rene stirred and turned his attention back to her.

"What do you mean?"

"I mean, riding horses, taking care of them. Have you been doing it long?"

Rene looked at Ines as if she was as interesting as the stream he had just been entranced by.

"I guess I've been doing it my entire life," he said with a laugh, "but I want to know about you. You were born in Lebanon, no? What was it like?"

Ines went on to explain the orchard, the ships, and everything else she could still remember, but it was as if a fog had rolled in and hidden many of her memories away.

"Do you miss home?" Rene asked.

"Cuba is my home," Ines said without pause.

Rene moved closer to her and placed his hand on hers, but Ines pulled her hand away.

"How many girls have you brought here before me?" Ines asked, although she wasn't sure she wanted to know the answer.

"None," he said, grabbing the canteen of water from the ground and drinking what was left, tapping the bottom to get out every drop.

"Do you take me for a fool?" Ines asked.

He stood up and held out his hand.

"You're the first girl I've ever brought to our ranch."

Ines narrowed her eyes as she watched his lips move as he spoke.

"I don't lie," he said.

Ines knew somehow that he was telling the truth. She took his hand.

"Let's walk." Rene's voice was soft but sure.

"What if they leave us?" Ines asked, glancing towards the horses.

"They won't," he said with a chuckle.

They continued to hold hands as they walked along the stream. Ines wondered if Rene noticed the beating of her heart through her hand or was bothered by the sweat that seemed to be dripping from her palms, but he didn't say a word. She felt as if they were growing closer without speaking. She pointed to small flowers or colorful birds and Rene would smile and do the same when he noticed the gray flash of fish in the stream or a butterfly fluttering above a bush. They walked for what must have been half an hour, but when they returned to where they'd started, the horses were still there.

"They really stayed," Ines said.

"Of course, they did. Did you doubt me?" Rene asked, contorting his face into a serious expression.

"If you want *me* to stay, change that tone," Ines said.

Rene laughed.

"I have a deep bond with the horses," Rene said.

Ines thought about the connection she felt to Palma and nodded.

They returned to the stable a little after noon. Raul took the reins from Ines when they returned.

"Did you enjoy the countryside, señorita?" Raul asked.

"I could stay here for hours," she said and looked at Rene.

Ines felt as if time moved differently on the ranch, or maybe it was her closeness to Rene that had altered her perceptions. She thought of these things as they walked back to the Jeep.

"You'll need to speak with my father if you want to see me again," Ines told him as she climbed up into the passenger seat.

Rene said nothing as they drove back to Las Piedras. Ines worried that her words were too forward and felt a fear well up within her that she would never see him again once he dropped her off.

When Ines returned home that day, Aida was outside in the courtyard, sketching a bird that was splashing and ruffling its feathers in the fountain.

"Forget something?" Aida asked without taking her eyes away from the bird.

A wave of realization crashed against Ines, as if a bucket of cold water had been flung on her. She'd completely forgotten about her sister.

"Don't worry, I told them that you went to Concha's house," Aida said. "Remember, next time you go to the beach, I'm coming."

As Ines approached her sister, the bird flew away in a flurry of wings and droplets of water.

"Aww," Aida said, "I was almost done anyway."

"I'm so sorry," Ines said.

"It's okay," Aida said and got up to go inside.

When they entered their home, Michel was sitting on one of the bottom steps of the stairwell and looked exhausted.

"How was the birthday party?" he asked Aida.

Aida began to go into details of the clown's magic tricks, and the pony that she was allowed a turn to ride.

"Is that where all of that horsehair came from?" Michel asked Ines as he pointed at her dress.

Ines looked down at her dress surprised as she'd been careful to wipe off any dirt or hair on the way back home. She felt her face flush.

"I'm only joking," he said.

Does he suspect something?

"That's not funny, Michel, Mama would kill me if I ruined a dress," she said, watching her brother closely and wondering how he could have found out.

Throughout dinner that night, Ines expected someone to mention Rene or her visit to his ranch, but no one did. She ate quickly and went to her room as soon as Papa dismissed them from the table. She filled several pages in her journal that night before bed, but her mind kept going long after she put down her pen, so she began to prepare the following week's lesson plan, but even that was almost impossible. Every thought was interrupted with the feeling of freedom she'd felt while riding Palma. Ines tried to look outside from her bedroom window to the street, but instead her own reflection stared back at her. She thought of Rene and how raw and unrefined he was. Even if she never spoke to him again, Ines knew she could never go back to what her life was like before.

The week after Ines visited the ranch, Rene came to the house to speak with her father alone. They met in Papa's study with the door closed. She would pass by every so often to try to hear any of their conversation, but they spoke softly, and Ines wasn't bold enough to open the door.

She wasn't sure exactly what had been said, but when her father approached her later that day, he didn't look as serious as she'd feared.

"You can see Rene again."

Ines rushed forward to hug her father and was grateful for whatever words Rene had chosen. He had chosen her.

As she hugged her father, she began to cry.

"I said you can see him again," her father said with a quiet chuckle.

Ines felt as if she'd lived that moment before, and a sense of dread began to fill her.

"I've never been this happy," she said but felt so afraid.

She had the overwhelming sense that the better her life became, the worse it would be when everything went away. Ines looked around their home from where she stood, still clutching her father, and knew that if she were to marry Rene, she would have to leave it all behind for a new home. The sense of freedom she'd felt when thinking of him was then replaced by a coldness that made the room feel empty. She knew that one day, everything would once again be left behind, but this time, it would be her choice.

Chapter 19

They didn't marry for many years. Rene was always busy on the ranch or at the bank, checking in to see that everything was being run smoothly while Ines spent her weeks in the classroom. It was only on certain weekends that they had time to see each other. Some weekends when Ines visited the ranch, Rene's farmhands and their families would throw parties, where they danced around a bonfire, played drums, and drank rum for hours. Ines had never felt the Caribbean breeze in that way, dancing along with them, sometimes until the golden traces of morning were already teasing at the sky. It was a freedom she'd only ever felt while around Rene. An entirely new world had opened itself to her, and she knew that there was no going back. Even though they only saw each other a handful of times each month, it was clear to both of them that their hearts belonged only to each other.

Rene talked often of marriage, but it was Ines who put her foot down, saying that she would only marry him after they'd known each other for at least ten years. She wasn't sure where the number had come from, but she was sure it was necessary. Rene would laugh at her unfounded conviction, but never protested or pushed the question. He was happy to live in the moment. The issue came when Ines' parents asked the question, sure it was Rene who dragged his feet, even when she explained that it was her own decision to postpone their marriage.

"You can marry someone else if he's taking too long, Ines," her father said during one of their more tense conversations, "your mother is worried about you, and we both want you to be happy."

They never seemed bothered that Michel and Johara were still not married, although they spent hours together, sometimes every day during the week, while telling others they were only good friends. When Ines told Concha and Isabella that she wanted to wait to be married, even they seemed confused by her decision.

"Is he seeing other women?" Concha asked.

"How is his temper?" Isabella asked.

"No, there's nothing wrong with him, I swear. I just want to know him better than anyone else," she told them.

Concha and Isabella would exchange confused glances but normally the conversation would end there.

Ines knew that it was only those ten years that would allow her to trust that Rene wouldn't change from one day to the next or leave her for some other woman who would try to take him away. In everything she did, there remained her fear of losing the things she cared about most. She imagined Rene being flung from his horse or their family being sent back to Lebanon in a rush of packing and tears. Ines wasn't sure where the images came from, but they manifested themselves as nightmares and plagued her nightly. Sometimes she even saw them during the day and only a stroll through the gardens or deep prayer could send them away. Ines only told Old Lady Nayibe about the dreams. She was convinced that they were omens of things to come and if she shared them with too many they would only come faster. They sat on the porch and Ines spent hours sharing her fears and nightmares with the old woman who still reminded her so much of her grandmother Aleia.

"Maybe they are omens," Nayibe said, holding her hand out for Ines to help her up from her chair. "But it's better to live with courage and eventually be proven right than to live in fear of them."

Nayibe had started to have trouble moving around her home and on multiple occasions would need Ines' help to walk around the property she had cared for on her own for so many years. When Ines visited, she would clean the house and prepare meals for the week, which led to constant protests from Nayibe.

"You really should come live with us," Ines told her.

"I made a decision many years ago that I would live and die in this home," Nayibe said.

She had become even more stubborn as she aged, so Ines knew that no matter how much she pressed the issue, she would never leave.

When Ines turned twenty-four, she felt that her fears had manifested into reality. They began as rumors at first. There were young men from the university who wanted things to change in Cuba, angry at the American-backed government that favored the rich and the tourists who flocked to their cities and beaches. Ines first heard the rumors from Michel, who had many friends attending university in Havana. He shared them over dinner, telling his family everything he'd heard. While her parents didn't believe the rumors, Ines knew they were true. She knew that although her dreams did not always come to pass, something was changing in Cuba, and it threatened the life she wanted so desperately to keep.

The first encounter Ines had with one of these "revolutionaries," as they began to refer to themselves, was a friend of Michel's named Javier who had invited them to hear him play music at a club in Havana. They went on a Saturday, Michel driving Johara, Rene and Ines to Havana. Although it was a sunny afternoon, when they entered the club, the world became dark. Clouds of sour cigar smoke rolled through the room like a fog.

"It smells terrible in here," Ines said.

"I can hardly breathe," Johara agreed.

Michel led them to an empty table near the bar as a band finished playing.

"Wait, he's getting on the stage now," Michel told them and pointed to his friend who was waiting at the stairs leading up to the stage.

The music began with an explosion of horns. Ines listened intently to the unique sounds each instrument made as Rene and Michel ordered themselves drinks.

"Do you like this kind of music?" Ines asked Johara.

"Not really," she said with a smile and looked over at Michel who had returned to the table, "but your brother does."

After the performance ended and another band had taken the stage, Javier joined them at the table.

"I didn't think you'd actually make it," he told Michel.

After Michel introduced everyone, his and Javier's conversation quickly turned to politics.

"What do you know of politics, Rene?" Javier asked.

Rene shrugged. "I'm a rancher, not a politician. I leave those things to men much smarter than me," he said.

"No, of course, I understand," Javier paused, "but being silent and ignorant is just as bad. You do realize Batista has run everything from the shadows for years, don't you? He quiets those who oppose him and does nothing to help the masses. He's creating an imbalance and change needs to be made to fix what is broken."

Rene stayed silent and looked at Javier. He picked up a glass of rum and took a sip, before asking, "So, what is your solution?"

No matter who he was speaking to, Rene remained calm and listened before he spoke. Javier, on the other hand, looked as if he wanted to reach across the table and hit Rene, but instead, he looked at Michel and continued.

"There are already people working towards this change. Look at the Castro brothers just a few months ago."

"They already failed once," Michel interrupted.

Ines had heard the rumors from Michel about an unsuccessful raid on an army base in Santiago de Cuba, led by Fidel and Raul Castro. It took place in the worst heat of the summer, record heat, to which Ines attributed the attack. She was convinced that without the breeze or the ocean, heat could take the gentlest man and turn him feral.

"But they were the flame that lit the fuse. There will be more men like them and not all of them will fail," Javier said.

"So, violence is your answer?" Rene asked.

He took another sip of his rum.

Ines noticed Javier's face growing red under the dim lights. She glanced over to the dancers in the center of the room and grabbed Rene's hand. He understood immediately and excused himself as they made their way to the dance floor.

Ines heard Javier loudly defending his position to Michel, "I'm not a fan of violence either, but sometimes, to create change, you must shake up those who are still asleep."

When the band finished their song and began playing one that they both recognized, Rene spun Ines and pulled her around the dance floor as if they'd practiced as dancing partners their entire lives. They laughed and joked as he pulled her close to him while their eyes and smiles spoke for them. Ines forgot about Javier's words as she danced with Rene. It wasn't until several years later that Ines once again heard the names Fidel or Raul Castro. By then, many things would have happened between that moment, as she danced salsa with Rene on the dancefloor, and when she eventually heard those names again. Both Isabella and Concha would be married, Isabella to a young man from Las Piedras who had been courting her for years and Concha to a wealthy businessman from Havana whom her father knew well. They would have children, making Ines an "aunt" to both Concha's son and to Isabella's twins, a son and daughter. Ines grew even closer to Rene in those years and rarely fought with her family.

As La Sirena grew at the hands of her father and brother, despite the unrest in other parts of the island, she worked diligently for her students, who continued to fill her with purpose. Ines visited Nayibe at least once a week and would spend hours gossiping with the old woman whom she loved as much as she had her own grandmother. Her life was perfect. As perfect as it had ever been. But Ines would remember that time as one remembers a dream. A fleeting haze of happiness that was more a feeling than a memory. Ines wished desperately for everything to stay exactly as it was, but the days went on, and slowly, just as sand disappears from a crack in a glass bottle, change came.

Chapter 20

Rene proposed to Ines on her twenty-eighth birthday. They were sitting in the sand on the bank of the stream where they'd first held hands several years before, panting after running through an afternoon rain. The rain was falling steadily, splashing into the stream as it passed them by. The trees above them rustled and blocked more raindrops from falling on them. It was there, as their chests heaved from running, laughing and feeling like children again, that Rene pulled out a ring from his pocket and asked Ines to marry him.

"You know I won't marry you for at least another year?" she asked over the tapping of the rain.

Rene laughed and shrugged, "I've waited this long," he told her.

Ines felt it was their mutual stubbornness that attracted them most to one another. While most other men would have given up long before then, and most women would have wanted to marry sooner, neither of them had given in.

"If you want to wait on the engage—"

"Yes," Ines said.

The same year they were engaged, the Castro brothers returned to Cuba. They wanted another chance at the Cuba they'd already failed to take. While the political unrest hadn't ended, Ines only became aware of it in glimpses. Her world had decreased in size as she gave the best parts of herself to the things that she cared about most. As they did almost every Sunday, Rene was over for dinner with Ines' family. They talked and laughed, passing food around the table as if they hadn't eaten at all that day. The house was filled with warmth.

"Not in the dining room," Papa said when he caught Aida feeding a piece of potato to Sombra, who had grown slow as he grew older, but no less hungry.

Ines laughed as Sombra stared at her father.

"How can you say no to that, Papa?" Aida asked.

"Very easily," Papa said.

As dinner was nearing its end, Ines announced that she had news to share with the family. As soon as she said the words her mouth felt as if it was filled with cotton.

"What kind of news?" Michel asked, looking at her as he wiped his mouth with a napkin, "because I have news too."

"You can go first," Ines told Michel, hoping her nerves would calm after he spoke.

Without protest, Michel announced, "I spoke to Javier earlier today."

Ines looked to her father, knowing his reaction to hearing Javier mentioned. As the years had gone by, Michel's friend had become more radical in his thinking, sharing information and philosophies with Michel that their father did not approve of.

"No politics on Sunday," her father said, taking a bite of the picadillo Mama had made. "Ines, what was your news?"

"Let him speak, Papa," Ines said, wanting to delay the inevitable announcement.

"As I was saying," Michel glanced at Papa, "the Castro brothers came back from Mexico. They tried to lead a coup against Batista and had dozens of men with them, but most of them were killed."

Johara, who sat next to Michel, took a bite of chicken fricassee and chewed. Ines watched her as she looked around the table with worry painted on her face as if she'd said the words herself.

"Oh, Michel, how are you hearing these things?" Mama asked, fear in her voice.

"Because he hangs around those no-good low-lifes who spout nonsense and then do nothing. Their minds are empty and their hands soft," Papa said.

Ines swallowed as her father straightened in his chair.

"It's important to know these things, Mama. Castro, his brother, and several of their commanders escaped into the mountains. They aren't finished." Michel turned to look at Papa, "I don't care what you say about my friends but know that change is coming whether we like it or not, and we need to be ready."

"Is this not exactly what they did before? This time they escaped to the mountains, but they will be back in prison or exiled again soon," Papa said.

As Michel and Papa began to argue back and forth, Ines felt her body go cold. A chill had entered the room and penetrated itself deep into her bones. Their voices became sounds that she could no longer understand. Ines knew in that moment that change was coming to Cuba and was certain it wouldn't be for the better. All of her nightmares had once again come back to her as she sat there at the table. She closed her eyes and saw fields stained in blood and buildings barred shut with their windows broken.

"Are you alright?" Rene asked Ines in a whisper and grabbed hold of her hand.

The warmth slowly returned to her body. The table had gone silent, the arguing stopped, and everyone was staring at Ines.

"You look as if you've seen a ghost," Michel said.

"Rene and I are engaged," Ines said.

At first, Ines wasn't aware that she'd spoken the words. It wasn't until the table came to life with celebration that Ines realized she'd said anything at all. Mama brought out the desserts from the kitchen while Papa opened what was, according to him, "a very old and very rare" bottle of wine.

"That's one way to end an argument," Michel said, before congratulating Rene with a slap on the back.

Ines once again felt as if she were in two places at once. Only Rene noticed that she wasn't herself, asking her several times what was wrong.

"I worked myself up dreading the announcement," she said while forcing a smile.

When the last echoes of dinner had faded away, and Rene had gone home, Ines was alone in her room with thoughts that kept her awake. They weren't the thoughts she'd had recently, excitement for her engagement or plans of the wedding; instead, her thoughts were of Cuba. She once again felt the strange, cold feeling she'd felt when her father and Michel were arguing. When she finally fell asleep, Ines dreamt of revolutionaries coming down from the mountains, like lava rushing down the sides of volcanoes, burning away the greens and browns of the countryside.

On Cuba's surface, nothing had changed after the Castro brothers returned, but deep down, everything had. It was as if termites had entered their island of trees. With the sugar industry not bringing the wealth it once had to Cuba, tourism, the American and European export, was more crucial than ever before. Ines knew La Sirena thrived because of the tourists who took her mother's designs back home with them, all around the world, while Rene and his father achieved their wealth by exporting cattle and other products to the Americas and other islands in the Caribbean. Cuba was a country of givers, sending so much from their island that eventually, there would not be enough left over for the Cuban people. That's what the revolutionaries believed. It was Cuba's reliance on foreign governments that the revolutionaries claimed had corrupted the politics of their country so profoundly. Ines didn't see the corruption no matter how hard she looked for it. She was a woman, a teacher, and an immigrant. She had no way of penetrating deeper into the island, to peel back all of the curtains and see what hid behind them. She saw the same buildings, statues, and trees that she had seen when she'd first arrived as a child. The beaches hadn't changed and neither had the birds, nor the sun, which was as bright orange as ever before.

As things continued to escalate in other parts of the island, life in Las Piedras continued on as usual. They were far away from most of the fighting, but could hear the occasional rumbles of gunfire, which sounded like thunder in the distance. Everything Ines and her family knew came from Michel, who claimed that attacks were becoming a daily thing the further he went towards the center of the island.

"I don't want you making your deliveries anymore," Mama begged Michel.

"You think the business can survive with only our one storefront here in Las Piedras?" Michel asked.

Papa agreed with Michel, but shared Mama's concern and decided any towns where violence was happening frequently would no longer receive deliveries of clothing.

"For all we know, we could be on the cusp of a third world war," Papa reminded them often.

While her father wasn't ignorant, his view of the world was limited to Cuba, and it did feel as though the world was crumbling around them. He was a man who prepared for the worst and hoped for the best, yet he usually kept his hope deep inside, especially as he grew older.

What began as small attacks that were only talked about in hushed whispers in homes and cafes started to become more violent and commonplace. Revolutionaries came to Cuba like flies to a carcass, or maybe, Ines thought, they came from the inside, there all along, hidden within their dying country, just waiting to be let out. When things began to escalate, it was difficult to be sure what was truth and what was fiction as rumors spread like a plague. While Castro was in the mountains, he and the survivors of his original campaign, as well as new converts, named themselves the 26th of July Movement. Although they didn't have many men, they used the hills and trees to hide and attack, making it impossible for government soldiers, who had them greatly outnumbered, to fight them head on. When the Presidential Palace in Havana was attacked, a real fear began to spread that the violence would reach them in Las Piedras.

Ines and her family continued to eat dinner together every night and as long as she and her siblings stayed in Las Piedras, Mama and Papa allowed them to leave the house to visit the park or the cinema. When Ines was with Concha and Isabella, they acted the same as always, but Ines could feel her own fear growing as it slowly went to once again consume her every waking moment. She wanted nothing more than for life to stay exactly as it was, but everywhere she looked she saw change. She saw things not how they were, but how she imagined they would become. Ines asked Rene often what he thought about everything that was happening, but he'd shrug and bring her thoughts to other things. He wasn't like everyone else, though, who ignored the news they were too afraid to face. He knew what was going on but did everything possible to enjoy the new reality they lived in.

"The people may be crazier, but the world is still the same," he would tell Ines.

Whether he knew it or not, if it hadn't been for Rene, Ines was sure she would have gone crazy herself in those early days of the revolution.

Ines would never forget the sound of her first explosion. It was a beautiful day in Havana and the streets were filled with people. The attacks had slowed in recent days, which had given many a sense that the violence was coming to an end. Rene wanted them to see a movie in the city, away from the watchful gaze of her family, who he was convinced made Ines even more afraid.

"You worry more when you're around your mother," Rene had said as he convinced her, "it'll be just one day. To forget everything. Nothing will happen."

They walked through the crowd towards the cinema where they were showing a film that had just been released. The movie theater in Las Piedras always played movies much later than when they were released in Havana, and the seats were lumpier and uncomfortable. On that day in particular, there was a line to enter the cinema in Havana. Ines and Rene had arrived a few minutes before the film began and were sure they would miss it if they had to wait out the line. They were deciding whether or not to leave when a man ran up to them with two tickets clutched in his hand.

"My girlfriend stood me up. Do you want them?" The man spoke in a strange staccato and was sweating profusely. Ines watched as his eyes darted from Rene's face to her own and before either of them could answer, he pressed the tickets into Rene's hand and ran off.

"That was strange," Ines said as she watched the man until he disappeared into an alley.

"He must've really liked the girl who stood him up," Rene said with a chuckle, "I guess we're staying then?"

Ines looked back to the line in front of the ticket office and nodded.

The movie was loud and filled with the sorts of sounds only possible in American movies. When the horses neighed, their cries filled the entire room, and Rene looked over to Ines, and whispered, "It's like the real thing."

Then, halfway through the movie, there was a sound that was different than the rest. It started as a low grumble as if a large truck was driving down the road. The room shook as well. Small dots of dust and dirt fell from the ceiling.

"An earthquake?" Ines asked Rene as the lights in the theater flickered to life and an attendant dressed in a red outfit rushed into the room. "There was a bombing not far from here!" he yelled and ran back out.

The theater came to life with movement and yelling. The sounds around the cinema became louder than the movie itself. Ines watched as a man in the row in front of them jumped over the legs of a woman who then screamed. The room went into an uproar as people began fighting each other to get to the exits as if a stampede of wild animals had been released.

"Let's go," Rene said and led Ines through an exit located behind the screen.

When they went through the door, daylight splashed across them. Ines looked into the sky and saw smoke rising not far from where they were. There was a bitter smell in the air.

"Take me home," Ines said. She could hardly get the words out.

They didn't speak on the drive back to Las Piedras. Each time Rene looked at Ines or tried to get her attention, she would look away at something out of the window. Silently she prayed and hoped that her family was safe. She looked out at the people in the streets of Havana who acted as if nothing at all had happened. Had they not seen or heard the explosion? Did they even know of the dangers that were so close by?

When she returned home, she ran around the house in a frantic search for her parents and siblings. They were all unaware that anything had happened.

"See why I tell you not to go to Havana?" Papa scolded her as he hugged her tightly.

"And you," Papa turned to look at Rene who had brought Ines inside, "how dare you put my daughter in danger. Go home. You've done enough for today."

Ines didn't look at Rene as he left and didn't call him until several days had passed.

The same night of the explosion, Abraham, his wife and Johara joined Ines and her family for dinner. Papa and Abraham's relationship had become more strained than ever before. Although they still worked together in La Sirena, it was the first time Abraham had been over in many months. Ines felt as if Abraham had become a stranger to her. She watched as he stared at Michel from where he sat next to Johara. Ines noticed the same look of hatred in his eyes that she'd seen so many years before on the day Michel had returned from the hospital after Bashir had died. Ines wasn't sure whether or not this was why he had grown so cold to them.

"The revolutionaries are saving this country," Abraham announced when the conversation at the table turned to politics.

"Ines was almost killed today in Havana," Papa told Abraham, "Can you guess who did it?"

Ines looked at her mother and Abraham's wife who both appeared to be holding their breath.

Don't poke a bull, Papa.

The argument that day ended with Abraham storming out, dragging his wife, and Johara behind him. After their guests left, Ines went to sit on the porch next to her father who was smoking a cigar. The wind gently rustled the palm fronds, which made a shifting sound like that of the maracas Ines had heard shaken in music clubs in Havana.

"Wouldn't it be better if people were like places and hardly changed?" her father asked.

Ines could smell the rum on her father's breath. She looked out at the courtyard, which seemed to have him transfixed.

"Is this how you felt in Lebanon?" Ines asked.

Her father turned his head to look at her.

"We aren't leaving Cuba," he said before looking back towards the courtyard and exhaling cigar smoke. "This land is the richest and most beautiful of all."

"But what if we need to leave?"

"No." He shook his head. "The problems that people bring will follow us anywhere we go. I'd rather face them here on this beautiful island."

Ines noticed her father's words beginning to slur.

"We left Lebanon to find more opportunities. Where can we find more opportunities than here? Look." Papa pointed up at the wooden carving hanging on the wall of La Sirena across the street. "Look at everything our family has built."

Ines looked around them. All she could see were things that people would want from them. Things that made her even more afraid.

<h1 align="center">Chapter 21</h1>

Ines hadn't visited Old Lady Nayibe in several months, the longest she'd gone without seeing her since living in Cuba and had heard from Mama that she was sick.

"What do you mean, sick? Why didn't you tell me sooner?" Ines asked her mother.

"She asked me not to," Mama replied, "You know how Nayibe is. She didn't want to worry you and ruin the excitement of your engagement."

Ines went to see Old Lady Nayibe immediately. There was no one to drive her, so she walked to her house, bringing with her a warm loaf of bread from the nearby bakery as she used to do as a child. The sky wasn't exceptionally beautiful, just a normal sky, but she remembered it perfectly. There was a long, wispy cloud that resembled the shape of Cuba. Ines wondered if that was how Cuba looked from above, in the eyes of God, surrounded by the deep, blue ocean.

When she arrived at La Casa de Nayibe, she noticed that the rose bushes looked wilder than she'd ever seen them before, and weeds erupted from the soil like hands reaching from their graves. Even stranger was that Nayibe wasn't on her porch, waiting for Ines as she always seemed to do. The porch was empty. Ines didn't knock when she entered through the front door.

"Nayibe, it's me," Ines called into the house.

From the moment she stepped inside, Ines knew that no one was in the house. It was empty, cold, as if all of the energy that once filled it had gone away. Ines opened every door and entered every room to be sure, but Nayibe wasn't home. She went back outside and walked around to Nayibe's garden. She didn't have to duck under the clothes hanger as there were no clothes drying. The small path of stones that led to the garden were overgrown with weeds like the grass in front of the house.

"Has it really been that long since I've been here?" Ines asked herself.

It had only been a few months, and she knew that weeds took time to grow. Maybe they were there the last time she'd visited, and she just hadn't noticed them? Rene was with her the last time. They came by to tell Nayibe that they'd been engaged.

"I could tell from your smiles," she'd told them.

As Ines entered the garden, she saw Nayibe sitting in the grass near the guava tree that still cast long, proud shadows along the rest of the garden. Nayibe's cane rested on her lap.

Without even turning to see who it was, Nayibe said, "Thank God you're here. I've been stuck sitting like this all morning. I couldn't get up."

Her words penetrated the iciness that had enveloped Ines' heart. They both laughed as Ines sat down next to her.

Ines tore off a chunk of the still-warm bread she'd brought with her and handed it to Nayibe. Ines was struck by how old Nayibe seemed. Her skin was papery and yellowed and her hand quivered as she reached for the bread. It seemed as if Nayibe had aged years in the months that Ines hadn't seen her.

"I'm an old woman, Ines. It's not your fault," Nayibe said as if reading her mind.

They sat and talked about everything except her illness. Nayibe never told Ines what it was, it was only later that she learned from her parents that Nayibe was dying from a disease of the liver, but there, in that moment, they spoke of happy things. She told Ines stories about Lebanon, all of which she'd heard before. Ines went inside several times and returned with water, fruit, and cheese as they ate and drank on the grass. The time went by so quickly that Ines wanted desperately for things to slow down, as they had when she rode horses with Rene, but time only seemed to go by faster as the sky darkened, and the afternoon turned to evening.

"I've been thinking a lot about this while I've been out here today," Nayibe began, "This guava tree, it has roots that go deep into the ground. To take it out, you need to dig and scrape then haul it somewhere else. It's not easy to uproot it," she said.

Ines looked at the guava tree, several of its fruit heavy and ripe, ready to be picked.

"I'm not like this tree. My body isn't stuck, fixed into the ground. When I die, I can be moved easily. Actually, then I'll be put back into the ground," she said with a laugh.

"Nayibe," Ines said, made uncomfortable by the thought.

Nayibe ignored Ines and continued, "But this tree, this tree will be here long after I'm gone. Even if no one cares for it and it dies, it will die standing, its roots still surrounded by earth."

Her eyes became unfocused as she spoke as if she were deep in thought.

"Let's not talk about those things," Ines told her, "You have so much time left. Here, let me make you dinner."

Nayibe refused, but Ines insisted.

"Okay, but only if you stay the night. I don't want you walking back home when it's dark."

Ines helped Nayibe to her feet and held her by the arm as they walked back inside.

"I need to use your telephone," Ines said as they entered the house, and she shut the door behind them.

With the money from her teaching, Ines had bought Nayibe a telephone the year before, but she had to beg her to use it and keep it plugged in. She and her mother would call Nayibe to gossip on the days they couldn't visit in person. Those calls were the only reason that Nayibe had agreed to keep the telephone. Ines called her mother and told her that she'd be staying with Nayibe that night. Afterwards, Ines and Nayibe cooked picadillo, the first Cuban dish Ines had ever tasted. Cooking was an unspoken language they shared. The house filled with the delicious smells of sizzling ground beef, spices, and peppers. Ines opened the doors and windows to allow the breeze to take the smoke out of the house, but the aroma of the food remained.

Ines went to her old room after they finished dinner. It was still the same as it had been when they'd stayed with Nayibe. Whenever Ines visited, she would look into her old room, convinced she could see the shadows of her younger self and Michel whispering to each other at night. It was the first time she would sleep in the room since they'd left, but it didn't feel strange to her. She knew she needed to stay there that night. Ines looked at the bed and part of her longed to go to sleep and wake up as a young girl again. Her eyes would open to a world where there were no explosions or gunfire ringing in the distance or nightmares of revolutionaries coming down the mountainsides.

She went and sat on the bed just as a tap came from the open door behind Ines. She turned to see Old Lady Nayibe standing in the door frame with a thick blanket draped over her shoulders. Ines got up from the bed and walked over to Nayibe. Her eyes looked tired but there was urgency when she spoke.

"I want you to live here when I'm gone," she told Ines.

"Stop saying such things," Ines said.

Nayibe hugged Ines with a strength Ines didn't realize the old woman still had, and felt like a child again in her arms, not wanting to ever let go.

When Ines woke up the next morning, she knew Nayibe had died. She wasn't sure if it had happened the night before or in the early hours of the morning, but when she stepped out of her bedroom, there was no doubt in her mind that she was the only living person in the house. Ines cried when she saw Nayibe. The old woman's face looked so at peace that Ines was sure her intuition was wrong, and that her friend was only in a deep sleep, but no matter how much Ines tried to wake her, Nayibe remained still. Ines felt as if she would be sick and ran from the room and outside to the garden. She breathed in the fresh air, clearing away her nausea and the stuffy air she felt constricting her inside the house. Ines looked at the guava tree then at the mountains in the distance and had the realization that Nayibe had died before she could see her home changed or taken away. This brought a serenity to the moment Ines had not asked for or expected.

After a few moments went by, she went back inside to call her mother, not looking at the room that housed her friend's body.

"Nayibe is gone," Ines said, her voice trembling as she spoke.

They buried her the next day. The heat was cruel in Cuba during summertime, which meant funerals needed to happen quickly. Most people had telephones in their homes, so they began spreading the word in town by calling the people who knew Nayibe and asking them if they knew anyone else who had known her. Ines had never heard of Nayibe having any family in Cuba, as she had lived a mostly reclusive life, so she was sure the list of people attending the funeral would be short, but the more people they called, including Doctor Karam, whom Ines hadn't spoken to in years, the longer the list became. Many shared memories with Ines of the fruit and vegetables they used to buy from her or remembered Nayibe as an amazing cook who had hosted wonderful get togethers many years before. It seemed Nayibe had lived multiple lifetimes before they'd met her.

When the funeral began, Ines was convinced there were more than one hundred people filling the chapel. Papa was set to be the only person to speak, recalling Nayibe's generosity as she welcomed them into her home and allowed them to stay with her when they'd first arrived from Lebanon. He read from a piece of paper and as his speech ended, Ines realized that if she didn't share her memories of Nayibe, she would regret it for the rest of her life. Mama's hand reached for Ines' as she stood up, but Ines ignored her and walked to the front of the chapel and began to speak without any idea what it was she was going to say. Her palms were sweaty, and her voice quivered when she began. All of the bodies in the pews seemed to disappear in front of her. As she spoke, she felt as if she'd gone to sleep and someone else was controlling her words. Ines saw Doctor Karam's mother, wiping her tears away as she listened. Many faces she didn't recognize looked back at Ines as if they'd known her, her entire life.

"Nayibe was my grandmother's best friend. When we arrived from Lebanon, we were told that my grandmother Aleia had died. These memories I'm sharing are for her as well, for Aleia and Nayibe, the two women I owe everything to."

When the ceremony ended and people started to leave, many approached Ines and shared their own fond memories of Nayibe. She thanked them as they left and was on her way to join Rene outside when a woman about her mother's age approached her.

"Ines?" the woman asked.

The voice was familiar. When Ines saw who it was, a woman with gray hair whom she didn't recognize, she nodded and tried to smile, but her face was tight with dried tears.

"I hear you're the one who put all of this together. Your words were beautiful. Thank you for all that you did for my aunt. I can tell how much you loved her."

"My family, and I did, yes. It's the least we could do. Nayibe was very important to us." Ines paused and looked at the woman. "Your aunt?"

The woman nodded and looked towards the coffin. Ines thought perhaps she was the niece of the person who built the coffin or who owned the flower company they'd hired.

"Nayibe," she said.

"Nayibe?" Ines asked, considering if it were some sort of mistake, sure that if Nayibe had family in Cuba, she would have told her. But her doubts left her when she listened intently to the woman's voice. The voice that came from the woman's mouth was one Ines felt didn't belong to her. She'd stolen the voice somehow. When the woman spoke, it was with Nayibe's voice.

Although they weren't alone in the chapel, she felt as if there was no one else in the room. People walked by them like flickering shadows.

"I came over a while after Nayibe first arrived." She looked once again at the casket and pushed back a strand of gray hair. "I haven't seen her in many years."

Ines studied her face to see if there were any traces of Nayibe's, but if there were any similarities, she didn't see them.

"My name's Maribel," she said.

"I don't remember you visiting when we lived with her," Ines said.

"It's not that simple," the woman with Nayibe's voice said.

Ines thought of the countless times she'd sat on the porch with Nayibe, drinking café con leche, eating fruit, and discussing whatever came to their minds. It was hard to believe that she never once mentioned family in Cuba. The only thing they never talked about in detail was how Nayibe's husband and daughter had died. Ines stared at the woman who called herself Maribel.

"Can we go somewhere quieter to talk?" Ines asked her.

Maribel agreed, and they walked out to the garden next to the chapel, on the opposite side from where everyone was exiting. They sat on a stone bench next to a bird bath that hung from an iron pole. Water sloshed softly as the wind moved the glass bowl back and forth on its chain.

"How did you hear about the funeral?" Ines asked when they sat down.

"I saw the news in the paper this morning," she said.

Michel had written an obituary for Nayibe and had given it to his friend in Havana who was an editor at one of the largest newspapers in Cuba. Normally the article wouldn't have been published so quickly, but Michel claimed that he owed him a favor.

Several guests had told them that it was because of the paper that they'd heard of Nayibe's passing.

Ines heard a loud boom in the distance and looked up to see storm clouds knotting in the sky above them. Her hand gripped at the iron arm of the bench. She remembered the explosion she'd heard in the cinema and her mind went wild with thoughts as she prepared her body to move, but no other sounds followed the first.

"I moved here when I was thirty and Nayibe had already lived in Cuba for several years," Maribel began, "I played with her daughter often when we were children…"

Maribel paused and stared at her hands.

"Did she tell you about my cousin? Abigail?" Maribel asked.

Ines nodded.

"But she never told me what happened to her," Ines said.

Maribel wiped away a tear from her cheek. Ines hadn't noticed that the woman had started to cry.

"Nayibe loved my cousin more than anything else and so did I, she was like a sister to me." Maribel paused as if searching for the words. "We would often get into trouble. One afternoon, we were playing in the barn behind Nayibe's house. My cousin and I loved to explore the barn and that day we closed all of the doors and shut the windows, so it would be as dark as possible, and used candles to light our way. As we played, Abigail's candle fell into a bale of hay. It lit immediately. The barn's walls were old and dusty, so the fire spread quickly. It felt as if only seconds had gone by before we were surrounded by flames and there was no way for us to get through."

Maribel looked at Ines again before continuing.

"We called for help until finally Nayibe's husband ran into the barn. It was full of smoke, and it was hard to see, but the next thing I knew, he lifted me into the air, carried me, and put me down in the grass outside of the barn. I saw him run back into the barn for my cousin, but he never came back out. When the rest of my family came, several minutes had gone by, and I was sitting there frozen, sobbing in the grass."

She didn't wipe the tears away as they flowed down her cheeks.

"I'm so sorry," Ines told her.

"I came to Cuba to ask for forgiveness from Nayibe, but every time I almost went to her home, my heart would freeze, and I decided it would be the next day. I've stayed in Cuba close to thirty years so I could one day be free of this guilt that has burdened me since I was a girl. Now she's no longer here to ask for forgiveness."

Maribel buried her head into her hands and began to sob. Ines hugged the woman she'd just met and held her close to her.

"Look at me," Maribel said between sobs, "I'm a grown woman crying in front of a stranger. I am so sorry."

"No, you are no stranger. Nayibe was like a grandmother to me. She was my best friend. I can tell you without any doubt that she forgives you," Ines whispered.

They sat there for a little while longer as Maribel's sobs came and went. When Maribel sat up and wiped her eyes with a handkerchief Ines had handed her, she looked down at her silver wristwatch.

"I have to leave," she said and stood up, "My husband and children are at home, and I didn't tell them where I was going. I'm so sorry about this, I don't know what came over me. I've never shared that memory with anyone since I came to Cuba all those years ago." As she got up to leave, Maribel turned to Ines and said, "Thank you."

She handed Ines a piece of paper and scribbled her name, telephone number, and address onto it.

"My husband's a powerful man, so if you ever need anything, anything at all, please don't hesitate to call."

A powerful man? Ines felt a strange weight to the words, as if something deeper was implied, but thanked the woman named Maribel all the same. Maribel hugged her goodbye as if saying farewell to an old friend before rushing back into the chapel.

Ines stayed outside for several minutes completely taken aback by everything Maribel had told her.

"Were you watching, Nayibe? Was what she said true?" Ines asked into the emptiness around her. The wind blew against her, ruffling her hair.

Rene ran up to her as she walked back inside the chapel.

"I've been looking everywhere for you," he said, his words thin and breathless, "We have to leave. They bombed the bridge and there are rumors of more attacks."

He didn't have to explain who "they" were, or which bridge he was talking about. It didn't matter. Ines knew the significance of his words: violence had found its way to their home.

"Where's everyone else?" Ines asked, thinking of her parents and siblings.

"They're fine, waiting for us. Come on. We're all going to the ranch. It's safer there," Rene said.

They rushed to the Jeep and sped off. Michel followed them with Aida, Mama, and Papa in his car.

As they drove, Ines kept looking out of the window at the long, black tail of smoke that snaked up into the sky. It reminded her of the smokestacks on the ship from when she was a child. This time instead of guiding her way, the smoke showed her what the world had become.

"Everyone's fine. I'm not sure how your brother knows these things, but he told us no one was hurt on the bridge. We're just being cautious," Rene told Ines. He looked at her as she sat silently while they drove. "It's okay," he repeated, "Everyone's okay."

Ines' face was pensive as she turned to look at Rene.

"Let's get married before the end of the year," Ines said.

Rene smiled wide.

"What brought that on?" he asked, looking at Ines then back at the road ahead, his smile never leaving his face.

Ines heard the words Maribel said echoing back to her. She didn't want to be like her, regretting decisions she'd made in the past.

"I'm not going to leave my life to fate," Ines said and looked back at her father's car, which followed them closely as they sped down the road. The smoke continued to rise in the distance and looked as if it were also following close behind.

Chapter 22

The bridge was repaired several months after the bombing and Michel was correct in that no one was killed. The damage hadn't been as bad as the attackers had hoped, but they had succeeded in instilling fear in Las Piedras. That damage, the fear of the world they all thought was safe, untouchable, wasn't as easily repaired. Ines visited the bridge once during the reconstruction and got as close as the government soldiers who had blocked off the area would allow her to. Even from a distance it was obvious where the bomb had exploded. Burn marks singed the surrounding stone and a huge chunk of the bridge was missing, including the side barrier where people would normally be standing with fishing lines cast out into the river. Ines remembered throwing rocks from the bridge as a child and had trouble imagining her own children doing the same. It was such a chaotic and violent world, and Ines wondered if it had always been that way. Had her parents worried about the same thing before Ines and her siblings had come into the world?

Rene had gone with Ines to see the bridge. As they looked at the damage, she squeezed his hand tightly. When he squeezed back, the fear left her, but only for a moment.

"Look at that," Rene said, pointing towards the river where chunks of debris stuck out of the river like teeth and caused water to swell and swirl around them.

The river filled with broken stones looked like a sign of what was to come. No one knew what came next, but Ines remembered her nightmares. Those visions of blood and destruction, the wild revolutionaries coming from the mountains, came into focus once again.

The same day that the bombs had gone off, miles of sugar crops had been burned not far from Las Piedras and a shootout between government soldiers and revolutionaries occurred in Havana. It seemed to Ines that the world as she knew it was disappearing around her. Many parents didn't want their students going to school, so her classes were canceled for several weeks after the bombing. This left Ines with even more time for her mind to wander and worry about everything that was happening. Michel shared news with the family, while Concha and Isabella, who also had their classes canceled, would tell Ines everything that they'd been hearing. Instead of eating together in the park, or walking through town, they saw each other in the safety of each other's homes.

"They burned some of my father's fields," Concha whispered to Ines and Isabella as they sat on Concha's veranda.

Concha looked at her housekeeper suspiciously as she brought out fruit for them to eat and waited for her to leave before continuing.

"Was anyone hurt? Ines asked.

"No one was burned or anything, if that's what you mean, but my father lost thousands. You should see him now. He looks like a ghost. White stubble all over his face, his eyes look so tired, and I think I even heard him crying one night in his study."

"Wow," Isabella said and looked at Ines as if asking whether or not her parents or Ines' would be next.

There was no one untouched by the revolution and it showed in the worried faces of everyone Ines saw walking the streets in Las Piedras. Every day it seemed there were fewer and fewer people outside as more news reports came in of the violence. The fear spread from household to household, and it wasn't just students not going to school. Many people refused to leave their homes altogether. More than half of the seamstresses at La Sirena refused to work in the weeks following the explosion. Some of them were afraid, but others protested the Cuban government, siding with the Castro brothers and their revolution, resulting in a strike that shut down the factory for several days. On the first morning of the strike, Ines was awakened by sounds coming from outside her window and looked out to see dozens of the seamstresses she'd known for much of her life crowding the street in front of La Sirena, raising signs above their heads and chanting. Her father went out into the street to calm them and get things back to normal, but nothing he did seemed to work.

"Our clothes are going to the people who are destroying our country," Ines heard one of the women yell at her father from the street.

Passersby had begun to gather as well, most likely amused by the drama. Ines watched as her father pushed past the small crowd in the street and walked into the factory. She prayed that the tide of women wouldn't crash against La Sirena and bring it crumbling down. As she watched familiar faces shouting and waving their fists, Ines felt as if the bombing of the bridge had shaken things loose that were once buried beneath the surface. Perhaps they had always felt that way. They must have. Ines felt the same strange fear she had as a child when watching her father from under the blanket in the back of his wagon as the man tapped the machete against his thigh. The women left after several hours of protesting, but Ines continued to look out of her bedroom window at La Sirena.

Things became disastrous when Papa learned it was Abraham who had organized the strike at the factory. It was no secret that Abraham sided with the revolutionaries, but no one could have guessed that he would go as far as to sabotage his own business. When Papa discovered this, he cut Abraham completely from La Sirena. This resulted in some of the worst fights Ines had seen in her own home, worrying at some points that Abraham, who was much larger than most men, would strike her father, seriously hurting him or worse. When he wasn't arguing with Abraham, Papa would argue even more with Michel, who tried to defend Abraham. Ines knew it was because of his relationship with Johara, but no one other than Ines was aware of their relationship, so she said nothing. The fighting in the house was deafening and mirrored the chaos of the world outside.

As a way to escape, Ines walked to La Casa de Nayibe often. Although it had been months since Nayibe had passed away, Ines was convinced she could sometimes feel her when she visited, especially when she sat by the guava tree in the garden. Ines kept up with the vegetables, fruits, and flowers doing everything as she was taught by Nayibe. A few days after her death, a lawyer had read Nayibe's will to Ines and her family, who were the only people named.

"There must be some mistake," Ines said when it was announced that La Casa de Nayibe, as well as the land where it stood, was left in its entirety to Ines.

While Nayibe had told Ines that she wanted her to have the house when she was gone, Ines hadn't realized something like that was possible. She left her jewelry and clothing to Mama and Papa, her book collection to Michel, and her paint supplies to Aida. To make the situation even more strange, Maribel wasn't present at the reading or included in the will. When Maribel had told Ines that she'd never gotten the courage to speak with Nayibe, Ines hadn't realized Nayibe hadn't even known she was in Cuba. This brought up even more questions that Ines wanted desperately to know the answers to.

Although the house was hers on paper, Ines didn't feel as if it truly belonged to her. It was the first house they'd lived in, in Cuba, but without Nayibe, being inside of it at times felt like a mausoleum. Ines did the chores around the house and property to feel close to her friend and to honor her wishes, but she would cry often when she walked through the empty house with all of its furniture exactly as it was while Nayibe was alive. Ines considered visiting Maribel and gifting her the house and the furniture inside, but she worried she'd take offense. The address Maribel had given Ines belonged to a residence in Havana, which completely wiped away any sort of courage Ines may have had. After the bombing near the cinema, Ines still had no intention of visiting the island's capital.

Ines was grateful when the school where she taught reopened but was surprised at the emptiness of her classroom. Out of the fifteen students normally present in class, only a handful of them were in their seats by the time classes began. Her parents urged her not to teach, reminding Ines that she wasn't in need of money.

"I don't teach so I can make money," Ines told them.

Even Rene, who was normally supportive of Ines and her teaching, asked her to stop for the time being.

"What if they target the schools?" her mother had said.

Even Michel agreed, adding, "They see us just as guilty as Batista himself."

The violence continued and began to escalate after the Presidential Elections in November. They huddled around the TV set in the living room, listening to the announcements as they were made in real time.

"The streets seem empty in Oriente and Las Villas today," the man on the TV announced, his voice sounding metallic through the speakers.

Many people were afraid to vote due to the threat of violence from the revolutionaries or even from the government itself. This was especially true of areas that were under rebel control. Papa and Michel had both voted that year, and surprisingly for the same candidate, Carlos Marquez Sterling. They had different reasons for doing so, which resulted in the usual arguments, but as it was announced that Sterling was leading in votes, their excitement was palpable.

"Now Cuba can have a chance at peace," Papa said.

Ines knew nothing of politics and neither did Rene. She was content to pray that whatever outcome was decided would be the best for Cuba. Her prayer was her vote, her way of giving something to their country's future. But as the results were announced, and Batista's choice of replacement, Andres Rivero Aguero, won, it was clear that the corruption the revolutionaries claimed to be fighting against had once again been more powerful than the Cuban people, and Ines realized her prayers were not enough.

"Disgusting," Papa said and shook his head the next morning. "This country will never grow into something better if we continue like this."

He smoked a cigar with a newspaper splayed out in front of him on the table. Michel was sitting next to him, also in shock. They'd just finished breakfast, but Papa had asked that they stay at the table to discuss the news as a family.

"When a wild beast is backed into a corner, it attacks. Who knows what the revolutionaries will do now? I don't want any of you leaving the house unless I approve. Is that understood?"

Papa looked at Ines and Aida.

"What about Michel?" Ines asked.

Her father didn't answer her question.

Once again Ines felt like her home had become a cell. She felt her being a woman had labeled her forever as a child, someone who needed to rely on others to survive.

The wedding was scheduled for the end of November, but due to more violence in Las Piedras after the election, a shooting near the square and another failed bombing on the same bridge that had been attacked before, they changed the date for December. Ines planned to have their wedding in the huge stone cathedral at the center of Las Piedras, sure that even the most radical revolutionaries wouldn't dare attack the house of God, but as the date drew closer, the head priest explained it would be impossible to be married inside the church itself.

"I'm sorry to say this, but it's still too dangerous. We want to keep our community safe and have decided against any large gatherings, including weddings, until things return to normal."

Rene and Ines were sitting in the priest's office, a holy place, but she could feel the bloodshed and corruption waiting for them just outside.

"Is there nothing we can do?" Ines asked.

The priest rubbed at his head, which was bald and reflected the lights in his office.

"Well, we could always have the ceremony in your home. In the eyes of God, you will be married, and that way we'll be sure that everyone in attendance will be safe."

Ines looked at Rene.

"Think about it tonight and come back tomorrow. There's no rush, we'll still be here in the morning."

"That's fine by me," Rene said to Ines later while they sat on a bench in the park outside of the church, "I'm happy as long as we're together. If you want to get married at home, let's do that."

Rene was always fine with everything, something that Ines both loved and disliked about him. She loved his reckless passion for life and ability to accept things as they were, but at times it felt as if she was the only one with a strong opinion.

"Are you sure?" Ines asked.

"Of course. Either way we'll be married. That's the whole point, isn't it?" he reassured her.

A green lizard scurried by her feet, and she pushed back the urge to chase after it. There she sat, in the same park she'd known most of her life, planning her wedding, and she was still the same little girl that she'd always been.

"Will we have it on the ranch?" Rene asked.

"Don't be silly," Ines said with a laugh, "do you really think my mother will let us have the ceremony anywhere other than her home?"

The next day, they went back to the priest with their decision, and he shared the dates he had available to perform the ceremony. There was only one date in December, and Ines had made up her mind that they would be married before the year ended, so they took it.

When they told Mama and Papa, Ines and Rene were sitting with them in the parlor. Mama exploded from her chair in excitement. Papa watched her, a thin smile on his face, as she paced around the room, listing all of the ways she would decorate the house and ensure everything was perfect for the ceremony.

"This shouldn't be much of a surprise," Papa said, "it's only been ten years."

"Let me enjoy this," Mama told him and continued to announce all of the things that needed to be done.

Aida heard the commotion and walked in with Sombra by her side. The dog had gone blind in one eye, which had turned a milky white. He walked over to Rene and began to lick his hands.

"What did I miss?" Aida asked and took a seat on the couch next to Ines.

"Your sister finally decided on the date for her wedding, and she's having it here," Mama told her.

"Congratulations!" Aida said.

She clapped her hands together then hugged Ines.

"When is it?" Aida asked.

"New Year's Eve," Rene said.

"That will be an amazing way to celebrate," Papa replied.

Ines told Michel later that night when he returned home from making deliveries. He looked exhausted; his eyes bloodshot with dark circles around them. With Abraham no longer working at La Sirena, Michel had begun to help Papa in the factory and still continued his deliveries. Aida had stepped in to help with customers in the store because Abraham no longer allowed Johara to come near their home or La Sirena. Michel's reaction to the news of her wedding wasn't what Ines had expected. His eyes were serious as he led her out to the garden. The moon was full, a pale white that illuminated the flowers around them.

"Ines, if I tell you something, do you promise not to tell anyone?" he asked.

Ines nodded and looked at her brother as she wondered what it was that he would tell her.

"Not a word to anyone, I promise. Now tell me," Ines said as her nerves began to bundle up inside her like a coiled snake.

Michel looked back towards the house and, convinced that no one was watching, whispered to Ines, "Johara and I are married."

Ines was speechless. The insects seemed to come to life all at once around them. A dog barked in the distance. There were no distant gunshots that night.

"Ines?" Michel asked and grabbed her by the shoulders, "not a word to anyone, right?"

"What do you mean married?" she whispered back.

"We married in secret," he said, "just the two of us and a few of our closest friends."

"And why would you go and do that? You didn't think Mama and Papa would eventually find out?"

Michel told Ines about Abraham and how involved he'd become with the revolutionaries. He explained that they'd left the home they rented from Papa and moved as far out of town as possible.

Michel had heard that Abraham was housing any wayward revolutionary who wandered down from the mountains in need of a safe place to stay.

"Please tell me you're not involved with them," Ines said.

"I'm not," he assured her, "but if Papa found out Johara and I are married, he'd disown me."

"Michel."

"You know I'm right," he said.

Ines didn't know what to think. Abraham had been her father's closest friend in Cuba until their falling out, and she didn't see hope of them reconciling, especially if he had become involved with the revolution.

"But how will you live together?" Ines asked Michel.

"One bridge at a time," Michel said.

Ines imagined the smoke rising from the destroyed bridge in Las Piedras.

"But for now, please don't say anything to anyone else. I had to tell someone, and you're the only person I can really trust. Even Mama may tell Papa if she feels guilty enough."

Ines saw her brother as a child again.

"I promise I won't," Ines swore to him.

Aida asked them where they'd gone when they returned inside. Ines only looked at her brother as he made up an elaborate lie about showing Ines a flower they'd planted as children that had grown exceptionally large.

Has he told me any lies just as easily?

Ines went upstairs to her bedroom and closed the door behind her as if shutting the door would protect the secret her brother had told her from the rest of their family. She felt sadness and fear for her brother. She'd always known how much he and Johara loved each other and could never imagine having to keep her own love for Rene a secret. Many girls, including Ines' friends, had fancied her brother, but for him, it was always Johara. Their bond only grew over the years, even as Cuba was torn in two and their own fathers chose opposing sides. A light rain began outside her window, which helped Ines fall asleep quickly. She dreamt of a white wedding dress and smoke.

Chapter 23

The day of their wedding was hectic and felt to Ines as if they'd thought of the idea the night before. Her mother ordered them around the home as if forgetting that it was Ines' wedding they were celebrating. They placed freshly cut flowers on tables, moved chairs, and prepared food. Ines had wanted to have the ceremony outside in the garden, but due to storms that were coming in, they decided it best to hold the ceremony indoors. They created an altar from a podium Papa kept in the factory and laid out a long, Lebanese rug down between the rows of chairs to serve as the aisle. Rene and Ines had been adamant about not having too large a crowd, but Mama hadn't listened, and the guest list increased daily.

"I don't think we need to invite Señora Ramirez. She didn't attend church on Easter Sunday, and I don't want the Father to feel uncomfortable," Mama announced as she went down the most up-to-date list of names she'd created several weeks before.

Rene and Ines only asked that their closest friends be in attendance, but everyone else on the list was up to Mama, Papa, and Rene's father, Domingo.

"And who are you bringing, Michel?" Mama asked one night over dinner.

Johara and her family were not invited to the wedding, and Ines didn't push the subject, knowing how easily Papa could lose his temper when it came to Abraham.

Michel shrugged.

"You really need to settle down, Michel, you can't keep this life of a bachelor forever, people will talk," Mama said.

While she meant well, Ines knew how painful those words must have been for Michel. The woman he was married to in secret wasn't allowed in their home. He was still expected to bring a date, so Ines asked Rene to ask one of his cousins if she would be willing to accompany Michel. Ines made it very clear that there was no chance of romance as Michel's heart belonged to someone else who wouldn't be able to attend.

"Who?" Rene asked as a sly smile played across his face.

Ines did her best to dance around the question, but her fiancé was quick, and she worried too much information would reveal Michel and Johara's secret.

While they prepared for guests, they could hear far off echoes of gunfire that sounded like the Chinese firecrackers Ines remembered from her childhood. The sounds didn't faze them anymore. They had become as common as a car driving by or the wind blowing through the fanned leaves of the palm trees outside. What did concern Ines and her family were the lights. Every few hours the lights would dim for a moment then come back as bright as before. They all looked around expectantly, as if their attention could keep the lights from going out completely.

Without looking away from the chandelier above them, Mama said, "People are getting ready for the festivities tonight. That's all."

Ines wasn't convinced and her stomach tightened each time the lights flickered.

By the time the wedding was set to begin, Ines was already exhausted. Guests had begun to arrive and fill their house with an excited energy that made it feel ready to burst at the seams. Ines was hidden in her father's study, hearing guests talking while the finishing touches were made to her dress. Mama had designed it herself, spending as much time sewing it as she had obsessing over the guest list. Aida, Concha, and Isabella were with them.

"Look," Mama said, turning Ines around so that her friends and sister could see.

"Beautiful," Aida said.

"You'll need to make my wedding dress," Concha said.

"You're already married," Isabella said.

"You never know," Concha said with a shrug.

Ines laughed.

"I love all of you," Ines said as she looked at her reflection in the long mirror in front of her. She was in the wedding dress of her dreams, but even then, her fears didn't leave her.

Ines could feel everyone's eyes on her even before she turned the corner and began walking down the aisle. The moment the music began, she grew hot, as if the guests' eyes had turned into one hundred small suns that penetrated through the wooden wall she stood behind. While she'd heard the same song at countless weddings as a child, that moment was the first time it filled her with fear. What if she fell? What if Rene ran? What if the gunfire came closer? Her father looped his arm through hers, and they began to walk together along the ornate carpet. The guests turned to look at Ines. They looked like seagulls as they twisted their necks to follow the slow procession. Their eyes were even hotter on her skin when she could actually see them, and Ines wanted nothing more than to become invisible.

As if on command, the chandelier and wall-sconces around them dimmed once again, but this time, they didn't come back to life. The music stopped on the down note and one gasp, made up of dozens of voices, was the only sound before a hush fell over the house and their guests. It was an overcast day, so only the dim glow of candles used for the ceremony illuminated the room. The priest looked to Ines and Papa, urging them to continue with a slight gesturing of his hand. One of their guests, Mama's friend Patricia, began to hum the bridal chorus, which helped keep their steps at the same tempo. More guests joined in, and they walked slowly down the aisle to where Rene was standing in his tuxedo, his hands wringing together in front of him.

Ines was married to Rene in her parents' home, to the sounds of humming and under the blanket of darkness. When the ceremony ended, everyone spoke and raised their glasses to toast the newlyweds. Domingo announced during his toast that his wedding gift was one of the houses on his property. He handed Rene a set of keys that opened a door she'd never seen before as Ines' friends and family clapped and cheered. Ines hadn't even considered where Rene would have wanted to live after they'd been married. She was so focused on getting married before things became even worse in Cuba that she assumed she and Rene would live in La Casa de Nayibe. Ines felt a wave of sadness and unease at the thought of leaving behind Nayibe, but she pushed the thoughts from her mind. That conversation would come later, and in that moment, Ines wanted to enjoy every moment of happiness that she could.

Once they'd eaten, their guests watched as a white town car pulled up in front of Mama and Papa's home and took Ines and Rene away to their honeymoon. They stayed in a hotel in a town several hours away from Las Piedras. A town where the violence still hadn't reached. It was close to the ocean, and they could hear the waves lapping against the rocks and sand from their hotel room. The night air was cool, so as soon as they checked in and left their things, they walked to the beach, not even bothering to change out of their clothes, at Rene's insistence. They walked hand in hand down the street towards the walkway that led to the beach, he in his tuxedo and Ines in the wedding dress her mother had made. Celebration echoed from inside the Spanish-style houses and hotels that stood like small mountains against the ocean.

"They must have heard we were married," Rene told Ines with a grin.

"In that case they would be in tears that I'm no longer available," Ines said.

They both laughed.

"What time is it?" Ines asked.

She knew their family and friends were probably back home celebrating both their marriage and the new year. Ines was grateful that they'd left and found time to be alone.

Rene pulled out a pocket watch.

"10:25 p.m.," he said and put the watch back into his jacket. "Plenty of day left."

"Does that thing even work?" Ines asked.

Rene shrugged then lifted Ines up into the air and carried her the rest of the way to the beach. There were many people out on the beach. Some were huddled around bonfires while others were readying fireworks to send off into the night sky once the new year came. Careful not to forget the direction of their hotel, Rene put Ines down in the sand as they found a more secluded part of the beach.

They stood at the edge of the ocean; the warm ocean water lapped at Ines' ankles. She looked at Rene's face as he looked out towards the dark horizon. It was a calm night, but Ines could feel the tide stronger than usual as it pulled at her. Water and sand moved back out to the Caribbean with each small wave. Rene held on to Ines' hand tightly as their feet sank deeper into the wet sand. Ines was sure the water would take her away if it wasn't for Rene holding on to her.

"Where should we live?" Ines asked him.

"Cuba, no?"

Ines laughed.

"Do you want to stay in Cuba forever?" Ines asked.

"Where else does the water show you so much of the blues and greens below?" Rene nodded towards the ocean that looked endless in the night.

"Well, of course Cuba, silly. What I meant was, where should we call home in Cuba? Your father's gift was so generous, but Nayibe left me her home."

Ines watched Rene, his jaw clenching and unclenching. Her stomach grumbled.

"I'll live wherever as long as we're together. My father can always rent out his house to someone else if that's your decision."

Ines jumped as a firework exploded above them. The red and green explosion of light reflected off the shimmering water surrounding them.

"Our own private fireworks," Rene said, smiling at her.

Without removing his tuxedo, Rene ran further into the ocean as water splashed madly around him.

"Come on in," he yelled before diving in under a crashing wave.

"I'll ruin my dress," Ines yelled back at him, but he was gone under the water.

She felt the same as she had when Rene had first taken her to ride horses on his ranch. Freedom was all Ines saw in the ocean in front of her as she splashed into the water and grabbed hold of Rene when he came up for air. As the fireworks burst around them that night, Ines had no way of knowing whether or not some of the sounds belonged to gunfire or violent, faraway explosions, but the fear didn't consume her as it normally did. For that night alone, the fear had left Ines. It was as if the world was preparing her for the new year that awaited them.

Chapter 24

There was a knock at their bedroom door before sunrise. Rene rolled over in bed next to Ines, one arm crossed over his face, but he was still fast asleep. She thought it must have been one of the hotel workers at the door, asking them if they would care for breakfast, so she ignored it at first, but the knocking continued.

"Someone's at the door," Ines said and shook her husband, who only mumbled and turned over on his side.

"Is this the rest of my life?" Ines asked and laughed quietly to herself.

She stood up and walked towards one of the large suitcases they'd brought with them and began to go through it.

"One moment," she called out.

Ines hadn't had a chance to hang anything the night before and although they'd only planned to stay there for three nights, they'd packed as if their honeymoon would last several weeks.

"Hurry up, Ines, open the door," said a voice she recognized immediately.

"Michel?" Ines asked through the door.

Only her mother, father, and Domingo had the address to their hotel. They were scheduled to be picked back up and taken to Las Piedras after three days and three nights. She gave up on looking for something to change into and walked towards the door in her nightgown.

She didn't remove the security chain and hid behind the door as she opened it.

"What are you doing here?" she whispered through the crack.

Ines was surprised to see Domingo standing next to Michel in the hallway.

"Tell my son to wake up," Domingo said, "we need to get back to Las Piedras."

"What do you mean?" Ines asked.

"There's a lot to explain," Michel said, "but it's not safe here. Hell, it may not be safe anywhere on this island anymore."

He looked down the hallway then back to Ines.

Rene joined Ines by the door, shirtless and rubbing his eyes.

"What's this?" he asked.

"Fidel claimed control of Cuba early this morning," Michel said, "nothing's happened yet, but there are rumors all over the street."

Ines felt as if the air had gotten thicker, and she couldn't breathe as easily as she could the night before. There was no way to know exactly what he meant, there hadn't been an election recently, but Ines knew in her heart that her vision had come true, and their island would soon be burning.

"Where are we going?" Ines asked but didn't unlatch the door as she ran over to her suitcase, this time picking out her clothes quickly and going to the bathroom to change.

"Are we going home?"

Ines pictured her mother's and father's house when she asked, but realized that she and Rene were married, so their home would be elsewhere.

La Casa de Nayibe. Ines shuddered.

She felt duty bound to live there, but the empty house scared her. Ines wasn't sure she could fill it with the same warmth she remembered as a child.

Once dressed, they followed Michel and Domingo back to Michel's car. Ines couldn't believe the things they told them as they drove back to Las Piedras.

How could it be that the government had just given up?

Ines looked out at the ocean where the water sparkled like gemstones in the early morning sun.

"Where did you hear all this from?" Rene asked.

"Friends," Michel said and looked back at Ines and Rene through the rearview mirror.

Ines felt something hollow making room inside her. The Spanish-style buildings, the palm trees, the countryside, the things she loved about Cuba looked different to her now. It was as if everything outside of the car had become dangerous.

The car ride wasn't long, but the orange sun was large in the sky by the time they were back in Las Piedras. It felt like the town hadn't slept through the night. More people than normal, even for New Year's Day, were out in the streets. Michel parked in front of their parents' home. Ines hurried inside through the courtyard with Michel while Domingo and Rene went to Domingo's car to get their gun belts and pistols and joined them a few minutes after. Mama was sitting next to Aida in the living room, her eyes glued to the television, while Papa had the radio on in his study, adamant that the radio would be the first with new information. Their entire morning was clouded with fear and confusion as they listened to any news that could illuminate what had happened. At her father's request, Michel and Rene made sure all of the doors were locked, and all of the blinds and curtains shuttered and drawn.

"As a precaution," Papa said.

He explained that he'd done the same at La Sirena that morning. The store and factory were already closed for the day due to the holiday, but he feared looting if things progressed.

Once the afternoon came, it was decided that they'd be going to Domingo's cattle ranch for safety. He had multiple houses on the property and some of them were vacant until the summer came, and he brought on more laborers.

"It will be safer to be in a larger group," Domingo insisted although Papa refused to go. He wouldn't leave his home, afraid that if he didn't keep an eye on La Sirena, the building would be gone by the day's end. Mama refused as well, not wanting to leave Papa behind and so did Bernita, who announced she would not leave the house so long as they were still living in it.

"You have to come," Ines told her parents frantically.

"We'll be fine, Ines," her mother reassured her, but Ines wasn't convinced.

Only at Rene's insistence did Ines finally agree to leave her parents in their home.

With just a few bags packed in a rush, Rene, Michel, Aida, and Ines went with Domingo to his ranch in two separate cars. Michel drove Ines, Aida, and Sombra, whom Aida wouldn't leave behind, while Rene rode with Domingo.

"That thing better not shed all over," Michel told Aida in a playful voice, but Aida's face, like Ines', was serious as she hugged Sombra who rested between Ines and Aida in the backseat.

The world had changed overnight. Everything was strange, as if they'd gone to sleep and awakened in another reality. Ines was now married, and the revolutionaries had taken control of their country. Ines prayed it was a dream, but as they drove through Las Piedras and passed by Fidel's supporters who had taken to the streets, chanting and cheering as they felt their fortunes shifting beneath their feet, Ines knew it wasn't a dream, but a nightmare.

The house they stayed in that night was a mile or so away from the house Domingo lived in with Rene's stepmother and younger sister. Even before Rene told Ines, she knew it was the home his father had gifted them at their wedding. There were three bedrooms and more than enough room for all of them. The house reminded Ines of Nayibe's, if slightly bigger. The radio was on constantly, spewing news updates that became more conflicting as the day wore on. The revolutionaries really had taken over their island, but no one knew what that truly meant. Ines thought of her parents and Bernita in the house across from La Sirena and she wished they were with them instead. She felt safer in the country, surrounded by miles of land all owned by Rene and his father. If the revolutionaries did come, they could see their fate before it was at their doorstep.

They only stayed in that home for three days and two nights, but it felt like much longer. Ines turned her head constantly to look out through the window in the direction of town, sure that at any moment she would see clouds of dust and caravans of military trucks driving towards them. But the only car she saw coming and going was Michel's, who seemed to be moving constantly.

"Careful you don't lead anyone back here," Rene told him.

"Where do you keep going, Michel?" Ines asked, but her brother wouldn't say a word.

On the second day when he returned, Johara was with him. They all ventured outside to greet her. It was the first time Ines had left the house, and she felt danger in every direction. Ines watched as Aida ran alongside Sombra in the fields and realized then how much she herself had changed.

Was the world always this dangerous, and I just hadn't noticed?

Ines wished she could run alongside her sister and forget her fear.

"Is this how you imagined our honeymoon?" Rene asked Ines, who tried to smile, but her mind was filled with other things.

The telephone conversations with her mother kept her informed of what was going on outside the safety of the ranch.

"There are people in the streets some nights, but nothing's changed," Mama said.

They spoke every morning and night, sharing news and rumors they heard from their friends and the media. There seemed to be a new update every minute, but most things in their world remained the same. Every time she closed her eyes, Ines was sure she would open them and see something else in Cuba had changed, but nothing did. The changes had been happening around them for years.

On the third day, it was clear that the dangers weren't as immediate as they'd feared, and Ines decided it was time to go home.

"Where exactly are we going after we drop off your sister?" Rene asked as he drove them back into Las Piedras.

Aida and Sombra were in the backseat, both resting their eyes. Ines knew he was asking whether or not she wanted to stay in the home Domingo had given them. They would be further out in the country and safer from the world around them.

"Nayibe's," Ines said.

Ines said the words with a certainty she didn't realize she had, but her mind was made up, they would live in Nayibe's old home. Rene nodded. Ines knew the concept was strange to both of them. They'd been robbed of the time necessary to get used to being married and becoming their own family.

It was dark by the time they dropped off Aida and left for Old Lady Nayibe's house. The drive to the house, which Ines had walked so many times, felt longer than before. She wouldn't be greeted by Nayibe when they arrived, the house wouldn't be filled with the sounds of her parents or other guests, it was her and Rene's house now. It was their turn to fill it. Ines felt the freedom she'd always wanted, and it overwhelmed her.

"Why are you crying?" Rene asked her.

Ines hadn't realized she'd been crying and didn't have an answer.

They drove up the road Ines' father had helped Nayibe expand several years before, so her neighbors' cars had an easier time making it up the hill. Rene's headlights cut through the dark as the Jeep bumped along the road that led up towards their new home. When Rene parked, Ines got out and dried her tears as she looked at La Casa de Nayibe as if seeing it for the first time. Rene stood beside her. The neighbors' lights, which had been on when they'd arrived, were turned off suddenly, so only the moon and the stars illuminated their surroundings. Ines looked at the rose bushes, the grass, the porch, all things that she'd grown up with and taken for granted. They were now completely under her care.

"Maybe the violence will finally end," Ines said.

Rene looked at her curiously as if wanting to ask a question.

"Maybe," he said.

For the first time since Ines had found out the house had been left to her, it felt like she belonged to it and it to her.

"Let's go inside," she told Rene.

Rene had the keys in his pocket, but he handed them to her as they reached the door.

"I think you should open it," he said.

Ines smiled and took the small key from him and guided it into the lock. With a twist and a push, they entered their home. Even as the world around them seemed unsteady and strange, they were a family now, and those walls of wood and stone granted them protection from the chaos that waited outside.

Chapter 25

Although the sun still rose every morning, casting its warmth across the island, it was as if a chill had fallen over Cuba. The island had belonged to Castro for only a few short years, but things were not as he said they would be, and the cracks were most visible from the inside. The hope Ines had that perhaps the revolution's violent tactics would end once Fidel and his men rose to power, that perhaps peace would finally come to the island after so much unrest, had all but disappeared. She watched in horror from her living room as live broadcasts showed the executions of hundreds of Batista's supporters and anyone else who stood against the revolution. Each time she watched the executions, Ines feared she would recognize the person being put to death while thousands of onlookers watched and chanted.

"Al paredon! Al paredon!" *To the wall! To the wall!*

The voices of the crowd came in through her television set like the voices of ghosts or demons. They haunted her. She could hear their hunger for blood and realized that perhaps she knew some of the people in those crowds. She imagined Abraham there, his arm raised, and his hand clenched into a fist as he shouted with the rest for blood to run down the wall. The thought made her angry as she stared at the television.

"Sharks. They're worse than sharks," Ines said.

When executions weren't being televised, Fidel would speak to his followers from La Plaza Civica, which Fidel had renamed La Plaza de la Revolución, in Havana. A sea of people stood in front of him, raising their hands to him in support.

"Turn that off," Rene said. "Who knows what it'll do to the baby," he told Ines, but she couldn't take her eyes from the screen or the bearded man who had changed everything.

She rubbed her hands along her pregnant belly and whispered, "You know I won't let anyone ever hurt you, don't you?"

Ines had become pregnant only a few months after she and Rene were married, but in her mind, she became pregnant only a few months after Fidel and his revolution rose to power. That was her new guidepost: Cuba before Fidel and Cuba after. Everyone she knew had been affected in one way or another. Ines was more afraid than ever to leave her home and would only do so to purchase groceries in Las Piedras, teach classes during the week, or visit her family in the home she'd grown up in, which she now urged them to leave and join her and Rene in La Casa de Nayibe, where she felt it was safer.

"No one will force us from our home," her father would say with a pride that scared Ines.

As Ines' belly grew larger, her fear seemed to grow in the same proportion. She refused to give birth in the hospital, afraid that her child would be taken from her, as some of the rumors explained could happen. So, when the day came, her mother and Bernita rushed over to La Casa de Nayibe along with Aida. Bernita had delivered several babies and although Ines was hesitant at first for Bernita to deliver her own child, she had grown to trust the old woman, who hadn't abandoned her parents like many other housekeepers, including Concha's, had abandoned the families they served.

"Señora Ines, please lie down." Bernita pointed to Ines' bed.

Ines still found it odd for Bernita to speak to her so respectfully.

When exactly had the world changed so much?

She did what her former housekeeper asked.

"We'll need a bucket of water, towels…" Ines stopped listening to Bernita's commands as Aida disappeared into the hallway to grab the necessary supplies.

"Did you know Bernita delivered all of her siblings?" Mama asked Ines as she handed her a cool glass of water.

Ines shook her head and realized there must have been so much about her childhood enemy she'd never known. Why hadn't she asked more about her in all those years of knowing her? Ines felt guilty, but before she could say anything to her mother or Bernita, the contractions became closer together and unbearably painful. She was in labor through the night and felt as if she'd entered a sort of trance. Her only clear memories were of Rene looking nervously into the room and quickly leaving when Bernita shooed him away. The pain was dizzying, and she squeezed her mother's and sister's hands tightly as she brought life into a world she feared.

One look at her son, and Ines decided on a different name than the one they'd chosen.

"We'll name him Rene," Ines whispered.

"What do you mean? Not Enrique?" Rene asked with a smile. He had been allowed to enter the room once the baby was born and wrapped in its blankets.

"Look at his forehead. It looks just like yours," Ines said.

Rene began to laugh harder than Ines had seen him laugh in many months, maybe years.

"You want to name our son after my forehead?"

"Strong and stubborn, just like your father," she told their son, whose name would be Rene from that day forward, but whom they would call Renecito.

The first to visit Renecito were Concha and Isabella. They arrived several minutes before Papa and Domingo, who were also on their way to meet their new grandson.

"He's perfect," Concha said as she lifted Renecito up gently and inspected him.

"He does look just like Rene," she said after Ines told them the name she'd chosen.

"He has your eyes, though," Isabella said.

It was true. Her son's eyes were a light blue, like a calm ocean. That's how her own eyes had been described to her, but she saw them differently when she looked into the mirror. They were more a gray blue, like the ocean just before sunrise. Ines wanted to know all of the things Renecito's eyes would see in his life and protect him from anything that could bring him pain. Ines noticed that her mother became tense when Concha and Isabella raised Renecito into the air, as if she were getting ready to catch him. Ines understood how she felt. She wanted nothing more than to shut all of the doors, bar them with wooden planks, and spend the rest of her days with just Rene and Renecito, locked away, safe from the world outside. At times, Ines feared that the walls would no longer be strong enough to keep the outside world away.

As another year went by, Renecito grew, and Ines saw even more changes come to Cuba. Now when she went to the market, there was only one grocery store she was allowed to purchase food from, and as luck would have it, the store was owned by one of their new neighbors, Señor and Señora Espinoza. Government officials had given her a small booklet containing slips of paper that could be used weekly in exchange for food. It was never enough. Hunger touched many homes, including her own. Both Ines and Rene heard of people buying more ration slips on the black market or even stealing them, just to get enough milk or bread for their families. They were lucky that on weeks when they needed more to eat, they could rely on the vegetables they grew in their backyard, or sometimes on the Espinozas, who would give them an extra bag of grain or bottle of milk.

"Your son will need this to keep growing big and strong," Señora Espinoza whispered to Ines, encouraging her to take the extra rations she handed her from behind the counter.

While at one point her days in Cuba had been filled with adventure, Ines now spent most of her days at home, but those days with her son were the most magical of all. Rene went to the cattle ranch or helped his father at the bank, but always came home in time for them to eat dinner as a family. Ines would usually use one of Nayibe's old recipes. She no longer taught her students and would only go to the park or into Las Piedras with her son if the news from the television seemed relatively calm. Most of her days were spent watching the television as Renecito sat calmly on her lap, hardly making a sound. When it was pretty outside, she would sit with her son near the guava tree as they both looked at it in wonder.

"It's beautiful, isn't it?" Ines asked Renecito as they looked up at the tree, and the distant mountains that framed it.

While her son still couldn't speak, she knew he agreed.

When visitors came, they were always surprised at how quiet and aware he was.

"Does he never cry?" Concha asked.

Concha and Isabella visited often, bringing their own children with them. Concha's son was older than Renecito, but when he was a toddler, he would scream as if he were being attacked by spirits. A stark contrast to Renecito.

"He really doesn't," Ines said. "Well, there is one thing."

Ines looked at Concha and Isabella with a sly smile on her face and got up to change the dial on the television set. When Fidel's face, with his long, bushy beard came onto the screen, Renecito began to cry uncontrollably. Several years later, when Renecito began to speak, he would refer to the bearded man as, "El Monstro," and run from the room in fear. Ines made sure he knew not to refer to him in that way in public, but this was all the indication she needed to know that her own instincts were correct to not trust the man who had won over the hearts of thousands. But while entertaining, this too scared Ines, who was sure that if someone heard Renecito's reaction, they would be reported to the government for being traitors and maybe end up on the television themselves.

Ines often forgot that not everyone was a supporter of the revolution, and she never knew whom to trust. This made her increasingly paranoid. She didn't completely trust her neighbors, even though they'd become friends. Many people Ines knew had accepted the changes blindly, unwilling to consider that perhaps the revolution did not have everyone's best wishes at heart. Ines kept her own dissent buried, afraid that if anyone found out, something terrible would happen to her family. She wondered how many others were the same as her. Still, Ines heard stories and rumors of other people in Cuba who rejected the new reality forced upon them and had plans to change things.

Ines found out by chance that Michel and Papa were part of the uprising against the revolution's regime. It was a Tuesday, and she'd stopped by the factory to visit her father at La Sirena before visiting her mother across the street in her old home.

"He's out to lunch," called one of the seamstresses who saw Ines standing in the office.

Ines thanked her with a wave and decided that she'd wait for him to come back.

"He's always gone when we visit now," Ines said to Renecito.

Her father was the only person running the factory at the time, but without the American tourists purchasing clothing in Cuba, business was much slower, and he could manage.

She helped Renecito down from his stroller, and he began to explore the office. Ines was grateful for the fan that spun above their heads.

"Bread," Renecito said.

"Let's get you some fruit instead," Ines said and walked over to the cooler her father kept under his desk. Renecito followed behind her.

Ines lifted the lid to find bananas and an ice-cold pitcher of water. The bananas were in the back of the cooler, so she had to kneel down to reach them, and that's when she saw it. Under the desk, taped against the wood, was a small, golden key. She didn't think anything of it and ripped two bananas from their stem.

"Bananas," she said in an excited voice.

"Look!" Renecito said from where he was squatting down next to Ines, "a key."

"It is a key," Ines said.

She sliced the banana and served it to Renecito, who sat back down in his stroller as he ate his snack.

Ines noticed a green, metal chest in the corner of the room that she'd never seen before. It had a lock on it. She wasn't sure how she wouldn't have noticed it in the past if the chest had been there before.

"I shouldn't, should I?" Ines asked Renecito.

His mouth was full of banana, but he nodded as he smiled at her, Rene's smile, and Ines couldn't help but smile in return.

"Good enough for me," she said.

Ines peered through the window at the seamstresses, who all seemed too busy sewing to pay her any attention. She moved quickly, sure that at any moment her father would come in through the door and find her going through his things. She removed the key, careful not to rip the tape. It was as if she were a young girl again, about to jump down the stairs with nothing but an umbrella. She knelt down in front of the metal chest and unlocked it. Her stomach filled with butterflies as she lifted the lid. She wasn't sure what she'd expected to find, but she hadn't expected the plain, men's clothes that were stacked neatly in the crate. All of the colors were dark green or brown. There was something else that was odd about the clothing, but she couldn't put her finger on it. It was then that she heard voices, and the door to the office began to open, and she knew her father had returned. Moving quickly, Ines locked the crate and ran over to kneel next to Renecito, dropping the key onto the floor with a clatter that she prayed her father hadn't heard.

"Oh, Ines," Papa said with genuine surprise in his voice as he stepped into his office.

There was a man with him that Ines didn't recognize. He wore a beret and smelled sour.

"You remember Miguel, don't you?"

Ines didn't. She was sure she would have remembered the man whose suspicious eyes seemed to move around constantly in his head.

"I don't think so. It's a pleasure," Ines said.

"Señora," Miguel said with a nod, tipping his beret slightly.

"How's my grandson?" Papa asked and walked over to Renecito.

"I found a key," Renecito told his grandfather.

"What's that?" Papa asked.

"He found this key on the floor. I'm not sure what it belongs to."

Ines wasn't sure why she lied, but she could feel the man's eyes on her as she handed her father the key that she'd picked up from the floor next to the stroller after placing it there only moments before. She watched her father's eyes closely, sure he looked in the direction of the crate.

"We were just stopping by to see everyone," Ines said as she stood up and walked around to the back of Renecito's stroller. "Is Aida next door?"

Her father shook his head.

"She's probably out painting somewhere. That sister of yours is more stubborn than you were, Ines," Papa said, "I can't get her to stay inside if I chain the doors shut."

"She always was," Ines said, forcing a laugh, "I'll stop by the house then. Say bye to abuelo."

"Bye, abuelo," Renecito said.

Ines said goodbye to her father, and the odd man he had brought with him.

As Ines pushed Renecito's stroller along the aisles of the factory—she wouldn't let him walk near the whirring machines—she asked one of the seamstresses, Marta, whom she had known since she was a child, if they'd been working on any new projects.

"Just the one," Marta said and held up a pair of pants that lay on the table next to her sewing machine.

Ines felt her heart pulse in her chest. The pants were the same simple design and dark green color of the clothes from the locked crate.

"Men's clothes," Marta said, "your father gave us the designs a few weeks ago. What do you think?"

"They look great," Ines said.

Marta tickled Renecito's feet before getting back to work, and Ines was left with even more questions than she'd had before.

Later that afternoon, when Rene returned home, Ines made up an excuse for them to visit her parents' house the next day.

"I think it'd be good for Renecito if we spent more time with them."

"We're over there at least once a week," Rene said.

"I'll call my mother now and let her know we're coming," Ines insisted, before Rene could reply.

All of her thoughts revolved around the clothing. When she took a shower that night and removed her own dress, which was one of her mother's designs from La Sirena, her hand scratched against the tag sewn into the fabric. That was when she realized what had struck her as strange about the clothing: there were no tags on any of them. The mermaid logo the seamstresses stitched into all of La Sirena's clothing was nowhere to be seen.

When they went to her parents' house the next day, the sky was overcast with a promise of rain. Renecito grabbed at the air above him that swirled in through the Jeep's open roof as they drove. When they pulled up to the street in front of her parents' home, Rene helped Renecito down from the Jeep. Ines and Rene each held one of Renecito's hands as he walked and jumped between them.

"Good morning!" Aida called out to them from where she sat in the courtyard.

She had a pad of paper in her lap and a pen in her right hand.

"Papa told me you're not working at the store anymore?" Ines asked.

"I can't stay cooped up in there," she said with a smile. "How's my nephew?"

She set down her paper and pen and lifted Renecito into the air.

"You're getting so big," she said.

When Ines was around Aida, she realized how much they'd both changed since they were young girls. Aida was now studying at the university, philosophy and other things, using her spare time to paint and draw as if her life depended on it. Ines wanted to urge her sister to work at La Sirena, where it was safer and where she would be helping their family, but she didn't say a word. It scared her at times how much she reminded herself of her mother.

When they went inside, Mama was in the kitchen preparing lunch as Bernita helped her.

"You're early," Mama said, walking over to them and kissing Renecito on the forehead.

"Where's Papa?" Ines asked.

"Where do you think?" she said and nodded towards his study. "He has guests, but I think he'll be finished soon. By the way, Michel will be here in a little while. He's running late with a delivery. Your father wanted me to tell you," Mama said as she went back to the stove.

Michel's marriage to Johara was still a secret to everyone but Ines. She was sure that during some part of that delivery, Michel would be visiting his wife, whom he still lived apart from. As Rene took Renecito outside to play in the garden, she watched them from a window, unable to imagine a life where their love had to be hidden away from the people they cared about most. She encouraged her brother, and even Johara, to say something to her parents, but they were afraid of the repercussions. Abraham and Papa still hadn't spoken since their argument. At times Ines wondered if their stubbornness meant that Michel and Johara's love was deeper, more powerful, than hers and Rene's, but that didn't matter to her. She couldn't imagine her life without the family she'd chosen and created.

When Michel arrived an hour or so later, he looked disheveled, and Ines noticed a tear in his white linen shirt. When he saw Ines looking at him, Michel tucked his shirt into his pants, hiding the rip in his shirt before walking towards her. Before Ines could say anything to him, two men in wrinkled suits walked out of their father's study. The men walked with their backs straight like palm trees, their arms moving at their sides at an even pace. Ines had seen the walk hundreds of times since the troubles began. It was the walk of a soldier.

"Who are they?" Ines whispered to Michel as their shoes tapped against the floor.

Michel shook his head. The men didn't even look in their direction.

"You know something. They're soldiers, aren't they? Why are they wearing suits?" Ines asked.

Michel shook his head again and shot Ines a glance that begged her to stop speaking.

"Michel, you—"

"Even if I knew something, I can't tell you," he said.

Ines looked around them and spoke so softly she could hardly hear herself. "You trust me with your own secret, don't you?"

Michel's face went red. Ines felt guilty after she'd said the words.

"I should never have told you."

"Told her what?" Rene asked as he walked up to them with Renecito in his arms.

Renecito's clothes were stained with dirt.

"Someone got messy," Michel said with a laugh. "Hello young, man."

Michel reached his hand out to Renecito for a handshake but was met with a small fist slamming softly into his palm.

"He got a little carried away playing outside in the garden. I swear he's faster than me," Rene said. "What were you guys talking about?"

Ines saw the gears in her brother's head turning.

"Come on, let's get you cleaned up for lunch," Ines said, taking Renecito from Rene.

Ines heard her father join them once she closed the door to the bathroom.

Their lunch that day was exactly how she remembered their family gatherings were before the world had gone upside down. They laughed and joked as if everything was normal, and maybe it was, maybe that was just the new normal that they would eventually grow used to. In that moment, Ines truly believed it. Sunlight came in through their dining room windows and her body felt warm and good. Ines forgot all about Fidel, the killings, the men in Papa's study; in that moment, her heart only had space for the warmth she felt with her family. Her mind let go of the uniforms she'd seen locked away in the crate, or the way Michel had arrived at their parents' house that afternoon. She wanted so badly for that moment, there with her family, to last forever, but like all things, the afternoon came to an end, and as they said their goodbyes, there was no way of knowing it would be the last time they would all be together for many long, difficult months.

Chapter 26

Papa and Michel were arrested two weeks after their lunch. It was in the middle of the night and Mama could hardly speak when she called to tell Ines, sharing little details of what had happened. Ines and Rene rushed over to her parents' home to find Mama sitting in the living room, in tears and making little sense, while Aida and Bernita were doing everything they could to calm her.

"What happened?" Ines asked Aida, who was busy fanning Mama.

Bernita took Renecito, who moved in and out of sleep, from Ines and walked off into another room.

Aida motioned towards the dining room, and they walked over while Rene stayed with Mama who didn't move from where she sat. Her back was hunched, defeated.

"They came at midnight. I was half-asleep and didn't see much. They were gone before I could get dressed and come down. I found Mama on the floor crying and yelling out at the open door."

They watched their mother as they spoke.

"I've never seen her like this, Ines," Aida told Ines.

Ines had. Twice. Once when she'd told her mother that Michel had fallen into the ocean, and the other when they walked between the rows of bodies in the cold room in the hospital. She said none of these things to her sister.

"Have we found anything else out? Why were they taken?" Ines asked.

The air became heavy when she spoke that last word.

Taken. The word carried a weight to it only someone living in Castro's Cuba could understand. It was the new boogeyman. People whispered about being taken as they looked around the room to ensure no one had heard. When someone was taken, it was expected that they would never be seen again until they were executed in the town square or locked away in prison without a fair trial. The thought of someone she cared about being taken kept Ines up at night, but she never truly believed it could actually happen. Especially not to Michel and Papa who were both such kind and honest men, but Ines was realizing that Cuba was no longer a country for kind and honest men.

Aida shook her head. "Nothing."

Ines looked out through the large dining room windows. The factory seemed dead without her father nearby. As she stared at the building, the pieces of a large puzzle tumbled down and came together in her mind, and she answered her own question. *The metal crate.*

"We have to do something," Ines said.

"What can we do?" Aida asked, "she's calmer now than she was earlier, so I don't know—"

"No, not for Mama. For Michel and Papa. Follow me," Ines said.

Ines told Rene that they would return soon, but to stay with Mama and Renecito, who had both fallen asleep. At first, he protested, but reluctantly agreed when he saw the determination in her eyes.

"Don't worry, we'll be back soon," Ines told Bernita who was sitting on a kitchen chair with Renecito sleeping in her lap.

Bernita nodded.

Ines ran her hand through her son's hair before leading Aida outside through the courtyard. The bubbling of the fountain brought back memories of Papa on the porch, frozen in time in the Cuba of her childhood. It took everything inside her to keep from crying. The street in front of La Sirena was so quiet it felt as if no one had ever stepped foot across it. Most people were inside once the sun had set. Aida and Ines must have looked like two ghosts walking across the empty street, Ines in the light pink dress she'd thrown on, and Aida in white.

"It looks different, doesn't it?" Aida asked her as she paused in the street to look up at the image of the mermaid.

Ines walked back to where her sister was standing and looked at the wooden mermaid who had once been so beautiful. It did look different. Ines had once been convinced that the mermaid looked exactly like her, but now it looked decrepit, as if it had aged badly in the years since Fidel had taken Cuba. The wood had been beaten by weather, the colors dull, as if at any moment the sign would fall free from its bearings onto the ground below in an explosion of dust.

Everything they'd been through, the life they'd created, would soon be nothing but dust carried away by the Caribbean breeze.

"Come on," Ines said and grabbed Aida's hand.

The front door to the factory was locked shut with chains and a padlock that Ines knew wouldn't open with her spare key. She tried the lock just in case but had assumed correctly.

"They must have locked the factory after arresting Papa and Michel," Ines said.

They walked around to the back entrance that led to Papa's office, but it was locked as well. Ines's stomach tightened, and she could see the town square so clearly, the far wall filled with bullet holes, and the ground stained with the faintest rust-colored stains. The night air was cool, but she was sweating.

"I have an idea," Aida said.

It was her turn to lead Ines. They walked towards the storefront, which by some miracle hadn't been locked with chains. They used the spare key and turned it, both of them smiling when they heard the distinct click. The door creaked open as they entered, as if warning them away. Ines imagined a sleeping soldier, left behind to guard the building, which should still have belonged to them, awoken from his slumber. He would rush over, his rifle pointed at their chests, and force them to the ground until he could clamp metal around their wrists. But nothing happened. There was no guard, just rows and rows of clothing, some hanging from racks, others folded, in tiny stacks of fabric. The thought occurred to Ines that it was likely no one would ever wear those clothes, and if they did, they would probably be the wives of soldiers or other revolution officials who would claim them as their own. They didn't turn on any lights, but the lamps from the street made it easy enough to see. Aida went behind the register and moved a rack of clothes that hid an old, wooden door that led between the factory and the storefront. It was the only door left as it was before their father had begun to remodel the buildings. Ines had forgotten all about it, and the soldiers hadn't found it.

"I knew it," Aida said.

They opened the door. It creaked angrily at them as they stepped inside the factory. It was as if a bomb had gone off. Clothes were thrown along the floor, bins were overturned, and damaged sewing machines lay on their sides.

"Wow… how can they do this? They've destroyed everything," Aida said as she righted a sewing machine.

Ines never thought she'd see the business her parents had poured everything into the way it was that night. But in that moment, her purpose guided her.

"Follow me. It should be in here," Ines said.

"What exactly are we even doing here?" Aida finally asked as they walked towards Papa's office.

Ines couldn't bring herself to say the words aloud. If she said them, then there would be no way to deny them. *"Our brother and father are criminals."*

When they entered their father's office, it was in shambles. Cabinets were turned over, drawers were pulled out, and papers were spread all over the floor. Ines went to where she'd seen the green crate the week before, but even after they searched under the broken cabinets and boxes, it was nowhere to be seen. The thought sank in that if they'd found the metal crate, they could have forced open the lock, or have several men carry it out with them, but she still wanted to find the key. Ines got on her hands and knees and began to look under the broken things.

"What are you looking for?" Aida asked.

"Hold on," Ines said.

She made her way to the desk where the key had been hidden before. It hadn't been flipped over like the others. Ines looked underneath the desk and felt a wave of relief when she saw the key taped as it had been a few days before.

She searched the room once more, but still couldn't find the crate.

"Can you please tell me what you're looking for?" Aida asked, growing frustrated.

"A green crate."

"Is it metal?"

Ines nodded.

"You should've said so sooner. There are a few of those in the store. Mama kept them in the same room she kept all of the discontinued designs."

Ines felt as if a sheet of cold water had splashed across her face.

Mama is involved?

They hurried back into the store but were blinded by headlights. A large truck rumbled by on the otherwise quiet street in front of La Sirena, filling the shop with light that made the clothes look like hanging bodies. Ines shivered as she imagined the scuffing sound the first soldier would make as he jumped from the truck and his boots scraped across the pavement. She could hear that sound so clearly. Ines looked at Aida who stared at her blankly, the breath held in her lungs. Just as her insides felt as if they would finally burst, the truck continued past their store, and the headlights disappeared as quickly as they'd come. Ines opened her eyes, not realizing she'd closed them.

"We have to be quick," she told Aida, wiping sweat from her forehead.

"Why didn't they search through here like they did in the factory?" Aida asked.

"I don't know," Ines said, "but if anything, it most likely means they'll be back soon. We need to be gone by then."

They rushed to the storeroom and entered an even smaller room where their mother kept discarded fabrics. The metal crates were hidden beneath several bolts of fabric and a mannequin that had lost an arm years before. The key Papa had hidden under his desk opened all three crates, and the locks tumbled to the ground one by one. The crates were filled with the same green and brown uniforms Ines had seen before.

"What are these?" Aida asked Ines as she held a long-sleeved shirt in front of her.

"They're uniforms for soldiers." Ines spoke the words aloud for the first time.

"But the revolution, they—"

"Not for Fidel's revolution," Ines said.

Aida looked at Ines with the same mixture of shock and understanding that Ines herself felt.

"We'll need to get rid of the clothes," Ines said.

She didn't feel fear in that moment. Her determination to help her family had filled her with a courage she'd all but forgotten she had.

"How?" Aida asked and put the shirt back into the crate.

The crate was too heavy for just the two of them to move, but Ines had an idea.

"We need to take the clothes out of the crates, and I'll need a car," Ines said.

"*We'll* need a car," Aida said, "I'm coming with you."

She snapped her fingers together and walked behind the counter next to the register.

"Papa kept a spare key somewhere in the store," Aida said as she searched through the drawers.

"Here it is," she said when she eventually found it taped to the top of one of the drawers, "you'd think Papa would've been more creative in how he hid things."

They both laughed for a moment, and the sound was strange to them in the empty store.

"I can do this alone from here," Ines assured her sister.

"But you don't have to," Aida said and began taking the clothes out of the metal crate and piling them onto the floor beside it.

Ines knew that there was no use arguing with Aida when her sister had put her mind to something.

"Okay," she said, "give me the key. I'll meet you out front."

Ines took the key and ran back to their parents' house, holding her dress at the hems as she ran. She felt relief when she saw the cars parked where they normally were. Ines entered one of them, her heart leaping from her chest when the motor roared to life after she inserted and twisted the key. She used all of the memories she had of Michel's driving lessons to bring the car around to the front of La Sirena where Aida was ducking down near the front door.

"You know anyone can see you standing there like that," Ines said as she got out of the car and opened the trunk.

"I feel like a spy, like one of those movies you like to watch," Aida said.

Ines smiled at her sister as they loaded the car with the clothing and left without another word. Ines immediately regretted not having Aida drive. Her hands were slick with sweat, making it hard to keep hold of the steering wheel unless she squeezed down as hard as she could. She hadn't driven a car since marrying Rene and it showed, but Aida didn't say anything about her driving, and Ines acted as confident as she could. Apart from the car and its rumbling engine, the streets remained empty and quiet.

"Do you think Papa and Michel will be okay?" Aida asked.

"Yes," Ines lied.

From that point on, Ines had no way of knowing what would happen and as they left town, she could only see the faintest traces of the Cuba she'd once known. They only had a few hours of darkness left once they arrived at La Casa de Nayibe, but their eyes adjusted slowly as the headlights went dark. The house that had once belonged to Nayibe looked like it had been waiting for them through the night. Ines looked at the neighbors' houses. They all had their lights off and no sounds came from them.

"Take these to the backyard," Ines whispered to Aida, grabbing an armful of the soldier's uniforms and walking to the back of the house.

They moved slowly as the ground was muddy from three days of consecutive rain. It took them several trips each to empty the car and used only the moonlight and stars to help them see.

"Now what?" Aida asked as they stood in the backyard with the pile of uniforms in front of them.

The night air blew softly against Ines and brought with it a dampness that she knew meant more rain. Ines looked at the guava tree as if it were speaking to her. She grabbed a shovel and began to dig a hole at the base of the tree. They took turns digging and hardly spoke to each other, but Ines could hear voices in the wind as she could as a child. She heard her grandmother Aleia's voice and also heard Nayibe. After hearing them, she couldn't remember what they said, but they gave her strength all the same. Ines blew at her hair, which kept falling into her eyes. When they finished, both Ines and Aida were dripping with sweat.

"Let's bury them," Ines said and began dropping the piles of clothing into the hole.

When they finished, they made the ground look as smooth as possible, but it was still obvious that something had been buried. Ines had been adding more vegetables to the garden, so the fresh earth didn't look out of place in the backyard, but just in case, Aida helped her bring over a bench and placed it down on top of their hiding place at the base of the guava tree. The darkness under the bench hid their work well. As they left, Ines glanced at her neighbors' windows, sure some of the blinds had moved since they'd arrived, but it could have been her imagination, and she was too exhausted to worry. Aida drove them back as Ines slept in the passenger seat.

"We're here," Aida said, nudging Ines awake.

Ines woke up with a start, not having remembered falling asleep. Had it all been a dream?

"And so are they," Aida said and pointed.

Two government cars were parked in front of La Sirena and a soldier stood in front of the factory door while another stood in front of the door that led into the store. It was raining now, so the glare from the streetlights made the soldiers look like twin shadows against the walls. There were probably more soldiers inside, continuing their search for evidence to use against Papa and Michel. Aida parked the car farther up the road and turned off the engine.

"Ready?" Ines asked her.

The rain soaked both Ines and her sister's clothing completely as they walked silently along the sidewalk and in through the courtyard. Ines watched the soldiers closely the entire way, afraid of one of them yelling out at them, "Hey, miss!" or something similar, but the soldiers didn't seem to notice them. Rene was asleep in the living room with Renecito on his lap and Mama slept in her chair nearby. Only Bernita was awake. She walked over to them without making a sound and helped them both change out of their dirty clothing and, as if knowing what they'd done, began washing the mud-stained clothes immediately.

"You should get some rest," Ines told Bernita, who she was sure hadn't slept at all that night.

"Don't be silly," Bernita said.

Ines changed into spare clothes she kept upstairs and joined Bernita in the kitchen where she continued to scrub away at her and Aida's soiled clothes. Ines felt a twinge of guilt as she watched the old woman. When her mother had first called to tell her that her father and brother had been taken away, she thought maybe it was Bernita who had been the one to report them.

I'm sorry.

She had misjudged her childhood enemy for so long.

Ines and Aida didn't want to wake anyone from where they slept in the living room, so they brought down blankets and joined them. Rene woke up for a moment, but Ines kissed him and told him to keep sleeping. Like they did sometimes as children, Ines and Aida placed their blankets at the center of the living room and lay down next to each other. Aida fell asleep quickly, but Ines was no longer tired. She wondered where her father and brother were sleeping. Were they separated from each other? Did they even have blankets where they were? Ines stared up at the Spanish-style ceiling above them and pictured the room where her father and brother were being kept. In her mind it was gray and cold and large centipedes crawled across the floor. Then, only for a moment, Ines thought of the town square and the firing squads, but quickly thought of other things. There was no way to tell how long she stayed awake with her mind turning like the ocean during a violent storm. She listened to the sound of rain falling softly outside and thought she could make out the soldiers' voices between the droplets. There was no way to be sure if she'd heard anything at all. Eventually, her eyes grew tired, and she was aware only that somewhere in Cuba, Fidel was sleeping peacefully in his bed.

Chapter 27

The day after Michel and Papa were taken away, Ines realized she was pregnant with their second child. She rushed to the bathroom soon after waking up and without time to close the door behind her, became sick multiple times. She felt a jolt inside her that radiated out as if trying to escape, and she knew instantly what it was, having felt that sensation only once before.

"How many days has this been going on?" Bernita whispered as she walked into the bathroom behind Ines and rested a hand on her back.

Ines was convinced that Bernita never slept.

"All week," she told her.

"You're with child?" Bernita asked.

Ines paused and looked at Bernita as if the answer would come to her from somewhere in the wrinkles on her face.

"I think so," Ines said finally, admitting it to herself for the first time since the morning sickness had begun.

Ines wiped her face and mouth with the back of her hand and realized she was sweating profusely.

"You need to rest," Bernita said.

"Please don't tell anyone," Ines said.

Bernita looked at Ines with a serious expression then shook her head.

"I won't. I'll watch after Renecito. If anyone asks, you're feeling a bit sick this morning from all of the excitement last night."

For all Ines knew, Bernita's lie was the truth, she was just worked up from the night before. She'd never been sick in the mornings when she was pregnant with Renecito, but she rested that day, in her old room, while the house buzzed with activity. Rene checked on her in the morning after he'd woken up. He didn't seem to believe she was just exhausted, unaware of what she and Aida had done the night before, but he didn't press the question and let Ines rest. She spent the day in bed, her mind going to her father and brother constantly as she watched from the window as the soldiers continued their search of La Sirena. They brought out files, loose papers, and even some bolts of fabric.

"They won't be bringing out any metal crates," Ines whispered as if someone could overhear her through the glass windowpane.

They stayed in her parents' house for the rest of the week, and the soldiers didn't return after the second day. A group of the bearded soldiers had entered her parents' home once they'd finished with La Sirena, going through her father's study as if it belonged to them, but after a few hours, they left. Before the sun rose every morning, Rene would go pick up his father, and they would drive out to gather information about Michel and Papa's arrests. Ines stayed with

Renecito, Aida, and her mother in her childhood home. At first, Mama wouldn't eat anything that Ines or Aida put in front of her and hardly spoke a word, only asking every so often if they'd heard anything new.

"Rene went to go find out more information," Ines said, but the words didn't seem to reach her mother.

When their mother did eat, she'd nibble on her food like an injured animal, and then push it aside with most of it untouched.

"Should we call the doctor?" Aida asked Ines one afternoon as they brought their mother's unfinished lunch into the kitchen.

"He can't cure this with medicine," Ines said.

They waited several days, hoping information would be their salvation, but they didn't learn anything. Rene and Domingo exhausted all of their contacts, some of them holding government positions, and although it was clear that Michel and Papa were suspected of treason against the revolution, they couldn't provide any other information.

"It's important you tell us anything you know," Domingo told Ines and Aida one afternoon.

Neither of them spoke of the metal crates or the uniforms they'd found inside.

After several days had gone by, Concha and Isabella visited, having heard the rumors in town. Ines made them all tilo tea, and they sat in the backyard, away from any wandering eyes or ears. They sat on wicker chairs near the garden.

"I can't believe you didn't tell us," Concha said.

"How's your mother?" Isabella asked.

"She's doing as well as can be expected," Ines told them.

Her mother still hadn't left her room since disappearing into it once the soldiers had gone. Ines looked up at the window into her parents' bedroom, but the curtains were drawn.

Birds chirped around them. It was a beautiful day to go to the beach or the park. They should have been there, talking while their children played together, running between the trees and along the sand. The thoughts felt strange to Ines as they spoke about her father and brother's arrests. They were thoughts for another reality.

"Good afternoon!" Concha said with a wave.

Ines turned to see Aida walking towards them with Johara by her side. Ines hadn't seen her secret sister-in-law in several weeks.

"I thought she wasn't allowed here?" Isabella whispered to Ines.

Ines greeted Johara, knowing in her heart how much pain she had to be hiding under the surface.

"Can I speak with you?" Johara asked Ines. Her eyes were red, and the skin around them inflamed.

Ines nodded.

"Aida, can you entertain Concha and Isabella for a few minutes?" Ines asked.

"She can try," Concha said with a laugh.

Johara and Ines walked towards the opposite side of the garden, where the flowers were in full bloom and gave off a colorful glow as the sun reflected off of the damp leaves.

"You know Michel and I are married?" Johara asked.

Ines was surprised by the question and looked behind her shoulder to see her sister and friends in the same place they were before.

"Yes," Ines said, lowering her voice.

Johara looked so much older than the last time Ines had seen her. Strands of gray mixed in with the beautiful blonde hair that she had admired as a girl.

"We can't let them rot in there," she said as her façade broke and tears began to stream down her face.

"I know," Ines said, moving towards Johara and hugging her.

Ines looked over to her friends and saw that they were now glancing in their direction.

"Does your father know?" Ines asked.

"That we're married? Of course not," Johara said, pushing away from Ines, "After what happened between our fathers, I can't even mention any of you around him. He thought of you as a second daughter, especially after Bashir—"

Her words caught in her throat.

"Can he help us?"

Both of them were surprised by Ines' question.

"Who?" Johara asked.

"Your father, can he help us get Papa and Michel released?"

"We both know how our fathers feel about each other now. Why would he?" Johara said.

"If he knows you and Michel are married, he may consider it. We're family now, after all," Ines said.

Johara was unconvinced and shook her head.

"He's a different person than you remember," she told Ines. "Maybe he'll even have you arrested for going there."

Ines felt sick at the thought that the man she'd seen as an uncle would do such a thing, but Johara was right, she wasn't sure who he was now. Ines didn't let Johara see her doubts.

"But is freeing your husband, my brother, not worth trying?" Ines asked.

Johara looked at Ines as if she'd said something she couldn't understand.

Finally, she said, "We'll see."

They went to visit Abraham the next day. Johara and her mother lived with Abraham in a small house far from town. It was as if he wanted to get as far away from Papa as possible, without leaving Las Piedras altogether. Rene drove Ines and Aida, who had insisted to come with them.

"I want to help Papa and Michel too," Aida had told Ines.

Sunlight reflected off of droplets of rain that rolled down the windshield as they drove. The humidity caused clouds of steam to form along the road. Ines tried to imagine how Abraham would look, and the words he would say when he saw her and Aida for the first time in many months. Nothing came to mind, though. All memories of the man she'd considered family had skewed and changed so much that even in her mind she could no longer recognize him.

When they arrived, Johara and her mother were sitting on the porch.

"It's so great to see you!" Johara's mother said, although her voice sounded strained.

"Come on, he's inside," Johara said.

The house was brighter than Ines had imagined. Vibrant colors and furniture made it seem as if they'd stepped into some sort of coastal museum instead of a house. Abraham was sitting on a beautiful orange couch that seemed out of place under his large frame. The television set in front of him was tuned-in to a live broadcast of Fidel speaking to his supporters in Havana.

"You both look well," Abraham said to Ines and Aida as they stepped inside.

He didn't invite them to sit down and instead stood up. He looked over at Rene for a moment and nodded. "Congratulations on your marriage," he added.

Though his words were kind, his voice was serious and unfriendly.

"Thank you," Ines said.

For all of the color and light in the room, the air was heavy.

"Would you like anything to eat? Drink?" Abraham's wife asked.

"They won't be staying long," Abraham said.

Ines could feel Rene tensing up next to her and begged him with her thoughts not to lose his temper. They were there for her family.

"So, what's this all about? All Johara said was that you both needed to speak with me."

Ines described what had happened to Michel and Papa. She described her mother's state and the lack of information they'd been able to receive.

"Serves them right. I knew they were opposed to the revolution, but I never thought them foolish enough to try a coup or whatever it is they did," Abraham said.

Ines was about to say something, defending her father and brother's innocence, but Johara interrupted her, "How could you say that?"

Abraham's demeanor changed, and he no longer tried to conceal his anger.

"Why do you care so much, Johara?" Abraham asked. "Don't tell me you have feelings for that boy?"

"We're married," Johara said and with a pause added, "and I'm pregnant."

A silence fell over the room.

Ines was as surprised as everyone else. It was as if the words had come out of her own mouth instead. *Both of us are pregnant.* She wanted to run to Johara and hug her tightly, but she stayed where she was and looked at Abraham whose face had turned red and trembled slightly.

"Out," he said and pointed at the door.

"Abraham, wait—" his wife said.

"Out of my house now! I won't have a daughter who lies and sneaks around with the son of my enemy. Worse, an enemy of our country! Get out before I make you leave. Get out. All of you," Abraham boomed.

Ines watched Abraham as they drove away. He stood on his porch with his arms crossed. She knew then that Johara had been right and regretted that she'd convinced her to reach out to Abraham for help. It wasn't just the revolution that had forced him and her family apart. His change had been gradual, and Ines couldn't believe she hadn't seen it sooner. His large figure became smaller and smaller as Rene drove them silently toward the main road. Johara sat in the back of the Jeep with Aida and looked as if she was doing everything she could not to cry.

"So, I have another sister now," Aida said with a lightness in her voice, "and another niece or nephew."

Ines turned and looked at her sister and Johara.

"That's right. We're family now."

"I hadn't even thought of that," Johara said. "I guess I have two sisters now."

"And the baby," Aida said with a smile.

"We just need to get Michel and your father back," Johara said, "you're my family now."

Ines reached back and squeezed Johara's hand. She thought of Renecito never seeing his grandfather or uncle again or the unborn children inside her and Johara never knowing them at all.

"What do we do now?" Aida asked.

No one spoke for a few minutes as the grumble of the engine lulled them into a contemplative silence. Rene was the first to speak.

"I have an idea," he said and looked at Johara through the rearview mirror. "Do you know how to contact Michel's friend from Havana?"

"Javier?" Johara asked.

"The one who wanted to argue about politics. We saw him play in Havana," Rene said.

"Yes, Javier. Umm… No, I don't think so. I don't remember Michel having spoken to him for quite some time," Johara said.

The car was silent as if all of the air had escaped through the open windows.

"I saw him recently," Aida said.

She rolled a fold in her dress between her fingers.

"What do you mean?" Ines asked, turning to look at her sister.

"I went off with some friends to Havana a few weeks ago," she said, looking down at her hands. "We wanted to sketch the scenes along the Malecon, capture the waves and sounds of people walking by in our drawings. While we were sitting, I remembered Michel's friend Javier and told my friends about him. We went to see if he was still playing, and he was."

Ines didn't say a word as a mixture of fear and anger danced inside her. While she herself had made her fair share of trips to Havana that her parents would have never allowed, there wasn't so much danger in the world then.

I'm becoming Mama. Ines looked at Aida who was no longer a child. She then looked out at the countryside. On the surface, the mountains, fields, and forests were as beautiful as the day they'd first arrived, but she wondered if even the island itself had changed while she hadn't noticed.

"Well, if everyone agrees, I can drive us to Havana, and we can check to see if he's at the club today," Rene said.

The thought of Havana reminded Ines of Maribel. She still had the piece of paper she'd given her at the funeral and had been carrying it around with her ever since. Ines reached her hand into her purse and felt around for the piece of paper. With everything going on, she'd completely forgotten about Nayibe's niece. *What had she said about her husband? He was a powerful man?* Ines continued to rummage around in her purse until she found the piece of paper Maribel had given her. Her address was scribbled in black. *Havana, Cuba* followed a street name Ines didn't recognize. While Maribel's telephone number was also scribbled there, Ines knew she needed to visit Nayibe's niece in person.

"Ines?" Rene asked.

"Let's go to Havana," she said.

Although Ines hadn't returned since the explosion, Havana was still the same as she remembered. There were fewer tourists than before, but the streets were still filled with people and music. Several buildings were boarded up while others had been replaced with stores or restaurants with new names, but the feeling was the same. The city still felt alive. Ines wanted to believe that nothing had changed after all, but she knew that hidden just beneath the painted walls and busy streets, the cracks were there. Her father and brother being locked away in some jail cell was a constant reminder that made it impossible to forget the new reality. Ines smelled fresh garlic and grilling meats as they walked along the busy sidewalks and wondered how the four of them looked. Rene held her hand tightly as if afraid she would take off running into the crowd, or maybe he feared soldiers would grab her and pull her away from him while he could do nothing but stand and watch. Johara moved as gracefully as she had when they were children, but she seemed more tired than Ines remembered. Aida, on the other hand, looked as if she was filled with energy as she took in all of the sights and sounds that surrounded them.

"I love Havana," she said, smiling, but her expression changed when she looked at Ines and remembered why they were there.

Ines looked at the address on the piece of paper.

"I'd like to stop here along the way," Ines told Rene and showed him the address.

"What is this?" he asked her.

Ines explained the note.

"And you want to go there now?" he asked.

"I do. Maybe her husband can help us somehow," Ines said, newly aware of a sureness in her voice.

Rene searched her face but said nothing.

When they arrived at the address, Rene, Aida, and Johara waited for her by the street while she knocked on the door. A woman, who wasn't Maribel, answered.

"Can I help you?" she asked, not opening the door completely.

"Good afternoon. I'm looking for Maribel, does she live here?" Ines asked.

The old woman looked past Ines to where Ines' family waited. Gray hair fell onto the woman's shoulder from a loose bun.

"Are you friends with Maribel and her husband?" the woman asked as she pushed back her thin strands of hair.

"Yes," Ines said after a slight pause.

"Then I can't help you. They don't live here anymore," she said and began closing the door.

Ines heard fear in the woman's voice, which caught her off guard, but she wasn't discouraged. She reached out and grabbed the door before it closed completely.

"Please," Ines said, "do they live close by? I was friends with Maribel's late-aunt Nayibe. She was like family to me. I just want to speak with Maribel, that's all."

The woman looked at Ines through the crack in the door before opening it again.

"Do you have a pen?" she asked.

Ines nodded and reached into her purse. The old woman told Ines the address quickly while she wrote it down.

Once she was done, the old woman grabbed Ines' arm and whispered, "If you don't know, Maribel's husband is with the revolution. A commander," and then looked behind Ines once again before adding, "Now please, leave me alone, and don't come here again," she said and closed the door.

When Ines returned to the group, she shared the new address, but didn't mention the warning she'd been given about Maribel's husband.

"I've heard of that neighborhood. Isn't that one of the ones *he* took for his men?" Aida asked.

They did their best not to say Fidel's name in public and referred to him as "he" so as to not alert any curious ears.

"Who is this woman again?" Johara asked.

Ines ignored them both.

"It should only be ten or so minutes up the road. I know it's getting late, so I'll go there while you three go to Javier's club. I'll meet you there afterwards," she told them.

Rene excused himself from Johara and Aida then pulled Ines away with him.

"What's going on?" he asked.

Ines knew if she told him that Maribel's husband may be one of Fidel's commanders, he would do everything he could to keep her from going.

"I'd like to see Maribel again, that's all. It's been several years since the funeral," Ines said.

"Is that really a priority? We came here to see if Javier could help us free your father and brother and then you brought up this address out of nowhere. Now there's a new address? I need to know what's going on."

Rene looked so afraid in that moment that Ines wanted to hug him tightly and tell him everything, but she knew he would stop her.

"You have to trust me, Rene," Ines said.

He did trust her, like he always had, and so she went to the house of Maribel and the commander alone, with no idea what to expect. She walked through the neighborhood that she'd hurriedly written down. The houses weren't houses at all but mansions. They seemed larger than Concha's house and were untouched from the scars of revolution. But around the mansions, walking or standing guard, were soldiers. There were soldiers everywhere.

"Barbudos," Ines said under her breath.

Bearded revolutionaries who had fought for Castro in the mountains were all around her. As she approached the address and walked towards the gate, Ines saw several soldiers standing guard along the front of Maribel's mansion. If Rene had been there with her, he would have forced her to keep walking, but he wasn't, and she was drawn to that house as if something was physically pulling her towards it. At first her heart sped up when she saw the soldiers, their rifles slung around their shoulders, but a calm came over her. She felt as if she wasn't alone, as though the spirits of her grandmother and Nayibe were there with her.

"Excuse me," Ines said to the closest guard, waving through the large, wrought-iron gate that made the walls around Mama and Papa's house feel small and useless.

The bearded man didn't move at first but looked her up and down.

"Do you have business here?" he called over.

The guard was young, probably not even in his twenties. Ines was sure it had taken him many months to get his beard to the length it was.

Ines checked the address on her paper once more to be sure.

"I'm here to see Maribel. I'm a friend of hers," she told the soldier as he walked towards her.

Ines looked at the rifle by his side which he'd grabbed hold of as he walked. She wondered if he was steadying it or if he was getting ready to use it.

"Oye, Raul, there's a lady at the gate that says she's here to see Señora Maribel," the young guard yelled over his shoulder.

"Who is she?" the man named Raul yelled back.

Ines couldn't see the man named Raul from where he was standing and realized there must have been even more guards around the mansion.

"Sorry, what was your name?" the young guard asked her.

He sounded like a child as he spoke, and Ines wondered how many years older he was than Renecito.

"Ines Di— Ines Aude."

Ines realized then that Maribel would only know her by her maiden name, if she remembered her at all.

"Ines Aude," the young soldier yelled over his shoulder once again. "Just wait right here," he said to her and walked back to where he was standing before.

Ines waited several minutes, grateful that the day was overcast and not too intensely hot. Finally, Maribel came towards the gate, an older guard walking beside her.

"It is you!" she said as soon as she saw Ines.

Maribel whisked Ines in through the heavy gate, which took two guards to push open.

She led Ines around to the back of her house where they were greeted by the most beautiful garden Ines had ever seen. It looked like heaven on Earth. Children played in a large pool nearby, being watched closely by a woman Ines assumed was one of their housekeepers.

"My children," Maribel said, noticing her gaze, "come, sit with me."

They sat down on a bench that reminded Ines of evenings watching the lightning bugs illuminating Mama and Papa's garden. Ines felt as if she were looking off at a long stretch of countryside as she took in the beauty of the property.

"Your home is beautiful," Ines told her.

"Oh, I'm so glad you're here. I'd been wanting you to visit since the funeral. We only moved here recently." A shadow passed across her face, only for a moment, before she was smiling once again. "How did you find us here?"

Ines told Maribel about the old woman, but didn't mention that Rene, Johara, and Aida were with her. She worried she would say something about the revolutionaries that would offend her, or worse, so when they first sat down, Ines spoke as little as possible. Luckily, Maribel did most of the talking. When the older woman spoke, Ines felt as if she was listening to Nayibe. She had forgotten how similar her voice was to Nayibe's and had to remind herself she wasn't a child sitting with Nayibe out on her porch. Ines felt chills crawl across her skin even as the sun warmed her. They spoke of Lebanon and reminisced on what little Ines remembered. Maribel told Ines of her children and when Ines mentioned that she used to be a teacher, she asked for advice for her youngest son, who was having trouble with his reading. When Maribel mentioned her husband, her tone changed. She explained that he was a good man who believed in a Cuba free of corruption, but it felt as if she were trying to convince herself of that fact. Maribel went on to tell Ines that her husband still didn't know her reason for initially coming to Cuba or that Nayibe even existed. Ines didn't find this as strange as when Maribel had told her the same at the funeral as she herself had begun keeping her own secrets, after all.

"How's your family?" Maribel asked.

"That's actually what I came here to talk to you about," Ines said.

Maribel looked at Ines curiously. Ines looked around them.

"Soldiers came in the night and took them away. It's been over a week, and they haven't been returned to us," Ines said.

"How could that be? I saw your father speak at the funeral. He seemed like such a kind, gentle person."

Ines felt the urge to cry again as she remembered her father.

"Has anyone told you anything? Have you found anything out?" Maribel asked.

"Nothing," Ines said and looked down at her feet.

"Horrible." Ines looked up to see Maribel shaking her head. "There's so much confusion going on that it's become hard to tell who the real criminals are anymore." Maribel sat up and patted down her dress before sitting back down. "You were like family to Nayibe, like a daughter. You were there for her when I could not be. No matter what you need, I will help you," she told Ines.

Ines was surprised by how easily she agreed. It was as if she'd been waiting years for that very moment.

"Here comes my husband," she said with a wave.

Ines looked in the direction of the mansion. A tall man walked towards them with two soldiers walking behind him on either side. The man wore a uniform the color of dark green palm fronds, the same that Fidel wore during his speeches on the television. Every part of Ines wanted to scream or run, but she didn't do anything. Every step Maribel's husband made felt longer than the one before until finally he was standing only a few feet away.

"Martin, this is Ines Aude. She's a childhood friend," Maribel said.

Ines was surprised by how easily Maribel said those words.

"Good afternoon," he said nodding towards Ines, "it's a pleasure."

Ines tried to force a smile, but without a mirror, it was impossible to know how she really looked, so she gave up and nodded in return.

"The pleasure is mine," Ines said.

Maribel explained to her husband that she'd known Ines since she was a little girl in Lebanon, more lies, but Ines didn't say anything to the contrary. Ines could recall every detail of Martin's face as Maribel spoke because he remained frozen like a statue. His jaw was prominent, his cheekbones sharp, and his forehead filled with perpetual lines of wrinkles. His light brown eyes seemed to shimmer while he looked at Maribel, as if they were the one part of him not completely turned to stone. Ines was certain it was the kindness in those eyes that Maribel knew, but she also wondered how many horrible things those eyes had seen.

"She needs our help," Maribel said, bringing Ines' attention back to her words.

Ines saw a slight twitch of annoyance flash across Martin's face before it returned to stone. There was silence for a moment.

"Uh, yes. My father and brother have been wrongly accused of a crime," Ines said, her hands fidgeting in her lap.

Ines was still sitting down, and was grateful for it, because she began to feel faint. The strength that had filled her earlier as she walked up to the mansion alone seemed to have disappeared, and she felt completely exposed under Martin's eyes. A cold exhaustion overtook her, and she was completely convinced that the commander could see through her words as if they were made of thin glass.

"Are they guilty?" Martin asked.

Even the wind seemed to slow then, the splashing in the pool, and the children's cries of laughter muted as Ines felt as if her head had been submerged in water.

"Martin that's—" Maribel began.

"Are they guilty?" Martin asked again.

His words were cold, but Ines answered them as honestly as she could.

"They are not guilty," Ines said.

The metal crates flashed into her mind and so did the wall where the firing squad executed prisoners of the revolution.

Martin didn't say a word, only watched her. Ines' words had been true. Michel and Papa were good men and to Ines they could never be guilty. In the eyes of God, she knew her family would be judged as good. Fidel was the guilty one. Men like Martin, who had done things she was sure Maribel had to convince herself were untrue, they were the guilty ones.

"Okay," he said, "Tell Maribel where they're being detained and their names. I will look into their case. Sometimes… mistakes can be made."

With that, Martin wished Ines a good day, and went back towards his house, the two soldiers following him like twin shadows.

Ines thanked Maribel as she left her home that afternoon.

"I only hope we can help," Maribel said, then added, "It's what Nayibe would have wanted."

Ines felt dirty as she walked out through the large metal gates. *Who exactly did I ask a favor from?* When she stepped out onto the street, the air returned to her lungs. It was as if the entire time she was around Commander Martin, her body had been holding its breath. When she joined Rene, Aida, and Johara at Javier's club, they told her that they'd had no luck. Javier hadn't been in for over a week and the club's owner had no idea when he was coming back.

"Maybe he was also taken," Rene said quietly so no one else could hear.

Ines shared with them her news, along with the details of where she'd been. Rene was so angry that he wouldn't speak with her as they drove back to Las Piedras. It wasn't until the next day that he said a word to her, but even then Ines wouldn't have changed her decision to go without telling them. For the first time in many months, with the promise of Maribel and her husband's inquiry, hope had returned to her.

Chapter 28

A week later, Ines received a message, in the form of a letter attached to her front door. She was granted a visit with her father and brother. They would have to wait another five days for their time slot, which would be just thirty minutes, and only two visitors would be allowed inside, but Ines didn't mind the restrictions. She ran screaming to tell Rene who hugged her immediately as she celebrated around the house. Johara, who had been staying with them at La Casa de Nayibe since Abraham learned of her marriage to Michel, came out of the guest bedroom and when Ines shared the news, her face, which had been marked from several days of crying, came back to life. Ines explained the rules around their visit, but Johara continued to smile.

"Just your seeing them gives me hope. Please tell Michel that he will be a father. He needs to know," Johara said.

Ines then called Aida. They both agreed that Ines and their mother would be the two who visited.

"We'll all be together soon, and I can wait until then. Mama needs to see them," Aida told Ines over the phone.

When Ines shared the news with her mother, she wasn't completely sure Mama had heard her, as she'd hardly acknowledged the news on the other line, but the next day when Ines took Renecito over for a visit, her mother was in the kitchen cooking for the first time since Papa and Michel had been taken. She looked so different from the woman who wouldn't leave her room, and Ines even noticed both the color and warmth had returned to her mother's face.

"You're going to see your uncle and grandfather very soon," Mama told Renecito as she lifted him into the air.

Ines didn't tell her that they would be the only two allowed to visit. She wanted her mother to focus on the excitement of the visit and not the grim reality that surrounded them. Mama spent the rest of the week tidying up the house with Bernita, getting things ready for Michel and Papa's eventual return. She repeated constantly that if they were going to allow them to visit, it was because they had been proven innocent and had only to wait for the process to run its course. Ines wanted so badly to share in her mother's optimism, but she knew what it was that her brother and father had done. At times she wondered if her mother had known as well, or even been involved, but those thoughts did not serve her. If Ines lost her mother as well, she didn't know what she would do.

When the day of the visit arrived, Mama was the first awake. She called Ines before the sun had risen and told Ines that she would begin preparing breakfast. When Ines and Rene arrived, they joined her for breakfast.

"Where's Renecito?" Mama asked.

"Johara is watching him," Rene said.

"Oh," Mama replied. Her tone made it seem as if she'd expected the answer.

It was then that Ines told her that only the two of them would be allowed into the jail that day. Ines watched her mother closely, worried she would be upset by the words, but she didn't seem to mind. Instead, she asked several times whether or not Ines thought it best if they arrived early. Ines was grateful to see her mother excited, but she herself felt an anxiety that made it difficult to breathe. All of the things that could go wrong made her wince from imagined dangers. Even as she dressed into an outfit her mother had chosen, her mind was only on the state of her father and brother. Ines had heard rumors of a building in Havana where people would be sent while they waited to be put to death by firing squad. Ines had no way of knowing whether or not that was where Michel and Papa were being held, but the thought haunted her. Being able to visit them was one thing, but to be released from a place like that may be impossible even with the help of Commander Martin.

Her fears took shape in her mind during the day as often as they did at night when she slept. Ines pictured the American who was said to be the most ruthless of all of Fidel's men, pointing his large cowboy gun at her father and brother's heads as he led them out to the wall where they would be killed like animals. She imagined Abraham in the crowd again, cheering with the rest of the smiling faces. She had visions of soldiers running down the mountainside. Ines saw the images so clearly while her mother spoke to her, but she smiled as if her thoughts were of happier things.

Rene drove them to Havana in Papa's car, which he fumbled around as if his hands were too big for the delicate controls.

"I prefer my Jeep," he would later say when Mama couldn't hear.

Ines' belly was already showing through her clothes, so she did her best to keep her arms resting on her lap in a way that any sign of the baby wouldn't show through. Ines caught her mother glancing at her belly several times as if she could see right through the fabric. Ines felt guilty that she still hadn't announced the news of their second child, even keeping it a secret from Rene, but until she knew Papa and Michel's fate one way or the other, she felt wrong telling them. She did everything she could to stay strong for her family, but when she thought of Renecito and their future child, living on an island that was now filled with so much fear and confusion, a weakness overtook her. The voices of hope versus those of fear fought in her head the entire drive from Las Piedras to Havana.

As they drove down the Malecon in Havana, Ines lowered her window to hear the waves crashing against the stone walls. She saw small fishing boats in the distance and wondered whether or not they would be bringing enough food home to their families that night. If they were lucky enough to have a large catch, how much of it would belong to the government? Everything was so limited since Fidel's revolution took power that it felt as if even the fish in the ocean were nearing the point of running out.

"What are you thinking?" Rene asked her.

"Look at the waves," she replied, "they're beautiful."

Mama agreed from the backseat.

None of them said a word about the prison or the impending visit.

Small stones crunched under the car's tires as they reached their destination. The prison was tucked away near the large harbor that had once welcomed Ines and her family to Cuba. The building was old, and sand colored with a flat roof that seemed to continue on endlessly in either direction. It was strange for such a horrible place to be so close to the beauty of the coastline. At one point, it may have been used for other things, like many of the other forts and castles Ines had seen along the coast. In those buildings, Ines had imagined princes and princesses walking along the ramparts, taking in the view of the Caribbean that seemed to glow green from under the water's surface. But as they parked in the designated area, after showing a guard their official letter she had received, Ines couldn't imagine any sort of royalty ever having lived in the building that contained the prison. She could only imagine hunger, sadness, and death existing within those walls.

As Ines and her mother stepped out of Papa's car, the ocean breeze whipped at their dresses.

"I'll wait right here," Rene told her, squeezing her hand through his open window, "Please be careful."

"We'll be fine," Mama said.

She grabbed Ines' arm, and they walked towards the prison. It was similar to the way Nayibe had grabbed Ines the day she'd died. Ines could feel her mother's arm bone as it dug into her side as if she were afraid to be any farther away from her daughter.

The closer they got to the entrance, the more Ines became convinced that the building would consume them the moment they entered, as it must have done already to other people countless times. How many people had entered there and actually been guilty? How many innocents had lost their lives to the sand-colored walls?

Are we guilty or innocent?

She wasn't sure which she was, having lied and kept secret the evidence of her family's disloyalty to the revolution, but she knew she could only be truly judged by the eyes of God. Ines had still wanted to ask forgiveness from the father in Las Piedras before their visit, but she was unsure whether or not he would report her if she told him of the soldier's hidden uniforms that burdened her soul.

As they walked ever closer to the building, the thought struck her that maybe Commander Martin had seen through her, and the letter was a way to get them into the prison where they would be arrested the moment they entered. Ines looked back at the car. Rene waved and for a moment Ines considered grabbing her mother's arm and running back towards him, but it was already too late. The guards at the entrance asked them their business and searched them before leading them through the halls that reminded Ines of the part of the hospital where they stored the bodies of the newly deceased. Ines shivered when they passed by cells that were filled with prisoners.

Most of the men were covered in dirt, their clothes stained so badly it looked as if they all wore the same color brown. Some of the prisoners smiled at her and called out obscenities while others said nothing or cried out for Ines and Mama to help them, claiming their innocence with shrill yells. Ines did not recognize any of the men, but the conditions they were in made her sick. She realized her father and brother must be receiving the same treatment, and the thought made her want to cry. Ines looked at her mother, who also seemed to be battling the same thoughts, but they continued walking past the cells and down the hallways. Eventually they were led inside a room that smelled like sweat and bleach. They sat and waited for over an hour. The only sounds were the clicking of a wall clock from the opposite side of the room and what sounded like men yelling or screaming from other parts of the fortress.

Ines bit at her lip.

"Don't do that. It's a bad habit," Mama said.

"I'm not a child, Mama," Ines reminded her mother.

Still, Ines did what she was told and was comforted by Mama's words that reminded her of her childhood.

Finally, with the groaning of the metal door, a shadow of a man was pushed forward into the room. The door was slammed shut behind him. Ines looked at her mother, sure there'd been some mistake, but when her eyes returned to the skinny man, she realized it was Michel who stood before them. Mama and Ines both stood up from their seats.

"Mama," Michel said, and burst into tears.

"Look what they've done to you," their mother cried.

Mama rushed towards him and embraced him like a child as he sobbed into her shoulder. Ines couldn't move from where she stood and realized her worst fears had not prepared her to see Michel in such a state. Her brother, who had teased her, played hide and seek with her, and supported her as they grew older together, had become almost unrecognizable. Purple streaks covered his arms, his lip was healing from some sort of wound, and only a small amount of his left eye was showing through swollen eyelids. His shirt was ripped on the side, so Ines could see his ribs through his bluish white skin, which seemed to have been stretched tightly against his body like the surface of a drum. When he hugged her, Ines felt as if the arms that wrapped around her could break at any moment. They stood there holding each other until she realized their father hadn't entered the room with him.

"Where's Papa?" Ines asked, pushing away softly from their embrace, afraid she would hurt him.

Michel did not answer her question.

"They keep asking us the same things. I don't think they've found what they're looking for," Michel said.

He looked to the door then pulled Ines towards the center of the room, his voice becoming a whisper.

"I need you to do something for us. I need—"

"Quiet, Michel. Don't say another word," Ines told him.

"But—"

"It's done," she said.

The words stayed in the room long after she'd spoken them. Mama took a seat at the table and looked at Ines and Michel as if they were strangers to her. Michel's eyes swam with both surprise and understanding. He nodded.

"Where's Papa?" Ines asked again.

Ines felt a numb heat creeping into her body and wanted to join Mama at the table, but she stayed where she was as if her feet had been fixed to the stone floor. Michel looked at Mama, his gaze frozen for a moment, before answering her.

"They took him off early this morning for more questioning," Michel said.

"How is he?" Mama asked.

"Honestly, I don't think he can survive here much longer," he said. "Whoever got you this visit clearly has authority. I haven't seen any other prisoners receive visitors. If it comes down to it, make sure Papa gets released even if it means leaving me in here."

"Don't say such things, you'll both be freed soon," Mama protested.

"Promise me," Michel pleaded.

"I promise," Ines said.

Michel looked at Ines with a ferocity she'd never seen before.

"Was it Abraham who helped you?" Michel asked.

"No," Ines said, "he's so much different than you remember."

A flash of Abraham on his porch as he watched them leave his house came back to Ines and disappeared just as quickly.

"And Johara? How is she?" Michel asked.

The metal door opened, and two guards entered.

"Visiting time is over," one of them said.

 The other grabbed Michel by the arm and began to take him from the room.

"Wait!" Ines whispered so only Michel could hear. "She's with child, Michel, Johara's with child."

Ines hoped Johara's message had reached his ears, but there wasn't any indication that he'd heard her.

The heavy door shut like the lid on a coffin.

Chapter 29

Three weeks passed without word on Michel or Papa. Throughout those weeks, Ines had stayed with her mother, who, as more days went by since the visit, had begun to show signs that her sadness was returning. She was once again eating less and would sometimes forget what day of the week it was, begging Ines to once more take her to visit Michel and Papa.

"I will try, Mama," Ines would say.

She did try. Ines called Maribel several times, but not once did she say whether her husband, Commander Martin, had gotten additional information about her father and brother's cases.

"Can we at least see them again?" Ines asked over the phone.

"I will try, Ines," Maribel said on the other line. "These things are not easy.

Hearing her own words repeated back to her made Ines feel helpless. *I will try.* Her mother was relying on her, but who could *she* rely on? She only had the words of a revolutionary commander's wife to comfort her.

Many visitors came to her parents' house. They came and went through the front door as if on constant rotation. Friends of Mama and Papa, some friends of Michel, and even curious nuns stopped by to check on the Aude family. Ines had never seen the house so filled with people since her wedding, but it felt emptier than ever before, and none of the visitors had the ability to help them. Rene continued to work on the ranch with his father, so Bernita and Johara helped Ines with Renecito as Ines and Aida once again cared for Mama. No one had noticed Ines' growing belly except Bernita, and Ines still hadn't told anyone else, including Rene. Ines' morning sickness had lessened, and she wore large, flowy dresses to hide the shape of her belly. The guilt of such a secret burned at her, almost as badly as what she had buried beneath the guava tree, but until her brother and father's return, she would not share the news.

The days went by so slowly. Ines wondered what she'd done in the eyes of God to deserve the torment of waiting for word on her family but hurried the thoughts from her mind.

They are still alive, and we will have them back.

She often watched the television with Aida and Johara, always making sure her mother wasn't nearby just in case it confirmed their greatest fears: her father and brother on the television alongside an announcement that they had been found guilty of treason. Or worse yet, of the wall, looming in the town center, blood and bullet holes covering it like decorations. A reminder of the fate that traitors shared. Each time the program ended without her hearing those words or seeing the images on the screen her hope was kept alive.

At night, Ines would walk outside into the courtyard or around their garden, sometimes stopping and looking at La Sirena, which seemed as dark as the cave she'd seen the day Michel and Bashir fell into the river. No light came from the building, and she knew how torn apart it was inside. Ines thought that at any moment the building would collapse into itself and disappear completely into a cloud of dust. Those glimpses of the factory, Mama and Papa's life's work, their mutual dream, left in such a state made Ines cry uncontrollably. She was sure no one could see her when she cried, and in those moments of release, Ines felt as if she could finally breathe.

Then, with as little warning as the day they'd been taken, Michel and Papa were returned to them. It was a Tuesday, late in the afternoon, and Ines ran into the courtyard at her mother's first cry, sure soldiers had come to take more away from them. Instead, Michel and her father were there, their clothes stained with dried sweat, dirt, and a color Ines knew must have been blood.

"My God, thank you! My lord in heaven, thank you!" her mother yelled out between her sobs.

"They didn't have any evidence," Papa told Ines as she approached him. He spoke the words slowly as if still in disbelief himself. "Michel told me about your visit. What did you do, Ines?" he whispered as he hugged her close to him. Ines felt his body against hers. It was an alien body, even more bony and frail than Michel's when they'd visited him in the prison.

Ines thought of Commander Martin and felt a knot in her stomach. What would he want in return? Then she thought of Maribel, and the image of Nayibe became clear in her mind. Somehow, they would be safe.

"Nothing, Papa. You're home." Ines sobbed into her father's shoulder.

She then turned towards Michel and hugged him.

It was as if all of the strength she'd shown in their absence had left her in that moment. Her fears had been kept away, contained by a commitment to bring her family back together. Now that she had them there in front of her, even if they looked and felt as weak as corpses, Ines could no longer hide her tears.

"What's this?" Michel asked, stepping away from their embrace. He looked down at Ines' belly.

She hadn't expected the question and felt her face warm as her mother and father also looked.

Ines turned to look at Rene who stood behind her and realized then that she no longer had to keep her secret.

"I'm pregnant," she said.

Rene went over to her and kissed his wife.

"What a beautiful day this is!" Mama exclaimed with a clap of her hands.

Papa smiled, but it was a tired thing.

"Wait, but what about Johara? Where is she?" Michel asked suddenly, taking his eyes away from Ines' belly. "Where is my wife?"

Ines was sure then that Johara's message of her being pregnant had reached her brother's ears after all but was shocked that the word had come from his mouth and immediately looked to her parents to see if they'd heard as well. At that moment, Johara appeared on the porch alongside Aida. Michel fell to his knees as Johara ran to him and grabbed hold of him as if it had been years since they'd seen one another.

Ines watched her parents. Her father looked at Johara and Michel as if unable to process all that had been said.

"Your wife?" Papa finally uttered. Ines watched her father; whose reaction was not one of anger.

"I knew all along," Mama said before pausing and looking at Aida, "You're about to have another niece or nephew."

"You told them?" Aida asked Johara.

"Told us what?" Mama asked. "Ines is pregnant."

"Oh, that," Aida said.

Johara turned to Mama.

"I am pregnant as well," she said.

That afternoon brought many revelations and with them crying followed by laughter and joy. But the joy did not last long.

Ines called Maribel to thank her for helping her father and brother, but when she heard the voice on the other end, it was once again Nayibe's.

"How can I ever repay you for your kindness?" Ines asked.

"By living without regret," Maribel said. To Ines' great sadness in later years, that would be the last time she and Maribel would ever speak.

Ines had hoped her father and brother's return would bring a sense of fullness that would make everything right in their lives, but this did not happen. Instead, the days that followed were filled with worried plans and whispered ideas. *Should they leave?* The question was repeated multiple ways and countless times, but Papa's answer was firm. He was a shadow of his former self, but he had enough strength in him to be adamant that he would not leave his home.

"I will not be scared away," he told them as they ate a Lebanese meal that Mama had prepared. It was the first time she'd cooked a large dinner since before they'd been taken.

Ines heard her father's words but could tell from his face and his slow movements that not only was he scared, but he was exhausted as well. She was like him and feared both staying and leaving. With their second child on the way, Ines knew she could not bear the fear of living under the revolution's regime for any longer. It had become all-consuming. Where would they go? Back to Lebanon? She wasn't sure things were better there.

"Don't we have cousins in America? Could we not go there?" Michel asked.

"No!" Papa exclaimed as he brought his fist down onto the table. "We will not leave."

It was at that moment that Ines realized her father would never leave, no matter how difficult things became. His pride would not allow it. Not unless something happened that made it impossible for him not to. Not unless Ines and her own family left first.

Ines watched her father and brother cautiously, afraid that at any moment they would do something foolish or the regime would change its mind and they would be taken away again. But nothing happened. Neither stepped foot in La Sirena, which still had not been returned to them, or met with any of the strange men that Ines had only ever seen in passing. They made several claims with the local government, but no one was able to give them answers as to when they would have their factory back.

"We were found innocent," Ines overheard Papa tell Michel angrily while in his study. "They can't keep our own business from us."

But they could, and from that moment on, they did.

Several weeks after the birth of their second child, a girl they named Lourdes after a town in France known for its miracles, and after months of going back and forth in her mind, Ines made the decision to leave Cuba. The thought of leaving scared Ines, but the alternative of staying terrified her. Rumors swirled that children could be taken away from their parents at any time, either by the revolution or by foreign governments who wanted to save them from Castro's regime. Either way Ines would not allow her family to be broken apart.

When she told Rene of her decision, her voice quivered, but he agreed immediately.

"My home is with you like I've said since the day we married. I see how afraid you are, and if leaving Cuba means you'll be free of that fear, then we'll leave."

That was all Rene said on the matter, which did not calm Ines' nerves. Part of her wanted him to grab her by the shoulders and shake her foolishness away, yelling, "This is our home! We cannot leave," but no such thing happened. Lourdes cried more than usual the night of her decision, but Ines welcomed the distraction. It was early in the morning when she finally fell asleep as thoughts of the island that they would soon be leaving behind swirled in her mind.

The sun was more orange than ever the day Ines went to the government office to make her decision official. The sky was a deep blue and birds chirped as palm trees shook in the breeze. Doubts came as she stepped into the government building located only a few minutes away from the park where she had so many memories. She was going to request that their names be entered into the raffle, which would give them the chance to leave. The decision to leave was not enough. The regime had to grant them approval and with luck their names would then need to appear in the selection, which could come at any time or never come at all. When the official, a young man with dark, curly hair and kind eyes asked Ines why she was leaving, she almost said, "to find a better home," but held her tongue, knowing that words like those could be punished. The man watched her as she replied, and Ines knew he probably thought her a traitor for wanting to leave their homeland.

"We have family in America. They wish for us to be with them."

The words tickled at her ears. They were half-truths. Ines did have cousins from Lebanon who now lived in America, but she wasn't entirely sure whether or not they remembered her. No, they weren't really her family. Her true family was there in Cuba, and she would need to leave some of them behind in order to save them all.

She told Concha and Isabella first. Things had recently been much calmer in Las Piedras than in previous months, so they went to the park with their children as Ines had always imagined they would one day. As their children played much like they themselves had played years before, the three women sat on a bench nearby.

"We entered our names into the raffle," Ines announced to them.

Neither Concha nor Isabella spoke for several moments and instead looked at each other in disbelief.

Isabella turned to look at Ines while tears began to well in her eyes.

"Oh, Ines, you can't leave, you can't—" Isabella began before Concha interrupted.

"It's amazing how peaceful things appear from here. From where we are sitting right now, it's as if we're once again in paradise, but we can't lie to ourselves, Isabella, this island no longer belongs to us," Concha said.

"You both should leave as well, it's not safe—" Ines said.

"No," Concha said, "maybe one day soon everything will be returned to us. No one knows for sure. And while there's still hope, I can't leave."

"Is it worth the risk to our families?" Ines asked.

Concha said nothing.

"Are you not afraid that the same thing that happened here will spread to wherever it is that you go? Can it be so much better somewhere else?" Isabella asked.

The calm of the afternoon, which was already so fleeting, disappeared entirely. The three friends sat in silence as their children continued to play. Ines realized then just how different all of their lives would be from that moment forward.

A week later, the inspector arrived. It was much sooner than Ines had expected. She was outside in the garden watering the vegetables with Lourdes in her arms, while Renecito played under the shade of the guava tree. She heard knocking from the front of the house and walked inside through the door she and Rene had added a few years before. When she opened the front door, a soldier was standing on her porch. He moved his fingers through his thick, matted beard.

"Buenos días," he said.

Ines returned the greeting and shushed Lourdes who had begun to cry in her arms. Her first thought was to be afraid of the man or the news he brought with him, but she knew why he was there. Ines wished Rene were home. She looked back towards the garden — a wild thought of the soldier digging just below the guava tree turned her blood cold. Then she thought of all of the things inside she had wanted to take to her parents' home, so they wouldn't be taken away by the revolution. As soon as he marked anything of worth down none of it would belong to them.

"I'm here to make the list," the soldier said.

Ines swallowed and nodded. She showed the soldier inside. He had a clipboard and several sheets of paper in front of him as he began moving through the living room, pressing down on the sofa, turning knobs on the television, and playing several notes on the piano. He began to make his way to the kitchen, marking things down as he walked in silence. It was then that Ines remembered some of the things her mother had brought with her from Lebanon that she'd given to Ines for safekeeping. Ines looked at the soldier and felt as if her heart would explode inside her chest. She'd forgotten to take them to her parents' home the week before. *Not those things.*

"Señor, may I go place the baby in the bedroom?" Ines asked.

He nodded.

"Pretend like I'm not here," he said with a smile.

Ines moved into her bedroom and shut the door behind her. She ran to the window and called out to her neighbor, Señora Espinoza, who several years before had given them extra food from their store. Although the store had been taken from them, Ines had never forgotten their kindness.

"Ines? Why are you whispering?" Señora Espinoza asked as she approached the open window from where she'd been working in her garden.

"Quickly, there's no time to explain. Take these things and hide them in your home," Ines said before adding, "And keep some of them for you."

Ines grabbed as many valuables as she could and handed them out through the window to Señora Espinoza. She listened for any indication that the soldier was approaching but moved as quickly as she could. When there was a light knock at the door, Ines closed the window and shooed Señora Espinzoa away.

"One moment," Ines called as she walked towards the door, wiping the sweat from her forehead. She realized then with a sinking feeling that the elephants her mother had brought from Lebanon were still resting on the shelf. It was too late to pass them through the window.

Lost things. No longer ours.

When she opened the door, the soldier looked at her then at the room. Lourdes lay in her bassinet where Ines had placed her. Had he glanced at the window?

"Once I finish in this room, I'm all done," the soldier said. Ines could see suspicion burning in his eyes.

Those final moments seemed to stretch for hours, and when he finally left, Ines cried uncontrollably in the living room until Rene returned home.

The next day, Ines went alone to tell her mother and father about the decision she and Rene had made. They were both in the living room listening to the radio when Bernita showed Ines inside. Mama sat on the couch and Papa in his armchair. As Ines told them of their decision, the room seemed to darken.

"No, you cannot leave. We cannot break up our family. This regime will not last forever and —" Papa was cut off as Mama walked up to him and placed her hand on his arm.

"Do you really want to leave?" Mama asked.

Ines weighed the words in her head. She felt as she had when she'd told Concha and Isabella. No, she did not want to leave, but her being strong and firm was necessary.

"Yes. For a better life."

"It is unreasonable. Renecito and Lourdes are so young. Do you really wish that life upon them? To give up all of this?" Papa raised his arms and signaled to the walls that surrounded them. "For what? Do you even know where you will go in America?"

Ines pushed her doubts away.

"You never really told me why you left Lebanon, Papa. Your answers were always vague. What went on when you and Mama made your choice to leave our home and come to Cuba?" Mama looked up at Papa as Ines paused. "In the end, it does not matter. You left for a better life. Not just for you but for all of us. When I leave for America, I am doing the same for my family, and I hope you will join me."

"I ask the same question: what waits for you in America?"

"One day you will wake from your dream and remember what you are," Ines said.

"And what is that?" Papa asked.

"Strong," Ines said.

Cuban music played through the radio from the corner of the living room, but it sounded as if it were coming from somewhere far away. Ines stared straight at her father.

"Go then," Papa said and stood up, walking in the direction of his study.

Ines watched as he disappeared around the corner.

"He'll come around, Ines," Mama told her.

"What about you? What about Aida? Michel and his family?" Ines asked as she began to cry. "Will you all stay here to die with him?"

Mama produced a handkerchief and dried Ines' tears.

"My heart will break if you leave Cuba, and I cannot be there with you, but I will not leave your father. I will pray, and if things continue to get worse, I know him. He will come around."

Ines left her parents' home that day feeling as if it would be the last time that she would ever see them. The thought ate away at her resolve. *Should we leave?* But she knew, deep down, no matter how many doubts filled her mind, there was no going back on her decision.

Chapter 30

Ines looked up from the journal and other things from the box that were now scattered in front of her. She could hear the soldier's voice as he spoke to Rene in the other room, but she still didn't know what they were saying. Ines placed the journal back into the box along with the other memories she'd pulled out.

"I'll take you with me in my heart," she said as she stood up and closed the door to her closet.

She looked around her bedroom once more, noting all of the things she hadn't been able to sneak out to Señora Espinoza or her parents. It had all been listed by the inspector and would belong to someone else now. For the second time, Ines filled the bag as quickly as she could.

This time, as she stepped back into the living room, she brought only one bag with her, and it was filled entirely with clothes for her, Rene, Renecito, and Lourdes.

The soldier looked up at her.

"Ready, are we?" he asked.

"Yes," Ines said, "we're ready."

He stood up and so did Rene.

"Don't forget that we know exactly what you have in here. Don't go trying to smuggle out anything of value." The man laughed, but it sounded angry.

"What happens now?" Rene asked.

"Now you leave," he said.

Before Ines left her home for the last time, she went out into the garden and looked up at the guava tree. The sun was high above her head and warmed her shoulders through her dress. She squinted her eyes, which were tight with dried tears.

"Goodbye, Nayibe."

Ines reached a hand down into the dirt at the base of the guava tree and let it run between her fingers. She prayed that Nayibe had heard her. She also prayed that no one would find the soldiers' uniforms she and Aida had buried at the base of the tree. She imagined the tree's roots growing around the pieces of fabric that would eventually dissolve and become absorbed into the earth. The orange sun above her head made Ines feel as if no time had passed since she was a little girl disembarking the ship, seeing the Cuban sun for the first time.

As she left her home, and the wind blew against her on the porch for the last time, Ines was sure she heard Nayibe's voice. The words she heard were as clear as they had been when she'd heard her grandmother's voice as a child, but in that moment, she didn't understand them.

You still haven't found it.

Ines wondered what it was she still hadn't found. The words repeated in her head as they made their way out of Las Piedras and towards the airport.

When they arrived, Ines felt a pressure in her chest. She already missed her family. She saw the faces of Papa, Mama, Michel, and Aida so clearly in her mind that she wondered how long her memory of their faces would last. Would they ever leave Cuba? And what about Concha and Isabella? Would they ever see each other again? The sounds that the airplanes made frightened Ines, and she struggled to understand what it was that kept them from falling from the sky like stones. As they walked through the airport, she felt eyes filled with judgment upon her. It was as if she and her family had committed unspeakable crimes. Ines knew that it didn't matter to them how or why they were leaving. They were leaving and that fact alone made them guilty. She knew the same thoughts went through the minds of the nurses who gave Ines and her family vaccinations in a small room in the airport that looked as if at one time it was used to store things. She could see it in the eyes of the soldiers who searched them once more before they boarded the plane. They were marked by their leaving. Stained by it. Ines knew then, without a doubt in her mind, that they would never return to Cuba. Ines held Lourdes tightly in her arms as she stepped onto the plane. Renecito was behind her, and Rene was behind him. She refused to take her seat until her son and husband had been allowed onto the plane and had taken their seats across the aisle from her and Lourdes. No one would take her children away. No one would break apart their family. When they finally took their seats in the cramped airplane, Ines breathed out a sigh of relief.

She rocked Lourdes in her lap as the world shook around them, and the airplane left the ground. Ines knew her daughter cried from the vaccination she'd received as well as from the sounds and vibrations that to her must have sounded as if everything around them was falling apart. And Ines thought, maybe everything was falling apart. Maybe everything already had. But she still had her husband, her children, and the hope that with their departure the rest of their family would join them in America. A sudden fear rose in her that at any moment the plane would be turned around, and they would be taken back to Cuba, but the plane did not change course. She looked over to Rene and Renecito who were sitting across the aisle from them. Rene smiled. It was a nervous smile, but it made Ines feel better all the same. She still had her family. They were still together.

Ines slid the window screen up and looked out. The island, surrounded by endless blue, became smaller and smaller behind them until it disappeared entirely.

She looked down at her fingernails, which were dirty with soil from Nayibe's garden. It was Cuban soil. They were so many feet in the air above the island, already so far away, but the island was still there with her.

Ines thought of the vegetables she'd pulled from the earth that morning.

Those will be the last vegetables I ever pick in Cuba.

Not once did she even consider whether or not they would return if Fidel ever lost power. How could she? He had taken everything from them so completely that it appeared he had the power of God himself and would rule over the island for all eternity.

They may be the last vegetables I ever pick in Cuba, but not the last vegetables that I ever pick.

Lourdes began to cry once more. Ines rocked her and continued to stare out of the window, watching the deep blues and greens of the ocean below, realizing that she may have sailed over those waters as a child when they'd arrived from Lebanon. Eventually, as they circled land, she could see the skyline of a city that looked as if it were made of crystal. The glass buildings reflected the sky, clouds, and ocean around them. They had arrived in Miami.

"Don't cry, mi cielo," Ines whispered to Lourdes, "we will be home soon."

About the Author

Andrew Diaz Winkelmann was born in Atlanta, GA and has an MFA in Creative Writing from Reinhardt University. Raised by a Cuban mother and an American father, he has a passion for writing stories that highlight varying cultures, and the immigrant experience. When he isn't working or writing, he and his wife, daughter, son and Rhodesian Ridgeback can be found traveling and hiking.